THE
SCARLET
GOSPELS

THE
SCARLET
GOSPELS

CLIVE BARKER

St. Martin's Press ☙ New York

For Mark, without whom this book would not exist

THE SCARLET GOSPELS. Copyright © 2015 by Clive Barker. All rights reserved. Printed in the United States of America. For information, address St. Martin's Press, 175 Fifth Avenue, New York, N.Y. 10010.

www.stmartins.com

Library of Congress Cataloging-in-Publication Data is available upon request.

ISBN 978-1-250-05580-4 (hardcover)
ISBN 978-1-4668-5955-5 (e-book)

St. Martin's Press books may be purchased for educational, business, or promotional use. For information on bulk purchases, please contact the Macmillan Corporate and Premium Sales Department at 1-800-221-7945, extension 5442, or write to specialmarkets@macmillan.com.

First Edition: May 2015

10 9 8 7 6 5 4 3 2 1

His friend demanding what scarlet was, the blind man
answered: It was like the sound of a trumpet.
—John Locke,
Human Understanding

PROLOGUE

Labor Diabolus

It raised my hair, it fanned my cheek
Like a meadow-gale of spring—
It mingled strangely with my fears,
Yet it felt like a welcoming.

—Samuel Taylor Coleridge, *The Rime of the Ancient Mariner*

1

After the long quiet of the grave, Joseph Ragowski gave voice, and it was not pleasant, in either sound or sentiment.

"Look at you all," he said, scrutinizing the five magicians who'd woken him from his dreamless sleep. "You look ghostly, every one of you."

"You don't look so good yourself, Joe," Lili Saffro said. "Your embalmer was a little too enthusiastic with the rouge and the eyeliner."

Ragowski snarled, his hand going up to his cheek and wiping off some of the makeup that had been used to conceal the sickening pallor his violent death had left on him. He'd been hastily embalmed, no doubt, and filed away in his ledge within the family mausoleum, in a cemetery on the outskirts of Hamburg.

"I hope you didn't go to all this trouble just to take cheap shots at me," Ragowski said, surveying the paraphernalia that littered the floor around him. "Regardless, I'm impressed. Necromantic workings demanded an obsessive's eye for detail."

The N'guize Working, which was the one the magicians had used to raise Ragowski, called for the eggs of pure white doves that had been injected with the blood of a girl's first menstruation, to be cracked into eleven alabaster bowls surrounding the corpse, each of which contained other obscure ingredients. Purity was of the essence of this working. The birds couldn't be speckled, the blood had to be fresh, and the two thousand, seven hundred, and nine numerals that were inscribed in black chalk starting beneath the ring of bowls and spiraling inward to the spot where the corpse of the resurrectee was laid had to be in precisely the right order, with no erasures, breaks, or corrections.

"This your work, isn't it, Elizabeth?" Ragowski said.

The oldest of the five magicians, Elizabeth Kottlove, a woman whose skills in some of the most complex and volatile of magical preservations weren't enough to keep her face from looking like someone who'd lost both her appetite and her ability to sleep decades ago, nodded.

"Yes," she said. "We need your help, Joey."

"It's a long time since you called me that," Ragowski said. "And it was usually when you were fucking me. Am I being fucked right now?"

Kottlove threw a quick glance at her fellow magicians—Lili Saffro, Yashar Heyadat, Arnold Poltash, and Theodore Felixson—and saw that they were no more amused by Ragowski's insults than she was.

"I see that death hasn't robbed you of your bitter tongue," she said.

"For fuck's sake," said Poltash. "This has been the problem all along! Whatever we did or didn't do, whatever we had or didn't have, none of it matters." He shook his head. "The time we wasted fighting to outdo one another—when we could have been working together—it makes me want to weep."

"You weep," said Theodore Felixson. "I'll fight."

"Yes. Please. Spare us your tears, Arnold," Lili said. She was the only one of the five summoners sitting, for the simple reason that she was missing her left leg. "We all wish we could change things—"

"Lili, dear," Ragowski said, "I can't help but notice that you're not quite the woman you were. What's happened to your leg?"

"Actually," she said, "I got lucky. He nearly had me, Joseph."

"He . . . ? You mean he hasn't been stopped?"

"We're a dying breed, Joseph," said Poltash. "A veritable endangered species."

"How many of the Circle are left?" Joseph said, a sudden urgency in his voice.

There was a silence while the five exchanged hesitant looks. It was Kottlove who finally spoke.

"We are all that is left," she said, staring at one of the alabaster bowls and its bloodstained contents.

"You? *Five?* No." All the sarcasm and the petty game playing had gone from Ragowski's voice and manner. Even the embalmer's bright paints could not moderate the horror on Ragowski's face. "How long have I been dead?"

"Three years," Kottlove said.

"This has to be a joke. How is that possible?" Ragowski said. "There were two hundred and seventy-one in the High Circle alone!"

"Yes," said Heyadat. "And that's only those who chose to be counted among us. There's no telling how many he took from outside the Circles. Hundreds? Thousands?"

"And no telling what they owned either," Lili Saffro said. "We had a reasonably thorough list—"

"But even that wasn't complete," Poltash said. "We all have our secret possessions. I know I do."

"Ah . . . too true," Felixson said.

"Five . . ." Ragowski said, shaking his head. "Why couldn't you put your heads together and work out some way to stop him?"

"That's why we went to all the trouble of bringing you back," Heyadat said, "Believe me, none of us did it happily. You think we didn't try to catch the bastard? We fucking *tried*. But the demon is goddamn clever—"

"And getting cleverer all the time," Kottlove said. "In a way, you should be flattered. He took you early because he'd done his homework. He knew you were the only one who could unite us all against him."

"And when you died, we argued and pointed fingers like squabbling schoolchildren." Poltash sighed. "He picked us off, one by one, moving all over the globe so we never knew where he was going to strike next. A lot of people got taken without anybody knowing a thing about it.

We'd hear about it later, usually after a few months. Sometimes even a year. Just by chance. You'd try to make contact with someone and find their house had been sold, or burned to the ground, or simply left to rot. I visited a couple of places like that. Remember Brander's house in Bali? I went there. And Doctor Biganzoli's place outside Rome? I went there too. There was no sign of any looting. The locals were far too afraid of what they'd heard about the occupants to take a step inside either house, even despite the fact that it was very obvious nobody was home."

"What did you find?" Ragowski said.

Poltash took out a pack of cigarettes and lit one as he went on. His hands were trembling, and it took some help from Kottlove to steady the hand that held his lighter.

"Everything of any magical value had vanished. Brander's urtexts, Biganzoli's collection of Vatican Apocrypha. Everything down to the most trivial blasphemous pamphlet was gone. The shelves were bare. It was obvious that Brander had put up a struggle; there was a lot of blood in the kitchen, of all places—"

"Do we really have to go back over all this?" Heyadat said. "We all know how these stories end."

"You dragged me out of a very welcome death to help save your souls," Ragoswki said. "The least you can do is let me hear the facts. Arnold, continue."

"Well, the blood was old. There was a lot of it, but it had dried many months before."

"Was it the same with Biganzoli?" Ragowski said.

"Biganzoli's place was still sealed up when I visited. Shutters closed and doors locked as if he'd gone on a long vacation, but he was still inside. I found him in his study. He—Christ, Joseph, he was hanging from the ceiling by chains. They were attached to hooks that had been put through his flesh. And it was so hot in there. My guess is he'd been dead in that dry heat for at least six months. His body was completely withered up. But the expression on his face could have just been the way the flesh had retreated from around his mouth as it dried up, but by God he looked as though he'd died screaming."

Ragowski studied the faces before him. "So, while you were having your private wars over mistresses and boys, this demon ended the lives and pillaged the minds of the most sophisticated magicians on the planet?"

"In sum?" Poltash said. "Yes."

"Why? What is his intention? Have you at least discovered that?"

"The same as ours, we think," Felixson said. "The getting and keeping of power. He hasn't just taken our treaties, scrolls, and grimoires. He's cleared out all the vestments, all the talismans, all the amulets—"

"Hush," Ragowski said suddenly. "Listen."

There was a silence among them for a moment, and then a funereal bell chimed softly in the distance.

"Oh Christ," Lili said. "It's his bell."

The dead man laughed.

"He's found you."

2

The assembled company, excepting the once-deceased Ragowski, instantly loosed a flood of prayers, protestations, and entreaties, no two of which were in the same language.

"Thank you for the gift of second life, old friends," Ragowski said. "Few people get the pleasure of dying twice, especially by the same executioner."

Ragowski stepped out of his coffin, kicked over the first of the alabaster bowls, and began working his way around the necromantic circle in a counterclockwise direction. The broken eggs and the menstrual blood, along with the other ingredients of the bowls, each one different but all a vital part of the N'guize Working, were spilled across the floor. One bowl rolled off on its rim, weaving wildly before hitting one of the mausoleum walls.

"That was just childish," Kottlove said.

"Sweet Jesus," Poltash said. "The bell is getting louder."

"We made our peace with one another to get your help and protect ourselves," Felixson shouted. "Surrender can't be our only option! I won't accept it."

"You made your peace too late," Ragowski said, bringing his foot down and grinding the broken bowls into a powder. "Maybe if there'd been fifty of you, all sharing your knowledge, you might have had a hope. But, as it stands, you're outnumbered."

"Outnumbered? You mean he has functionaries?" Heyadat said.

"Good God. Is it the fog of death, or the years that have passed? I honestly don't remember you people being this stupid. The demon has imbibed the knowledge of countless minds. He doesn't need backup. There's not an incantation in existence that can stop him."

"It can't be true!" screamed Felixson.

"I'm sure I would have said the same hopeless thing three years ago, but that was before my untimely demise, Brother Theodore."

"We should disperse!" Heyadat said. "All in different directions. I'll head to Paris—"

"You're not listening, Yashar. It's too late," Ragowski said. "You can't hide from him. I am proof."

"You're right," said Heyadat. "Paris is too obvious. Somewhere more remote, then—"

While Heyadat laid his panicked plans Elizabeth Kottlove, apparently resigned to the reality of her circumstances, took the time to speak conversationally with Ragowski.

"They said they found your body in the Temple of Phemestrion. It seemed an odd place for you to be, Joseph. Did he bring you there?"

Ragowski stopped and looked at her for a moment before saying, "No. It was my own hiding place, actually. There was a room behind the altar. Tiny. Dark. I . . . I thought I was safe."

"And he found you anyway."

Ragowski nodded. Then, trying to keep his tone offhand and failing, he said, "How did I look?"

"I wasn't there, but by all accounts appalling. He'd left you in your little hidey-hole with his hooks still in you."

"Did you tell him where all your manuscripts were?" Poltash asked.

"With a hook and chain up through my asshole pulling my stomach down into my bowels, yes, Arnold, I did. I squealed like a rat in a trap.

9

And then he left me there, with that chain slowly disemboweling me, until he'd gone to my house and brought back everything I'd hidden. I wanted so badly to die by that time I remember that I literally begged him to kill me. I gave him information he didn't even ask for. All I wanted was death. Which I got, finally. And I was never more grateful for anything in my life."

"Jesus wept!" Felixson yelled. "Look at you all, listening to his babble! We raised the sonofabitch to get some answers, not recount his fucking horror stories."

"You want answers!" Ragowski snapped. "Here then. Get yourself some paper, and write down the whereabouts of every last grimoire, pamphlet, and article of power you own. Everything. He's going to get the information anyway, sooner or later. You, Lili—you have the only known copy of Sanderegger's *Cruelties*, yes?"

"Maybe—"

"For fuck's sake, woman!" Poltash said. "He's trying to help."

"Yes. I own it," Lili Saffro said. "It's in a safe buried below my mother's coffin."

"Write it down. The address of the cemetery. The position of the plot. Draw a goddamn blueprint, if you have to. Just make it easy for him. Hopefully he'll return the favor."

"I have no paper," Heyadat said, his voice suddenly shrill and boyish with fear. "Somebody give me a piece of paper!"

"Here," said Elizabeth, tearing a sheet from an address book she pulled out of her pocket.

Poltash was writing on an envelope, which he had pressed up against the marble wall of the mausoleum. "I don't see how this saves us from his tampering with our brains," he said, scribbling furiously.

"It doesn't, Arnold. It's merely a gesture of humility. Something none of us have been very familiar with in our lives. But it may—and I make no guarantees—it may hold sway."

"Oh Christ!" said Heyadat. "I see light between the cracks."

The magicians glanced up from their scrawling to see what he was talking about.

At the far end of the mausoleum, a cold blue light was piercing the fine cracks between the marble blocks.

"Our visitor is imminent," said Ragowski. "Elizabeth, dear?"

"Joseph?" she said, failing to glance up from her fevered scribbling.

"Release me, will you, please?"

"In a minute. Let me finish writing."

"Release me, god damn you!" he said. "I don't want to be here when he comes. I don't ever want to see that horrible face of his again!"

"Patience, Joseph," Poltash said. "We're only heeding your advice."

"Someone give me back my death! I can't go through this again! Nobody should have to!"

The swelling light from beyond the mausoleum wall was now accompanied by a grinding sound as one of the enormous marble blocks, at about head height, slowly pushed itself out of the wall. When it was roughly ten inches clear of the wall, a second block, below and to the left of the first one, began to move. Seconds later a third, this time to the right and above the first, also began shifting. The glittering silver-blue shafts of light that had begun this unknitting came in wherever there was a crack for them to steal through.

Ragowski, enraged at the indifference of his resurrectors, resumed the destruction of Kottlove's necromantic labors where he'd left off. He grabbed the alabaster bowls and hurled them against the moving wall. Then, pulling off the jacket he'd been buried in, he got down on his knees and used it to scrub out the numbers Kottlove had scrawled in the immaculate spiral. Dead though he was, beads of fluid appeared on his brow as he scrubbed. It was a dark, thick liquid that collected at his forehead and finally fell from his face and spattered on the ground, a mingling of embalming fluid and some remnants of his own corrupted juices. But his effort to undo the resurrection began to pay off. A welcome numbness started spreading from his fingers and toes up into his limbs, and a lolling weight gathered behind his eyes and sinuses, as the semiliquefied contents of his skull responded to the demands of gravity.

Glancing up from his work, he saw the five magicians scrawling madly like students racing to finish a vital examination paper before the tolling of the bell. Except, of course, the price of failure was rather worse than a bad mark. Ragowski's gaze went from their toil to the wall, where six blocks were now on the move. The first of the six marble blocks that had responded to the pressure from the other side finally slid clear of the wall and dropped to the ground. A shaft of frigid light, lent solidity by the marble cement dust that hung in the air from the unseated block, spilled from the hole and crossed the length of the mausoleum, striking the opposite wall. The second block dropped only moments later.

Theodore Felixson began to pray aloud as he wrote, the divinity at his prayer's destination usefully ambiguous:

"Thine the power,
Thine the judgment.
Take my soul, Lord.
Shape and use it.
I am weak, Lord.
I am fearful—"

"It's not another 'Lord' we need in here," Elizabeth said. "It's a goddess." And so saying, she began her own entreaty:

"Honey-breasted art thou, Neetha,
Call me daughter, I will suckle—"

while Felixson continued the thread of his own prayer:

"Save me, Lord,
From fear and darkness.
Hold me fast
Against your heart, Lord—"

Heyadat interrupted this battle of supplications with a bellow that only a man of his considerable proportions could have unleashed.

"I never heard such naked hypocrisy in my life. When did you two

12

ever have faith in anything besides your own covetousness? If the de-mon can hear you, he's laughing."

"You are wrong," said a voice from the place out of which the cold light came. The words, though in themselves unremarkable, seemed to escalate the wall's capitulation. Three more blocks began to grind their way forward while another two dropped out of the wall and joined the debris accruing on the mausoleum floor.

The unseen speaker continued to address the magicians. His voice, with its glacial severity, made the harsh light seem tropical by contrast.

"I smell decaying flesh," the demon said. "But with a quickening per-fume. Someone has been raising the dead."

Yet more of the blocks toppled to the ground, so that now there would have been a hole in the wall large enough to allow the entrance of a man of some stature, except for the fact that rubble blocked the lower third of the space. For the entity about to make its entrance, however, such mat-ters were easily resolved.

"Ovat Porak," it said. The order was obeyed instantly. The rubble, lis-tening intently, divided in a heartbeat. Even the air itself was cleansed for him, for as he spoke every particle of cement dust was snatched from his path.

And thus, his way unhindered, the Cenobite entered into the pres-ence of the six magicians. He was tall, looking very much as he did in those volumes of notable demons that the magicians had pored over in recent months and weeks, vainly looking for some hint of frailty in the creature. They had found none, of course. But now, as he appeared in the flesh, there was a distinct sense of humanity in his being, of the man he had been once, before the monstrous labors of his Order had been performed. His flesh was virtually white, his hairless head ritual-istically scarred with deep grooves that ran both horizontally and verti-cally, at every intersection of which a nail had been hammered through the bloodless flesh and into his bone. Perhaps, at one time, the nails had gleamed, but the years had tarnished them. No matter, for the nails pos-sessed a certain elegance, enhanced by the way the demon held his head, as though regarding the world with an air of weary condescension.

13

Whatever torments he had planned for these last victims—and his knowledge of pain and its mechanisms would have made the Inquisitors look like school-yard bullies—it would be worsened by orders of magnitude if any one of them dared utter that irreverent nickname Pinhead, the origins of which were long lost in claim and counterclaim.

As for the rest of his appearance, it was much as it had been depicted in the etchings and woodcuts of demonic listings for millennia: the black vestments, the hem of which brushed the floor; the patches of skinned flesh exposing blood-beaded muscle; and the skin tightly interwoven with the fabric of his robes. There had always been debates as to whether the damned soul who wore this mask of pain and its accompanying vestments was a single man who'd lived many human lifetimes or whether the Order of the Gash passed the scars and nails on to another soul after the labors of temptation had exhausted their present possessor. There was certainly evidence for either belief in the state of the demon before them.

He looked like a creature that had lived too long, his eyes set in bruised pools, his gait steady but slow. But the tools that hung from his belt— an amputation saw, a trepanning drill, a small chisel, and three silver syringes—were, like the abattoir worker's chain-mail apron he wore, wet with blood: confirmation that his weariness did not apparently keep him from taking a personal hand in the practicalities of agony.

He brought flies with him too, fat, blue-black flies in their thousands. Many buzzed around his waist, alighting on the instruments to take their share of wet human meat. They were four or five times the size of terrestrial flies, and their busy noise echoed around the mausoleum.

The demon stopped, regarding Ragowski with something resembling curiosity.

"Joseph Ragowski," the Cenobite said. "Your suffering was sweet. But you died too soon. It pleases me to see you standing here."

Ragowski tensed. "Do your worst, demon."

"I have no need to pillage your mind a second time." He turned and faced the five quivering magicians. "It's these five I came to catch, more for closure than the hope of revelation. I've been to magic's length and breadth. I've explored its outermost limits, and rarely—very rarely—I've mined the thoughts of a truly original thinker. If as White-head said, all philosophy is footnotes to Plato, then all magic is footnotes to twelve great texts. Texts I now possess."

Lili Saffro had started to hyperventilate a little way into the demon's speech and now reached into her purse, digging frantically through its chaotic contents.

"My pills. Oh Jesus, Jesus—where are my pills?"

In her jittery state she lost her grip on one end of her purse, and its contents fell out, spreading across the floor. She went to her knee, found the bottle, and snatched up her pills, oblivious to everything but getting them into her mouth. She chewed and swallowed the large white tab-lets like candies, staying on the ground, clutching her chest, and taking deep breaths. Felixson spoke, ignoring her panicked outburst.

"I have four safes," he told the demon. "I've written down their where-abouts and their codes. If that's too much trouble for you I'll fetch them myself. Or you could accompany me. It's a big house. You might like it. Cost me eighteen million dollars. It's yours. You and your brethren are welcome to it."

"My brethren?" the Cenobite said.

"Apologies. There are sisters in your Order too. I was forgetting that. Well, I'm sure I own enough works for you to pass around. I know you said you've got all the magic texts. But I do have a few very fine first edi-tions. Nearly perfect, most of them."

Before the demon could respond to this, Heyadat said, "Your Lord-ship. Or is it 'Your Grace'? Your Holiness—"

"Master."

"Like . . . like a dog?" Heyadat said.

"Surely," Felixson said, wanting desperately to please the demon. "If he says we're dogs, then dogs we are."

"Well stated," the demon said. "But words are easy. Down, dog."

Felixson waited for a moment, hoping this had just been a throwaway remark. But it was not.

"I said down," the Cenobite warned.

Felixson began to kneel. The demon went on.

"And naked. Dogs go naked, surely."

"Oh . . . yes. Of course. Naked." Felixson proceeded to undress.

"And you," the demon said, extending his pale finger toward Kottlove. "Elizabeth Kottlove. Be his bitch. Naked as well, on your hands and knees." Without further prompting, she started to unbutton her blouse, but he said, "Wait," and walked toward her, the flies rising up from their blood-clotted dining places as he moved. Elizabeth flinched, but the demon merely reached out and placed his hand on her lower belly.

"How many abortions have you had, woman? I count eleven here."

"Th-that's right," she stuttered.

"Most wombs would not survive such unkindness." He clenched his fist, and Elizabeth let out a little gasp. "But even at your advanced age I can give your abused womb the capacity to finally do what it was made to do—"

"No," Elizabeth said, more in disbelief than denial. "You couldn't."

"The child will be here soon."

Elizabeth was out of words. She simply stared at the demon as though she could somehow make him take pity on her.

"Now," he said, "be a good bitch, and get down on all fours."

"May I say something?" Poltash said.

"You may try."

"I . . . I could be very useful to you. I mean, my circle of influence reaches to Washington."

"What is your offer?"

"I am simply saying, there are a lot of people in high office who owe their positions to me. I could make them report to you with a single phone call. It's not magical power, I grant you, but you seem to have all you need of that."

"What are you asking in return?"

"Just my life. Then you name the names in Washington you need at your feet and I'll make it happen."

The Cenobite didn't reply. His attention had been claimed by the sight of Felixson, who was standing in his underwear, with Elizabeth beside him, still preserving her modesty. "I said naked!" the demon snapped. "Both of you. Look at that belly of yours, Elizabeth. How it swells! What about those tired tits? How do they look now?" He pulled off the remains of her blouse and the brassiere beneath. The dry purses of her breasts were indeed growing fuller. "You'll do for one more breeding. And this time you won't be scraping it out of your womb."

"What do you think of my offer?" Poltash asked, vying for the demon's attention.

But before the demon could respond, Heyadat interrupted. "He's a liar," he said. "He's more of a palm reader than an advisor."

"Shut your fucking mouth, Heyadat!" Poltash said.

Heyadat continued. "I know for a fact that Washington prefers that woman Sidikaro."

"Ah. Yes. I have her reminiscences," the demon said, tapping his temple.

"And you pass it all on to your Order, right?" Heyadat inquired.

"Do I?"

"Surely, the other members of your Order—"

"Are not with me."

Heyadat blanched, suddenly understanding. "You're acting alone—"

Heyadat's revelation was interrupted by a moan from Elizabeth Kottlove, who was now on all fours beside the Cenobite's other dog, Theodore Felixson. Her belly and breasts were now round and ripe, the Cenobite's influence powerful enough to already have her nipples leaking milk.

"Don't let that go to waste," the Cenobite said to Felixson. "Put your face to the floor and lick it up."

As Felixson too eagerly bent to his task, Poltash, who had apparently lost all confidence in his offer, made a mad dash for the door. He was two strides short of the threshold when the Cenobite threw a look into the passageway from which he'd come. Something glittering and serpentine there sped from the other side of the wall, crossed into the chamber, and caught Poltash in the back of his neck. A beat later three more came after it, chains, all of them ending in what looked like hooks big enough to catch sharks, wrapping themselves around Poltash at the neck, chest, and waist.

Poltash shrieked with pain. The Hell Priest listened to the sound the man made with the attentiveness of a connoisseur.

"Shrill and inexpensive. I expected better from one who lasted this long."

The chains rent themselves in three different directions, trisecting Poltash in the blink of an eye. For a moment the magician stood there looking dazed, and then his head rolled off his neck and hit the mausoleum floor with a sickening plop. Seconds later, his body followed after, spilling his steaming intestines and stomach, along with their half-digested contents, onto the ground. The demon raised his nose and inhaled, taking in the aroma.

"Better."

Then, a tiny gesture from the Cenobite and the chains that had ended Poltash's life snaked across the floor and slithered up the door, wrapping themselves around the handle. Tightening themselves, they pulled the door closed and raised their hooked heads like a trinity of cobras ready to strike, dissuading any further attempts at escape.

3

"Some things are better done in private, don't you think, Joseph? Do you remember how it was for us? You offered to be my personal assassin. And then you shit yourself."

"Aren't you a little tired of all this by now?" Ragowski replied. "How much suffering can you cause before it fails to give you whatever sad, sick thing it is you need?"

"Each to their own. You went through a phase when you wouldn't touch a girl over thirteen."

"Will you just do it already?" Ragowski said.

"Soon. You are the last. After you there'll be no more games. Only war."

"War?" said Ragwoski. "There'll be nobody left to fight."

"I see death has not made a wise man of you, Joseph. Did you really think this was all about your pitiful secret society?"

"What then?" Heyadat asked. "If I am to die, I'd like to know the reason!"

The demon turned. Heyadat looked into the shiny darkness of his eyes, and as if in answer to Heyadat's question the Cenobite spat a word in the direction of the open wall. A flight of twenty hooks, trailed by glinting chains, came at Heyadat catching him everywhere—mouth, throat, breasts, belly, groin, legs, feet, and hands. The Cenobite was bypassing the torture and interrogation and going straight to the execution. Lost in his agonies, Heyadat babbled as the hooks steadily worked themselves deeper into his three-hundred-and-fifty-pound body. It was hard to make much sense of what he was saying through the snot and the tears, but he seemed to be listing the books in his collection, as though he might still be able to strike a bargain with the beast.

"... the *Zvia-Kiszorr Dialo* ... the only ... remaining ... of Ghaffari's *Nullll*—"

The Cenobite then called seven more chains into play, which came swiftly, sweeping around Heyadat from all directions. They hooked themselves into his shuddering body and wrapped themselves so tightly the fat man's flesh oozed from between the rusted links.

Lili edged herself into her corner and covered her face with her hands. The others, even Kottlove, who appeared now to be eight months into her term while Felixson hammered at her from behind, looked up as Heyadat continued to chatter and sob.

"... Mauzeph's *Names* ... n-n-names of ... Infernal Territories ..."

All twenty-seven chains had now secured themselves in the man's body. The Cenobite murmured another order and the chains proceeded to tighten further, pulling on Heyadat's body from several directions. Even now, with flesh and bone under unbearable stress, he continued to list his treasures.

"... oh God ... Lampe's *Symphony*, the ... the ... the Death Symphony ... Romeo Refra's ... Romeo Refra's—"

"*Yellow Night*," Ragowski prompted. He was watching Heyadat's torment with a dispassion perhaps only a dead man could have worn.

"... yes ... and—" Heyadat started to say.

There the list stopped, however, as Heyadat, only now comprehending what was happening to him, unleashed a stream of pleading cries, all rising in volume as his body was subjected to the contrary demands of the hooks. His body could not withstand the claims made upon it any longer. His skin began to tear and he started to thrash wildly, his last coherent words, his entreaties, overtaken by the ragged howls of agony that he now unleashed.

His belly flesh succumbed first. The hook there had gone deep. It ripped away a wedge of bright yellow fat ten inches thick and some of the muscle beneath. His breasts came next: skin and fat, followed by blood.

Even Lili watched now through her fingers as the spectacle escalated. The hook in Heyadat's left leg, which had entered behind his shinbone, broke it with a crack that was loud enough to be audible above Heyadat's screams. His ears came off with scraps of scalp attached; his shoulder blades were both broken as the hooks there pulled themselves free.

But despite the thrashing, the screams, and the reflecting pool of black blood below his body now so large it lapped against the hem of the Cenobite's vestments, the demon was not satisfied. He issued new instructions, using one of the oldest tricks in magic: Teufelssprache.

He whispered instructions and three new hooks, larger than any that had come before—their outer edges sharp as scalpels—flew at the exposed fat and flesh of Heyadat's chest and stomach and sliced their way into his interior.

The effect of one of the three was immediate: it pierced his left lung. His screaming stopped and he began to gasp for air, his thrashing becoming desperate convulsions.

"Finish him, in mercy's name," Ragowski said.

The Cenobite turned his back on his victim and faced Ragowski. The demon's cold, lifeless stare caused even Ragowski's stiff reanimated flesh to prickle.

"Heyadat was the last man to give me orders. You would do well not to follow in his footsteps."

Somehow, even after experiencing the hand of death itself, Ragowski still found himself afraid of the calculating demon who stood before him. Taking a deep breath, Ragowski conjured what courage he could.

"What are you trying to prove? Do you think if you kill enough people in the worst ways imaginable they'll give you a name like the

Madman, or the Butcher? It doesn't matter how many abhorrent tortures you devise. You'll always be the Pinhead."

The air went still. The Cenobite's lip curled. Quick as a flash, he reached out for Ragowski, seized the dead man's scrawny throat, and pulled him close.

Without taking his black gaze off Ragowski for an instant, the demon lifted his trephine from his belt, activating the device with his thumb as he brought it to the middle of Ragowski's upper brow. It fired a bolt through Ragowski's skull and then retracted.

"Pinhead," Ragowski said, undeterred.

The Cenobite made no reply. He simply hooked the trephine back on his belt and put his fingers into his own mouth, seeking out something that lodged within. Finding it, he drew the thing out—a small, slick, blackened hunk, like a diseased tooth. He returned his fingers to the hole in Ragwoski's skull, inserting the object and letting go of Ragowski's throat in the same moment.

"I'm guessing I'll be dead soon, right? To paraphrase Churchill, I'll be dead in the morning, but you'll *still* be Pinhead," Ragowski growled.

The Cenobite had already turned his back on Ragowski. The hooks that held Heyadat in place had clearly waited for their master to turn back to them before they performed their coup de grâce. Now, blessed with his gaze, they showed their skills.

The hook, a weapon that the demon had affectionately named the Fisherman's Hook, was attached to a chain that had found purchase in the ceiling. It suddenly and swiftly tore through the roof of Heyadat's mouth, lifting his entire body clear of the ground. The moment the Cenobite's gaze landed upon the rusty blood-caked links, eruption followed eruption. Heyadat's hands split in two, the feet the same. The huge bulk of his thighs was gouged from groin to knees. His face was stripped of skin, and the three deeply embedded hooks in his chest and stomach pulled out heart, lungs, and entrails all at once. Surely a faster autopsy had never taken place.

Their task complete, the hooks dragged what parts of him they'd claimed through the pools of blood, back toward the place from whence they'd come. Only one remained: the Fisherman's Hook, from which the empty and significantly lighter carcass of Yashar Heyadat hung slowly swinging back and forth, the drooping doors of his stomach—bright with fat—flapping open and closed.

"All the fireworks were red again tonight," the Cenobite said, as though bored of the whole affair.

Felixson, still rutting like a dog, pulled himself out of Kottlove and retreated from the spreading blood. Seeking purchase, his hand landed on something soft. He turned and his face fell.

"Lili . . ." was all he said.

The demon turned his head to see what Felixson saw. It was Lili Saffro. The sight of Heyadat's slaughter had apparently been too much for her. She was slumped dead against the far wall. There was a stricken expression on her face, and her hands still clutched at her chest.

"Let's be done with this," the demon said, turning to face the three remaining magicians. "You. Felixson."

The man's face was all snot and tears. "Me?"

"You play the dog well. I have work for you. Wait for me in the passage."

Felixson didn't need to be told twice. Wiping his nose, he followed the demon's instructions and fled for the exit. Though Felixson was going naked into Hell on the heels of the creature who had slaughtered almost every friend he'd ever had, he was happy with his lot.

So happy, in fact, that he scurried through the ragged door in the mausoleum wall to wait for his new master to come to him and never once looked back. He went far enough down the passageway to be reasonably certain he would not hear the screams of his friends and then he squatted against the crumbling wall and wept.

4

"What's wrong with me?" Ragowski said.

"You're infected with a tiny sibling of mine, Joseph. A worm, made from a piece of me. I passed it from its crib beside my cheek into the hole in your skull. Its body is filled with tiny eggs that need only the presence of warm, soft nourishment to be born."

Ragowski was not a stupid man. He understood completely the significance of what he'd just been told. It explained the unwelcome fullness in his head, the churning motion behind his eyes, the tang of bitter fluid draining from his nose and down the back of his throat.

Ragowski hawked up a wad of phlegm and spat at the Cenobite, who deflected it with a tiny motion of his hand. When it hit the floor, Ragowski saw the truth of the matter. It wasn't phlegm he'd brought up; it was a little knot of worms.

"You're an asshole," Ragowski said.

"You have the rarest of opportunities to die twice and you waste your breath with banal insults? I had hoped for more from you, Joseph."

Ragowski coughed and in the midst of the hacking lost his breath. He tried to recover it, but his throat was blocked. He dropped to his knees, and the impact was sufficient to burst the fragile panel of his skin so that veins of worms fell from his anatomy, littering the ground around him. Mustering the last of his will, he lifted his head to defy his destroyer with his stare, but before he could do so his eyes dropped back into their sockets, his nose and mouth following quickly after. In seconds his face had gone entirely, leaving only a bowl of bone brimming with the Cenobite's writhing descendants.

There was a shrill shriek behind Ragowski, and finally finished with him, the demon turned toward the din, only to find that in his preoccupation with Ragowski's demolition he had missed the only pregnancy Kottlove would ever take to full term. The shriek had not come from her, however. She was dead, slumped on her back and torn in two, killed by the trauma of the infant's birth. The thing that the demon had created in her, however, lay in a puddle of its own fetid fluids shrieking in the tone the demon had mistaken for its mother's voice. The creature was female and, at a glance, virtually human.

The demon surveyed the mausoleum. It was indeed a comprehensive spectacle: the pieces of Poltash sprawled at the door; Heyadat's head and mutilated carcass still swaying slightly as it hung from the Fisherman's Hook; Lili Saffro, forever frozen, her body ravaged by time, her face a distressing testament to the empirical power of fear itself, her life claimed by the only Thing to which every soul must answer; and finally, Ragowski, collapsed into little more than a mess of bone and worms.

The worms, disrespectful guests that they were, had already begun to desert his remains in search of another feast. The first of the departees had found pieces of Heyadat in one direction and the half-mangled corpse of Elizabeth Kottlove in the other.

The Cenobite knelt between Kottlove's bloodied legs and selected a blade from his belt. Taking the purple clot of the child's birth cord in one hand, he severed it and tied it into a knot. He then found her mother's blouse, mercifully unstained, and wrapped the child in it. Even swaddled, she continued to make a noise like an angry bird. The demon regarded her with a curiosity entirely devoid of concern.

"You're hungry," he said.

The Cenobite stood, holding on to one end of the silk swaddling, and released the child, letting her unroll high above her mother's corpse. The baby tumbled, then dug her claws deep into the blouse and clung there, looking into her caretaker's eyes, issuing a reptilian hiss as she did so.

"Drink," he instructed.

He shook the fabric to which his creation clung, and she fell upon her mother's corpse. Getting up onto all fours, the child made her erring way to Elizabeth's left breast, where she kneaded the cooling flesh with her hands, which had already sprouted uncommonly long fingers for an infant so young. And when Kottlove's milk began to once more flow from her lifeless bosom the child suckled greedily.

The demon then turned his back on the child and returned from whence he came, his loyal dog Felixson, waiting in the wings.

As the bricks and mortar moved back into their original positions, sealing themselves behind the departing demon, the child, still growing, was now easily twice as large as she had been at birth. It was a little after dawn when the Cenobite left the mausoleum, and by that time his progeny had already emptied both breasts and was tearing her mother's chest open for the meat inside. The cracking of the corpse's breastbone echoed loudly around the small, musty room.

The naked girl's anatomy was undergoing a violent growth, and every so often could be heard the sound of pain, muted because it came through gritted teeth. Utterly unaware of her father's desertion, the young demon girl moved about the room like a pig at a trough, gluttonously devouring the remains of the once-powerful magicians, effectively erasing the last remnants of an order of magic that had moved behind the shadows of civilization for centuries.

By the time the police arrived, alerted by the unwitting soul who discovered the hideous spectacle that was the mausoleum—a frail and broken groundskeeper who vowed he would never again set foot in a cemetery—the girl, fully a woman after less than twelve hours, was gone.

BOOK ONE

Past Lives

Three may keep a secret, if two of them are dead.

—Benjamin Franklin, *Poor Richard's Almanac*

1

Two decades ago, Harry D'Amour had turned twenty-three in New Orleans, drunk as a lord on Bourbon Street. Now here he was in the same city that had taken terrible wounds from hurricanes and human greed but had somehow survived them all, its taste for celebration unscathed. Harry was drinking in the same bar on the same street, twenty-four years later. There was music being played by a jazz quintet led, believe it or not, by the same trumpet player and vocalist, one Mississippi Moses, and there were still one-night love affairs happening on the little dance floor just as there had been almost a quarter of a century before.

Harry had danced then with a beautiful girl who claimed to be Mississippi's daughter. While she and Harry danced, she told him that if they wanted to do something "bad tonight"—Harry remembered perfectly the way she'd smiled as she said "bad"—then she had a place where they could play. They'd gone up to a little room above the bar where her papa's music could be heard loud and clear coming up from below. That little fact should have warned Harry that this was a family affair and that men who have daughters can also have sons. But all of his blood had gone south once he had his hand up her dress, and just about the time he had slid a finger into the moist heat of her the door opened and the girl made a pantomime of being surprised to see her two brothers, who were now standing in the room looking almost convincingly upset. The two intruders into Harry's bliss had played out a scene they probably performed half a dozen times nightly: informing him that their lovely little sister was a virgin and that there wasn't a man in the bar who would ever testify to having seen him if they dragged his Yankee carcass to a tree hidden behind a wall just a minute's walk from there, where a noose was already hanging, waiting for a taker. But they assured him that they were reasonable men and if D'Amour had enough money on him they could maybe overlook his transgressions—just this once, of course.

Naturally, Harry had paid up. He'd emptied his wallet and his pockets and almost lost his best Sunday shoes to the taller of the two brothers, except that they had been too big for him. The brothers knocked Harry around a little as he made his exit, tossing his shoes back at him and leaving the door open so he could make his escape, the lighter for a few hundred bucks but otherwise unharmed.

All these years later, Harry had come to the bar half-hoping to find the girl still there, changed of course by the passing of so many years but still recognizable. She wasn't there and neither were her ostensible brothers. Just the old jazz musician, eyes closed as he played, riffing on the bittersweet love songs that had been old when Harry had first heard Mississippi Moses play them all those years ago.

None of this nostalgia, however, did much to improve Harry's state of mind; nor did his reflection, which he caught in the age-eaten mirror behind the bar whenever he looked up. No matter how much liquor he downed, it refused to blur, and Harry saw all too clearly the scars of battle and time. Harry noted his own gaze, which, even when hurried, had taken on a distrustful cast. There was a downward tug at the corners of his mouth, the consequence of too many unwelcome messages delivered by unlovely messengers: notes from the dead, subpoenas from infernal courts, and the steady flow of invoices for the services of the janitor in Queens who would burn anything in his furnace for a price.

Harry D'Amour had never wanted a life like this. He'd attempted to make a normal life for himself, a life untainted by the secret terrors whose presences he had first encountered as a child. The keeping of the law, he had reasoned, would be as good a bastion as any against the forces that stalked his soul. And so, lacking the smarts and the verbal dexterity required of a good lawyer, he became instead a member of New York's finest. At first the trick seemed to work. Driving around the streets of New York, dealing with problems that reared from the banal to the brutal and back again twice in the same hour, he found it relatively easy to put to the back of his mind the unnatural images that stood beyond the reach of any gun or law that had been made.

That wasn't to say that he didn't recognize the signs when he sensed them, however. A gust of wind carrying the scent of corruption was enough to call up a black tide from the base of his skull, which he only managed to drive back by sheer force of will. But the labor of normality took its toll. There wasn't a single day in his time as a cop in which he hadn't needed to cook up a quick lie or two to keep his partner, an occasionally affable family man known affectionately as Sam "Scummy" Schomberg, from knowing the truth. After all, Harry wouldn't wish the truth upon anyone. But the road to Hell is paved with the bubbling mortar of good intentions, and ultimately Harry's lies and half-truths weren't enough to save his partner.

"Scummy" Schomberg's nickname, however lovingly used, was well earned. Besotted as he was by his five children ("the last four were accidents"), his mind was never far from the gutter, which, on nights when he was on duty and the mood struck him, ensured that he'd spend time driving up and down the squalid streets where hookers plied their trade until he'd found a girl who looked healthy enough ("Lord knows I can't take some fucking disease home") for him to arrest and then subsequently set free once he'd received some complimentary service in a nearby alley or doorway.

"Another Jack?" the bartender asked Harry, shaking Harry from his reverie.

"No," Harry replied. A memory of Scummy's libidinous leer had come into Harry's head, and from there his mind ran in quick autonomous leaps to the last moments of his partner's life. "Don't need that," Harry spoke more to himself than the bartender as he rose from his barstool.

"Sorry?" the bartender said.

"Nothing," Harry replied, sliding the ten-dollar bill he'd left toward the man as though he were paying him not to ask any more questions. Harry needed to get out of here and put his memories behind him. But despite his alcoholic haze, his mind was still faster than his feet and, his protests notwithstanding, it brought him back to that terrible night in New York, and he instantly found himself sitting in the patrol car down on 11th Street waiting for Scummy to get his rocks off.

2

Scummy and his chosen receptacle were out of sight, down some steps leading to the basement of a building. The place was empty, its doors and windows bricked or boarded up more thoroughly than Harry ever remembered seeing before. He glanced at his watch. It was ten after two in the morning, in the middle of June. Harry was getting a little antsy, and he knew why. His body always knew before his brain that something bad was in the vicinity.

Harry tapped impatiently on the wheel, scanning the deserted street for some clue to the whereabouts of whatever was inspiring the irritation in his system. As a kid he'd called it his UI, which stood for "Unscratchable Itch." Adulthood hadn't offered him any reason to change the name, so the UI was still in the private vocabulary he'd created to help him put some order into the mental chaos its presence had always produced.

Was there something under the flickering lamp on the other side of the street? If it existed, it did so at the very limit of his eyes' power to separate substance from shadow. The Possible Thing seemed to Harry tomovewithaferalfelinegrace.No.He'dhaditwrong.Therewasnothing—

But even as he formed the thought, the Possible Thing confirmed his initial suspicion by turning back and retreating into the shadows, its muscular form shifting like breeze-quickened water as the shadows erased it. The Thing's departure, however, failed to ease the I in Harry's UI. It hadn't been the cause of his prickling skin. No, that was still nearby. He opened the door of the patrol car and got out, moving slowly so as not to attract attention. Then he studied the street from end to end.

A block and a half up 11th he saw, tethered to a fire hydrant, a goat. It looked both pitiful and unlikely there on the sidewalk, the peculiarities of its anatomy—distended flanks, bulging eyes, bony skull—positively alien. Harry got out of the undercover patrol car, leaving his door open, and started to walk toward his partner, his hand staying instinctively to the handle of his gun as he did so.

Harry was three strides across the street when he felt the UI come over him like a tidal wave. He stopped, glancing at the short stretch of empty sidewalk that lay between him and the darkened stairway where Scummy had gone with the girl. What was taking so damn long?

Harry took two tentative steps, calling to his partner as he did so.

"All right, Scummy, zip it up. Time to move."

"What?" Scummy shouted. ". . . Oh God, that's good. . . . You sure you don't want in on this, partner? This bitch'll—"

"I said it's time, Sam."

"*Uno momento,* Harry . . . just one . . . God damn . . . oh yeah . . . oh yeah, just like that . . . Scummy likes that. . . ."

Harry's gaze went back to the goat. The front door to the building outside which the animal was tethered had opened. Blue lights burned within, like candle flames, fluttering at a midnight mass. Harry's Itch rose beyond the unbearable. Slowly, but with purpose, he crossed the cracked sidewalk to the top of the stairs and glanced down into the murk where he could vaguely make sense of Scummy lounging against the wall, his head back while the hooker worked on her knees in front of him. Judging by the sloppy, desperate sounds of the job she was doing, she wanted the cop to shoot his load already so she could spit it out and go.

"God damn it, Sam," Harry said.

"Christ, Harry. I hear you."

"You've had your fun—"

"I ain't come yet."

"How about we find another girl on another street?"

As he spoke, Harry glanced back at the goat, then at the open door. The blue candle flames had ventured out into the street, detached from wick and wax. They were lighting the way for something. Harry's gut told him he didn't want to be around when the Something finally showed itself.

"Oh, you're good," Scummy said to the whore. "I mean really good. Better than my fucking brother-in-law." He chuckled to himself.

"That's it," Harry said, and he went down the remaining stairs, losing sight of both the light-attended doorway and the goat as he caught hold of Scummy's jacket shoulder. Harry pulled his partner away, the girl dropping forward onto her hands as D'Amour dragged Scummy up the stairs.

"What's going on?" she demanded. "Does this mean you're booking me?"

"Shut up," Harry said in a hushed tone. "You're not getting booked. But if I ever see you on this block again—"

There was a wretched shrieking from the goat at that moment, which lasted a full three seconds as it echoed in the preternaturally still night air. Then the sound abruptly ended, leaving them once more in silence.

"Fuck. Fuck. Fuck," Harry said.

"What was that?" Scummy asked.

"A goat."

"What? I didn't see no goat—"

"Scummy?"

"Yeah?"

"On three we're going to make a run for the car, okay?"

"O . . . kay. But—"

Harry cut in, speaking with a hushed urgency. "There is no but, Scummy. You look at the car and you keep looking at the car till you're in and we're away. Anything else and we're dead men."

"Harry, wha—?"

"Trust me. Now come on."

"Ah, Christ, my zipper's stuck."

"Forget your fucking zipper. Nobody's going to be looking at your dick, I promise you that. Now move."

Scummy ran. Harry, following fast behind, looked down the street as he made his way silently to the car. The goat's throat had been opened, but it was far from dead. Its robed slaughterer stood there, holding the thrashing animal by the legs, its head pulled back to make the partial throat cut gape and speed the flow of blood.

The goat's life force came out of it in spurts, like water from a faulty faucet. The goat and butcher were not the only presences in attendance, however. There was a third member of the party, his back to Harry. As Harry crossed the street toward the car, the third member turned to look back. Harry caught a glimpse of his face—a mangled smear of formless flesh like a hunk of discarded clay—before the man plunged his hands into the goat's spurting blood.

Scummy had made it halfway to the car, then, contrary to Harry's instruction, looked at the unsightly tableau. It had stopped Scummy in his tracks. Harry transferred his gun from right hand to left and used the right to grab hold of Scummy's arm.

"Come on."

"You see that?"

"Let it go, Scummy."

"That ain't right, Harry."

"Neither is getting a blow job from a teenage runaway."

"That's different. People can't be slaughtering fuckin' goats in the street. It's fuckin' disgusting." Scummy took out his gun. "Hey, you two degenerates with the goat. Do not fuckin' move. You're both under arrest."

So saying, he started to walk toward them. Harry cursed under his breath and followed. Somewhere nearby, no more than two or three blocks over, the whooping of an ambulance siren reminded Harry that somehow the rational world was still a stone's throw away from this wretched scene. But Harry knew it didn't matter. These types of things, all pieces of one unknowable mystery, threw up veils around themselves that made seeing them clearly a difficult thing for ordinary eyes. If Scummy had been alone he would likely have driven past this grotesquerie without even registering its existence.

It was only because Harry was with Scummy that he saw, and the knowledge of that was like a stone in Harry's guts.

"Hey, assholes," Scummy hollered, his shouts echoing back and forth between the façades of the deserted buildings. "Stop that shit."

The two men did the worst possible thing in response: they obeyed. Harry sighed as the butcher let the goat drop to the ground, its black legs still twitching. And the clay-faced man who'd been washing his hands in the blood raised himself from his stoop and turned to face the two policemen.

"Oh Christ alive," Scummy murmured.

Harry saw the reason for Scummy's blasphemy; what had been an undefined gob of flesh two minutes ago was now organizing itself. The claylike matter that Harry had first seen had now shifted; there was almost a nose, almost a mouth, and two holes like thumbprints where the eyes should have been. The clay man started toward them, steam rising from his blood-soaked hands.

Scummy stopped advancing and threw the briefest of looks at Harry, just long enough to catch Harry's tiny nod back toward the car. In that time, the clay man's protean features had finally settled on a mouth, which he now opened, and a low noise escaped him, like the warning growl of an angered animal.

"Watch out!" Harry said, and the thing went from a walk to a run in two strides. "Go! Go!" Harry shouted, and, leveling his gun, shot at the thing once, twice, and then seeing the bullets slow the creature's run to a stagger, his blood blooming on its shirt where he had been hit, Harry fired three more rounds: two to the torso and one to the head. The creature stood a moment in the middle of the street, looking down at his bloody shirt, his head slightly tilted as though in mild puzzlement.

Behind him, Harry heard Scummy getting into the car and slamming the door. He gunned the engine, the wheels squealing as the car U-turned and pulled up to Harry.

"Get in!" Scummy yelled.

The creature was still examining his wounds. Harry had a moment's grace, and he took it. Turning his back on the beast, Harry scrambled over the hood of the car, threw open the door, and flung himself into the passenger seat. Before he'd even closed the door, Scummy accelerated. Harry caught a glimpse of the creature as they raced past him and saw, as if Harry were perfectly still and able to take in every detail of the moment, the creature's heavy head rise, showing two tiny dots of light burning in his thumbhole eyes. The beast was pronouncing a death sentence with his stare.

"You gotta be fucking kidding," Harry said.

"That bad, huh?"

"Worse."

They were already almost a block past the creature, and for a few deceitful moments Harry thought perhaps he'd misread the look in the enemy's gaze and they might actually be able to reach the safety of a busy street unharmed. But then Harry's Itch returned, just in time for his partner to shout, "Jesus fuck!"

Harry looked back to see that the enemy was giving chase and he was closing in on the speeding vehicle with every stride. The beast had raised his steaming bloodstained hands in front of his body, palms out, fingers spread freakishly wide. As he ran, his hands became brighter, like the dull embers of a fire woken by a sudden wind. Sparks were flying off his hands now, yellow-white, turning to smoke, darkening as they did so.

Harry turned on the siren and emergency lights in the hopes that the creature was of the rare breed that could be felled by such tactics. But, far from dissuading the enemy from his pursuit, the alarms seemed instead to lend speed to his heels.

"Fuck! It's almost on us, Harry!"

"Yeah."

"How many bullets did you put in that fuckin' thing?"

"Five."

"Fuck."

"Just keep driving."

"Fuck."

You know any prayers, Scummy?"

"Not one."

"Fuck."

And then the beast was on them, slamming his burning hands down on the rear of the car with such strength that the front end kicked into the air. For a few seconds the wheels were off the ground, and by the time they hit the street again the enemy was smashing through the back window. The stink of frying goat's blood filled the car.

"Out!" Harry yelled.

Scummy threw open his door. The car was still moving, but Scummy was out anyway. Harry felt the heat of the enemy's hands behind his head and smelled the hairs on his neck burn up. He had his door open— only an inch, but it was open. Then he grabbed the dashboard with his left hand to put some force behind his exit and threw himself against the door.

Clean, cool air met him for a second; then so did the street. He tried to roll into the fall, failed, and landed on his head, rubbing the side of his face skinless on the cracked asphalt until he finally came to a halt. The adrenaline in his veins forgave his body its frailties, at least for a few seconds. He got up, wiping dirt and blood from his eyes, and looked for Scummy. Scummy was standing ten yards from Harry, half-hidden by the black smoke of the burning car. He had his gun pointed directly at Harry.

"Scummy, what—"

"Behind you!"

Harry turned. The beast stood in the smoke-laced air, no more than two yards from where Harry was standing. His human garments had been largely burned away by the blaze he had started, and it gave Harry an unwelcome view of just how pleasurable the beast was finding all this madness. His penis was standing up in bliss, its mottled head unsheathed. The hair around its base was burning, so that the member seemed to rise from a thicket of flame. And if the rock-hard salute wasn't proof enough of the beast's contented condition, the smile on his face was.

He raised his right hand. The flames were now out, leaving the hand black and smoking but otherwise undamaged. The only places where the memory of fire remained were in the lines of the monster's palms, which were still bright with heat, the embers glowing brightest at the dead center of his hands. Harry wanted to pull his eyes away from the spot, but they wouldn't come unglued, at least not until he'd watched the place in the center of the beast's hand burn brighter still and finally issue a fleck of white fire that flew past Harry's head, missing him by inches.

He had time, in his stupefied state, to be thankful that the beast has missed his mark. Then Harry realized that of course the fiery fleck wasn't meant for him. He turned, yelling to Scummy, but both the motion and the warning were slow—too slow, as though the air around him had the consistency of tar.

Harry watched Scummy, standing a dozen yards away, watching with the same tar-trapped eyes, powerless to do anything as the fleck of white fire approached and struck him in the throat. Scummy slowly raised his free hand to brush it off, but before his hand could reach it the fleck burst and two bright lines of fire raced around his neck, one going left and the other right, circling fully 'round and meeting again at his Adam's apple.

For a moment, the air around Scummy's head flared up, shivering and shimmering like a wave of heat over scorched earth. But before Scummy could utter a word, a sheath of flames sprang up and swallowed his face. His head was on fire, from his Adam's apple to the bald spot he'd forever been combing his hair over. That's when Scummy began screaming. Terrible gutteral cries like silverware being run through the garbage disposal.

Time continued to unravel at the same indolent rhythm, obliging Harry to watch the heat at work on his partner's flesh. Scummy's skin grew redder and redder in the blaze, shiny beads of fat appearing from the pores and bursting as they ran over his face. Harry started to raise his hands to remove his jacket—his mind just clear enough to imagine he might still smother the flames before they did any real harm. But as Harry made to move, the beast grabbed Harry's shoulder, spinning him around, and pulled him close. Now facing the wretched creature, Harry watched as the creature held his smoldering hand out and cupped it just below Harry's chin.

"Spit," the creature said, his voice matching his misshapen appearance.

Harry did nothing by way of reply.

"Saliva or blood," the beast warned.

"That's easy," Harry said.

Harry didn't know why this thing needed anything from him, nor did he particularly like the idea of the creature owning a piece of him, but the proposed alternative was clearly worse. He did his best to summon a wad of spittle, but the offering he dropped into the beast's hands was meager. The adrenaline had left Harry's mouth as dry as a set of sun-bleached bones.

"More," the beast said.

Harry went deep this time and brought up the good ripe stuff from every pocket of his throat and mouth, gathered it, rolled it, and spat it with gusto into the beast's palm. It was a nice piece of work, no question. To judge by the crude, lipless smile on his face, the beast was well pleased.

"Watch," he said.

Then he wrapped the hand into which Harry had spat around his erection.

"Watch?" Harry said, glancing down in disgust.

"No!" the creature said. "Him. You and me. We watch him." As the beast spoke, he began to work his rod with long, leisurely strokes. His free hand still rested on Harry's shoulder, and with overpowering force he turned Harry back toward his partner.

Harry was appalled to see that the damage done in the few seconds Harry's gaze had been averted had already rendered Scummy unrecognizable: his hair had burned away entirely, and his naked head was a bubbling ball of red and black; his eyes were virtually closed by the heat-swollen flesh, and his mouth hung open, burning tongue sticking out like an accusing finger.

Harry tried to move, but the hand on his shoulder kept him from the job. He tried to close his eyes against the horror, but the creature, though he was standing behind Harry, somehow knew that he was disobeying his instruction. The beast pushed his thumb into the clenched muscle of Harry's shoulder, penetrating it with the ease of a man pressing his thumb into an overripe pear.

"Open!" the beast demanded.

Harry did as he was told. The blistered meat of Scummy's face had started to blacken, the swollen skin cracking open and curling back from the muscle.

"God forgive me, Scummy. God fucking forgive me."

"Oh!" the beast gasped. "You dirty-mouthed whore!"

Without warning, the beast unloaded. Then he gave a shuddering sigh and turned Harry to face him once more, the two lighted pinpoints of his eyes seeming to burrow into Harry's head and scratch at the back of his skull.

"Stay out of the Triangle," he said. "Understand?"

"Yes."

"Say it."

"I understand."

"Not that. The other thing. Say it, like you did before."

Harry gritted his teeth. There was a definitive point where his flight was overridden by his fight, and he was fast approaching it.

"Say. It," the beast said.

"God forgive me," Harry said through gritted teeth.

"No. I want to have it in my head for later. Give me something good to work with."

Harry mustered the voice of entreaty as best he could, which, as it turned out, wasn't very hard.

"God. Forgive me."

3

Harry woke around noon, the sound of his partner's screams nearer than his liquor-soaked memories of the previous night's birthday celebrations. The streets outside his room were gratifyingly quiet. All he heard was a bell, calling those who were still faithful to a Sunday mass. He ordered up some coffee and juice, which came while he was showering. The day was already humid, and by the time he'd dried himself he'd already started work on a fresh sweat.

As he sipped his coffee, strong and sweet, he watched the people to-ing and froing in the street two stories below. The only pair in any hurry were a couple of tourists with a map; everyone else was going about their business at a nice mellow speed, pacing themselves for the long hot day and the long hot night that would surely follow.

The phone rang. Harry picked it up.

"Are you checking up on me, Norma?" he said, trying his best to sound human.

"Got it in one, Detective," Norma said. "And no. It wouldn't do me much good, would it? You're too good a liar, Harry D'Amour."

"You did teach me everything I know."

"Watch it, now. How was the birthday celebration?"

"I got drunk—"

"No surprise there."

"—and I started thinking about the past."

"Oh Lord, Harry. What have I told you about leaving that shit alone?"

"I don't *invite* the thoughts in."

Norma spat out a humorless laugh. "Honey, we both know you were born with an invitation stamped on your forehead."

Harry grimaced.

"All I can say is what's already been said," Norma continued. "What's done is done. The good and the bad both. So make peace with it or it'll swallow you whole."

"Norma, I want to do what I came here to do and get out of this goddamn city."

"Harry—"

But he had already gone.

Norma pursed her lips and hung up the phone. She knew what to expect from Harry D'Amour, but that didn't mean she was inured to his brooding, tortured façade. Yes, Otherness had a way of finding Harry wherever he went, but there were things that could be done about that—measures that could be taken if one was so inclined. Harry D'Amour never took those measures because, Norma knew, Harry D'Amour loved his job. More important, he was damn good at it, and, as long as that was the case, Norma would forgive him his transgressions.

Norma Paine, black, blind, and admitting to being sixty-three (though the truth was probably closer to eighty or more), sat in her favorite chair by the window of her fifteenth-floor apartment. It was from this spot that she had spent twelve hours of every day for the last forty years talking to the dead. It was a service she offered to the recently deceased, who were, in Norma's experience, often lost, confused, and frightened. She'd seen the departed in her mind's eye since infancy.

Norma had been born blind, and it had come as quite a shock to her when she first realized that the benign faces she could remember looking down at her in her cot were not those of her parents, but those of the curious departed. The way she saw it, she was lucky. She wasn't really blind—she just saw a different world from most other folks, and that put her in a unique position to do some good in the world.

Somehow if someone was dead and lost in New York, sooner or later they found their way to Norma. Some nights there were phantoms lined up half a block or more, sometimes just a dozen or so. And occasionally she would be so inundated with needy phantoms that she would have to turn all hundred and three televisions in her apartment on—all playing relatively low, but tuned to different channels, in a new Babel of game shows, soap operas, weather reports, scandal, tragedy, and banality—in order to drive them all away.

It wasn't often that Norma's counseling of the recently dead overlapped with Harry's life as a private investigator, but there were always exceptions. Carston Goode had been one such case. Goode by name, good by nature—that was how he'd styled his life. Goode was a family man who had married his high school sweetheart. Together, they lived in New York with five kids to raise and more than enough money to do so, thanks to fees he charged as a lawyer, a few good investments, and a deep-seated faith in the generosity of the Lord his God, Who took—as Carston was fond of saying—"best care of those who cared best about Him." At least that had been his belief until eight days ago, when within the space of a hundred seconds his well-ordered, God-loving life had gone to Hell.

Carston Goode had been on his way to work, bright and early, eager as a man half his age to be in the thick of things, when a youth had darted toward him through the throng of early birds on Lexington Avenue and snatched Carston's briefcase right out of his hand. Lesser men would have yelled for help, but Carston Goode was more confident in the state of his body than most his age. He didn't smoke or drink. He worked out four times a week and only sparingly indulged in his passion for red meat. None of these things, however, stopped him from being felled by a massive heart attack just as he came within two or three strides of the felon he'd decided to chase down.

Goode was dead, and death was bad. Not simply because he'd left his beloved Patricia alone to raise their children or he wouldn't now get to write the book of personal revelations about life and the law that he'd been resolving to do every New Year's Eve for the past decade.

No, the truly bad thing about Goode being dead was the little house in the French Quarter of New Orleans that Patricia didn't know he owned. He had been especially careful to keep all knowledge of its existence a secret. But he had not factored into his arrangements the possibility that he'd drop dead in the street without the least warning. Now he was faced with the inevitable dissolution of everything that he'd worked so hard to appear to be.

Sooner or later, somebody—either Patricia going through the drawers in his desk or one of his associates dutifully tidying up the work Goode had left unfinished at the firm—would turn up some reference to number 68 Dupont Street in Louisiana and, tracking down the owner of the house at the address, would discover it had been Carston. And it was only a matter of time before they would go down to New Orleans to find out what secrets it would reveal. And the secrets were abundant.

Well, Carston Goode wasn't about to take this lying down. Once he adjusted to his less corporeal state, he next learned the way the system worked on the Other Side. And, putting his skills as a lawyer to work, he very soon had jumped to the front of a long line and found himself in the presence of the woman he had been assured would solve his problems.

"You're Norma Paine?" he said.

"That's right."

"Why do you have so many televisions? You're blind."

"And you're rude. I swear, the bigger the bully, the smaller the dick."

Carston's jaw dropped.

"You can see me?"

"Unfortunately, yes."

Carston looked down at his body. He, like every ghost he'd met since his death, was naked. His hands instantly moved to his withered penis.

"There's no need to be offensive," he said. "Now please, I have money, so—"

46

Norma got up from her chair and walked straight at Goode, murmuring to herself.

"Every night I get one of these dead-ass fools think they can buy their way into Heaven. There's a trick my momma taught me," she said to Goode, "once she knew I had the gift. It's called Ghost Pushing." With the palm of her left hand, she shoved Goode in the middle of the chest. He stumbled backward.

"How did you—"

"Two more of those and you're gone."

"Please! Listen to me!"

She shoved again. "Make that one. Say good night—"

"I need to talk to Harry D'Amour."

Norma stopped dead in her tracks and said, "You've got one minute to change my mind about you."

4

"Harry D'Amour. He's a private investigator, right? I was told you know him."

"What if I do?"

"I have urgent need of his services. And like I said, money is no consequence. I'd prefer to talk directly to D'Amour, after he's signed a confidentiality agreement, of course."

Norma laughed, hard and long.

"I never cease . . ." she started to reply, her words having to compete with her unfettered amusement, ". . . never . . . cease to be amazed . . . at how many absurdities can be uttered in perfect seriousness by folks like you. In case you haven't noticed, you're not in your law offices now. Ain't no use in hanging on to your little secrets, 'cause you've got nowhere to put them except up your ass. So talk, or I'm gonna leave you to find some other ghost talker."

"Okay. Okay. Just . . . just don't send me away. The truth: I own a house in New Orleans. Nothing fancy, but I use it as a place to get away from . . . my responsibilities . . . as a family man."

"Oh, I've heard this story before. And what is it you do in the little house of yours?"

"Entertain."

"I bet you do. And who are the entertained?"

"Men. Young men. Legal age, mind you. But young nonetheless. And it's not what you think. No drugs. No violence. When we meet, we make . . . magic." He spoke the word quietly, as though he might be overheard. "It's never serious. Just some bits of nonsense I got out of old books. I find it keeps things spicy."

"I still haven't heard a compelling reason to help you. So you had yourself a secret life. Then you up and died and now people are gonna find out. That's the bed you made. Make your peace with what you were and move on."

"No. You misunderstand. I'm not ashamed. Yes, I fought what I was at first, but I came to terms with that a long time ago. That's when I bought the house. I don't give a shit what people think or the legacy I left behind. I'm dead. What does it matter now?"

"That's the first sensible thing you've said all night."

"Yeah, well, there's no use denying it. And like I said, that's not the problem. I loved every moment I spent at that house. The problem is that I loved my wife too. I still do. So much that I can't bear the thought of her ever finding out. Not for me, but because I know it would destroy her. That's why I need your help. I don't want my best friend to die knowing she didn't really know me. I don't want our kids to suffer the fallout of her wounds and my . . . indiscretions. I need to know they're going to be okay."

"There's enough in that story to make me think you might be a decent human being under all those layers of lawyer and liar."

Goode didn't raise his head. "Does that mean you'll help me?"

"I'll talk to him."

"When?"

"Lord, but you're impatient."

"Look, I'm sorry. But every hour that passes makes it more likely that

Patricia—that's my wife—is going to find something. And when she does, that's when the questions start."

"You've been dead how long?"

"Eight days."

"Well, if your adoring wife loves you as much as you claim, I think it's reasonable to assume that she's far too busy grieving to be going through your papers."

"Grieving," Goode said, as though the idea of his wife's anguish concerning his death had not really come into focus until now.

"Yes, grieving. I take that to mean you haven't been home to see for yourself."

The lawyer shook his head.

"Couldn't. I was afraid. No. I *am* afraid. Of what I'll find."

"Like I said, I'll see what I can do. But I'm making no promises. Harry's a busy man. And weary, though he won't admit to it. So be warned: I care about his welfare as if he were my own flesh and blood. If this business in New Orleans goes sour because of something you fail to tell me here and now, I'll have an undead lynch mob chase down your lily-white ass and hang you up from a lamppost in Times Square until Judgment Day. Understand?"

"Yes Miss Paine."

" 'Norma' is fine, Carston."

"How did you—"

"Oh, come on now. I can see your dead, naked ass and you don't know how I know your name?"

"Right."

"Right. So here's what we'll do. Come back tomorrow, early in the evening. I'm less busy then. And I'll see if I can persuade Harry to join us."

"Norma?" Carston mumbled.

"Yes?"

"Thank you."

"Don't thank me yet. When you hire Harry D'Amour, things have a tendency to become . . . complicated."

5

The subsequent meeting had gone smoothly enough, the dead Mr. Goode giving Harry the number of a security box filled with cash ("for those little expenses I didn't want my accountant asking me about") from which Harry could take as much as he felt appropriate for fees, flight, and hotel costs, with enough left to cover whatever problems might pop up that would need "Monetary Lubrication" to ease them away. All of this brought D'Amour to where he now stood: before Carston Goode's House of Sin.

It wasn't much to look at from the outside. Just a wrought-iron door in a twelve-foot wall with the number painted on a blue and white ceramic tile and set in the plaster beside it. Carston had been able to supply Harry with a detailed description of the kinds of incriminating toys Harry would find in the house, but he hadn't been in any condition to supply keys. Harry had told him not to worry. Harry had never met a lock he couldn't open.

And, true to form, he had the gate open in under ten seconds and was walking up the uneven paved path that was bordered on either side by pots of various shapes and sizes, the mingled fragrance of blossoms as intense as a dozen shattered perfume bottles. Nobody had been there to take care of Goode's garden in a long time, Harry noticed. The ground was slimy with decayed petals, and many of the species in the pots had perished for want of attention. Harry was surprised at the state of the place. A man as organized as Goode would surely have made arrangements to keep his garden looking nice and neat, even when he wasn't there to view it. So what had happened to the gardener?

Four strides farther, Harry reached the front door and he had his answer. There were thirty or more fetishes nailed upon the door, some small, clear bottles containing scraps of God knew what, and one small clay representation of a man, his cock and balls no longer between his legs—but tied with glue-caked string around his face. The genitals were upside down, so that his testicles could be painted as eyes and his penis as a jutting nose that was daubed bright red.

Not for the first time during this trip Harry glanced around looking for some hint that his employer's spirit was somewhere nearby. Harry had been in the company of phantoms often enough to know what tiny signs to look for: a certain strangeness in the way shadows moved; sometimes a low-velocity hum; sometimes the simple silence of nearby animals. But Harry sensed nothing in the sunlit garden to suggest he had Goode's company. It was a pity, really; it would have made the search-and-destroy mission ahead a damn sight more entertaining if Harry had known the owner of the House of Sin was witnessing everything.

There was a thick line of what was undoubtedly dried blood poured across the house's threshold, its sacrificial thrashing source catching the lower half of the door in its death throes. Harry took out his pick again and quickly opened the two locks.

"Knock, knock," he muttered as he turned the handle.

The door creaked but failed to move. He worked the handle back and forth a few times to be sure it was functioning, then put his shoulder to the job, with all hundred and ninety-seven pounds of him to back it up.

Several of the bagged fetishes gave up the smell of their contents as he pressed against them: a dust of incense and dead flesh. Harry held his breath and forced the door.

There was more creaking, then one loud crack that echoed against the courtyard walls and he was in, stepping away from the fetishes before he took another breath. The air was cleaner on the inside than out. Stale, yes, but nothing that instantly set off alarm bells. Harry paused for a moment. The phone in his pocket rang. He answered.

"Impressive. Every case we've done together you've been on the line as soon as I step into—"

"Shit?"

"No, Norma. The house. I've just stepped into the house. And you knew it. You always do."

"Lucky, I suppose," Norma said. "So is it a den of sodomy?"

"Not at the moment, but the day is young."

"Are you feeling better?"

"Well, I ate several pastries and had three cups of the best damn coffee I ever drank. So, I'm ready to go at it."

"Then I'll leave you to it."

"Actually, I got a question for you. We got fetishes covering the front door, some jars with some kind of shit in them, a little clay man with disfigured genitals, and blood on the threshold."

"And?"

"Any idea what that's all about?"

"Doing what fetishes do. Somebody's trying to keep the wrong things out and the right things in. Do they look new?"

"A week or so, judging by the blood."

"So it wasn't Goode's doing."

"Definitely not. Besides, this is fairly elaborate stuff. Is it possible Goode did serious magic down here?"

"I doubt it. Way he talked, he was using the magic as a way of getting his guests naked. He might have bled a chicken or drew up some phony circle to give it some flavor, but I don't think it was anything more than that. Regardless, be careful. They do things differently down there. Voodoo is potent shit."

"Yeah, and some of it's on my shoe."

The conversation ended there. Harry pocketed his phone and began his search.

6

Harry had only signed off with Norma for a minute, no more, when his exploration of the three small downstairs rooms brought him into contact with a patch of intensely cold air in the kitchen, which was a sure sign of a presence from the Other Side. He didn't attempt to retreat from it or spit out the dozen verses he could recite that essentially meant "Get thee the fuck out of my way." Instead he stood perfectly still, the air so chilled his breath formed a dense cloud at his lips, while the cold patch circled him and circled again.

Back in New York, when Harry finally left the force he had sought a different type of protection. His queries soon brought him to one Caz King, a tattoo artist known for his expertise in arcane symbology. Caz tattooed visual defenses against dark forces on the bodies of his clients.

Upon his instruction, Caz attempted to commit to Harry's body every alarm system in his arsenal that was applicable to all forms of nonhuman life that Harry might encounter. Caz had done a thorough job, because the symbols and codes were soon fighting for space. Best of all, the alarm system actually worked. Even now, one of the small identification tattoos Caz had drawn on Harry was twitching, telling him that his chilly, unseen visitor was something called a String Yart, a harmless, nervous entity that resembled, in the words of those who'd studied them, a monkey made of loosely configured ectoplasm.

Harry uttered the command, "No go, Yart," the first two words calling into life the complex design Caz had spent a month of nights inking onto Harry's chest. The design was intended to be a universal repellant and it worked beautifully.

Harry felt the ink get a little hotter under his skin and then suddenly the patch of cold air left his vicinity. He waited a few seconds to see if there were other curious presences here who also wanted to inspect him, but nobody came. After two or three minutes of looking around the kitchen and finding nothing even vaguely interesting, Harry went into the other two rooms on that floor. One had a dining table, polished but still much scratched. There were large metal fixtures beneath each corner of the table, placed there, he assumed, to make binding someone to the table easy. But that was all Harry found in either room that he'd need to deal with before leaving.

Upstairs, however, was a different story. On the floor inside the first of the three bedrooms there was a four-foot-high bronze statue of a satyr in a state of extreme arousal, the lewd mischief of his intent wonderfully caught by the sculptor. Carston, it soon became apparent, had quite an eye for erotic antiques.

On one wall of the first bedroom was an arrangement of Chinese fans spread to display the elaborately choreographed orgies that decorated each one. And there was more antique erotica on the other walls. Prints that looked like illustrations to pornographic rewriting of the Old Testament, and a large fragment from a frieze in which the orgiasts were interlocked in elaborate configurations.

There was a double bed in the room, stripped back to a stained mattress, and a dresser, which contained some casual clothes and a few letters, which Harry pocketed unread. Buried at the back of the middle drawer, Harry found another envelope, which contained one thing only: a photograph of what he took to be the Goode family, standing beside a pool, frozen forever in a happier time.

Finally Harry had an image of Goode—his grin unforced, his arm tightly clasping his happy spouse to his side. The kids—three girls, two boys—all seemed as guilelessly happy as their parents. It had been good to be Goode that day, no question. And much as Harry scrutinized the father's face, he could see no sign that Goode was a man with secrets. All the lines on his face were laugh lines and his eyes gazed into the camera lens without a trace of reticence.

Harry left the picture out on the top of the dresser for later visitors to find. Then he moved on to the next room. It was in darkness. Harry stayed at the threshold while he found a light switch.

Nothing he'd seen in the house so far had prepared him for what came into view when the single naked bulb hanging at the center of the room went on. Here, finally, was something he could entertain Norma by describing: a leather sling hanging from the ceiling supported by heavy-duty rope. It was a black hammock designed for those special folks who rested best with their legs held high and wide.

The windows in the room were sealed up with blackout fabric. Between the window and where Harry stood was a comprehensive collection of sex toys: dildos ranging in scale from the invasive to the inconceivable, whips, switches, and old-fashioned canes, two gas masks, coiled lengths of rope, plastic cylinders with rubber tubes attached, screw-down presses, and a dozen or so items that looked like esoteric surgical equipment.

It was all meticulously clean. Even the faint pine odor of disinfectant was still present. But however bizarre and intense the ceremonies of pain and violation here had been, they had left nothing in the room that caused Caz's tattoos to warn Harry of imminent trouble. The room was clean, by both bacterial and metaphysical standards.

"I see your point, Mister Goode," Harry murmured to the creator of this chamber of possibilities, absent though he was.

Harry moved on to the next room, which he fully anticipated would contain proof of further escalation in Goode's debaucheries. He opened the door, which was the only one *inside* the house that had sigils etched into it. Harry was unsure whether it was for keeping unwanted guests out or dangerous elements in, but he was certain he would soon find out. He flipped on the light—another bare bulb hanging on a ragged cord—to illuminate a room that, compared to the previous one, was a model of decorum. The windows were blacked out here too and, like the rest of the room, they were painted a light gray.

Harry's tattoos gave off a warning twitch when he stepped over the threshold. He'd come to be able to interpret the subtle differences in the signals over the years. This warning was the equivalent of a blinking amber light. Some kind of magical working had been performed here, it told him. But where was the evidence? The room contained two plain wooden chairs, a bowl filled with what had been dog food, he guessed, its dried-up remains still attracting a few lazy flies.

With its bare boards and its blacked-out windows, the room was certainly set up for magic. There were two oddities in the room's construction, which Harry had noticed the moment he surveyed the room: the right-hand window was placed too close to the corner of the room, which meant either that the architect had done a lousy job or that the room had been shortened at some point in its sordid history, with the faux wall put up to create a very narrow and as yet unseen fourth space.

Harry went over to the wall, looking for some way in, the multiplying of the signals from his tattoos indicating that he was indeed getting warmer in his ghostly game of Marco Polo. Harry looked down at the palm of his left hand where Caz had painfully drawn the Searcher's Sigil. For an instant Harry was back on 11th Avenue and the hand was not his but that of the demon.

"*Spit!*" Harry heard the word bounce off the walls in the claustrophobic space.

"Go fuck yourself," Harry said, and drove the vision from his head as he pressed his tattooed hand to the wall.

Now he was on to something. A silent imperative, one that didn't slow its work by traveling by way of thoughts, took hold of Harry's hand and moved it over the wall, lower and lower, until his little finger was brushing the ground. Harry felt the Searcher Sigil's exhilaration at the hunt, quickening as his hand closed on its invisible quarry. There was a mark on the gray paint barely darker than the rest of the wall. And before Harry even realized it, his hand had already elected his middle finger to finish the job. It pressed lightly on the spot, there was an audible click, and then Harry was obliged to stand back as a door, exquisitely concealed by the gray paint, swung open on silent hinges.

Mr. Carston Goode apparently had more to hide than his extensive collection of toys, and absurdly satisfied at the discovery, Harry stepped inside the small room to find out what. Like its predecessors, this tiny room had but a single bare bulb to illuminate it, but whereas there had been nothing in the previous rooms that was of any great interest to Harry, this narrow passage was another story entirely.

One wall was given over to books, the scent of their antiquity powerful. It was a smell that Harry's six years as a pupil at St. Dominic's All Boys Catholic School had taught him to abhor. It brought back too many unwelcome memories of the casual brutalities of the place. There were the usual rulers across the knuckles and canes on bare buttocks, of course, but many of St. Dominic's staff had other appetites that a beating wouldn't placate. The Fathers all had their favorites. But Harry had been spared the private lessons, as they were commonly called. He'd had more kick in him than any of the Fathers were willing to handle.

But as they say, hurt people hurt people, and the pupils themselves played their own version of the game. Harry had been their victim on several occasions, and the library was their location of choice. Father Edgar, the library's overlord, was often absent from his desk, dealing a harsh hand to boys who were lax about returning books. It was there between the stacks that the strong took the lesser, and it was there that Harry, his head pressed to the floor while he was used, learned to loathe the smell of old books.

Waving away the scent and its unbidden memories, Harry scanned Goode's secret library speedily, pausing only when he came upon titles of particular interest. Goode's limited but nonetheless impressive library included the Carapace Derivations, a series of books that had undoubtedly driven more inept practitioners to self-slaughter than anything else on these well-stocked shelves; two thin volumes, their author unnamed, that seemed to be illustrated guides to suicide; a few books on Sex Magick (the *K* used, he guessed, as a nod to Crowley's explorations in this territory); and *The Frey-Kistiandt Dialogues*, a grimoire that reputedly only existed in an edition of one (which he was now holding in his hand), which was rumored to have been found in the ashes of the Yedlin—the child genius of Florence who had been burned in one of the Savonarola purges. Harry's insatiable curiosity could not lessen the temptation to put its legend to the test. He raised the open book to his face and breathed deep. It smelled of fire.

Harry suddenly saw Scummy's face, with his eyes spilling from their sockets as they burned, and he quickly closed the book. He'd seen more than enough of Goode's collection, he decided.

He turned his attentions from the shelf of books and looked to the other wall. There he found a few more rows of shelves. These were given over to the kind of stuff Goode had probably used to get his young, impressionable guests in the mood: candles of red and black wax in the form of phalluses; a row of bottles intricately decorated with multicolored beads that were filled with, when Harry uncorked them, eye-stinging liquor, some of it vaguely smelling like brandy or whisky but clearly adulterated with Goode's secret ingredients, whatever they were. Some were herbal, Harry's nose told him; much else was not. God knows what prescription medications Goode had ground up and dissolved in this "sacred potion": tranquilizers, most likely, and perhaps a few magic pills designed to cure erectile dysfunction.

All of this would have to go, of course, as would most of the other contents on these shelves: the phials of white powder, which he presumed was cocaine; the row of little fetish dolls with the faces of young men snipped from photographs and attached to the heads of the dolls with safety pins, along with a second set, this one of their genitals, similarly clipped and pinned, but between their legs. Harry counted them. There were twenty-six dolls there in what he took to be Carston Goode's harem. Harry would have to take some advice from a local expert in these dolls before he committed them to the flames, just to make sure that it wouldn't cause all twenty-six young men they represented to ignite where they stood.

Having explored the upper shelves, Harry now went down on his haunches, knees popping as he took a closer look at the middle rows. There were a number of large jars with vacuum-sealed lids used for homemade preserves. But the contents of these jars weren't as benign as blackberry jam and pickled onions. They contained dead things in a solution of what was probably formaldehyde: some freakish (a two-headed rat, an albino toad, its eyes bright red) some decidedly sexual (a human penis, a jar entirely filled with testicles, like pinkish eggs, a fetus with an endowment long enough to wrap around its own throat), and some that had simply rotted or disintegrated in the preserving fluid, leaving pieces of unrecognizable gristle in the murk. These, like the dolls, he would need the experience of some local expert to safely dispose of.

Taken in their entirety, the items suggested that Goode's interest in magic went a long way beyond the theatrics required to get a bunch of guests naked. Sure, a few of the freak-show items might have been used as props to lend veracity to a faked ceremony, but that didn't explain the library or the row of dolls with their pinned-on portraits.

He went down on his knees to search the shadowy recesses of the bottom shelves. There were more jars lined up there, but behind them his blind hand came to rest on something very different. A small box, perhaps four inches square, which when he brought it out into the light proved to be intricately carved on all six sides with golden-etched designs.

Harry knew what it was the instant he had it in the light. It was a puzzle box, a piece more valuable and more dangerous than all of the rest of Goode's collection put together.

7

Harry's fingers moved over the box without need of his instruction, eager to familiarize themselves with the feel of the thing. The box released a host of stimuli through his inquiring fingers that made Harry feel good all the way down to his guts, and then, having proffered this taste of bliss, suddenly withdrew it, leaving Harry feeling empty. He tried to duplicate the motions he'd made when he'd first picked the box up, but the bit of bliss was not to be had a second time. If he wanted more of the same, Harry knew from the stories, he would have to solve the puzzle that the box presented.

Harry stood up and leaned on the bookshelves to take a better look at the glittering device. He'd never laid eyes on one until now. Named after their French designer, the devices were known simply as Lemarchand's Boxes. In more knowing circles, however, they were also branded with a more truthful name: Lament Configurations. They existed in unknown numbers all around the world. Some, like this one, were in hiding, but many were out in the tide of human affairs and appetites, where they made terrible mischief. To solve the puzzle box was to open a door to Hell, or so the stories said. The fact that most of the people who solved the puzzles were innocents who'd chanced upon them was apparently a matter of indifference to Hell and its infernal agents. A soul, it would seem, was a soul.

Even though he knew all too well the danger a Lament Configuration presented, Harry could not quite persuade himself to put it back behind the specimen jars. Harry let the twitching pleasure in his fingertips slide over the box once more. That briefest of contacts the Configuration had teased him with had been rapturous, and his fingers couldn't forget the feeling, and, without even his instructing, his hands were investigating the box as if reacquainting themselves with an old friend.

Harry watched them, feeling oddly remote from their frenetic motion and remoter still from the possibility of consequence. He could stop this at any moment, he told himself; but why stop so quickly when he could feel little trills of pleasure moving up through his fingers to his hands, to his arms, to his whole weary system? He had plenty of time to call a halt to this before it got hazardous. But in the meantime why not enjoy the panacea that the box provided as it eased the aches in his joints and his back and sent a rush of blood to his groin?

In this moment, the not-so-distant memory of Scummy, the humiliations at St. Dominic's, and the countless other ghosts of far too many pasts caused Harry no pain at all. They were all part of a pattern, like the sides of a Lemarchand's Box; with time, it would all come to fit in some grand design, or so his untethered thoughts persuaded him. There was suddenly a subtle vibration from the box, and Harry struggled to focus more clearly on the nature of the power in his hand. It was veiling itself from him, he knew—hiding its darker purpose behind the gifts of pleasure and reassurance.

Put it down, he told himself. But his body had been unpleasured for so long (some Calvinistic streak in him denying anything that smacked of self-indulgence as though it might weaken him when the battle began in earnest, as one day he knew it would) that this finger-marrow joy was enough to seduce him momentarily from the narrow road he had been so obsessively walking.

In short, he did not put down the box but continued to investigate it with something very close to tenderness. The puzzle was succumbing to him with an ease that inspired suspicion at the rim of his thoughts. It was showing its innards to him, their surfaces as intricately inscribed as the six external walls. His fingers could do no wrong now. They slid, they pressed, they stroked; and to each stimulus the box responded with its own flourish: sliding open to reveal an interior maze work of mechanisms that blossomed and seeded.

Harry would have been lost to its beguilements had a sudden rush of purposeful arctic air not enveloped him, turning the sweat of excitement on his back and brow to a suit of ice water. The spell was broken instantaneously, and his fingers—this time moved by his own instruction—dropped the open box at his feet. It made an uncanny sound in the narrow passage, as though something much larger had struck the ground. The String Yart had returned.

"Oh, for God's sake," Harry said.

To Harry's astonishment, he got a reply. Two of the small jars on the upper shelf flipped and fled to the floor, shattering. The phantom's presence had put such a chill on Harry that his teeth were chattering.

"No. Go. Yart," Harry said, his voice laced with irritation.

The cold air dissipated. No sooner had the Yart heeded Harry's command than a banal tinkling tune rose from the ground, its source the Lament Configuration that lay gleaming among the scattered jars and their withered contents.

"The hell . . . ?" said Harry.

This was what Goode was attracting Harry's attention to. Though he'd let go of the box, the damn thing had made its solving its own responsibility. This was a new kink in the lore of the box for Harry. Whenever he'd found reference to the Configuration the victim had signed his own death warrant by solving the box's puzzle himself.

"These things don't solve themselves, right?" Harry asked the air.

Several of the smaller bottles knocked against one another.

"Now that reply I'm not so sure about?" Harry said.

The ghost passed behind the books, knocking every third or fourth volume onto the floor.

"Whatever you're trying to tell me—"

Harry stopped, unfinished, because his question was in the process of being answered. And the answer was yes. The box was indeed solving itself; pieces of its internal anatomy slid into view and were lifting the box up. The parts coming into view were asymmetrical, causing the box to topple sideways. Now it had room to instigate the next stage in its self-solving: a three-way separation of its top surface, which caused the unleashing of a discernible ripple of energy that carried the subtle but distinct odor of curdled milk.

The box's maneuvers gathered speed and, staring down at it, watching the device perform, Harry decided it was time for this game to end. He raised his foot and brought it down on the box, intending to break it. He failed. Not because his weight wasn't sufficient to do the job, but because the box had a defense mechanism for which he had not accounted, somehow forcing his foot aside as it came within less than an inch of its target so that it slid around the box like a rubber sole on wet rock. He tried again, and again he failed.

"That's fucked," he remarked, sounding a damn sight less nonchalant than he felt.

The only option remaining was to get out of the place before the fishermen who'd cast this glittering bait came for their catch. He stepped over the box, which continued to resolve its own conundrums. That, Harry reasoned, was a good sign indicating that the door to Hell was not yet open. But he'd no sooner taken comfort in this thought than the walls of the passage proceeded to shake. Minor tremors escalated in seconds to what felt like blows being delivered against the narrow space from all sides. All the items on the shelves that had not already been knocked off by Goode's ghost now came down: the rest of the books, large and small; the specimen jars; and all the other bizarrities in the dead man's collection.

The walls on which the shelves had been secured were fracturing from floor to ceiling and beams of cold light pierced the cracks. Harry knew from experience the nature of that light, and the company it kept. A casual observer might have called it blue, but that missed all its nuances. This was a plague pallor, the color of grieving and despair.

Harry didn't need to rely on his Unscratchable Itch, because Caz's handiwork was going crazy, warning him with every twitch and thrum that this was not a good place for him to be. He was in the process of taking the tattoos' advice, kicking aside all that had been cleared from the shelves so as to get back to the exit. But as he did so, curiosity got the better of him and for a moment he paused to look through the widening crack behind the shelves to his right.

The gap in the wall was at least a foot and a half wide and getting wider. There would be, he guessed, some unforeseeable horror coming through the passage between here and there; a glimpse was all he needed, enough to be able to report something even juicier than he'd anticipated to Norma.

But to his surprise and mild disappointment, there were no demons in immediate view. What he could see, through the shifting crack in the wall, was a vast landscape. He took a quick glance around at the other cracks, but he saw only the same dead, cold light and heard only the sound of a harsh wind, which was blowing across the wilderness in front of him, raising up all manner of trash from the ground—nothing particularly hellish, just plastic bags, sheets of filthy paper, and brown dust. It looked like a war zone.

He could see now the patterns of old, cobbled streets crisscrossing the wasteland, and in some places the rubble of an old building that had presumably once stood on the spot in question. In the middle distance, however, emerging from behind the slow veil of gray smoke, entire buildings, miraculously saved from the bombardment that had leveled everything else, still stood tall. In better times they had been beautiful, he knew, which surprised him. They looked like refugees from the old cities of Europe in their elegance.

The gap in the wall had now opened to the width of a door, and Harry had advanced a step or two through it without even being conscious of having done so. It wasn't every day that a man got a glimpse of the Pit. He was determined to take as much from this opportunity as he could. In his hunger to make sense of the entire vista, however, he had neglected to look down at his feet.

He was standing on the top step of a steep flight of stone steps, the base of which was erased by a yellow-gray mist. And from that mist a figure was emerging. It was a naked man, his limbs scrawny, his belly a pot, the muscles of his chest covered by a layer of fat that resembled rudimentary breasts. But it was the man's head that drew Harry's astonished gaze. The man had clearly been the subject of a vicious experiment, its consequences so severe that Harry was astonished the patient still lived.

The man's head had been sawed open through the bone, from the top of his skull to the base of his neck, slicing down the middle of his nose, mouth, and chin, leaving only his tongue entire, which lolled from the left side of the man's mouth. In order to keep bone and muscle from returning to their natural position, a thick rod of rusting iron, maybe five inches long, had been driven a finger length down into the gap in the sundered head.

The iron rod did more than simply separate the halves, however; it also—by some trick in its design—forced the half faces away from the frontal position, directing the man's gaze off at forty-five degrees in each direction. This cruel surgery left its victim with a vaguely reptilian likeness, his bulging eyes staring out in different directions, and as a result with every few steps he took he turned his head one way or the other so to fix his gaze again on Harry.

How any human being's anatomy, much less his sanity, could have survived such vicious reconstruction was beyond comprehension. But survive he had, and with countless other parts of his anatomy also sliced and shaved and hammered and threaded, the man loped up the stairs toward Harry with distressing ease, as though this was a condition with which he had been born.

"And time to go," Harry said to himself, though his curiosity was a long way from being sated.

He knew how he was going to seal the door, presuming the conventional method of reversing the work—closing the box that had caused the connection to be made in the first place—was not available. He'd use one of three pieces of magic—Universal Incantations (magicians called them U-eez)—that would do the job without need of much preparation.

The bisected man continued to lope up the steps toward him when a penetrating voice rang out from the mist.

"Felixson. Hurry."

The bisected man froze.

At last, the presence of this mutilated thing upon the steps made sense. It was not here alone. It was the property of some greater power, which had apparently quickened its ascent, so that its form slowly became clearer. It was male, dressed in the ageless black vestments of the Cenobites, an infernal order of priests and priestesses.

But this wasn't just any Cenobite going about his business of catching souls in a net of promised ecstasies. This was a figure in Hell's pantheon whom many who could not have named three angels could recognize. Somebody had even thought up a nickname for him that had quickly grown in popularity. He was called Pinhead, a name, Harry now saw, that was as insulting as it was appropriate. A pattern of grooves resembling the rigorous design of a chessboard, its squares, as yet undifferentiated, had been carved into his sickly flesh, and where the lines crossed, the pins that had earned him his moniker (not pins at all, in truth, but hefty nails) had been hammered into bone and brain.

Harry didn't let the shock of recognition hold him for more than a moment. He took a backward step into the narrow, chaotic room behind him and uttered five words of a Universal Incantation:

"Emat. Thel. Mani. Fiedoth. Uunadar."

The demonic Hell Priest heard the incantation and yelled up to his beast:

"Take him, Felixson! Be quick!"

Already the matter between worlds was knitting together in response to Harry's instruction, a thickening veil between this world and Hell.

But Felixson, the bisected man, was quicker than the incantation. Before he even reached the top of the stairs he leaped for the breach, his body tearing the veil open as it plunged through. Harry retreated to the door that took him out into the empty gray room. But the morbid curiosity, one of countless shades of curiosity Harry possessed, kept him from leaving the tiny hidden room before he had a closer look at the creature named Felixson who now entered the narrow room and seemingly forgot his purpose the moment he did so. Harry watched as this halved man lowered his abominable head to scan the remnants of Goode's library.

And then, to Harry's' astonishment, Felixson spoke, or came as close to doing so as his divided palate allowed.

". . . Bookshh . . ." he said, specks of spittle flying from his mouth.

A kind of tenderness had come into his manner, and he went down on his haunches, both sides of his head smiling.

"Books?" Harry murmured as Felixson lovingly picked over the litter of Carston Goode's secret library.

Harry's voice was enough to break the creature from his reverie. Felixson dropped the book he had been lovingly examining and looked past the fallen cabinet at Harry.

"You! Shtay!" Felixson said.

Harry shook his head.

"Nope."

Harry raised his hand and slid it behind the bookcase that stood between him and Felixson, pushing with all his might. The room was far too narrow to allow the bookcase to fall very far. It struck the shelves on the other wall, shedding the last of its contents.

As it toppled, Harry pushed against the door, which had swung closed, and stepped out into the gray room. Behind him, he heard the noise of splintering wood as Felixson tore at the cabinet so as to get to the door. Harry turned back and slammed it closed. It locked automatically, and the invisible door illusion was instantly complete once more. It didn't remain that way for long, however. Seemingly possessed with an inhuman strength, Felixson thumped against the door with intent. It flew open, splintering off its hinges.

"Die now, Detective!" Felixson said, stepping out of the small room.

Before Harry could process Felixson's impossible knowledge of his profession, a light within the narrow room blazed with sudden ferocity, illuminating everything with the deranged lucidity of lightning blasts. As if punctuating the display, a hook-headed chain leaped out of the tiny room and whipped toward Harry, whining as it flew in his direction. Felixson's response was to instantly drop to the ground, doing his pitiful best to protect his heads as he did so. Meanwhile, the tattoo Caz had recently added ("because," Caz had stated, "you fuckin' earned it, man") was itching wildly, its unpleasant news flash unequivocal: *This is a death threat.*

But Harry wasn't the hook's target. Its bull's-eye was the door behind him, and the hook and chain threw themselves against it with considerable force. The door slammed shut and the hook snaked down to the handle, wrapping the chain around the mottled metal knob several times. Finally, interest gave way to a more levelheaded panic, and it was then that Harry scrambled to the door and attempted to pull it open. He succeeded in getting it open a few inches before he felt a sharp pain in his neck and a rush of wet heat, which divided at his shoulder, running down over his back and chest.

An unseen hook had pierced him, but Harry paid it no heed and continued trying to haul the door open, gritting his teeth against the pain he knew would come when he tore himself free. Loosing a stream of profanities, Harry pulled on the door, but the hook in his shoulder dug in deeper and then the chain to which it was attached tightened, and Harry was hauled away from the door and any hope of escape.

8

"Do not bother to run, Harry D'Amour," said the Cenobite, releasing Harry from the chain's grip. "For there is nowhere to go."

"You . . . know my name," Harry said.

"And you, no doubt, mine. Tell me, Harry D'Amour, what words you've heard whispered that have moved you to put aside the comforts of the commonplace to live, as I am told you live, engaged in constant conflicts against Hell."

"I think you got the wrong Harry D'Amour."

"Your modesty nauseates me. Be boastful while you have the breath for it. You are Harry D'Amour: private investigator, scourge of Hell."

"Sounds to me like those nails are touching too much gray matter."

"You are a magnificent cliché. And yet, you have sown hope in too much undeserving dirt. Against all expectations it grew and spread and, wherever the chance of its survival was slimmest, it prospered, your gift to the damned and despairing. A gift I shall now extinguish."

The Cenobite made a gesture with his left hand and another hook and chain came through the door, this one weaving over the boards like a snake and then suddenly leaping at D'Amour's chest. Harry felt the design of interwoven talismans Caz had inked on his chest convulse, and the hook was thrown back with such force that it slammed against the opposing wall, burying the sharpened point into the plaster.

"Inspiring," the Cenobite said. "What else have you learned?"

"Hopefully enough to keep me from looking like that poor shit," D'Amour said, referring to the still-deferent Felixson.

"Appearances deceive. You should know that. You are in the presence of one of your world's most renowned magicians."

"What—" The words suddenly struck a chord in D'Amour's memory. Over the last several years, the world's most powerful magicians had been systematically and ritually slaughtered. Nobody knew why. Harry, acting like some kind of detective, was beginning to put the pieces together.

"Felixson?" he said. "I know that name. That's . . . Theodore Felixson?"

"Last of the High Circle."

"What the fuck happened to him?"

"I spared him his life."

"If that's what salvation looks like, I'll pass."

"War is but a continuation of diplomacy by alternate means."

"War? Against who? A bunch of pampered magicians?"

"Perhaps you'll find out. Perhaps not. Thank you for accepting your bait by opening the box."

"Bait? This was a fucking setup?"

"You should be honored. Though I fail to see what sets you apart from the rest of the vermin, your reputation precedes you. I propose a test. I'll leave Felixson here to do away with you. Should he fail at his task, I shall return to you with an offer you'd dare not refuse."

The Hell Priest turned to leave.

"You want me to fight this crippled mess?" D'Amour said.

"As I said, appearances deceive."

With that the Cenobite unclipped a machete and a hook from his belt and threw them down before Felixson, who quickly snatched them up,

feeling the weight of them. A mischievous double grin, all the more gro-
tesque for its simple sincerity, appeared on his broken face.

"Hook!" he shrieked in excitement to the Cenobite, who was making
his way back to the passageway into Carston Goode's hidden library.
"You never . . . give . . ." He was working hard to shape the words.
". . . hook."

"To the victor I will bestow more spoils."

There was, briefly, a noise like very distant thunder. Then it was
gone, and so, Harry sensed, was the Hell Priest.

"Just the two of us then," Harry said, and before Felixson could move
to attack, Harry took out his gun and fired twice into Felixson's heart.
The bullets put two holes in Felixson's heart, but they did not kill him,
and the magician's mouths turned upward in an arrogant sneer.

"Stupid Da More. Can't kill Felixson. Not never!"

"You say that like it's a good thing."

"Is best!"

"You are so wrong," D'amour said.

"You die. Find out who is wrong," Felixson said, flicking the length
of chain toward Harry like a whip as he came toward him.

Felixson pointed toward Harry and spoke incomprehensibly to the
hook. It flew from Felixson's hands, came at Harry, and dug into his
groin, cutting through tender flesh and exiting out through a second
spot: two wounds for the price of one.

Harry howled in pain.

Felixson wrenched the chain back and tore through the flesh of
Harry's thigh. The hook returned to him and he addressed it once again.
Once again, the hook came at Harry, and caught his groin in the oppo-
site flank.

"Good now," Felixson said. "Only one more hook hook then bye to
little Da More."

Harry barely had time to react to Felixson's promise of unmanning.
His attention had been drawn to the door out into the passageway. It
was shaking violently, as though stampeding animals were trying to
break through.

"What *is*?" Felixson asked, his attention now focused on the door as well.

"I don't have . . . a fucking clue," Harry said, clinging to consciousness.

The door wasn't going to hold much longer against the beating it was taking. The wood around the hinges and lock was cracking now, throwing off splinters and flakes of paint.

"Who there?" Felixson said. "I kill Da More. If you come."

Felixson growled and jerked the chain back, tearing the hook from D'Amour's other thigh in one clean motion. The veins in D'Amour's neck bulged as he unleashed a guttural gurgling groan.

"You see!" Felixson screamed at the door as he ran an affectionate palm down over the lethal curve of the blood-drenched hook.

Felixson chattered a third incantation and, again, the hook-headed chain began snaking its way toward Harry like a slothful cobra, its head held high as it wove toward Harry's crotch. A panicky collage of sexual images broke through Harry's terror: masturbating behind the gym at St. Dominic's with Piper and Freddie; the girl (was it Janet or Janice?) he'd fucked on the overnight bus to New York; and the weeping adulteresses who were eager to sin a little more by offering to double Harry's rate. All of this and a hundred other memories ran through his head as the instrument idled its weaving way toward his manhood.

And then, without warning, it ceased its leisurely approach and struck. Harry wasn't about to let this thing unman him without a fight. He waited until the hook was an inch from the front of his pants and then reached down and grabbed the hook with his right hand and the chain just behind the hook with his left. The chain instantly started to thrash wildly to free itself of Harry's grip.

"Stupid!" Felixson yelled. "You worse make!"

"Shut the fuck up!" Harry yelled at Felixson. "Ass-licking cretin!"

"Kill Da More!" Felixson yelled to the serpentine chains.

Harry's sweaty hands were steadily losing their grip on the blood-encrusted metal. A few seconds more and it would be in him. The hook inched closer to his crotch as his sweat-slicked palms failed him more with every moment. Castration was imminent. Harry saw, in his mind's eye, the hook digging into the meat of his cock.

He gripped the chain with the last of his strength and loosed a primal howl of protest and, as if on cue, the door finally succumbed to those who wanted to be inside. The lock flew off, and the door was thrown sideways, slamming so hard against the adjacent wall that large gobs of plaster rained down in the room like a dusty hailstorm. Harry felt a blast of icy air break against his face. Harry's friend the String Yart had broken past the sealed door and was with him once again. But this time, Harry sensed, the Yart wasn't alone.

Unfortunately, the opening of the door had not distracted the butcher's hook from its ambitions. It still intended to gouge out Harry's groin, and even Harry's white-knuckled grip could not prevent the chain from pushing closer to him by increments. Harry felt the cold presence of a spirit moving around his hand, its coolness welcome. The cooling presence refreshed his weary body, dried his palms, and put strength back into his sinews. He pushed the serpent chain away from his groin a good six inches, then threw the thing to the ground and put the hook beneath his knee.

"Take that, fucker!" Harry said.

The snaking chain was far from happy with this new arrangement. Even trapped beneath Harry's weight, it still tried to slide itself out and it was only a matter of seconds, Harry knew, before it succeeded, for the wounds on his thighs were bleeding copiously and whatever was left of his strength would be gone very soon. But the ghosts' presences calmed and comforted him. He was no longer alone in this battle. He had allies; he just couldn't see them. It appeared, however, that Felixson could. The man's eyes had swelled up, and he laid his gaping head first on his left shoulder, then on his right, moving around on the spot where he now stood as he attempted to assess the strength of his new enemies, talking to them all the while.

"Felixson will catch and make eat you!" He reeled around, snatching up at the invisible spirits, muttering curses or incantations, or both, as he tried to catch hold of just one of the phantoms swirling around the room.

With its summoner's attention redirected, the chain slowly lost its will to act and its thrashing died down. Very cautiously, Harry took his knee off of the hook and picked it up. As he moved, the adrenaline shock left his body and his light-headedness returned. This time he was afraid that he wouldn't be able to hold on to consciousness. He had help, however, as one of the cold spirits, apparently sensing his distress, wove through his body like an ethereal balm.

Though the pain was not diminished, the spirit coaxed him away from it and into some chamber of his soul where he had never been before. It was numinous, this place, and filled with little games to enchant his pain-wearied body.

Then, the presence inside him seemed to speak. Harry heard it say, *Get ready,* and as that final syllable of its utterance reverberated in him the balmy dream evaporated and Harry was back in the room with Felixson, who, impossible as it was to believe, seemed to have gone a hell of a lot crazier. He had some invisible thing pinned against the opposite wall and was tearing into it. In its agony, the unseen victim was releasing a high-pitched shriek.

"Tell dead friends!" Felixson said, his speech decaying as his frenzy grew. "Tell them all dead how you. Tell to them Felixson will shit them! To messing in Hell's business? Never! Hear? Tell!" He twisted his fingers in the empty air and his voice rose an octave. "I hear no tell!"

Though Harry couldn't see the phantoms, he could feel them and their agitation. Felixson's commands only seemed to make them angry. The whole room began to vibrate, the old boards throwing themselves back and forth across the room in their fury, opening cracks in the plaster every time they struck the wall.

Harry watched as his allies dislodged several pieces of ceiling plaster, and in the clouds of dust that rose from the floor when they fell he seemed to see the ghosts, or at least their vague outlines. Cracks appeared in the ceiling, zigzagging across the plaster. The bare bulb swung back and forth, making Felixson's shadow cavort as the phantoms moved around the room, their hunger to destroy this place and Felixson palpable. It was clear that they were working to pull the room apart. Plaster dust was filling the room like a white fog.

Felixson turned his gaze back at Harry.

"Harry Da More I blame! He pays!"

Felixson reached for the chain, and Harry watched as the plaster fog was swept aside by a phantom, its descent mirrored by a second phantom coming from the opposite direction and intersecting at the chain. The chain, struck at the precise spot where the ghosts crossed, blew apart, leaving a length of perhaps eighteen inches of loose metal still dangling from the hook. The blow had formed a wound in Felixson's brow. The magician was unprepared for this. He cursed and wiped away blood from his right eye.

Then, two more phantoms converged not only on the remainder of the chain but directly onto the hand that held it. Before Felixson could loose the chain from his grasp, the spirits converged on his hand. When they met, fragments of flesh, bone, and metal blew outward. With Felixson wounded and unarmed, the spirits took it upon themselves to continue the destruction of Carston Goode's den of iniquity. The whole place rocked as the phantoms shook its foundations. The bulb in the middle of the room flared with unnatural brightness and just as quickly burned out.

Harry realized it was time to move. He was perhaps two strides from the door when the second tattoo Caz had given him, a warning sigil in the middle of his back, sent out a pulse that spread throughout his body. He swung round just in time to throw himself out of the way of Felixson, whose lips were drawn back to expose jagged, flesh-shredding teeth. Felixson's teeth snapped in the air where Harry's head had been two seconds before and the momentum of the lunge carried Felixson forward, slamming him into the wall beside the door.

Harry didn't give Felixson an opportunity to go after him a second time. He was out through the door and into the passageway. The ghosts were in a crazed state, and they were everywhere, tossing themselves back and forth. They slammed into the walls like invisible hammers.

The plaster had been cleared off by now, exposing wooden slats beneath. There was a din of destruction from the other end of passageway, which suggested the stairs were being taken apart with the same gusto as the walls, but the dust and the darkness conspired to limit Harry's sight to a foot in front of his face and no more. Despite the sounds of un-making before him, he had no choice but to risk it.

Meanwhile, the floorboards groaned and twisted, spitting out the nails that had held them in place. Harry ventured over them as fast as he dared, past the sling room, which was now a wall of suffocating dust, and on over the cavorting boards. The wooden slats were succumbing to the strikes of the hammer-bodied spirits even more quickly than the plaster. Harry crossed his arms in front of his face to protect it from the splinters that pierced the air. He was walking blind. For a third time the cool presence intervened, entering Harry and speaking in the blood that thundered in Harry's ears

Back! Now!

Harry responded instantly, and as he jumped back Felixson charged past him, his mouth vast, and from it a solid howl emerged, which suddenly dropped away. The stairs were gone, and something about the way Felixson's howl had diminished told Harry's instincts that there was now a void beneath the house into which the Cenobite's lapdog had been dispatched. Judging by Felixson's faraway howl, it was deep, and there was likely no way anyone would ever be able to climb out of it if, or rather when, the house folded up and fell.

Harry turned back in the direction he'd come. He quickly and carefully headed to the back room, trying not to focus on the passageway as it collapsed beneath him, the boards digging away into the blackness over which he was leaping.

By the time he returned to the room, the plaster dust had almost cleared, sucked away by emptiness below. There was only a single un-reliable patchwork of wooden slats left between Harry and the hole. But at least now he had a clear view of his last hope and his only target: the window. Trusting his feet to know their business, he crossed the room without incident. There was a ledge perhaps four floorboards in front of the window, but it didn't look as though it was going to be there for long. The boards had already lost most of their nails.

Harry started to pull at the blackout fabric that had been secured to the window. It had clearly been nailed to the frame by an obsessive, but had been done several years before, Harry guessed, because the fabric, though thick, had begun to rot through after several summers of extreme humidity and when he pulled at it the material tore like paper. The light of the outside world came flooding into the room. It wasn't direct sunlight, but it was bright nonetheless, and it was more than welcome.

Harry peered out of the window. It was a long way down, and there was nothing on either side. A drainpipe would have been adequate. A fire escape would have made a climb down plausible. But no, he was going to have to jump and hope for the best. He pulled on the window's edge, trying to raise it, but it was sealed shut, so he turned around and tore up one of the floorboards, making his ledge even narrower. As he turned back toward the window with his weapon, he caught sight of something from the corner of his eye and glanced back to see that he was no longer alone in the room.

Battered, bloody, and covered in dust—his teeth bared, his eyes narrowed to slits of fury—Pinhead's rabid dog, Felixson, stood staring at Harry. Far though Felixson had surely fallen, he had climbed his way back up, intent on finishing the bloody business between them.

"You've done some dumb fucking things, D'Amour . . ." Harry said to himself.

Felixson came at him suddenly, the boards he had sprung from splintering as he leaped. Harry threw the wood he'd been carrying at the window, shattering the glass, and put all his effort into getting out. A crowd of people had gathered out on the sidewalk. Harry caught a few fragments of the things they were yelling—something about him breaking his neck, something about getting a ladder, or a mattress, or a sheet—but despite all the suggestions, nobody moved to help in case they missed the moment when Harry jumped.

And two seconds later he could have, had he been free to do so, but Felixson wasn't about to lose his prey. With one last bound, the living monstrosity cleared the chasm between them and caught hold of Harry's leg, digging his fingers, their strength clearly enhanced by the merciless fusing of metal and flesh, deep into the bleeding holes in Harry's thighs.

Though Harry was in tremendous pain, he didn't waste the remaining energy he had by voicing it.

"All right, fuckhead," he said. "You're coming with me."

And with that he threw himself out of the window. Felixson held on to Harry as far as the window ledge, and then, perhaps out of a fear of being seen, he let go.

Harry landed hard on a patch of asphalt. He was familiar enough with the sound of breaking bones to know that he'd surely shattered a few. But before he could ask any of the onlookers for a ride to the nearest hospital, the house gave up a long growl of surrender and then collapsed, folding up and dropping down through what was left of the structure, the walls flying apart in places, and in others entire sections of wedded brick toppling in mounds. It happened with astonishing speed, the entire structure dropping away into the earth in less than a minute, its collapse finally releasing a dense gray-brown cloud of dust.

As the walls succumbed, so did Harry's body. A wave of shudders passed through him, and once again his sight was invaded by a pulsing blankness. It did not retreat this time but pressed forward from all directions. The world around him narrowed to a remote circle as though he were looking at it through the wrong end of a telescope. The pulse of pain maintained rhythm with that of the invading nullity, all moving to the beat of his drumming heart.

Very far off, in the place from which his consciousness was departing, Harry saw somebody approaching him through the crowd: a bald, pale, diminutive man with a stare so penetrating that he could feel its intensity even though he was almost a world away. The man moved through the crowd with uncommon ease, as though some invisible presence cleared the way for him. The sight of the man lent Harry's besieged senses a reason to hold on a little longer, to resist the encroaching emptiness that threatened to erase the place where he walked. It was hard, though. Much as he wanted to know who this intense Lilliputian was, Harry's mind was closing down.

Harry drew a ragged breath, determined at least to tell this man his name. But he had no need.

"We should leave now, Mister D'Amour," the man said. "While everyone is still distracted."

The man then reached out and took gentle hold of Harry's hand. When their fingers made contact, a wave of forgiving warmth passed into Harry's hand and the sting of his wounds retreated. He was comforted as a babe in its mother's arms. And with that thought, the world went black.

9

There were no dreams at the beginning. He simply lay in the darkness, healing, and now and then he would rise to the surface of consciousness because somebody was talking about him near the place where he slept or perhaps in the hallway outside. He had no desire to wake and become a part of the conversation, but he heard the talk, or fragments of it at least.

"This man belongs in a hospital, Dale," said the voice of an elderly man.

"I don't believe in hospitals, Sol," said the man who was Dale, his voice a playful Louisiana drawl. "Especially for someone like him. He wouldn't be protected there. At least here I know nothing can get to him. For Pete's sake, there was a *demon* at that house on Dupont Street."

"The same house he leveled?" the man called Sol replied.

"*He* didn't do that."

"How can you be so sure? I don't like it, Dale," Sol said. "Anyway, what the hell possessed you to go over to Dupont Street in the first place?"

"You know about my dreams. They tell me where to go, and I go. I learned a long time ago not to ask questions. That's just trouble. I showed up, there *he* was. I only got him back here by giving him a little of my energies. He was close to collapsing the entire time."

"That was foolish. Skills like yours should be kept secret."

"It was necessary. How else was I going to get him out of there unseen? Look, I know it's crazy, but I know we need to help him get well."

"Fine. But once he's healed, I want him out."

Dale, Harry thought. The name of his savior was Dale. Harry didn't know who the other man in the conversation was but was sure he would meet him when the time was right. Meanwhile, there was that comfortable darkness to curl up in, which Harry did, certain in the knowledge he was safe.

There were other conversations, or fragments of conversations, that came and went like night ships moving past him in the darkness. And then came the day when, without warning, everything in Harry's dreaming state changed. It started with Dale talking to him, his face close to Harry's so he could tell him what he needed to in a whisper.

"Harry dear, I know you can hear me. You're getting a visitor today. Solomon's just gone to pick her up. Her name's Freddie Bellmer. She and Sol have been friends for a long time. Sol thinks Miss Bellmer may be able to get your body to mend a little more quickly. Though between you and me I sometimes wonder if you're not perfectly happy stayin' asleep in there. I know you've had some hard times. That spill you took being one of them. Oh, and I'm sorry to report that your cell phone did not survive the fall. But I digress; as soon as Solomon got you cleaned up, and I don't mind telling you I was a tiny bit jealous he didn't let me stay and watch, he called me in to see your tattoos. I don't know what all of them mean, but I know enough. They're protections, aren't they? Lord, you seem like a man that needs a lot of those. I . . . How shall I put this . . . ?"

He paused, as though looking for the right words, or, if he already had the words, he was looking for the most diplomatic way of using them. Finally, he began to speak again, though it was plainly difficult.

"I . . . I always knew—even when I was small, y'see—I knew I wasn't quite the same as the other boys. When my mother died—I never did know my father—I came to live with my uncle Sol. I had just turned six, and the moment old Uncle Sol laid eyes on me he said, 'Lord, look at the colors coming off you. That's quite a show.' That's when I knew I would have to live a different life than most folks. There'd be secrets I'd need to keep. Which is fine. I'm good at keeping secrets. And I don't know what it is about you, but I just wanted you to know that whenever you do decide to wake up, I will gladly lap up anything you want to tell me about the world outside this stinky old town. And I look forward to the trouble we'll get into together. I don't know what it is yet, my dreams haven't shown me, but I know it's a doozy—"

Then, the whispering was replaced by Solomon's deep voice.

"Are you kissing him?"

"No," Dale replied calmly, without turning around. "We were just talkin'."

It wasn't Solomon who replied, but a new voice, that of Miss Bellmer. Her voice was deep and severe. It wasn't as softly feminine as Harry had expected. But then neither, as Harry would soon find out, was the owner of the voice.

"If you're done playing doctor, I would recommend that you step away from the bed," Miss Bellmer said to Dale, "and let me take a look at the patient."

Her voice grew louder as she approached the bed; then Harry heard the springs protesting as she sat down. She didn't touch Harry, but he felt the proximity of her hand as it moved over his face and then down his body.

There was nothing said; both Solomon and Dale were too much in awe of Miss Bellmer to interrupt her during the examination of the patient.

Finally, Miss Bellmer spoke:

"I don't recommend keeping this man under your roof a moment more than you need to. The physical wounds are healing nicely. But . . . I have somewhere . . ." she said as she rummaged through her bag, ". . . something that will get him up on his feet a little quicker."

The weighty Miss Bellmer got up.

"A teaspoon of this in half a cup of warm water."

"What does it do?" Dale asked.

"It will give him bad dreams. He's a little too comfortable in the dark. It's time he woke. There's trouble coming."

"Here?" Solomon said.

"The entire world does not revolve around you and your house, Solomon. It's this one here—your Mister D'Amour—that has some very bad things coming his way. Call me when he wakes up."

"Is he in danger?" Dale asked.

"Honey, that's an understatement."

10

Before leaving, the provocative Miss Freddie fed Harry his nightmare potion. The subtle energies her touch had released still pulsed through his body long after his three caretakers had left him to sleep. It was a different kind of sleep now, however, as though Miss Bellmer's tonic had subtly reordered his thoughts.

Fragments of meaning flickered in the darkness, two or three frames cut from the home movies of *The Devil and D'Amour*. No two demons were ever quite the same. They all had their own monstrous proclivities and they rose to visit Harry from deep within his subconscious. There was, of course, the clay-faced creature who had murdered Scummy and pleasured himself to the sight. There was also a chattering imbecile called Gist, who had come very close to killing Harry in a plunging elevator, a decade ago or more. There was Ysh'a'tar, the New Jersey Incubus Harry had caught giving Holy Communion one Sunday morning in Philadelphia. Another was Zuzan, the unholy assassin who'd taken the life of Harry's friend and mentor, Father Hess, in a house in Brooklyn. Others Harry couldn't even put a name to, perhaps because they didn't even have names. They were just dreams of mindless malice that had crossed his path throughout the years, sometimes on an empty street long after midnight but just as often on the crowded avenues at noon when Hell's creatures went about their vicious business in plain sight, defying human eyes to believe that they were real.

After a while, however, the parade of atrocities dwindled, and Harry sank back into the darkness from which the arrival of Miss Bellmer had stirred him. How long he stayed there, recovering his strength, and healing, he had no idea, but certainly many hours. When he did finally rise from that healing darkness again it was to the sound of rain. And it was no light shower. The rain was lashing against the window, and the din reminded him suddenly of how very much he needed to piss.

He forced open his eyes and saw that he was in a room lit only by the illumination from the lamps outside in the street below. He threw off his sheet. He was completely naked, and he saw no sign of his clothes, which had been in a dusty, bloody state after all that had happened on Dupont Street. Noticing his nudity, he saw, for the first time, the wounds that he had been dealt. He looked down at them. The flesh looked raw, but when he touched the place he felt no more than a mild discomfort. These people who'd rescued him clearly knew their business as healers. He pulled the sheet off the bed, wrapped it loosely around his torso, and left his sickroom in search of a place to relieve himself. There were three candles set in simple, white bowls along the wall just outside his room. Harry saw that he was on the second floor of a somewhat large French Colonial–style home.

"Hello?" he called. "I'm awake. And naked."

Except for the sound of rain beating down on the roof, Harry's calls were met with silence. He moved on down the carpeted hallway, passing two more bedrooms, until he finally found a bathroom. Its tiled floor was chilly beneath his bare feet, but he didn't care. Unwrapping the bedsheet, he raised the toilet seat and unleashed the contents of his bladder with a blissful sigh.

He went to the sink and ran the hot water. The pipes chugged and stuttered, the noise they made echoing off the tiled walls. He splashed some water on his face and examined his pallid complexion in the mirror. The noise in the pipes was getting louder; he realized he could now feel their lamentations through the floor. Then, there was another sound, rising from the chug and shudder of the pipes.

It sounded as though somebody was throwing up—here, in the bathroom with him. It wasn't hard to trace. The noise was coming out of the bath, or rather out of its plughole, which, Harry now saw, was throwing up a gruel of dark gray water, bringing up with it a tangled mass of long black hair and what looked like recycled chunks of excrement. An unmistakable stench came to meet him from the darkness, that of human remains.

It was a smell with which Harry was woefully familiar, though it still carried power. The smell wasn't just repugnant; it was also a distracting reminder of rooms he'd stood in and trenches he'd uncovered where the dead lay in corruption, their skins barely containing the maggot motion they were home to.

Caz's handiwork twitched. No doubt about it: Harry had been awake for less than five minutes and already he was in trouble. The filthy waters and their sickening freight had come to do him harm. How exactly they might do so was not a puzzle he had any desire to see solved. He snatched his makeshift clothing off the edge of the bath, wrapped it once more around his middle, and tucked it in on itself as he went to the door. He'd closed it when he'd come in, but given that there was neither a key nor a bolt to secure any further privacy, he was surprised to find that when he pulled on the knob the thing refused to move.

It was an unwelcome reminder of the doors on Dupont Street—some of which had been visible, some contentedly wrapped in hooks and chains, all conspiring against his next breath. He turned the polished knob in both directions, hoping to chance upon the trick of its release, but there was more than a faulty mechanism keeping the door from opening. He'd been sealed up in here with—with what, he didn't know.

He glanced back at the bath. The hairs that had appeared from the plughole had now risen up from the surface of the water in several places and were knitting themselves together, forming what was unmistakably the rough outline of a head, the cavorting waters rising up into it, like fish caught in a net. Harry dragged his sight off this bizarrity so as to focus his attentions on getting the door open. He grabbed the knob with both hands and proceeded to shake the door with deserved violence, coaxing it to open.

"Open up, you sonofabitch!"

But there was no movement, no sign, however minimal, that the door was succumbing to his assault. He gave up on the handle and tried another approach: pounding on the door with his fists and yelling for someone to save him. He shouted over and over, but there was no reply—only the sounds of the thing that was with him in the room. Twice he looked back at the bath as he pounded on the door, and on each occasion the raw human form being sewn together with hair and water and shit was closer to completion.

With the first glance, Harry saw only the head, shoulders, and rough sketch of its torso. On the second glance, the torso had been completed, all the way down to its sexless groin, the boneless arms moving more like tentacles than human limbs. The hair hadn't even attempted to craft hands from its tangles. Instead it slithered and coiled together until it had given itself two hammerhead-shaped fists, one of which it slammed against the wall with astonishing force. The tiles it struck shattered, sending shards far enough to prick Harry's skin.

The excremental stench had steadily grown in intensity as the creature rose up and out of its birthplace, the sting so sharp it brought tears to Harry's eyes. He wiped them away with the heel of his hand, and with his sight momentarily cleared he looked around for something he could use to defend himself. All he had was the sheet he was wearing. It wasn't much, but it was better than nothing. He untucked it, glancing up at his hammer-handed adversary. The creature was stepping out of the bath now, shedding globs of gummy, greasy fluid as it did so.

The stink was overpowering. There were fresh tears welling in Harry's eyes again, but he hadn't time to clear his vision. The thing was out of the bath swinging its left arm back over its right shoulder as it lurched toward Harry. As it did so, Harry opened the sheet and threw it high and above the fetid waters of the enemy's head. The sheet landed on the creature and clung to it like leaves on a wet sidewalk.

The creature was clearly disoriented. Whether Harry had actually blinded the beast for a moment, which seemed unlikely, or he'd simply confused it for a short time, the effect was the same. The thing swung its hammer-hand high, intending to shear off Harry's head, but in the four or five seconds between the blinding and the blow Harry had dropped down onto his haunches and out of the hammer's path.

The beast's blow missed Harry by inches, but for the first time since walking into this vision Harry felt the healing wounds from the Hell Priest's hooks break open with the sudden movement. His hand went down to the injuries in his thighs and the blood spilled down the sides of his legs and onto the linoleum beneath him.

Harry dragged his bleeding ass across the floor in the hopes of putting some distance between himself and the hammers. Only when his spine hit the tiled wall and he could go no farther did he dare look up at the foe. The sheet had proved more valuable than he'd expected; soaking up the gray filth that churned between the woven hairs of its head and back, the sodden sheet clung relentlessly to the creature, much to its visible frustration.

The creature reached up trying to rid itself of the burden, but its hands were made for murder, not for tending shrouds, and in its frenzy it threw its whole body back and forth, causing some of its fluids to escape the fragile cage of its making.

The creature stumbled and, for a single heart-quickening second, Harry feared the creature was going to fall on top of him, but it reeled around and fell the opposite way, striking the door. The falling weight of water and filth in the ungainly body of the thing was enough to knock the door from its hinges so that it toppled out onto the carpeted landing.

The fall tore a zigzag laceration up the side of the creature, and dark liquid matter poured forth from the wound and was instantly absorbed by the carpet that sat beneath its protesting body. Harry watched in fascination as the creature bled out, leaving behind only a corpse of hair and feces that vaguely resembled a human form.

As Harry struggled to pull himself to his feet, he heard Dale's voice.

"Harry? Are you all right?"

It sounded as though Dale were in the room with him. Harry, still in shock, scanned the room with his eyes and saw the wallpaper flicker like blown candle flames. Harry sighed.

"Gimme a break," he said. "There's no fucking way I'm dreaming."

And then he woke up.

11

"I've called Miss Bellmer," Solomon said as Dale and Harry sat down in the living room with their strongest drinks of choice to talk about what had happened during the last few days. Solomon, a man no younger than seventy-five, was lanky and tall, with a shock of gray hair. He stood nearly a foot taller than Dale and was easily thirty years his senior. "Have you any enemies, Mister D'Amour?" he asked.

"I lost count before I graduated high school," Harry said.

"Really now?" Dale said, a hint of arousal in his manner.

"Well, that settles it," Solomon continued. "Something followed you down here and decided to have you murdered while you were away from your usual protectors."

"Protectors?"

"The folks in your life who know who you *really* are," Dale offered.

"I guess that would be Caz and Norma."

"That's it?" said Solomon. "You don't trust a lot of people, do you?"

"Most of the people I used to trust aren't around anymore."

"Oh, honey," Dale said. "I'll be your friend."

"I'm sorry," Solomon said.

"It's fine," Harry said. "Some die too soon. Most live too long."

Before anyone had time to reply, somebody rapped sharply on the front door.

"That'll be Miss Bellmer," Solomon said. "You two stay here."

Solomon went to open the front door and Harry's Unscratchable Itch started its familiar song. Harry squirmed in his seat.

"What on earth's wrong, Sol?" Harry heard Miss Bellmer saying out in the hallway. "You look troubled."

"Oh, no more than usual," Solomon replied.

"Well, thank the Lord for small mercies. How's the patient?"

"He's doing fine."

Upon which words Solomon brought Miss Bellmer into the room. Freddie Bellmer looked more than a little surprised to see Harry. Aside from her reaction, Harry noted that Miss Bellmer had a beautiful face: high cheekbones, huge, dark eyes, and lips so perfect they looked carved. But he also saw that there was something about her height (she was easily as tall as Solomon) and her clothes (though brightly colored and voluminous, they carefully concealed the shape of her body) that created a distinctive ambiguity about her.

"Your tonic seems to have done its job," Solomon said.

"So it has," Miss Bellmer said.

"Detective D'Amour, meet Miss Freddie Bellmer," Solomon said. "She's been a friend of mine since . . . well . . ."

"Since before I was *Miss* Bellmer," she said. "As I'm sure your patient has already deduced. Isn't that right, Detective?"

Harry shrugged as he rose to shake Bellmer's hand. "I'm off duty."

Dale snickered. Bellmer smiled an abundant smile, which somehow felt like a denunciation to Harry. She took Harry's hand in hers. Her calloused hands belied her dainty handshake.

"You are a lot livelier than the last time I saw you," she said.

"I have a strong constitution."

"Without a doubt. But I do have a warning for you, Mister D'Amour. I didn't just look at your physical wounds; I looked at the important things too. The will. The soul. Lord, but you must have had some hard times. You're nothing but one big psychic scar. I never saw such a mess in all my life."

"Takes one to spot one."

Dale tried hard to cover up a smile, but he was clearly enjoying the show.

"Grow up, Dale," said Miss Bellmer. "You stupid queen."

"At least this queen can still tell you to suck his dick," Dale said.

Now it was Harry who tried covering a smile.

"Children. Play nice," Solomon said.

Miss Bellmer sighed, her hand going to her brow. "Sol, darling, do you by any chance have some vodka in the house?"

"Coming right up," Sol said, and he went in search of vodka, leaving Miss Bellmer to pick up her conversation with Harry.

"So how do you feel?" Miss Bellmer said.

"Alive," Harry said. Then he leaned in close to Miss Bellmer and whispered, "No thanks to you. Admit it; you were surprised to see me when you walked in. I remember your voice. I remember what happened when you visited me. And something tells me that if that disgusting beast in my dream had caught me, we wouldn't be having this conversation right now. So what I'd like to know is, to whom did you sell your soul, and for how much?"

Miss Bellmer smiled, cleared her throat, and said, "I'm sure I have no idea what you're talking about, Detective."

"Very convincing," D'Amour said as he turned away from Bellmer and made his way carefully back to the couch.

"Freddie, you may want to reapply your blush, dear. You've gone white as a sheet," Dale said.

"Fuck off, Dale," Bellmer said, her voice deepening. "As for you, D'Amour, I'd tread lightly if I were you. I've got powerful friends in high places. Very fucking high. I'm protected."

"Take it from me," Harry said. "They really don't care about little people like us. We're cannon fodder to them."

"You don't know who they are."

"Whatever you say, *sir*. I promise you, come the day, you'll be out in the rain the same as me."

Harry's response had sown sufficient doubt in Miss Bellmer's head to silence her.

Bellmer's lips were pinched tight as though she was doing her best not to give D'Amour any more rope with which she could be hanged.

"I've never seen you so quiet, Freddie," Dale said, happy to fan the flames. "What's the matter, doll? Cat got your cock?"

Bellmer wagged a long, well-manicured finger at the two men. "I've got something special lined up for a whole bunch of people. And you're both on the list now. Mutts like you go straight in the ground. I'll make you dig the hole yourself. Then I'll kick you in, and cover you up. Neat. Cheap. Anonymous."

"Christ almighty," said Dale. "Where did that come from?"

"You already tried to kill me once," said D'Amour. "If you try it again, I might not like it."

"We'll see how much you like it when you're eating dirt, mother-fucker. Take my advice. Go the fuck home."

"Freddie?" Solomon said. "What's come over you?"

Solomon had emerged from the kitchen with an unopened bottle of vodka and four shot glasses and had caught the tail end of her speech. Freddie turned and saw the disappointment on her old friend's face.

"Sol," Bellmer said, attempting to compose herself. "I came to warn you. This man's dangerous. I think—"

"*I think* you should leave," Sol said.

Freddie Bellmer took a moment to digest Solomon's words. When it was clear he was not going to rescind them, she whipped her long straight hair over her shoulder and consulted her watch, which looked minuscule on her broad, thick wrist.

"Look at that," she said, trying to maintain a modicum of composure. "I'm late for my next patient."

And, without saying good-bye, she was out through the door. There was a moment of silence, and then Dale spoke.

"I always knew he was a cunt."

12

Harry took the noon flight out of New Orleans the next day. He had tried to offer Solomon and Dale some money for their many kindnesses, but of course they wouldn't take a cent, and Harry knew that to press them would only cause discomfort, so he made his thanks and gave them his card before going back to a rainy, gray New York.

When he got home, he was pleased to find everything just the way he liked it. His apartment was chaotic, and his kitchen was littered with beer cans and boxes of Chinese food that had turned into little ecosystems of mold. He left it all for another day. What he wanted most was some more sleep, this time he hoped without the potentially fatal dreams. He took off his jacket and shoes as he staggered to the bed, and dropped down onto it. He was barely in the process of pulling up the cover when sleep overwhelmed him and he sank into its depths unresisting.

After sleeping almost twenty-six hours, Harry slowly allowed his aching body to familiarize itself with the state of wakefulness, and after a healthy interlude of inner debating he got up out of bed and made his bleary-eyed way into the bathroom.

As the water poured over him, Harry imagined that it cleaned him not only of his body's naturally collected oils but also of the events of the past few days. And as the water did its best to sluice away Harry's memories, his thoughts went to his wounds. He looked down and saw that his thighs looked almost totally healed, though he knew he was going to have a couple of shiny new scars to show for it. All in a day's work, he thought.

A half hour later—showered, dressed in clean clothes, and carrying a comfortably concealed, fully loaded revolver—he was out on the street, heading toward Norma's place. He had much to tell her. The rainstorm had moved on, and the city sparkled in the late summer sun.

His mood was good, even optimistic, which was rare. Goode may have lied about more than a few things, but at least the money in his lockbox was real and, because of it, Harry could finally pay the back rent he owed—three months' at least, perhaps four—and maybe even buy a pair of shoes that didn't leak. But after that, he'd be back to square one.

The problem with being a P.I. whose career was periodically hijacked by forces beyond his control wasn't that unnatural forces left him covered in dust and blood; it was the fact that they typically didn't pay well. That said, there was an undeniable pleasure to be had from knowing something about his beloved city's secret life that other people didn't, mysteries that the expensive beauties who gave him chilly looks if they caught his admiring gaze, or the high-octane executives with their thousand-dollar haircuts, would live and die never knowing.

New York wasn't the only city in the world that had magic in its blood. All the great cities of Europe and of the Far East kept their own secrets as well—many more ancient than anything New York could boast—but there was nowhere in the world that had such a concentration of supernatural activity as Manhattan. For those like Harry who'd trained themselves to look past the glorious distractions the city offered, evidence could be seen just about anywhere that the island was a battlefield where the better angels of human nature perpetually warred with the forces of discord and despair. And nobody was immune.

Had Harry been born under a star less kind, he might well have ended up among the city's nomadic visionaries, his days taken up with begging for enough money to buy some liquid oblivion, his nights spent trying to find a place where he could not hear the adversaries singing as they went about their labors of the dark. They had only ever sung one song within earshot of Harry, and that was "Danny Boy," that hymn to death and maudlin sentiment that Harry had heard so often that he knew the words by heart.

On his way to Norma's, he stopped in at Rueffert's deli and bought the same breakfast he'd bought there whenever he was in the city every day for the better part of twenty-five years. Jim Rueffert always had Harry's coffee poured, sugared, and hit with just a dash of cream by the time he'd get to the counter.

"Harry, my friend," Jim said, "we ain't seen you in a week, at least. My wife says, 'He's dead,' and I say, 'Not Harry. No way. Harry doesn't die. He goes on forever.' Isn't that right?"

"Sure feels that way sometimes, Jim."

Harry left some money in the tip jar—more than he could afford, as usual—and headed out the door. As he exited the shop, he collided with a man who seemed to be in a hurry, even if he didn't appear to know where he was headed. The man grunted, "Not here," and surreptitiously slipped a scrap of paper into the palm of Harry's hand. Then the man wove around Harry and continued on down the street.

Harry took the stranger's advice and walked on, curiosity speeding his step. He turned a corner onto a quieter street, not planning a particular route, just wondering where he was being watched from, and who by, that the messenger should warn him the way he had. Harry checked the reflections in the windows on the opposite side of the street to see if anyone had followed him, but he saw no one. He kept walking, the paper crumpled up in his left fist.

About two-thirds of the way down the block was a florist's store called Eden & Co. He went in, taking the opportunity to glance back down the street. If he was being followed it was not, his ink and his instinct told him, by any of the half-dozen people who were walking in his direction.

The air in the flower store was cool, moist and heavy with the mingled perfumes of dozens of blossoms. A middle-aged man with an immaculately trimmed moustache that followed the line of his mouth like a third lip appeared from the back of the store and asked Harry if he was looking for anything in particular.

"Just browsing," Harry said. "I, uh, love flowers."

"Well, let me know if you decide on anything."

"You bet."

The man with the perfect moustache stepped through a beaded curtain at the back of the shop and immediately started up a conversation in Portuguese, which Harry's arrival had apparently disrupted. No sooner had the man begun than a woman came back at him speaking twice as fast and in an obvious rage.

While their heated conversation went on, Harry wandered around the store, looking up now and again to see if there was anyone watching from the street. Finally, having convinced himself that he was not being spied upon, he opened his fist and smoothed out the piece of paper. Before he read a single word, he knew it was from Norma:

Don't go to my apartment. It's bad. I'm in the old place. Come at 3 a.m. If you itch, walk away.

"A message?" a woman's voice asked.

Harry looked up. He barely had time to bite back the *Christ!* he almost muttered at the sight of her. Three-fourths of the woman's face was a rigid mass of smeared and indented scar tissue. The remaining quarter—her beautiful left eye and brow above it (plus the elaborately coiffed wig, which was a mass of curls)—only seemed to make the erasure of the rest of her face seem even crueler. Her nose was reduced to two round holes; her right eye and mouth were shorn of lashes and lips. Harry fixed his attention on her left eye and stumbled over his reply, which was simply a repeating of her question.

"Message?" he said.

"Yes," she said, glancing down at the scrap of paper in his hand. "You want this with the flowers?"

"Oh," Harry said, breathing a sigh of relief. "No, thank you."

He quickly pocketed the message, nodded, and left the flower shop and its bad omens behind him.

Harry took the note and his puzzlement over its contents, along with a fierce hunger, to Cherrington's Pub, a dark, quiet watering hole that he'd found the first day he'd come to New York. It served old-fashioned food with a minimum of fuss, and they knew him so well that he only had to slide into his corner and give a little nod to a waitress named Phyllis and there'd be a large bourbon—no ice—on his table within sixty seconds, sometimes less. Having a routine that bordered on stagnancy had its benefits.

"You're looking good, Phyllis," Harry said as she brought him his drink in record time.

"I'm retiring."

"What? When?"

"End of next week. I'm going to have a little party on Friday evening, just for the staff and a few regulars. You in town?"

"If I am, I'll be here."

Harry studied her. She was probably in her mid-sixties, which meant she'd been edging toward forty when Harry first found the place. Forty-something to sixty-something was a lot of life, a lot of chances come, gone, and never coming round again.

"You gonna be okay?" Harry said.

"Yeah, yeah. I'm not planning on dying or nothing. I just can't take this place anymore. I don't sleep nights. I'm tired, Harry."

"You don't look it."

"Aren't guys like you supposed to be good liars?" she said as she headed away from the table, saving Harry from fumbling for a reply.

Harry settled back into the corner of the booth and pulled out the note again. It wasn't like Norma to be scared. She lived in what was unequivocally the most haunted apartment in the city. She'd held advice sessions for the dead for more than three decades—hearing stories of violent deaths by those who'd experienced them firsthand, murder victims, suicides, people killed crossing the street or stopped in their tracks by something dropped from a window. If anyone could have honestly claimed to have heard it all before, it was Norma. So what was it that had made her leave her ghosts, and her televisions, and her kitchen where she knew the location of everything down to the last teaspoon?

He looked at the clock above the bar. It was six thirty-two. He had eight hours to go. He couldn't wait that long.

"Fuck this three in the morning crap," Harry said. He downed his bourbon and called over to Phyllis, "Time to close out the tab, Phyllis!"

"Where's the fire?" she said, sauntering back to Harry's booth.

"I've got to get someplace faster than I thought."

He tucked a hundred-dollar bill in her hand.

"What's this for?"

"You," Harry said, already turning toward the door. "In case I don't make it to your party."

13

Harry stepped out of the cab on the corner of 13th and Ninth. The intersection was not Harry's true destination. A few blocks farther down in what had been a well-kept building that had once housed lawyers and doctors, including psychiatrists. It was in the waiting room of one of the latter, a psychiatrist by the name of Ben Krackomberger, M.D., that Harry had first met Norma Paine.

After the events of Scummy's death, Harry had been taken off active duty. Harry's version of the events that led to that night his partner lost his life proved to be a bigger bite than the department could chew, so they sent him to Krackomberger, who in a courteous but insistent fashion kept pressing Harry on the details of what he "imagined" he'd seen.

Harry would go through it all again and again, moment by moment, foiling Krackomberger's attempt to catch Harry out with some inconsistency from telling to telling. Finally the doctor said, "It comes down to this, Harry. In the end, your version of what happened that day is preposterous. In less serious circumstances I'd call it laughable."

"Is that a fact?"

"Yes."

"So I've been pouring my fucking heart out to you—"

"Calm down, Mister D'Amour."

Harry rose to his feet. "Don't interrupt me. You're telling me that all this time, you've made me go over and over it, and you were laughing inside?"

"I didn't say— Please, Mister D'Amour, sit down, or I'll be obliged to have you forcibly—"

"I'm sitting. Okay? Is that okay?" Harry said, taking a seat on the table that rested between the good doctor and his therapy couch.

"Yes, but if you feel the need to get up again, then I suggest you leave."

"And if I do, what will you put on my papers?"

"That you are unfit for service due to extreme delusional states, almost certainly brought on by the trauma of the incident. Nobody is calling you crazy, Mister D'Amour. I just need to give your superiors an honest assessment of your condition."

"Extreme delusional states . . ." Harry said softly.

"People respond to the kind of pressure you've had to endure in very different ways. You seem to have created a kind of personal mythology to contain the whole terrible experience, to make sense of it—"

He was interrupted by a series of crashes from the next room, where Krackomberger's secretary sat.

"It's not me!" a woman's voice—not that of the secretary—said.

The doctor got up, making a mumbled apology to Harry, and opened the door. As Krackomberger did so, several magazines sailed past him and landed on the Persian carpet in the doctor's office. Suddenly the hairs on the back of Harry's neck stood on end. Whatever was wrong next door, it wasn't just an irate patient, Harry's UI told him. This was something altogether stranger.

He took a deep breath, got up, and followed Krackomberger through to the waiting room. As Harry did so, the doctor retreated, stumbling over his own feet in his haste.

"What the hell's going on in here?" Harry said.

Krackomberger looked at him, his face drained of blood, his expression crazed.

"Did you do this?" he said to Harry. "Is it some kind of practical joke?"

"No," said the woman in the waiting room.

Harry followed the woman's voice and saw her. She had the high cheekbones and the lavish mouth of a woman who had once been a classic beauty. But life had marked her deeply, etching her black skin with frown marks and grooves around her downturned mouth. Her eyes were milky white. It was obvious that she couldn't see Harry, but regardless, he felt her gaze upon him, like the softest of winds blowing against his face. All the while something in the room was having a fine time of it, overturning chairs, sweeping half the contents of the secretary's desk onto the floor.

"It isn't his fault," the woman said to Krackomberger. "And it isn't mine either." She clutched her walking stick and took a step in their direction. "My name is Norma Paine," the blind woman said.

Krackomberger stood frozen in a daze. Harry took it upon himself to speak for the doctor.

"He's Ben Krackomberger. And I'm Harry. Harry D'Amour."

"Not the same D'Amour who was involved in that mess with the dead cop?"

"The *very* same."

"It is a pleasure to meet you, Mister D'Amour. Let me offer you a bit of advice," she said to Harry as she pointed a finger at Krackomberger. "Whatever this man tries to tell you about what you did or didn't see, just agree with him."

"What? Why would I do that?"

"Because people like him have a vested interest in silencing people like us. We rock the boat, you see?"

"Is that what you're doing right now?" Harry said, nodding to the framed pictures that were coming off the walls, one by one. Not simply falling but being lifted off by their hooks, as if by invisible hands, then thrown down so violently the glass shattered.

"As I said before, I'm not doing this," Norma said. "One of my clients is here with me—"

"Clients?"

"I talk to the dead, Mister D'Amour. And this particular client doesn't feel as though I'm paying enough attention. Doctor Krackomberger. Say hello to your brother."

Krackomberger's chin quivered. "Im-impossible," he muttered.

"Warren, yes?" Norma said.

"No. Warren is dead."

"Well, of course he's dead!" Norma snapped. "That's why I'm here."

The doctor looked utterly bewildered by this piece of logic.

"She talks to the dead is what she's saying, Doc," Harry put in.

"I'm not speaking Swahili," Norma said to Harry. "I don't need an interpreter."

"I don't know," Harry said, looking at Dr. Krackomberger. "He looks pretty confused."

"Try and pay attention, Doctor," Norma offered. "Your brother told me to call you Shelly, because that's your middle name and not many people know that. Is it true?"

". . . you could have found that out any number of ways."

"All right. Forget it," Norma said, turning her back on the doctor. "I need a brandy. Mister D'Amour, would you like to join me in a little toast to the idiocy of psychiatrists?"

"I would happily drink to that, Miss Paine."

"Warren," Norma said, "let's go. We're frightening innocent people."

She was speaking, Harry supposed, of the receptionist who had taken refuge under the desk when the pictures started to drop and hadn't emerged since.

"Wait," Krackomberger said as they headed for the door. "You're blind, aren't you?"

"And you're perceptive," Norma said.

"Then . . . how can you possibly see my brother?"

"I don't have any idea. I only know I can. The world is invisible to me but perfectly clear to you. The dead are invisible to you and perfectly clear to me."

"You're telling me you can see my brother? Right now?"

Norma turned back and stared into the office. "Yes, he's lying on your couch."

"What's he doing?"

"You really want to know?"

"I asked you, didn't I?"

"He's masturbating."

"Jesus. It's him."

From that chance encounter the friendship of Harry and Norma sprang. And like much that happens by chance, this collision of souls could not have been more essential for both. Harry had been doubting his sanity in those recent weeks—the fuel for that fire supplied by Dr. Krackomberger—and suddenly there was Norma, talking to the supernatural as if it was the most natural thing in the world, something that was happening across the city every moment of every day.

It was she who had first said—when Harry unburdened himself of what he'd seen the day of his partner's death—that she believed every word of it and that she knew men and women around the city who could tell stories of their own that were evidence of the same Otherness, present in the daily life of the city.

As Harry drew within sight of the old building, he was surprised to find just how much it had changed over the years. The windows were either boarded up or broken and there'd apparently been a fire at some point in the building's history, which had gutted at least a third of the place, scorch marks blackening the façade above the burned-out windows. It was a sad sight, but more significantly, it was a troubling one. Why would Norma leave the comfort of her apartment for this godforsaken corner of nowhere?

All the doors were severely locked and bolted, but it wasn't a problem for Harry, whose solution to such a setback was always old-fashioned brute strength. He chose one of the boarded-up doors and pulled off several of the wood planks. It was a noisy, messy business, and if there'd been any kind of security patrolmen guarding the building, as several prominently placed signs announced there were, they would have certainly come running. But as he suspected, the signs were bullshit, and he was left to his own devices without interruption. Within five minutes of beginning his labor he had denuded the door of its boards and picked the lock that lay behind them.

"Nice work, kid," he said to himself as he stepped inside.

Harry took out a mini flashlight and shone it into the room. He saw that everything that had distinguished the modestly elegant lobby in which Harry now stood—the deco sweep of the design on the mirrors, the etchings in the tile underfoot, and the shape of the lighting fixtures—had been destroyed. Whether the destruction was the result of a crude attempt to take up the tiles for resale and bring down the mirror and light fixtures intact for the same purpose or the place simply had been smashed by drugged-up vandals with nothing better to do, the result was the same: chaos and debris in place of order and purpose.

He walked through the litter of glass and tile shards until he reached the stairs; then he began to ascend. Apparently there were easier ways into the building than prying open one of the doors as he had, because the sharp smell of human urine and the duller stink of feces grew stronger as he climbed. People used this place, as a toilet, yes, but probably to sleep in as well.

He eased his hand around the revolver tucked snugly in its holster, just in case he found himself discussing real estate law with any bad-tempered tenants. The good news was how very inactive his tattoos were. Not an itch, not a spasm. Apparently Norma had made a smart choice for a bolt-hole. Not the most salubrious of surroundings, but if it kept her safely hidden from the adversary and its agents, then Harry had no qualms.

Dr. Krackomberger's office had been suite 212. The plush beige carpeting that had covered the passageway leading up to it had been rolled up and removed, leaving just the bare boards. With every second or third step Harry took, one of them creaked and Harry grimaced. Finally, Harry reached the door of his onetime psychiatrist's office and tried the handle, expecting it to be locked. The door opened without protest, and

Harry was faced with yet another spectacle of vandalism. It looked as though somebody had taken a sledgehammer to the walls inside.

He chanced a word: "Norma?" Then several words: "Norma? It's Harry. I got your message. I know I'm early. Are you here?"

He went through into Krackomberger's office. The books that had lined the doctor's walls had not been taken, though it was obvious that at one point they'd all been stripped from the shelves and a pile of them used to make a fire in the middle of the room. Harry squatted beside the makeshift fire pit and tested the ashes. They were cold. Finding nothing more, Harry took a peek inside Krackomberger's private bathroom, but it was as trashed as the rest of the place. Norma was not here.

But she had led Harry to this place for a reason; of that he was certain. He chanced a glance at the bathroom mirror and there he saw, scrawled on the surface of the grimy glass, an arrow drawn in ash. It was pointing downward, toward the lower floors. Norma had left him a bread crumb. Harry left the office where he'd met his sightless friend so many years ago, and headed to the basement.

14

The members-only club that had once occupied the basement of the long-forgotten building had been designed for elite New Yorkers with more outré tastes than could be satisfied at the sex emporiums that had once run along Eighth Avenue and 42nd Street. Harry had glimpsed it in operation many years before when he'd been hired by the building's owner—one Joel Hinz—to do some detective work regarding his wife.

Despite the fact that Hinz ran an establishment dedicated to hedonism of every stripe directly under the feet of the city's lawmakers, he was a deeply conservative man in his personal life and was genuinely distressed when he began to suspect his wife of being unfaithful.

Harry had done his investigations and about three weeks later had brought confirmation in the form of incriminating photographs of Mrs. Hinz to the grieving Mr. Hinz in a large manila envelope. As Hinz had requested, he'd sent his assistant J. J. Fingerman to take Harry down into the club and get him a drink and a quick tour of the premises. It was quite an eye-opener: bondage, whipping, caning, water sports—the club offered a smorgasbord of perversities, practiced by men and women, most of them dressed in costumes that announced their particular proclivities.

A fifty-year-old man whom Harry recognized as the mayor's right hand was tottering around on stiletto heels in a frilly French maid's outfit; a woman who organized celebrity fund-raisers for the homeless and the destitute was crawling around naked with a dildo impaled in her ass, from the base of which hung a tail of black horsehair. On the main stage one of the most successful writers of Broadway musicals was tied to a chair having the flesh of his scrotum spread out and nailed to a piece of wood by a young woman dressed as a nun. To judge by the state of the lyricist's arousal, the procedure was pure bliss.

When Harry's tour had ended, he and Fingerman returned to Hinz's office and found his door was locked from the inside. Rather than wait for the keys to be located, Harry and Fingerman kicked the door open. The cuckolded husband lay sprawled over his desk where the photographs Harry had taken of Mrs. Hinz in her various liaisons were spread. The photographs had been spattered with the blood, bone fragments, and brain matter that had emptied in all directions when Hinz had put his gun into his mouth and pulled the trigger.

The party was over. Harry had learned a lot that night about the close relation of pain and pleasure, in certain situations, along with what fantasy and desire could drive people to do.

Harry found a cluster of light switches at the top of the stairs and flicked them on. Only two of them worked, one turning on a light directly over Harry's head, which spilled down the black-painted stairs, the other turning on a light in the booth where guests had paid their entrance fee and received a key for a little changing room where they could shed their public skins and don the masks of who they really were.

Harry cautiously headed down the stairs. There were a few small twitches and a flutter of activity in one of his tattoos: the rendering of a ritual necklace that Caz had dubbed the Scrimshaw Ring. While many of Caz's tattoos were simple talismans and made no pretense to solidity, the Scrimshaw Ring had been so meticulously rendered in the trompe l'oeil style, the shadow beneath it so dense that it made the necklace appear to stand proud on Harry's skin.

Its function was relatively simple: it alerted Harry to the presence of ghosts. But given that the spirits of the dead were everywhere, some in states of panic or agitation, others simply taking the air after the suffocations of death, the Scrimshaw Ring discriminated nicely and did not alert Harry's presence to any revenants except those that posed the greatest possible threat.

And apparently there was one such ghost—at *least* one—in Harry's immediate vicinity now. Harry paused at the bottom of the stairs, contemplating the very real possibility that this was another trap. Perhaps it was a ghost hired by the powers he'd confronted and embarrassed in New Orleans. But if they wanted revenge why come all this way to send only a few phantoms? They could frighten the unwitting, to be sure, but Harry was scarcely that. A little spook show wasn't going to leave him trembling. Harry pressed on.

The club seemed to have been left in the very state it had been in when Hinz put a bullet through his brain. The bar was still intact, the bottles of hard liquor still lined up, waiting for thirsty customers. Harry heard the glasses stacked underneath the bar start to chime as one of the ghosts began its performance.

When he ignored the noise and continued his advance, the spirit threw several of the shot glasses into the air. They were then pitched down onto the bar with such violence that a few of the flying shards struck Harry. He didn't respond to the display. He simply made his way on past the bar and into the big room with the Saint Andrew's cross set on the stage, where whip wielders once showed off their expertise.

Harry ran his light around the room, looking for some sign of the presence here. He stepped up onto the dais, intending to continue his search for Norma backstage, but as he crept closer toward the velvet curtain he heard a noise off to the right. His gaze shot in the direction of the sound. The opposing wall there had an array of canes, paddles, and whips hung on it—maybe fifty instruments in all. A few of the lighter items dropped to the floor and then one of the heavy wooden paddles was pitched in Harry's direction. It hit his knee, hard.

"Ah, fuck this!" he said, jumping off the stage and walking straight into the assault. "My tattoos are telling me you're a threat. But I'm not remotely intimidated by whoever you are, so if you go on throwing shit at me I will spit out a syllogistic that'll make you wish you'd never died. I promise you."

Harry had no sooner voiced this threat than one of the biggest whips on display was pulled down off the wall and drawn back, in preparation for a strike.

"Don't do it," Harry said.

His warning went disregarded. The phantom wielding the whip either was very lucky or knew its business. With the first strike it caught Harry's cheek, a sharp sting that made his eye water.

"You dickhead," he said. "Don't say I didn't warn you." He started to speak the syllogistic, which was one of the first he'd ever learned:

"E vuttu quathakai,
Nom-not, nom-netha,
E vuttu quathakai,
Antibethis—"

He was barely a third of the way through the utterance, but the incantation was already revealing the presences in the room. They looked like shadows thrown up on steam, their edges evaporating, their features scrawled on the air like an artist was working on the rain. There were three of them: all men.

"Stop the syllogistic," one of them moaned.

"Give me one reason why I should."

"We were only following orders."

"Whose orders?"

The phantoms exchanged panicky looks.

"Mine," said a familiar leathery voice from the darkness of the next room.

Harry let his guard down immediately. "Norma! What the hell?"

"Don't torment them, Harry. They were only trying to protect me."

"All right," Harry said to the phantasms. "I guess you guys get a reprieve."

"Stay at your posts, though," Norma said, "He could have been followed."

"Not a chance," Harry said, all confidence as he walked into the back room.

"Famous last words," said Norma.

Harry tried the light switch, and the wall-mounted lights went on, the bulbs red so as to flatter the nakedness of the old customers' gristly hides.

Norma was standing in the middle of the room, leaning on a stick, her hair gray, going to white, unpinned for the first time in all the years Harry had known her. Her face, though still possessed of the elegant beauty and power of her bones, was slack with exhaustion. Only her eyes had motion in them, the colorless pupils appearing to watch a tennis match between two absolutely equal players—left to right, right to left, left to right, right to left, the ball never once fumbling.

"What in God's name are you doing down here, Norma?"

"Let's sit. Give me your arm. My legs are aching."

"They're not being helped by the damp down here. You should be more careful at your age."

"We're neither of us as young as we used to be," Norma said as she led Harry through to what had been the room where the players only went when they were in the mood for the extreme games. "I can't do this much longer, Harry. I'm damn tired."

"You wouldn't be damn tired if you were sleeping in your own bed," Harry said, looking at the tattered mattress that had been laid on the floor, strewn with a few moth-eaten blankets to keep her warm. "Christ, Norma. How long have you been down here?"

"Don't worry about that. I'm safe. If I was in my own bed now I'd be dead. If not today, then tomorrow, or the day after. Goode set us up, Harry."

"I know. I walked into a serious trap at his place. Barely made it out alive."

"God, I'm sorry. He was damn convincing. I think I'm slipping. This never would have happened if I were a younger woman."

"He got us both, Norma. He was working with some powerful magic. You know all the magicians that have been murdered? One of them is still alive. Well . . . depending on your definition."

"What?"

"It's a long story, but I know who killed them. A demon. I met him at Goode's house. He's a serious player."

"Oh Lord. I was afraid of that. That's the other reason I'm holed up in this filthy place. I think they wanted to split us up. As soon as you left, my apartment was compromised. I felt the bad juju coming and I got the fuck out of there, but quick! There's roads open, Harry. Roads that should be closed, and there's something coming down one of those roads—or maybe all of them—that means me and you and a whole lot of other people harm."

"I believe it, but that doesn't change the fact that you can't stay here. This place is disgusting. We have to relocate you to some place where you won't be sleeping on a damp floor with rats running over your feet. Not to mention what's been done on that mattress. You can't see the stains, Norma, but there's a lot of them, in a variety of colors."

"You got a place in mind?"

"As a matter of fact, I do. I'm going to get everything ready, and then I'm coming back for you, all right?"

"If you say so."

"I do. I'll see you soon. We're gonna make it out of this thing. I promise."

As he gave her a gentle kiss on the cheek she caught hold of his hand.

"Why are you so good to me?" she said.

"As if you didn't know."

"Indulge me."

"Because there is nobody in the world who means more to me than you. And that's no indulgence. It's the plain truth."

She smiled against his hand. "Thank you," she said.

Harry regarded her affectionately for a moment, then without saying a word turned and went in search of a safer haven.

BOOK TWO

Into the Breach

The ineffable thing has tied me to him; tows me with a cable I have no knife to cut.

—Herman Melville, *Moby-Dick*

1

The Monastery of the Cenobitical Order was a large-walled compound built seven hundred thousand years ago on a damned-made hill of stone and cement. It could only be entered by one route, a narrow stairway that was carefully watched by the monastery guards. It had been built during a time of imminent civil war, with factions of demons in constant skirmishes. The head of the Cenobitical Order, his identity known only to the eight who had raised him from their number into that High Office, had decided that for the greater good of the Order he would use a tiny part of the vast wealth they had accrued to build a fortress-sanctuary where his priests and priestesses would be safe from the volatile politics of Hell. The fortress had been built to the most rigorous of standards, its polished gray walls unscalable.

As the years had passed and the Cenobites were less and less in the streets of the city that Lucifer had designed and built (a city called, by some, Pandemonium but named Pyratha by its architect), the stories about what went on behind the sleek black walls of the Cenobitical fortress proliferated and the countless demons and damned alike who glanced its way all had favorite stories about the excesses of its occupants.

Between the monastery and Hell's great city, Pyratha, sat the vast shantytown called Fike's Trench, where the damned who did service in the mansions, temples, and streets retired to sleep, and eat, and, yes, copulate (and, if they were lucky, produce an infant or two who could be sold at the abattoir, no questions asked).

The stories of the fortress and the monstrous things that went on behind its walls were exchanged like currency, growing ever more elaborate. It was an understandable comfort to the damned, who lived with so much terror and atrocity in their daily lives, that there be a place where things were even worse—where they could look and tell themselves that their situation could be worse. And so each man, woman, and child nurtured acknowledgments that they were not among the victims of the fortress where the unspeakable devices of the Order would scour even the most treasured of memories. And in this fashion, the damned existed within the framework of something approximating a life; living in excrement and exhaustion, their bodies barely nourished, their spirits unfed, they indulged in the almost happy thought that at least a few others suffered more than they.

All this had come as a shock to Theodore Felixson. In life he'd spent much of the fortune his workings in magic had earned him (what he'd liked to refer to as his *will*-gotten gains) on art, always buying privately because the paintings he collected moved, when they moved at all, outside the sniffing range of the museum hounds. All the pictures he'd owned had related in some way to Hell: a Tintoretto of Lucifer falling, his wings torn from his body, trailing after him into the abyss; a sheaf of preparatory studies by Lucca Signorelli for his fresco of the damned in Hell; a book of horrors that Felixson had purchased in Damascus because its unknown creator had found a way to make the meditations of each hour turn on sin and punishment. These had been the most horrific pieces in his rather sizable collection on the subject of the infernal, and not one of them even remotely resembled the truth.

There was an elegant symmetry to Pyratha, with its eight hills ("one better than Rome," its architect boasted), which were crammed with buildings of countless styles and sizes. Felixson knew nothing of the city's rules, if it had any. The Hell Priest had referred to it in passing on one occasion only and spoke of it with the contempt of a creature who thought of every occupant of Pyratha as a subspecies, their mindless hedonism matched only by their lavish stupidity. The city that Lucifer had built to outdo Rome had fallen, as Rome had fallen, into decadence and self-indulgence, its regime too concerned with its own internal struggles to cleanse the city of its filth and return it to the disciplined state it had been in before Lucifer's disappearance.

Yes, surprising as the architecture of Hell was to Felixson, finding out that the angel who had been cast down from Heaven for his rebellious ways was absent from his throne defied all expectations, even if it did make a certain amount of sense. As above, so below, Felixson thought.

There were countless theories concerning Lucifer's disappearance and Felixson had heard them all. Depending on which story you chose to believe, Lucifer either had gone mad and perished in the wastelands, escaping Hell entirely, or was walking the streets of Pyratha disguised as a commoner. Felixson didn't believe any of it. He kept his opinions on the subject, and all other opinions for that matter, to himself. He was lucky to be alive, he knew, and though the torturous surgeries had destroyed his abilities to form an intelligible sentence, he was still fully capable of thinking clearly. If he bided his time and played his cards right, sooner or later, he knew, an escape route would present itself, and when it did he'd take it and be gone. He'd return to Earth, change his name and his face, and renounce magic for the rest of his days.

That had been the plan right up until he realized that living without power wasn't the nightmare he'd envisioned it to be. He had been among the most accomplished and ambitious magicians in the world, but holding on to that position had taken staggering amounts of energy, will, and time. When he finally allowed himself to learn from the Cenobites, he discovered that the matters of his soul, the complex business of which had first drawn him into the mysteries of his craft, had been neglected entirely. It was only now, as a slave to a demon, that Felixson was again free to begin the long journey of self-within-self, the journey from which the getting of magic had distracted him. Living in Hell kept him aware of the possibility of Heaven, and he'd never felt more alive.

Felixson stood at the bottom of the steps that led up to the gate of the fortress with a message clutched firmly in his recently mangled hand. The epistle he held had been given to him by one of Hell's messengers, the only objectively beautiful beings in the underworld. They existed for the sole purpose of ensuring that Hell's dirtiest dealings always came wrapped in a pretty package.

Ahead, he could see Fike's Trench and, beyond it, the whole of Pyratha. On the road heading toward him marched a small army of Hell's priests and priestesses, a procession of three dozen of the Order's most formidable soldiers. Among them, Felixson was proud to say, stood his master.

Felixson took his eyes off the smoking spires of the city and returned his gaze to the approaching procession of Cenobites. A wind had sprung up, or rather *the* wind, for there was only one: it blew bitterly cold and stirred up the scents of rot and burnt blood that perpetually filled the air. Now, as the acrid wind grew in strength gust by gust, it caught on the black ceremonial robes of the Cenobites and unfurled the thirty-foot flags of oiled human skin that several of the priests and priestesses held so that the flags snaked and snapped high above their heads. The holes in the hides where the eyes and mouths had been looked to Felixson as though the victims were still staring wide-eyed with disbelief at the sight of the flying knives that undid them, forever screaming as their skin was expertly stripped from muscle.

The bell in the fortress tower, which was called Summoner (it was the same bell, in point of fact, those that had opened Lemarchand's Configuration always heard tolling far off), was now ringing to welcome back the brothers and sisters of the Order to the fortress. Upon seeing his master, Felixson knelt in the mud, head bowed so deferentially that it touched the ground as the procession climbed the steps to the fortress gate. With his head firmly planted in the dirt, Felixson extended his arm, the missive he carried held high in front of him.

His lord stepped out of the procession to speak to Felixson, and the Cenobites continued to make their way past him.

"What is this?" his lord said, snatching the letter from Felixson's hand.

Felixson turned his muddied and divided head, twisting it to the left so he could study his lord's reaction with one eye. The Cenobite's face was inscrutable. Nobody knew how old he was—Felixson was smart enough not to ask—but the weight of his age sat on his countenance, carving it into something that could never be manufactured, only chiseled by the agonies of loss and time. Felixson's tongue rolled out of his head, landing in the mud and shit–caked street. He didn't seem to mind. He was in thrall to his master.

"I am called to the Chamber of the Unconsumed," the Hell Priest said, staring down at the letter in his hand.

Without another word, the Cenobite turned against the tide of the members of his Order and moved toward Pyratha. Felixson followed, naïve to the details but loyal to the end.

2

After the filth of the Trench, the streets of the Hell's city were comparatively clean. They were wide and, in places, planted with some species of tree that needed no sunlight to survive, their black trunks and branches and even the dark blue leaves that sprang from them gnarled and twisted as though every inch of their growth had been born in convulsion. There were no cars on the streets, but there were bicycles, sedan chairs, and rickshaws—even a few carriages drawn by horses that had almost transparent skin and fleshless heads so flat and wide (their eyes set on either edge of these expanses of bone) that they resembled manta rays stitched upon the bodies of asses.

In the streets, word of the Cenobite's appearance went out before him, and at each intersection even the busiest traffic was held up by demons in dark purple uniforms (the closest things Pyratha had to a police force) so that the Cenobite could make his way through the city undeterred by a single citizen.

As he passed, most of the citizens either made signs of devotion—touching navel, breastbone, and the middle brow before inclining their heads—or, if officers, went down on their knees to demonstrate their veneration. It wasn't just hybrids and demons who dropped to the ground—so did many of the damned. The Hell Priest paid them no heed, but Felixson drank it all in.

Up close, the buildings they hurried past seemed even more impressive to Felixson than they had from the hill on which sat the monastery. Their façades were decorated with what looked like intricately rendered scenes of Lucifer's personal mythologies. The figures were designed to be contained within a rigorous square format, which brought to Felixson's mind the decorations he'd once seen on the temples of Incas and Aztecs. There was every kind of activity pictured in these decorations: wars, celebrations, and even lovemaking—all very graphically depicted. As he had paced a long period in the hushed and claustrophobic cells of the fortress, only able to see the city for a few stolen minutes now and then, it gave Felixson a sense of something vaguely resembling contentment to be given so much to feast his eyes upon.

"*There*," the Hell Priest said, tearing Felixson from his reverie.

Felixson looked up to see the Cenobite pointing at what was easily the tallest building in the city. It rose higher than the eye could see, piercing the pitch-black sky. For all its enormity, the building was entirely void of detail. A windowless, featureless spike, its façade was the very essence of mundanity. The palace was a true work of art, a building so bland it wasn't even appealing enough to be considered an eyesore. It was a joke, Felixson guessed, its architect found quite amusing.

As they came to within three steps of the summit, a door opened inward, though there was nobody visibly doing the job. Felixson noticed the tiniest tremor in the Hell Priest's hand. The Cenobite cast his lightless eyes up at the stone spectacle that rose high above them, and then said, "I am here to be judged. If the judgment goes against me, you are to destroy every one of my endeavors. Do you understand?"

"Evry tings?" Felixson said.

"Don't succumb to sentiment. I have all I need here." He tapped his temple with the broken and poorly reset forefinger of his right hand. "Nothing will be lost."

"I do, Master. I do can."

The Cenobite offered a subtle approving nod, and together they stepped inside.

3

The Palace of the Unconsumed was as devoid of features inside as it was outside. The foyer was thick with infernal bureaucrats in gray suits, tailored to accommodate whatever physical defect afflicted the damned. One, with a ring of football-sized tumors growing out of his back, had his suit neatly encircling each of the pulsing protuberances. Some wore fabric hoods that reduced their expressions to two small eyeholes and a horizontal rectangle for their mouths. There were sigils sewn into the fabric, their significance outside Felixson's field of knowledge.

The drab passages were lit with large bare bulbs, the light they gave off never entirely solid but flickering—no, fluttering—as though the source of light was alive inside. After turning the corners of the passageways six times—every one of them committed to memory by Felixson—they came out into a place of startling splendor. Felixson had assumed the entire building was a hive of featureless corridors, but he was wrong. This area was an open space, bathed in light, and consisting only of a single, reflective metal tube, perhaps ten feet wide, that ran all the way up from the floor to the ceiling, which was set so far above their heads it remained unseen.

The Cenobite pointed to the darkness above them and said a single word:

"There."

Their ascent was accomplished via a wide spiral staircase that sat within the reflective tube. Each of the metal steps were welded to its core. But even here in this elegant construct, the infernal touch hadn't been neglected. Each of the steps was set not at ninety degrees to the core, but at ninety-seven, or a hundred, or a hundred and five, each one different from the one before but all sending out the same message: nothing was certain here; nothing was safe. There was no railing to break the slide should someone lose their footing, only step after disquieting step designed to make the ascent as vertiginous as possible.

The Cenobite, however, was defiant. Rather than climb the stair close to the column where he could at least enjoy the illusion of safety, he ascended hewing always to the open end of the step, as if daring fate to take its due. Sometimes the preceding step had been crafted so as to incline more precipitously and ascending to the next step took a considerable length of stride, yet somehow the Hell Priest managed to make the climb with effortless dignity, leaving Felixson to follow behind, clinging desperately to the core. Halfway into their journey, he started to count the stairs. Felixson got to three hundred and eighty-nine before the Hell Priest disappeared from sight.

Nearly breathless, Felixson continued his ascent and found an archway, more than twice his height, at the top of the stairs. The Cenobite had already stepped through it and was surprised to find that there was no guard—at least none visible—at the threshold. Felixson went on after his master, keeping his head declined so far that he couldn't see anything of the chamber into which his master had led him. Felixson saw that they were in a large dome, which was surely two hundred feet high at its apex, though with his head bowed it was difficult to judge accurately. The entire chamber seemed to be carved from white marble, including the floor, which was icy cold beneath the soles of his feet, and though he did his best to keep from making a sound, the dome picked up every tiny hint and lobbed its echoes back and forth before adding them to the reservoir of murmurs and steps and quiet weepings that ran like a gutter around the farthest edge of the floor.

"Far enough," somebody said, their command folding into a thousand tapering echoes.

A breath-cremating heat came at Felixson and the Priest from the center of the dome. The only object in the circular room was a throne so far beyond the dimensions of a piece of ordinary furniture that it deserved a better, as yet uninvented word. The thing was made of solid blocks of metal, nine or ten inches thick: one slab for the high back, one for each arm, one for the seat, and a fifth running parallel with the arm slabs but set beneath the seat.

Flammable gases blazed from six long, wide vents, one on every side of the throne and two directly beneath it. They burned with sapphire flames, which intensified to an aching white, flecked with red motes at their cores. The gases rose high above the back of the flame, which was itself easily ten feet tall, and drew together, braiding themselves into a single blazing column. The heat inside the dome would have been lethal had the dome not been pierced with several concentric rings of holes, housing powerful fans to extract excess heat. Directly above the throne, the chamber's spotless white marble was scorched black.

As for the throne itself, it was virtually white-hot, and sitting in it, his pose formal, was the creature whose indifference to the blaze had given him his apt moniker: the Unconsumed. Felixson had heard of him in whispers. Whatever color his skin had originally been, his body was now blackened by heat. His vestments and his shoes (if ever he'd worn them) and his staff of office (if ever he'd carried one) had burned away. So too all the hair from his head, face, and body. Yet somehow, the rest of him—his skin, flesh, and bone—was unaffected by the volcanic heat in which he sat.

The Hell Priest stopped in his tracks. Felixson did the same, and even though he had been given no order, he went down on his knees.

"Cenobite. Do you know why you have been summoned?"

"No."

"Come closer. Let me better see your face."

The Cenobite approached within perhaps six strides of the throne, showing no concern for the incredible heat that emanated from the spot. If he felt it, he showed no sign.

"Tell me of magic, Cenobite," the Unconsumed said. His voice sounded like the flame: steady and clean but for those flickering motes of scarlet.

"A human artifice, my Sovereign. Yet another of man's inventions designed to grasp divinity."

"Then why should it concern you?"

It wasn't the Unconsumed who spoke but a fourth presence in the chamber. An Abbot of the Cenobitical Order made his presence known as he emerged from the shadows behind the Unconsumed's throne and made his way at processional speed across the chamber. He carried the staff of the High Union, which was fashioned after a shepherd's crook, shouting condemnations as he approached. Behind his back, the Abbot had commonly been called the Lizard, a nickname he'd earned from the countless scales of polished silver, each set with a jewel, that had been hammered into every visible inch of his flesh, assumed to cover his entire body.

"We have found your books, Priest. Obscene volumes of the desperate workings of men. It's heresy. You are part of an Order," the Abbot continued. "Answerable to its laws only. Why have you been keeping secrets?"

"I know—"

"You *know* nothing!" the Abbot said, slamming his rod against the cold marble, punishing the Cenobite's ears with its din. "A Cenobite is to work within the system. You seem content to work outside that system. As of this moment, you are exiled from the Order."

"Very well."

"And personally," the Abbot continued, "I would have you executed. But the final judgment lies with the Unconsumed—"

"—and I see no punishment in execution," said the Unconsumed. "You are never again to set foot in the monastery. Your belongings have been confiscated. You are banished to the Trench. What happens to you there is not my concern."

"Thank you," said the Hell Priest.

He bowed, then turned and headed for the archway. Wordlessly, he and his servant exited the chamber and began the long descent.

4

Caz kept odd hours, but there was an emergency buzzer hidden in a niche in the brickwork beside the front door, which only a select group of people knew about. Harry used it now. There was some static on the intercom and then:

"Caz isn't home right now."

"It's D'Amour. Let me in."

"Who?"

"Harry. D'Amour."

"Who?"

Harry sighed. "Harold."

Sixty seconds later Harry was sitting on Caz's overstuffed sofa, which occupied fully a quarter of his living room. Another significant fragment was taken up by books, his places in them marked. His subjects of interest could scarcely have been more eclectic: forensic pathology, the life of Herman Melville, the Franco-Prussian war, Mexican folklore, Pasolini's murder, Mapplethorpe's self-portraits, the prisons of Louisiana, Serbo-Croatian Puppeteers—and on and on, the towers of books looking like a bird's-eye view of a major metropolitan city. Harry knew the etiquette of the books. You could pick something out of the stacks and flip through it, but it had to go back in the same place. You could even borrow them, but the price of a late return was always something disgusting.

Of all the men Harry had ever called his friend, Caz was easily the most intimidating. He stood six feet six inches tall, his body a mass of lean, tattooed muscle, a good portion of it done in Japan by the master who'd taught Caz the skill. Caz wore a coat of ink and color that stopped only at his neck, wrists, and ankles, its designs a compendium of classic Japanese subjects: on his back was a samurai in close combat with a demon in a rain-lashed bamboo grove; two dragons ascended his legs, their tongues interwoven as they wrapped around the length of his dick. He was bald and clean shaven, and had anyone caught sight of him coming out of a bar at two in the morning, shirtless and sweaty, they would have stepped out onto the street rather than get in his way on the sidewalk.

He cut an intimidating figure, to be sure. But one glance at his face and it was a very different story. Caz found some source of delight in everything, and as a result he had an unmatched kindness in his eyes. There was scarcely a time when Caz wasn't smiling or laughing out loud, the one significant exception being that portion of his day he spent drilling pictures and words on other people's bodies.

"Harold, my man, you look serious," Caz said to Harry, using a nickname Harry allowed him and only him to use. "What's troubling you?"

"If I'm going to answer that question, I need a drink first."

Caz prepared his specialty (Bénédictine with a pinch of cocaine) in the little office behind the store, and Harry told him everything that had happened so far, every damn bit of it, sometimes reaching back to his earliest encounters.

". . . and then this thing with Norma," he said to Caz. "I mean, they got us both, y'know? How could we both have been fooled? I rarely see her frightened, Caz, maybe twice in my life, but never like this. Never hiding in some shit hole because she's afraid of what's going to come for her."

131

"Well, we can get her out of there tonight, if you'd like, my man. We can bring her here. Make her feel comfy. She'll be safe."

"No. I know they're watching."

"They must be keeping their distance then," Caz said, "'cause I haven't had a twinge."

He turned his palms over, where two of his synthesized alarm sigils had been inked by an ex-lover of his in Baltimore.

"I haven't felt anything either," said Harry. "But that might mean they're getting smarter. Maybe they're running some interference signal, y'know, to block our alarms. They're not stupid."

"And neither are we," Caz said. "We'll get her somewhere safe. Somewhere . . ."—he trailed off and a Cazian grin appeared on his face—". . . in Brooklyn."

"Brooklyn?"

"Trust me, I know *just* the person. I'm going to go over there now. You go back to Norma. I'll call you when everything's ready."

"I don't have a phone," Harry said. "Lost it in the demolition."

"Fine," Caz said. "I'll knock. Any idea how many are after you guys?"

Harry shrugged. "No. I can't even figure out why they'd choose now. I've been in the same office since I started out. And she's been in that same apartment doing her thing all these years. There was never any trouble from the Pit before. What do you think they want?"

"You," Caz said. "Plain and simple."

"What?" Harry said. "No. If they wanted me, they'd come for me. Christ knows they do it often enough."

"Yeah," said Caz. "But they always fail."

5

Harry came back to the basement sex club to find Norma in conversation with a ghost she introduced to Harry as "Nails" McNeil, who had not come in search of Norma but had wandered in on a lark to reacquaint himself with his favorite old stomping ground.

"He loved getting crucified at the summer and winter solstices," Norma told Harry. Norma listened while the invisible presence added something to this. "He says you should try it, Harry. A crucifixion and a good blow job. Heaven on Earth."

"Thanks, Nails," Harry said. "But I think I'll stick to plain old masturbation. On that note, while we wait for Caz to get here, I'm going to settle down for a couple hours of sleep on the stage next door. The scene of many of Mister McNeil's finest hours, no doubt."

"He says, 'Sweet dreams.'"

"That's pretty much out of the question, but it's the thought that counts. I brought some food, Norma, and a pillow, and some brandy too."

"Oh my stars, Harry. You shouldn't have gone through so much trouble. And you don't need to stay either. I'm perfectly fine."

"Indulge me."

Norma smiled. "We'll keep our chatting down," she said.

Here was a first, Harry thought as he tossed the pillow down on the stage in preparation of sleeping beneath a cross on boards that had no doubt seen their share of bodily fluids. There was probably something significant about that, he thought vaguely, but he was too damn tired to get very far with the notion. Sleep overcame him quickly, and despite Nails McNeil's good-night wish, Harry's dream—in the singular—was not sweet. He passed the dazed hours dreaming he was in the back of the cab that had brought him here, only the familiar streets of New York were now a near wasteland, and his driver—far from ignorant of what was pursuing them—simply said over and over, "Whatever you do, don't look back."

6

The Hell Priest left the fortress and exited the city without a word, Felixson following close behind. Only when they finally reached the threshold of the monastery did the Hell Priest speak.

"Do you see that stand of trees a mile to our left?"

"Yes."

"Go and wait. I will come for you."

They separated once they were inside the gates. Under ideal circumstances the Hell Priest would have seen his duties accomplished at more leisurely a pace than he'd now been obliged to accept. But he was ready to move, for there had been many years of preparation and it was a relief to finally have the grim business before him under way. When he'd thanked the Unconsumed, he had been sincere.

All of what he was about to do depended on possessing much magic, of course. That had been the key to this endeavor from the beginning. And it was no small pleasure to him to discover that most of his fellow Cenobites, if the subject of magic and its efficacy were to be brought up in conversation, had nothing but contempt for it; that fact made what was about to happen all the more ironic.

He went directly to the row of anonymous buildings that ran along the wall on the far edge of the fortress where the slope on which it stood fell away. They were called the Channel Houses. To compensate for the gradient, the wall on that side was twice as high as at the front, the top of it crammed with iron spikes that pointed in, out, and up. These were in turn covered with barbs that had snared hundreds of birds, many of them caught in the process of picking at earlier victims. Here and there among the iron and the bones were a few recent captives, occasionally fluttering frantically for a few seconds and then settling again to gather their strength for another futile attempt at freedom.

The original purpose of the Channel Houses had long been forgotten. Many of them were completely empty. Some were repositories of chain-mail aprons and gloves that had been used for vivisections on the damned, the blood-gummed equipment tossed and left to the flies. Even they, having fed and bred several generations there, had exhausted the usefulness of the stuff and gone.

Nobody now came there, except the Hell Priest, and even he had only come twice: once to elect a hiding place for his own contribution to the Order's tradition of torment, the other to actually hide them away. In point of fact, it had been the sight of the birds on top of the wall that had inspired the simple but elegant solution of how he could bring the news—news he had spent many months of study refining—to its recipients. Using the lethal knowledge he had culled from his researches and the only book in his secret library that did not concern magic, *Senbazuru Orikata or How to Fold One Thousand Cranes*, the oldest known volume on the art of origami, he had gone about his secret work with an eagerness he had not remembered feeling for the better part of a human lifetime.

Now, as he entered the sixth Channel House, where his labors lay sleeping in a large birdcage, he felt that eagerness once again, chastened by the knowledge that there would be neither time nor opportunity to do this twice, so he could not afford error. Since he'd first brought his secret work here the Order had swelled in number, a circumstance he had planned for. He had to fold the new identities into his flock with a fine brush and an ink called Cindered Scale. This would take only a few more minutes. As he worked, he listened for any sounds besides those of the dying birds—a whisper, a footfall, any sign that he was being sought—but inscribing the Execution Writs on the extra papers he'd folded and left unmarked for this very situation was finished without interruption. He put the papers together in the cage with the others he had crafted, and as he did so a feeling almost utterly foreign to him insinuated itself into his thoughts. Puzzled, he struggled to name it. What was it?

He made a hushed grunt of recognition when the answer came. It was doubt. But as to its source, he was woefully ignorant. He wasn't doubting the efficacy of the working in which he was about to engage. He was certain it would more than suffice. Nor was he doubting its mode of delivery. So what was it that troubled him?

He stared down into a cage of folded paper birds while he puzzled over his unwanted emotion. And all at once it came clear. The doubt was rooted in certainty, certainty that once the magic he had labored over in this room was free to go about its business there was no turning back. The world he had known for almost as far back as his memory stretched was about to change out of all recognition. He was moments from unleashing utter chaos, and the doubt was simply reminding him of the fact. It was testing him. It was asking of him: *Are you ready for the apocalypse?*

He heard the question in his head, but he answered it with his lips. "Yes," he said.

With the doubt defined and replied to, he went on with his work, picking up the cage and taking it to the door, which he opened as he set the cage down on its threshold.

For safety's sake he took a gutting knife from his belt, prepared for the unlikely event that he would be interrupted. Then he spoke the words, which were African in origin and had taken him some time to master, punctuated as they were with grunts and delicate expulsions of breath.

The Hell Priest watched the cage as he spoke. The incantation sometimes required a second and even a third repetition, so he was drawing breath to repeat the syllables when there was a slight shift in the heap of folded papers. It was followed almost immediately by another movement, and another, the urge to live spreading through the occupants of the cage. In less than a minute, nearly a hundred origami cranes came alive, flapping their paper wings. The only sound they were capable of making was the one they were making now: paper rubbing against paper, fold against fold. They knew what they'd been made to emulate and they fluttered against the door in their hunger for release.

The Hell Priest had no intention of releasing them all at once. That risked too much attention being drawn to their source. He opened the cage and let fewer than ten of them go. They hopped around on their folded feet, stretching their wings as they did so. Then, as though by mutual consent, they all beat their paper wings, took flight, and rose up above the Channel Houses. Three of them landed on the roof of Channel House Six, cocking their heads to stare back down at their caged brethren. The remainder, having circled the Channel House once to orient themselves, flew off, and the remaining three who came to perch on the gutters followed seconds later. The spectacle of the first few departing had driven the ninety or so that were still in the cage into a mad frenzy.

"Your turn will come," the Hell Priest said to them.

If they understood him they chose not to take notice. They flapped and fought and repeatedly flung themselves against the bars. Despite the weight of the iron cage and their own frailty, they still managed to make the cage shake. The Priest opened the door a couple of inches and let another dozen out, quickly latching the door again to watch what this second group would do. As he'd suspected, not one of them wasted time perching on the Channel House roof, as the three from the first group had done. Instead, they all flew up immediately, circling around to orient themselves before quickly going their various ways. The cold, hard wind was blowing again, and the Priest watched his folded birds that looked like scraps of paper billowing in from the chaotic sheets of the city, knowing that anything more than a cursory glance would break the illusion, for the scraps were not in thrall to any specific wind; they were obviously flying in very different, and very precise, directions.

With the gift of this illusory wind, he decided to throw caution to it and let all of the birds have their freedom. He tore the cage door off its simple hinges and the bars broke where they were welded to the framework of the cage. He pulled the front of it away, standing clear of it as the paper flock rose up in a chaotic tangle of folded wings and beaks.

None of them languished. They had work to do, and they were eager to do it. They rose up after a few seconds and hopped or fluttered to the doorway. From there they set off to do their work. The whole business, from his tearing open the cage to liberate the birds to the departure of the last of them, had taken perhaps three minutes.

He didn't have long now. As a result, he didn't wait in the Channel House but headed out at a brisk walk so as to be seen on the busier paths that ran between the blocks of cells. In doing so, however, he was not providing himself with an alibi. In point of fact, he had no need of one, because in a short time none of those who saw him there would be alive to testify. His only concern was that the presence of the birds would be discovered. But, to his satisfaction, their existence went unnoticed by his brothers and sisters. He was wonderfully alive in those glorious minutes of anticipation.

His senses quaking, he climbed the steps to the wall above the gate and looked across at the city. The usual fires were burning here and there, and on the second-closest bridge he saw a violent crash between the regime's guard, they in their black and silver uniforms, and an unruly mass of citizens who were forcing the guard's retreat by simple superiority of numbers.

Homemade fire bombs were lobbed among the guards and emptied in sprays of orange flame, the victims dowsing the fire by throwing themselves off the bridge into the water. But the fire was immune to its oldest enemy; the burning guards would dive deep to extinguish the flames only to surface and instantaneously reignite. He could hear the guards shrieking as they were consumed. It was business as usual.

But then came a cry from much nearer by. He heard a wail emanate from within the monastery behind him. Before it died away there were another two and almost immediately three or four more. None were cries of pain, of course. These were souls who had lived in a state of perpetual self-elected agony so as to earn a place within the Order, and the execution that the Hell Priest had composed was designed for efficiency, not indulgence.

When one of the Hell Priest's paper soldiers found an intended victim the Writ's baleful influence took effect, and when that happened they had only eight or nine heartbeats left to them, each one weaker than the one that preceded it. The shouts he heard were of disbelief and rage, and none of them lasted very long.

There was panic among those who worked for the dead and dying members of the Order, however, the damned who, like Felixson, had slavishly served their masters in any way they were called upon to do so. Now their masters were falling down, their mouths frothing, and the slaves were crying out for help only to find that the same thing was likely happening in every other chamber of the monastery.

The Hell Priest finally entered the monastery, walking the pathways between the cell blocks looking left and right but only fleetingly. His brothers and sisters were in their last death throes. Priests, priestesses, deacons, and bishops all lay where they had fallen, some at the threshold, as if all they'd needed were a breath of fresh air, others visible only as an outstretched limb seen through a half-closed door.

What they had in common, these many dead, was blood. It had been expelled from their bodies with convulsive force, just as the Hell Priest had planned in his drawing of the Writs. The death spasms he had willed upon them were a cruelty of his own invention and only plausible because the laws of magic were doing to the body what nature could not. Once the Writs reached their victims, they reconfigured in a matter of seconds the organization of their innards, so that their bodies became blood-filled pitchers disgorging everything in two or, at most, three convulsions.

Only two times as he walked around the cell blocks did he confront living victims. On the first occasion somebody caught at the hem of his vestments. He looked down to see a priestess with whom he had worked several times in the collecting of souls. She was in extremis, blood pouring forth from every pore in her body. He pulled his robes from her weakening grasp and moved along quickly.

On the second occasion, he heard someone call out from a cell he was passing. There he saw, leaning against the wall a foot or so from the door, an excessively corpulent brother in black spectacles whom he had never liked, nor been liked by in turn.

"This is your doing," the cumbersome priest said from within his cell.

"You are mistaken," the Hell Priest said.

"Traitor!"

He was raising his voice as he became more certain of his accusations, and rather than encourage him to shout still louder by moving on, the Hell Priest stepped into the cell, fully prepared to dispatch the accusing Cenobite with hook and hand. Once inside, the Hell Priest saw the unfolded remains of his Execution Writ lying on the floor. For some reason, perhaps because of the great weight of his corpulent brother's body, it had not yet taken effect on him.

". . . murderer . . ." the fat one said.

This time he didn't shout his accusation, though he clearly wished to, for his face had grown suddenly pale and loud noises stemmed from his innards. Death was seconds away.

The Hell Priest backed away from his dying brother. As he did so, two things happened simultaneously: the fat one reached out and caught hold of the front of the Hell Priest's vestments, and then he convulsed, his obese body disgorging a stream of hot blood that hit the Hell Priest's face with such force that it stung his flesh.

The Hell Priest took hold of the fat one's hand and, with a single squeeze, broke all of his fingers in a bid to free himself from the grip. Before he could liberate himself, there was a second convulsion, more powerful than the first. The contents washed over the Hell Priest like a tidal wave, and as the dying obese brother slid down the wall his grip on his murderer weakened, as his life finally gave out. The Hell Priest turned his back on his brother and left the cell, emerging into the tumultuous halls, his bloodied condition no bad disguise.

He decided he'd seen more than enough. Not because the sights overwhelmed him. He was, in fact, quite proud to see the successful fruits of his labors. But this was only the first part of his plan. It had gone off without a hitch and it was now time to move away from here and attend to his rendezvous with Felixson. But as the Hell Priest came in sight of the fortress gates, one of which was open only a little way, he met, or rather heard, the third survivor.

"Stand still, Priest," said a weakened voice.

He did as he was commanded and, looking off to his right, saw the Abbot, semi-recumbent, being pushed on a two-wheeled vehicle, attended by physicians who administered to him from all sides. The Abbot's weakened frame had been aggravated by the great spillage of blood down his reptilian chin and out the front of his exquisitely decorated robes. Blood still trickled from the corners of his mouth and negotiated its way between the scales of metal and gems. More came when he spoke, but he cared not. He had survived the torment that had left the whole of his Unholy Order dead, all except for himself, and this other who stood before him.

He studied the Hell Priest, his golden eyes ringed with small scales set with sapphires, giving away no clue to his thoughts. Finally he said, "Are you immune to this sickness that has taken us?"

"No," the Hell Priest said. "My belly is twisted up. And I am bleeding."

"Liar. *Liar!*" He pushed his attendants away from him, left and right, and stepped off the device that brought him here, coming at the Hell Priest with startling speed. "You did this! You murdered your own Order! I smell their blood on you!" The jewels flickered with color, rubies and sapphires and emeralds concealing completely the rotting body beneath. "Confess it, Priest. Save yourself the stink of your own flesh burning."

"This is no longer my Order," the Hell Priest said. "I am but a citizen of the Trench, come to collect my belongings."

"Guards! Arrest him! And summon the inquisitors from—"

His orders were silenced by the Hell Priest's hand over his throat. The Priest lifted him up, which was no small feat, for the heaviness that the

142

jewelry added to the Abbot's body weight was substantial. Still, the Priest lifted him and pressed him against one of the cell block walls.

With his free hand he scraped at the Abbot's decorations, digging his fingers beneath the silver and jewels adorning his face and tearing them away. The Abbot's flesh was soft with rot beneath, like soap too long left in hot water, and when the Priest began to remove the carapace it came away readily. In a matter of seconds he had exposed half of the Abbot's face. It was a pitiful sight, the flesh barely adhering to the bone.

And yet there was no fear in the Abbot's eyes. He drew breath enough through the Priest's stranglehold to say, "It seems we are united by a secret. You are not the only one with magic to wield. I am alive now only because of workings I prepared many years ago. You can kill me now, but I promise I will take you with me."

He stared unblinking at the Hell Priest as he declared his immunity, and the Hell Priest knew his promise to be true; he could already feel the connection the Abbot was forging between them.

"There is much I can do short of your destruction," the Hell Priest said.

"And the longer you take to do it, the closer the inquisitors get."

The Hell Priest stared into the Abbot's eyes. Finally, he dropped the Abbot to the ground.

"Another day, then," the Hell Priest said, and made his exit.

The Hell Priest arrived at the edge of the forest and found Felixson waiting for him, loyal dog that he was.

"Is done?" Felixson said.

"Yes," the Hell Priest said, looking back as a fresh din kicked from the fortress.

There was some confusion around the gates, an argument about whether they should be left open for the dignitaries or closed against the hoi polloi. It was a consequence of what he'd done that he'd not foreseen.

The Order had always jealously preserved its privileged state, executing outside the gates anyone who had violated the law or entered without the mandatory triple-signed permission papers. But it would be impossible to seal the fortress and its secrets off from prying eyes now;

there were too many corpses that would need to be tended to, too much blood to clean up. And with the Abbot in the state of mental instability in which he'd been left, there wasn't a single authority in the fortress.

In time, a few absentee Cenobites would return, having by chance escaped slaughter, and the predictable infighting would begin. But for now, there were only a few confused guards at the gates, the dead inside, the damned who'd served them, and no doubt a swelling congregation of flies.

7

"Harry?"

Harry opened his eyes and sat up. Norma was at the edge of the stage.

"Are you awake?"

"I am now. What's wrong?"

"Somebody's trying to get in, Harry. The spirits are doing their best, but they say they can't keep them out much longer."

"How many are there?"

"Two. What do you want to do?"

"I want to take a piss."

He came back from his bathroom break with a bottle of brandy in hand. He took a hit off the bottle, handed it to Norma, and made his way up the stairs to the front door.

The alcohol had quite a kick and, with nothing to soak it up, he all but lost his footing on the darkened stairs as he ascended. But he got to the top without breaking any bones, slid the bolts aside, and opened the right-hand door. There was no way to do it quietly. The door grated over the accrual of debris as he opened it. It was still dark outside, which meant Harry couldn't have been sleeping for very long.

Norma's ghosts, he sensed, had come with him, and he addressed his invisible companions as he climbed up the garbage-strewn steps to street level. "I'm not getting any twitches. That's a good sign. But if something goes wrong get back to Norma and get her out the back way, okay? The fire exit had chains on it, but I broke them, figuring you'd have your pals watching the alley. So you just get going with her; don't wait for me. I can look after myself and I'll find you wherever you end up. I hope to God one of you is listening, because if I ever lost her . . ."

He trailed off there, unable to give voice to his fear. He was at the top of the steps now, and rather than loiter outside the hideaway he wandered to the intersection, checking in all directions. There was no one around, and the traffic was light.

He idled around the block, pausing to light up the stub of a cigar, which he felt—contrary to the connoisseurs who wouldn't touch anything that had been near a flame—was nicely pungent after a couple of hours of being smoked, then tenderly put out, smoked again, then extinguished once more. Now it was ripe as an old sock, and nurturing it to life gave Harry the perfect excuse for lingering here and assessing the state of the street.

He got to the end of the far side of the block and pulled on his cigar only to find that it had conveniently died on him again. He took out a tattered book of matches he had in his jacket pocket and tore one match off, to give himself a nice hot flame to rekindle his stinker. As he bent his head to the task, his peripheral vision caught sight of a man and a woman approaching him from the north end of the block. The woman was small but fierce looking; the bald man at her side was easily a foot and a half taller than she.

It was Caz and he had brought company. Harry drew on his cigar to get a good, fragrant cloud going. He glanced in their direction but did nothing that could be construed as a signal. Then, turning his back on them, he retraced his path around the building, waiting until Caz and company had turned the corner, at which point Harry headed back down the garbage-littered steps and waited.

Only when they reached the top of the flight and began their descent did Harry go inside and wait for them to follow. Harry had met Caz's friend once before. He remembered her name was Lana. She was barely five feet tall, but every inch of her was solid muscle. Her body had more ink on it than Harry's and Caz's combined, but it wasn't because of her passion for the art form. Every bit of her skin, face included, was a living, breathing scroll—an encyclopedia of arcane writs and sigils that, she said, "barely kept the spirits at bay." The woman was a magnet for the supernatural. Harry was happy to see her.

"I brought her along in case we had some problems," Caz said when he entered the building.

"Hi, Harry," Lana said. "Good to see you again."

She extended her hand, which Harry took. Her grip almost crushed his fingers.

"Lana," Harry said, the epitome of restraint.

"She's got an apartment she'll let us have for as long as we need it."

"Anything for Norma," Lana said.

"So let's get her moved, shall we?" Caz said. "I've got my van parked just down the street. Shall I bring it around?"

"Yeah. We'll be up here by the time—" He stopped. Then quietly said: "Damn."

"Visitors?" Lana said, eyes darting about as she took in the surroundings.

"Something. I just felt a twitch in the ink. But it's gone. It could have been something passing over. You never know in this damn city. Let's just get the lady out of this shit hole. Five minutes, Caz?"

"Five'll do'er."

"Lana, come with me, will you?"

"You got it, boss man."

Harry detected a note of sarcasm in her voice but chose to ignore it as he guided her back through the dimly lit maze.

"Jesus, Mary, and Joseph," Norma said as they came into her room. "What are *you* doing here?"

"Sorry. He said he was a friend of yours," Lana said.

"You know I'm talking to *you*," Norma said.

"I'm not going to let you get sick, Norma. A lot of people depend on you. Me included. So we've decided that you're staying at my place."

Harry winced, waiting for Norma to come back at Lana with some other objection, but she just sat there, a smile forming on her face.

"What's so funny?" Harry said.

"Nothing," Norma said. "It's just nice to have you all bullying me around for my own good."

"So we're having a pajama party?" said Lana.

"Yes, we are," Norma said.

"No arguments?" said Harry.

"Nope."

She was still smiling.

"Sadomasochistic ghosts are one thing," said Harry. "But this? This is weird."

8

There was a goodly number of signs that something of substantial consequence was about to happen in New York tonight. For those with the sense to read the signs—or hear them or smell them—they were everywhere: in the subtle elegance of the steam that rose from the manholes on several avenues, in the pattern of gasoline spilled from every automobile collision that involved a fatality, in the din of tens of thousands of birds circling over the trees in Central Park where every other night they would be sleeping and silent at this hour, and in the prayers the homeless souls muttered as they lay concealed for safety's sake where the garbage was foulest.

The churches that stayed open through the night hours for those in need of a place to calm their hearts saw more souls come than they would surely see in half a year. There was no pattern to these men and women, black and white, shoeless and well-heeled, unless it was the fact that tonight they all wished they could cut from their mind's configuration the part that knew—had always known, since infancy—that the great wound of the world was deepening, day on day, and they had no choice but feel the hurt as if it was their own, which of course in part it was.

The trip to Brooklyn had been eventless so far. Caz had taken Canal Street and crossed the Manhattan Bridge.

"We're heading for Underhill Avenue," Lana said as Caz brought them over the bridge onto Flatbush. "Left on Dean Street, go straight for four blocks, then right."

"Holy goddamn shit stop the van," Harry said in a single breath.

"What is it?" Caz asked.

"Just stop!"

Caz put on the brakes. Harry looked into the rearview mirror, studying what he saw there as he murmured, "What the hell is *he* doing here?"

"Who?" more than one voice demanded.

From the cover of Hell's timberland the Hell Priest would have happily lingered and watched how the farce of death was developing within his former place of residence, but he had more urgent business. He took three strides, which brought him to the barbed thicket that surrounded the forest, marking its end. Its gnarled branches were so intricately intertwined that it looked as solid as a wall. The Cenobite thrust his hands into the knotted thicket, the barbs tearing open his flesh. He pushed in as deep as his wrists, and then he grasped the tangled branches and pulled them hard. There were several small flashes of white light from the severed branches, and they spread outward in all directions.

Felixson watched in awe. He'd seen plenty of workings more spectacular than this, but to feel the power it was generating—that was worthy of his wonderment. The thicket grove was in the transforming grip of his master's energies, and its brambles were suddenly pliant and swaying like thorny seaweed in the grip of a furious tide.

Seconds before it happened, Felixson could feel the old feeling in his stomach and balls, the feeling that meant the work he was doing—or in this case witnessing—was about to erupt from mere theory into reality. He held his breath, the significance of the maneuvers he was watching now so far beyond the rudimentary state of his own magic skills that he had no idea of the consequence it would have.

The entire grove was shaking. Felixson could hear noises like distant fireworks, boom upon boom upon boom. There was fire striking fire in every direction. Felixson glanced up at his master's face and to his astonishment saw there an expression he'd never seen before: a smile.

"Cover your face," the Hell Priest said.

Felixson did as he was instructed and covered his face with his hands, but his curiosity had the better of him. He peered up between his fingers and watched as the spectacle continued to escalate. The smile had not left his master's face. Indeed it grew clearer, Felixson saw, as the Hell Priest lifted his arms into the pose of the triumphantly crucified. The response from the energies was instantaneous. They wrapped themselves around his arms and fingers.

Something was imminent, Felixson knew, and he couldn't bring himself to look away.

Harry looked back at Lana. "How close are we to your place?"

"Another mile or so. What the fuck is going on?"

"Good," Harry said. Then he opened the door and got out of the car. "Everyone wait here. This can't be a coincidence."

"Shouldn't we be—"

Harry silenced Caz's protests with a flick of the wrist, looked left, then right. The street was empty. The only other vehicles besides Caz's van had been abandoned and stripped of all but their paint. And not a single light was burning in any of the nearby houses. Despite the inhospitable atmosphere, none of Harry's tattoos were tingling. Either this was the real deal or it was one hell of a mirage.

Harry crossed the street and shouted at the diminutive man standing on its corner, "Hey! Dale! Are you lost or something?"

Dale looked up at Harry as though he hadn't even noticed the presence of another soul.

"Harry?" Dale asked. He stepped into the street, giving five percent

of his attention to Harry and devoting the rest to taking in his surroundings.

"Hell of a thing, seeing you here," Harry said.

"I just go where—"

"Your dreams tell you to. Right. I remember. And your dreams told
you—"

"To stand in this exact spot, at this exact moment."

"Did they tell you I'd be here?"

Dale smiled. "No. But it's a nice surprise," he said, his voice full of
honeyed sincerity.

"Sol and Bellmer didn't feel like coming?"

"Sol never comes along. And Miss Bellmer . . . well, she was found
dead last night with her giant clit stuffed in her mouth. And it wasn't
the clit they cut off."

"So much for friends in high places."

"Good riddance, I say."

"Don't see me crying, do you? So, want to take a ride?"

"Oh. The van? No. I'm afraid that's not in the cards."

"The wha—"

Harry stopped short. Every drop of ink on his skin suddenly unleashed a war cry, the sound of a thousand silent air-raid sirens all
going off at once. It was like a kick in his belly. His breath went out of
him, and he dropped to the ground, blind to everything but the din of
his ink. Dimly he heard Caz yelling to him to, "Get up, get up; Norma
says we've got to get out of here!" Then somehow Caz was kneeling
beside him.

"Fuckin' A! Your fucking ink is having a primal scream," he said.

Then, as suddenly as the sound had risen, it fell. Harry opened his
eyes and his senses came back to him. He took everything in: Caz and
Dale were staring down at him; Norma was listening to the wind.

"Everyone," Harry said weakly, "meet Dale."

"As in 'Alan-a,'" Dale said. "Charmed."

As everyone traded hellos, Harry took a deep breath and slowly got
to his feet.

"He's a friend I met in New Orleans. He's good people, aren't you, Dale?"

"Easy there," said Caz.

"I'm fine," said Harry.

"Didn't look fine," said Lana.

"I'm. Fine," Harry said. "It just got very loud. Very fast."

"It must be getting close," said Dale.

"I guess. Whatever it was, it was big," Harry said. "We should go now. Before it gets here."

"Before what gets here?" Lana said.

Dale turned and answered her question.

"Hell."

"Damn. There's going to be a breach point here," Norma said. "Something in another pale wants access to this place and . . . I'll be damned." Norma stopped short. "I just realized there aren't any ghosts here." She half-turned and directed her face to the sky. Then, after a few seconds: "Not a one."

"What's that noise?" Caz said.

It had suddenly begun all around them, not one sound but many. Harry turned to the spot, listening for the source.

"It's the houses," Harry said.

Windows were rattling against their frames, locked doors vibrating as though they were about to tear themselves open. Loose tiles on the roofs were shaken free and slid down, smashing on the ground below, while from inside the houses came the noise of innumerable domestic objects dancing to the same summons. There was an escalating din of objects falling and smashing—crockery, bottles, lamps, mirrors—as though each house was being vandalized at the same time.

"Looks like we're in for a fight," Caz said.

"God damn it," Lana said. "Wrong place. Wrong time. Story of my fuckin' life."

Caz reached beneath the driver's seat of his van and pulled out a piece of rolled carpeting. He laid it on the sidewalk and, crouching down, unrolled it, calling out to his friends as he did so.

"Anyone want in on this?"

Harry glanced at the selection of knives and other lethal tools that were laid out on the two-foot-long piece of threadbare carpet. The longest was a much-scratched machete (which Harry had had need of once before), and there was a selection of six other blades, the longest a substantial hunting knife, the smallest a knife Caz had been given on Valentine's Day by a butcher he'd once dated.

"No thanks. Too many bad memories. But give Norma a knife."

Caz nodded and made a selection for Norma. Dale picked up the machete.

Still, the loosed energies on the streets took their fill on the houses, blowing some of the windows in and some out, as though there was something almost tidal about the rising powers. All at once, the streetlights went out and, despite Harry's earlier protestation, Caz put a knife into Harry's hand. Harry nodded in agreement.

"Your tattoos?" asked Caz.

"Berserk," said Harry.

"Any ideas?"

"None I like."

9

The entire wood was in a bewildering complex motion, the air around the Hell Priest a cosmos of mote-freighted paths, so elaborately intertwined that in places they formed knots through which the traffic of light fragments continued to flow. Shock waves spread from the spot in all directions, their force pressing the bright dust away from the epicenter, creating in the process an expanding sphere of steadily more concentrated matter.

"Get inside," the Hell Priest said to Felixson, who had retreated into the softened thicket as a safe place from which to watch the events unfold.

He trusted his master and immediately did as he was instructed, moving out of the thicket. Still crouched over, he stepped through the wall of flaming brush. It was quick, but it wasn't pleasant. The hair on his head and body was instantly seared off. The clothes he had made himself in a pitiful attempt at propriety burned to gray ash in a second, adding fire to cleanse his groin. He now looked like a child down there, he thought, his manhood reduced to a nub, his balls tight against his body. But he was safe inside the still-expanding sphere, and close to his master.

Then the Hell Priest quickly scrawled something upon the air, leaving a few black characters in front of him. "I'm unlocking the restraints I put on your memory."

"Re . . . traints?"

"Of course. Without them, you would have gone mad long ago. But I have need of your assistance. There. A small part of what you knew has been restored. Use it sparingly, and in my service, and I will reward you with more, by increments."

A few narrow doors had suddenly opened in Felixson's head, each one a book, its contents a piece of his power. The knowledge brought with it a tiny piece of his history and he was suddenly mortified at his state: a freakish, prostrate gibberer, his hairless groin and inadequate genitals humiliating. He would cover himself as soon as he had an opportunity. But for now he put the problem of his metaphorical and literal nakedness aside and returned his attentions to his master.

"The gift is most welcome, Master," he said, finding that the power to form a coherent sentence had also been restored. Whether it was on purpose or an unintended side effect of his master's working, Felixson knew not, but he knew enough not to question it.

"Remember that," said the Hell Priest.

"Of course. Your generosity—"

"Not the gift, Felixson. *Master.* Remember my name. Forget it for an instant and I'll wipe you clean. You won't even remember to crouch when you shit."

"Yes, Master."

As he trembled, his mind filled with doors opening and closing in howling winds that had sprung up from compass points he could not even name, and in those winds came words and phrases arbitrarily loosed from the remembered pages.

The place where he had stepped into the blazing thicket was becoming brighter by orders of magnitude. So bright indeed that Felixson had to avert his eyes and, shielding his face with his right hand, he studied what he could see at this oblique angle. The Hell Priest wasn't smiling now; Felixson was fairly certain of that. Indeed there were signs suggesting that even the Hell Priest was taken aback by the scale of this eruption.

"Watch," the Cenobite had said, "every detail." And then the remark from which Felixson had taken the greatest comfort: "The future will want to know."

How much better might the Hell Priest be persuaded to treat him now that he wasn't simply a naked runt of a man but had witnessed a part of his master's journey toward apotheosis? Nor was it just any part; it was the beginning he'd witnessed, the purging of the old, the piercing of his flesh, and the striking of a spark that was going to blossom, if he judged the Priest's nature and ambition correctly, into the conflagrations that would change the shape of history forever.

Felixson's speculations ceased there. The Hell Priest was walking toward the ignited air, and Felixson followed step for step. The brightness divided around them, but not without leaving traces of its energies that, as they advanced, broke against their faces.

The effect upon Felixson was not unlike that of his first snort of very pure cocaine—the heart quickening, the skin suddenly hot, the senses more alert. The sudden rush of confidence was there too, and it made Felixson want to pick up the pace of their advance, eager to see what, or who, lay on the other side of this bright passage.

Felixson saw a sliver of that other place now: specifically, a dark street, by night, with some figures retreating from the spot where he and his master were emerging. Felixson was disappointed. This wasn't the way he'd expected it to be, not at all.

They were almost at the end of their passage now: two more steps and the Hell Priest was standing on asphalt—another two and Felixson had joined him. This was the place where Felixson had done his time wearing the mask of a magic man—Earth—and memories flooded him. It wasn't the sight of the street and the dark houses that pricked Felixson's memory most deeply, however; it was the smell of the city air and of the sidewalks. A feeling of intense loss overwhelmed him for a moment as he thought of his once-charmed life—of love, and magic, and friends, all of it, and all of them, dead.

If he hadn't quickly governed himself, tears would have blinded him and this outward display of weakness on this of all occasions would have been the end of him. His punishment, he knew, would be severe in contrast to the already-limitless acts of unspeakable butchery that could be found in his master's grimoire.

It was difficult after the blaze of the passage and the onslaught of familiar, unwanted recollections to make much more than rudimentary sense of the scene into which he and his master had stepped: lightless street, lightless houses, lightless sky, and some figures, visible only because they were illuminated by the wash of brightness from the fire-framed door through which he and his master had emerged.

A young woman caught his eye first, her loveliness a welcome respite from the innumerable forms of ugliness that existed in the place he had just left behind. But there was nothing welcoming on her face. Her gaze was fixed on the Cenobite, of course, and while she watched him her lips moved, though he could not catch a word of what she was saying.

"D'Amour!" the Hell Priest called, his voice, though never loud, easily heard.

Felixson turned, startled by his master's words. They had come back to Earth for the detective. They had come back, Felixson assumed, to finish what they'd started in New Orleans.

Felixson, naked as the day he was born, searched the musk for the man his master was summoning. There was a short man who wielded a machete and a bemused look. Next to him was a tall, broken-nosed fellow who seemed to be protecting a blind black woman. Like the younger woman, there was no hint of welcome in her expression; she had curses on her lips, no doubt of that.

And then, from the darkness off to their left, much closer to the doorway than any of the others, walked a man with a face that showed the marks of a life lived hard. Felixson had only a moment to scan the man's scars, because the man's eyes demanded his attention and they would not be denied. He seemed to look at both the Hell Priest and Felixson at the same time.

"Nobody touched your goddamned box," D'Amour said. "You shouldn't be here."

"I no longer have need for the box and its games," the Hell Priest said. "I have begun my sublime labor."

"What in fuck's fuck are you talking about?" said Harry, tightening his grip on the knife Caz had given him.

"I have brought an end to my Order, so as to begin an endeavor I have been planning for most of your life. A life, it would seem, that refuses to be snuffed out. You have survived that which no man ought. I have given great thought to the choice of eyes that should witness the birth of the new world. I have need for a mind that will preserve the events that are to unfold from this moment on. I have chosen you, Harry D'Amour."

"What? Me? What about fuckstick over there?" He threw a ragged gesture out toward Felixson. "Why not him?"

"Because Hell has made you its business. Or you have made Hell yours. Perhaps both. I would be excused nothing by a witness such as you. Indeed I encourage you to seek out the tiniest sign of frailty in me and, should you find any, magnify it in your final testament."

"My final testament?"

"You won't simply witness what is going to unfold in Hell from this point outward; you will make a testament of it, wherein my acts and my philosophies will be recounted in full detail. They will be my Gospels, and I will forbid you nothing in their chapters and verses, as long as it is observed truth, however far from my ideal of myself I may fall.

"Your job is to witness. To see and remember; changed perhaps by the sights you will have seen, but amply rewarded."

Norma reached out to D'Amour, starting toward him, but Caz caught hold of her arm and gently restrained her. He couldn't restrain her tongue, however.

"I know how these deals end up," Norma said. "There's always a catch. Always a trick."

"I have made my intention clear," the Hell Priest said. "What is your decision, Detective?"

"Somehow the words 'fuck you' don't seem strong enough," Harry said.

As if in response to the Priest's anger, the flames around the fiery door suddenly lost the parity of their brightness, tainted by the darker colors, as though something was being burned alive, its boiling blood darkening the blaze. Pieces of its fire-withered stuff tumbled from the walls of conflagration, sending up columns of black-gray smoke that eclipsed the flames.

"What part of 'fuck you' don't you understand?" Lana said.

The demon uttered an indecipherable order as he made a counter-clockwise flick of the wrist. The action sent Lana flying across the street at speed. She crashed against a chain-link fence, knocked unconscious before her head even hit the ground. Though the demon's incantation went unheard, his message was clear; the demon possessed a power he wasn't supposed to have.

"What is your answer now, Detective?" the demon said.

By way of reply, Harry pulled out his gun and walked toward the Cenobite, firing as he did so. He didn't bother wasting bullets on the torso—even minor demons could take a lot of lead and not be slowed by it. Instead he aimed for the head. If he could, he'd take out the bastard fuck's eyes, Harry thought. He leveled the Colt, aiming as carefully as speed would allow, and fired. The bullet entered the Cenobite's cheek an inch below the left eye, and the force of it jerked back his head. He didn't lift it again, and this offered Harry a clear shot at the creature's throat, which he took. It opened a hole in the middle of his throat, and air whistled out.

From behind him Harry heard Norma yelling, "Let go of me! *Harry?* Help me!"

Harry glanced back to see that Pinhead's accomplice had slipped past Caz and had grabbed hold of Norma's hair. He held a crescent-bladed knife, like a small scythe, pressed to the lower portion of her abdomen. By the crazed look in his eyes and the vicious way he pushed the point of the weapon into her it was clear that he would be happy to eviscerate her if Harry or his compatriots made one false move. Caz held his lanky arms in the air and was pleading with the thing.

"Take me," Caz said. "Let her go."

"I like them vulnerable," Felixson said, backing away toward the hell gate.

Out of the corner of his eye, Harry saw that Dale was making a slow move toward the magician, apparently unnoticed. Harry felt a momentary sense of relief. And then the Priest uttered an incantation. Harry felt a stinging in his sinuses and turned to see that the Cenobite was leaking a dark, ominous ooze that was so potent it was dissolving the asphalt upon which it fell.

The black ooze was a dark blood that ran from the wounds Harry had inflicted in the demon. The blood followed the lines of the scars on the Cenobite's face—down, across, down, across—until the drops cascaded down his neck and forked off toward each arm.

The blood dance held Harry's gaze for a long moment, long enough for the power accruing in his adversary's hands to reach critical mass. The Priest flicked his hands toward Harry and a few stinging flecks of the black venom broke loose and burned Harry's gun hand.

An idea formed in Harry's mind, and before he had time to rethink it he advanced toward Pinhead, taking off his jacket. As he did so, Pinhead unleashed another burst of his murderous mud that Harry quickly dodged. Harry was determined not to give the bastard a third chance.

"What are you doing, D'Amour?" Pinhead demanded.

As if in answer, D'Amour wrapped his jacket around his hands, and then, with no time to formulate a clear plan, he used it to catch hold of the demon's arms. It was a move that had proved effective before, so, Harry thought, it couldn't hurt to attempt it a second time.

Pinhead let out a cry that had a measure of fury in it but was mostly repugnance and outrage. The wild thought flashed through Harry's mind like sweet lightning. And his notion proved true. The demon had for so long lived uncontaminated by the proximity and, certainly, the touch of humanity that a rush of revulsion passed through him and momentarily gave Harry the advantage. He used it. Before the demon could entirely regovern his will, Harry pressed the demon's arm toward the ground between them. The churning filth continued to erupt from the creature's fingers, the asphalt it struck cracking and scattering fragments in all directions.

Harry wrenched the creature around, but with such violence and suddenness that the flow of filth emanating from his arms was spat off into the dark street. It hit Caz's van, the metal shrieking as it was torn open, the muck apparently throwing itself around inside the vehicle, causing more damage than seemed possible.

Five seconds later the gas tank exploded in a fat blossom of yellow and orange fire. There apparently was something combustible in Pinhead's killing muck, because the flame instantly followed the trail of filth back toward the demon.

It came with incredible speed, faster even than the demon could summon the words to extinguish it, and crawled up the poisonous arms that Harry had been gripping. Harry had barely let go of the remnants of his jacket, which was all but eaten away, when the fire consumed it and a burst of searing energy struck him so hard he was hurled to the ground.

The demon was blown back, and the conjuration of poison and flammable filth seeping from his arms disappeared as though it had never existed. The demon rose to his feet and tried once more to concentrate his efforts on reclaiming the mystical killing force of his black blood.

The trouble was that this magic wasn't any part of his training as a Cenobite; it was something he learned from an obscure magical treatise—the *Tresstree Sangre Vinniculum*. He had been certain he'd mastered it, but there was instability in the summoned matter that the treatise had made no mention of: once a taunting element had been introduced—D'Amour's filthy presence at the Cenobite's left, the fire on the right—the equations were catastrophically thrown off.

Had he exited Hell using the conventional methods, he simply could have utilized his hooked weapons of choice, but that option was no longer available to him. And in calmer circumstances he would have quickly scanned the contaminating outside forces and dispatched them, but with the confusion of the moment and his defenses compromised he had no option but to retreat.

He took three quick backward steps toward the threshold, looking for Felixson as he did so. The Priest noted that, to Felixson's credit, he had taken hold of the blind woman, whom he'd judged to be the second-likeliest source of trouble on this field of battle.

Felixson's maneuver had had the effect of driving the whole of Harry's entourage back. The two males, one a wan, brutish thing, the other a diminutive fey specimen, were on their knees, in thrall to an incantation of dubious efficacy.

Both men were forcibly resisting; the taller of the two's body was twitching with the effort it took to pull himself up, but it was clear that he was seconds from breaking free of Felixson's magic manacles. Clearly, there was nothing to do but go and leave D'Amour and his allies to the elements. However, given the strength he sensed in the attachment between D'Amour and the blind woman, the demon realized that something could still be recovered from this failed coup.

"Felixson! Bring the blind meat with you."

"Don't you fucking dare!" D'Amour shouted.

As ever, the magician was quick to obey his master's words and, ignoring D'Amour and his empty threat, pulled Norma toward the burning door, dick and balls flapping as he wrenched her closer to its fiery archway. She fought furiously, scratching and kicking at Felixson over and over, but none of her blows were powerful enough to make him release his grip.

The scene was too much for Harry: the all-too-crisp night air, the scent of infernal fire, the imminent loss of another partner at the hands of a malformed beast. The combination was too specific in its repetition to be believed and it rendered Harry utterly immobile.

When the magician turned, the last of his powers over Caz and Dale went out. Caz, freed from Felixson's hold, got to his feet and immediately went in pursuit of Norma. But Felixson had gained the door by now and in a few strides he and his captive were through it and gone from sight, leaving only the demon on the threshold.

Lana had finally regained consciousness and picked herself up from off the ground, though her short waking exposure to Pinhead's toxic secretion had left her feeling nauseated and unsteady. The demon disregarded them entirely. He continued to step back through the gate and into the bright passageway beyond. In that little time, the flames from which the door was formed had already started to diminish.

"Do something!" a man's voice said somewhere very far from Harry. "Jesus Christ! Harold! Fucking wake up!"

Harry snapped to attention. It was Caz who had been screaming at him. He looked about and found that his friends were bruised and battered but heading directly toward him, toward the porthole through which one of the most notorious demons in Hell's army had just fled with his best friend. Harry realized he had no time for measured decisions; he had to move, but quick.

"Right behind you, asshole," he heard himself say.

Hell had come for Harry D'Amour on this street and, failing to catch him, had taken Norma Paine instead. Now Harry would go after her, even if he had to go alone. Without even thinking, Harry leaped through the gate.

Harry heard Caz yell something behind him, but with the flames dying out and the passage through becoming harder and harder to see Harry didn't dare risk looking back. Another two, three strides and he drew a breath that was denser—no, dirtier—than the breath that had preceded it. And two strides later he ran into what felt like fresh cloths hauled from a pail of hot water and shit being pressed against his face and thrust down his throat as though to smother him.

His momentum faltered, his heart hammering as he tried to keep panic from overcoming him. It was the greatest of his terrors—smothering—and he was sorely tempted to retreat a step, or two, or three, back into the crisp, merciful air of the world at his back. But his friends were at his back now.

"Fuck. *Me*," Lana said in short, suffocated bursts.

Harry looked at them with disbelief in his shit-teared eyes.

"This is my fight. You have to go back," Harry said.

"My dream told me to be here," Dale said. "And here I will stay."

"We're not leaving you, or Norma, behind," Caz said.

"No way," said Lana.

"You guys sure about this?" said Harry.

"Not at all," said Caz.

Harry nodded. They pressed on. No more was said as they made their way through the miasma, never once looking back.

10

From the first, Hell surprised them—even Harry, who had caught a fleeting glimpse of its geography in Louisiana. They stepped out to the other side of the place of passage into a far from unpleasant sight: a grove in a forest of antediluvian trees, their branches so weighed down with age that a small child could have picked the large, dark-purple-skinned fruit simply by reaching up. However, none such child had been on duty to harvest the fruits and as a result they littered the ground, the sickly stink of their corruption only one part of the stew of smells that had added its own particular horror to the oppressive stench that had stopped Harry in his tracks as he'd passed from Earth into Hell.

"Goddamn," Lana said, "I thought the roaches in my apartment were big." She was looking down at the brown-black insects that appeared to have a close familial relation to the common cockroach, the main difference being they were perhaps six times larger. They covered the ground at the base of the trees, devouring the food that had fallen there. The sound of their brittle bodies rubbing against one another, and of their busy mouthparts devouring the fruit, filled the grove.

"Anybody see Pinhead?" Harry said.

"Is that his name?" Lana said. "Pinhead?"

"It's a name I know he hates."

"I can see why," Dale said, chuckling to himself. "It's not a very kind nickname. Or even accurate for that matter."

"Is he some kind of big noise in Hell?" Caz asked.

"I don't know," Harry said. "I'm sure he thinks so. I just want to get Norma back and fuck off out of here."

"That's a good plan in theory. But the execution might prove a bit more difficult," said Caz, gesturing toward the door through which they'd come, or rather toward the place where it had once stood. The door was no longer there.

"I'm sure we'll find a way out," Harry said. "It's easy enough to get in. We should all—"

"Back off, you little freak!" Lana shrieked, interrupting Harry's suggestion.

It didn't take long to figure out why. Dale was wiping blood from the knife Caz had given him. Without warning, he had stuck a knife into the meat of Lana's palm. It was a nasty wound. When Caz caught hold of Lana, whose face was already gray and clammy, he persuaded her to raise her hand and keep it raised so the blood could drain. The blood coursed down her arm, soaking her blouse in the process.

"What the fuck!" Lana blurted. "I'll kill you!"

Caz maintained his hold on her. Dale cracked a mischievous smile. Harry moved between them as a buffer and faced Dale, closing his hand around the hilt of his knife once more.

"Mind explaining what the fuck that was, Dale?" Harry asked.

"He's fucked! What else do you need to know?" Lana said.

"Dreadfully sorry. Really I am. It simply needed to be done. The dreams told me. I recognized the moment and got swept up in it."

"I think your friend might be disturbed, Harold," said Caz.

"I'm gonna be sick," Lana said.

"No, you're not," Caz told her. "Don't look at your hand. Look at me." He shrugged off his battered leather vest and pulled off his black T-shirt, tearing it up into bandage-width strips. "I'll have all of this out of sight in just a few seconds," he promised Lana. "You're going to be fine."

"This fucking sucks. That's the hand I use for . . . uh . . . you know."

Caz smiled, doing his best to get the wound bound tightly enough to stop the flow of blood. Harry, meanwhile, watched Dale closely, who was trying his best to apologize. But his supplication fell on deaf ears.

None of Harry's alarms were sounding when he pointed them toward the diminutive man, but then again he was smack-dab in the middle of that no-longer-fabled land where villains were supposedly dealt their karmic justice and, as a result, his tattoos were behaving erratically. Harry went with good old-fashioned intuition and separated Dale from the group.

"You're on probation," Harry said. "Out in front. Any other tricks and I let Lana have her way with you."

"Can't I now?" Lana said.

"Just wait," Dale said. "You'll see. The dreams are never wrong. I found you, didn't I, Harry?"

There was silence for several seconds, at least among the two-legged occupants of the grove. The roaches continued their seething sibilant song among the decaying fruits.

Finally, Harry spoke, ignoring Dale's question.

"Let's prioritize here. At the risk of stating the obvious, this isn't going to be easy. We need to find Norma as fast as we can, avoid the powerful demon that wants me as his slave, and then get the fuck out of Hell. I'm sure we'll encounter some heinous, unthinkable, soul-scarring shit along the way, but hopefully we all make it out alive."

His friends fell silent. Lana gripped the tender flesh of her wounded hand close to her chest and snorted, "Good pep talk, Coach. I feel much better now."

11

Norma had been sitting what she judged to be many hours now in a darkness within a darkness. For the first time in her life she saw nothing at all. Her blindness oppressed her. She longed to be cured of it—to be able to see something of the demon and his human underling, the one with the breath of a man who had an ulcerous stomach. Though the world as sighted people saw it was a closed book to her, she saw what they could not: the presence of phantoms—everywhere—their faces, ripe with need and unspent passion, trailing their hunger like pollen from flowers that were past their hour but refused to wither and disappear.

These sights had been, until now, more than adequate compensation for whatever spectacles she'd been denied. She had envied the sighted masses who walked the streets below her apartment nothing as long as she had her ghosts. But there were no ghosts here. She heard the dusty whispering that she knew was a sign of their presence, but no matter how loudly she called out to them, no matter how hard she willed them to appear, they would not come.

"You are alone," the Cenobite said.

She flinched. She had not heard him come in. It made her uneasy. Usually she knew in her bones when something—anything—was nearby. But the demon was quiet. Too quiet. And he stank. God almighty, he stank! Her sensitivity to the nuances of smell was another gift of her sightlessness, and this creature stank to high heaven. This was a being who trafficked, of course, with demons; their countless varieties of bitterness were all over him. So too was blood, as of the overpowering scent off a butcher's apron. Whiffs of it came off whatever instruments of hurt hung from his waist.

But the strongest scent was also the oldest—it was the perfume of his transgressions. There were other smells too, some of which she could name—incense, books, sweat—and far, far more that she had no name for.

He had spoken to her scarcely at all except to remind, as if she did not already know, that he was an expert in the provision of suffering and that if she did anything to irritate him she would instantly have firsthand knowledge of his expertise. Only when her nerve endings and her sanity had given up ("and only then," he had said) would she be granted an undignified death.

So she had not moved.

She'd stayed in the darkness within the darkness and done her best to reach out past the horrors to some comforting memory: the face of a happy revenant, one whom she'd directed to the place where his loved ones would be, or the fine, happy times she'd had with Harry and a bottle of brandy, reminiscing about some shared craziness. But for some reason the memories gave her no pleasure now. There was a stone in her stomach and it weighed her down, stopping her from flying off into the past.

She was therefore glad, in point of fact, that the demon had finally condescended to come back into her presence, even with his bitter scents invading her senses. In that, she was at least saved from boredom.

"The detective and his band of misfits will surely have come for you," he said. "I will keep you alive. Despite your friend's protestations, he has already begun his work as my witness."

Then, without warning, he hit her in the stomach. The blow bent her double. There she stayed, gasping for air. Before she could catch her breath, he went at her face with a left, then a right, then another left, each blow a loud, stupefying sound in her head. There was a moment's hiatus, and then he came back at her, physically unbending her by seizing hold of her shoulders and lifting her up as he threw her against the wall. Again the breath went from her, and her legs, which were going increasingly numb, threatened to fold up beneath her.

"No," he said as she began to slide. "You stay standing."

He put his right hand around her throat to hold her head up and with his left proceeded to strike her again and again, delivering hammering blows to her liver, her heart, her kidneys, to her breasts, to her gut, to her sex, and then up to her heart again, twice, three times, and down through the same already tender, aching places.

It was pleasure he was feeling, she was certain. Even now, as she barely held on to consciousness, some part of her that could never relinquish the study of body language heard the little exhalations of contentment emerge from the demon when he stood back for a moment and reveled in the tears and anguish on her bloodied and swollen face.

She felt his stare like a subtle pressure upon her, and knowing that he was finding joy in her suffering, she pulled together every thread of strength in her soul and she brought those tears up behind her face to deny him the satisfaction. She knew it would piss him off, and that knowledge only strengthened her.

She closed her mouth and coaxed the threads of strength into turning up the corners of her lips into a Gioconda smile. Her eyes she also closed, slowly lowering her lids to conceal from him her frailty. There would be no more tears now, nor shouts of pain. The threads had sewn the expression in place. It was a mask; whatever she truly felt was hidden behind it, unreachable.

He released the clamp of his hand from her neck, and she slid down the wall, her legs folding up beneath her. He pressed his booted foot against her shoulder, and she toppled over. After that, he delivered one vicious kick to her body, cracking several ribs, and another to her throat, which really tested the strength of her mask. It held, however. Knowing what was coming next, she tried to bring her hand up to her face to protect it, but she wasn't fast enough. His boot got there first, one straight kick to the face, blood bursting from her nose. Another kick at her face and now, finally, she felt the darkness within a darkness wrapping her in its blanket of nullity, and she was grateful for its imminence. The demon raised his foot and brought the boot down hard on the side of her head. It was the last thing she felt.

Oh Christ, she thought, *I can't be dead! I've so much left unfinished!*

Funny, she didn't feel dead, but then wasn't that the most common thing she heard from her visitors? And if she wasn't dead, why could she see for the first time? And why was she hovering nine or ten feet above the place where her body lay against the wall?

The demon—what did Harry call him? Dick face? Pinprick? Pin*head*! That was it. He was backing away from her, his breathing ragged. It had taken no little effort for the Cenobite to brutalize her the way he had. And having stepped away, he changed his mind and approached her again, kicking her hands away from her face.

He'd made a real mess of her, no doubt about that, but she was very pleased to see that her enigmatic smile was still in place, defying him. There was a sliver of satisfaction in that, no question, however hard the rest of the news was to take.

Aside from the obvious, she found it impossible to think of the demon as a Pinhead. That was a school-yard insult or the name of a pitiful sideshow freak. It did not belong to the monster standing over her body now, his body shaking with excitement from the beating he had just delivered.

The demon retreated a few more steps, still looking at what his brutality had achieved, and then reluctantly withdrew his gaze and turned his attention to the little weasel of a man who had just entered the room and was lingering by the door. She knew without need to hear his voice that this was the creature who'd first caught hold of her on the street back in New York, whispering all manner of obscene threats into her ear to keep her from resisting his hold on her. He was more pitiful to look at than she'd imagined, a wizened gray thing, throwing peasant rags over his naked body. And yet on his face—even now after what he'd done to her by hauling her here—she saw the remains of what had surely once been a man possessed of luminous intelligence. He had laughed much once, and pondered deeply too, to judge from the lines left by old laughter on his cheeks and frown marks on his brow.

As she studied him, she felt herself plucked away from the room where her beaten body lay. Some invisible tether was pulling her through this building, which was a maze of once-beautiful rooms, grand halls where plaster rotted and fell away from the walls and the mirrors decayed, their gold leaf frames flaking and crusting over.

Here and there, as she made her unintentional departure, she caught sight of the remains of places where others—prisoners of circumstance like herself—had been tortured. The remains of one such victim lay with his legs in the furnace, where a fierce fire had once burned, consuming his extremities somewhere above the knee. The victim had died long ago, his flesh long since petrified, leaving behind something that resembled a bronzed diorama that paid tribute to a murder scene.

She saw the victim's ghost too, hanging in the air, forever tethered to his agonized remains. The sight of him gave her comfort. She didn't understand this seemingly abandoned place, but she would be able to learn from its ghosts. They knew a lot, the dead. How many times had she said to Harry they were the world's greatest untapped resource? It was true. All they'd seen, all they'd suffered, all they'd triumphed over—lost to a world in need of wisdom. And why? Because at a certain point in the evolution of the species a profound superstition was sewn into the human heart that the dead were to be considered sources of terror rather than enlightenment.

Angelic work, she guessed; some spiritual army, instructed by one commander or another to keep the human population in a state of passive stupefaction while the war raged on behind the curtain of reality. The order had been carried out, and instead of being allowed to comfort humanity's collective soul, the dead became the source of countless tales of terror, while the phantoms that were their spirits made manifest found themselves shunned and abominated until, over the generations, mankind simply taught itself a willful blindness.

Norma knew what a loss there was in this. Her own life had been immeasurably enriched by the dead. Much of the human rage and appetite for war and its atrocities might have been soothed away by the certain knowledge that the threescore years and ten of our biblical span were not the full sum of things but rather a thumbnail sketch for a glorious, limitless work. But this knowledge would not come to light in her lifetime.

Norma had only ever shared her thoughts on this with one living person: Harry. But she had listened countless times to ghosts unburdening themselves of their anguish at being unseen, unable to comfort their loved ones by simply saying, "I'm here. I'm right beside you." Death, she had come to realize, was a two-sided mirror of griefs: that of the blind living, who believed they'd lost their loved ones forever; the other of the sighted dead, who suffered beside their loved ones but could not offer a syllable of comfort.

Her reverie was broken as she passed through the roof of the building and the light of Hell washed over her. She had assumed that at some point her sight would desert her, but it did not.

As the building fell away beneath her, she was granted a bird's-eye view of the wilderness through which the Cenobite and Felixson had brought her. She hadn't really expected infernal regions to resemble anything that the great poets and painters and storytellers evoked throughout the millennia, but she was still astonished that they had fallen so far short of what her spirit's eyes now saw.

The sky contained neither sun, nor stars, which was predictable enough, but what it did contain was a stone the size of a small planet. The stone reached high above the immense landscape that spread out below, and it threw off fissures like lightning bolts, through which brightness poured. The effect upon the vast panorama was uncanny.

This was scarcely a promising environment, but still it found a way to grow, even prosper. On the slopes of the hills beneath her, long white grass swayed in some infernal wind and here and there bushes grew, the branches barbed and knuckled but bearing small colorless flowers. Her mind began to run wild once again. Where was this journey taking her? Did it even have a destination, or was she simply loosed from her body and fated to wander Hell for eternity?

Regardless of her will or intent, the invisible tether continued to pull her toward its unknown purpose, and as it did her spirit began to sink toward the ground. In a few seconds she was moving inches above the level of the white grass. Some distance ahead of her was a small forest. The canopy of upper branches was intricately knotted, except for perhaps thirty or forty wild ones that had freed themselves and grew like sticks of black lightning. Large black birds were perched on several of the knotted branches, fighting with beaks and claws for the choicest spots. She was so distracted by the sight of their feuding that she didn't notice the people emerging from the darkness beneath the trees until she was almost upon them.

Then she smelled blood, and everything went white.

12

Dale, forced to the front by Harry, had been leading the way, but now, as they had barely stepped foot out of the forest, he turned and stared at his followers.

"It's close!" Dale said.

"Keep walking, dickhead," Lana said.

"Harry, your friend's being weird again!" said Caz.

"We talked about this, Dale," said Harry.

"No, no, no," said Dale in full southern charm mode. "It's about to happen. You will all be very happy, I promise. And then when it's over, dearest Lana, I do hope you'll think better of me."

"You're fucking creepy, man," Lana said. "All I know is I'd feel a whole lot better if . . . I'm—" She stopped, abruptly changing her tone from irritation to bewilderment. ". . . *What?*" she said, her voice hushed as she lifted her injured hand to her face and examined the injury as though seeing it for the first time. Fresh blood was running from underneath the bandages. *"I'll be damned . . ."* she said in the same soft voice. *"Harry?"*

"I'm right here, Lana," Harry said.

"... *I think I'm dead ...*" she said softly, followed immediately by a commanding, "Get out! Who the fuck ... *I will not get out.*"

"Don't fight it, Lana," Dale said. "It's your blood. It's how she found us!"

"Fight what?" Harry said, approaching Dale, his tone serious. "What did you do?"

"Whoa," Caz said, tightening his grip on one of his knives. "Is this like a demonic possession thing? I'll kill the little dude right now if I have to. Shit's bad enough as it is."

"*Everyone shut up. It's me, Norma,*" said Norma, from somewhere within Lana.

"Who said you could hijack me?" Lana protested.

"Norma?" Harry said, turning to Lana, his eyes narrowing in disbelief.

"*Yes, it's me. I don't know—*" The words ceased as Lana shook her head again, determined to dislodge her unwelcome guest. "What the fuck is happening here?"

"Lana. Let Norma speak," Harry said.

"Fuck off!" Lana snapped. "I've been possessed before. It's not a feeling I like."

"She won't stay long, honey," Dale said. "I promise."

"Just let her say what she needs to say," said Harry. "This is why we're here."

"Okay," Lana said, nodding as she drew a deep breath. "Just let me catch my bearings. I've never had a friendly ghost inside me."

"You've never had anything friendly inside you," Caz said.

"I'll remember that next time you're drunk and you can't find a *man.*"

Caz pursed his lips.

"Oh, I am *sure* there's always a willing man for you," Dale said, eyeing Caz, a smile on his mischievous face.

Caz, caught off guard, looked at Dale, flushed.

"Okay," Lana continued. "I'm ready. Let's get it over with so we can get out of this shit hole and go back to the shit hole I'm familiar with."

She closed her eyes and let out a deep, deep breath. Then:

"*My goodness.*"

"Norma!" said Harry. "That really you?"

"*'Fraid so, Harry. Oh Lord, I think I might be dead. That bastard just finished beating the living shit out of me.*"

"Pinhead? Hands-on?"

"*Hands. Feet. Last time I saw him, he was stomping on my head.*"

"I'm going to fucking kill him."

"*It's a lovely thought, Harry. Thank you. But it's not going to be easy. He's not your ordinary sadomasochist from beyond the grave— Oh dear, I think it's time to go already.*"

"Lana! Let her stay!"

"*It's not Lana. . . . It would appear I'm not dead after all. My body's wondering where the hell my mind went.*"

"Do you know where your body is?"

"*Yeah. Some big-ass building straight down this road. Looks like it was really fancy back in the day. But it's falling apart, now. Listen to me, Harry. You all got to get out of here. I don't want anyone dying on my account.*"

"No one's dying. And we're not leaving without you."

"*Oh, for Christ's sake, Harry. Listen to me. He's too strong. Whatever you think you've got up your sleeve, it's not going to be enough.*"

"I'm not going to leave you down here, Norma. Whatever happens, I'm going to—"

Lana's eyes opened, and there was a brief flash of confusion on her face; then it cleared and Lana said, "Is that it?"

Harry sighed. "That's it. Thank you, Lana. You were great."

"No problem," she said, fluttering her eyes. "Just as long as she doesn't plan on being a permanent tenant."

"She doesn't."

"Is she dead? Because that's what freaks me out, having a dead person in here with me."

"She's alive," Harry said. "For now."

"Oh, and Dale?" Lana said.

"Hmm?" Dale said.

"Next time, tell me what the fuck you need to do before you do it. You cut me again without me approving—even for a good reason like that one—I'll rip your cock off."

Norma woke into a place of pain; in her head, her stomach, her back, her legs, she could feel every blow.

"Get her to her feet, Felixson. And hurry. We have business in the city. It's time to put an end to that ridiculous regime. Better sooner, while they're still arguing among themselves. Get her up, and if she won't walk, then carry her."

"But Master, would it not be better to simply kill her?" Felixson said.

The Priest stopped his preparations and fixed his icy gaze on Felixson. Without uttering another word, Felixson bowed his head in apology, repeatedly, and approached the still bloodied and bruised Norma, then leaned in close to her face and uttered a quiet monologue. Norma got a whiff of Felixson's foul breath, which only added insult to her copious injuries.

"I know you're listening to me, you black cunt. I don't know what he wants from you, but I don't intend to carry you all the way to the city, so I'm going to make life a little easier for the both of us. I can't heal you—I don't have that much power—but I can give you an Epoidiatic Opiate. It will put the pain out of sight and mind, for a while."

"Will it . . . take . . . my wits?" Norma murmured through the blood in her mouth.

"What do you care? Take what you're given and be grateful."

He glanced away for a moment, just to confirm that he and his Epoidia weren't being witnessed. They weren't. The Priest had once again begun his preparation—an incantation of some sort—when Felixson began muttering an incantation of his own under his breath. He was good; she had to give him that. She felt the opiate spreading through her body, its warmth removing all traces of pain.

"That should do it," he said.

"Oh my Jesus, yes."

"Just remember to moan and sob every now and then. You're supposed to be in pain, remember?"

"Don't worry; I'll give him a good show."

"Get up!" Felixson then said loudly, grabbing Norma's arm and pulling her to her feet.

Norma let out a ragged series of cries and curses, but the fact was the incantation was so strong it had even taken away problems not caused by the demon: arthritis, stiffness, the general pain created from the business of being—all gone. She felt better than she had in years. So what if the Epoidia was only covering up the problem? She would happily live in this opiated state as long as she could. Next time she had a moment alone with him, she'd try to get him to teach her the trick he'd used, so she could give herself another fix of it when this one wore off.

Then her thoughts turned to Harry and his gang of Harrowers. Norma didn't like the idea of any of them, friends or not, traveling to this wretched place for her sake. But she knew that Harry wouldn't take her advice. And she couldn't blame him; were the roles reversed, she'd ignore his requests just as he, no doubt, was ignoring hers.

"What are you thinking, woman?"

The question came from the Cenobite.

"I'm just nursing my wounds."

"Why nurse wounds you cannot feel?"

"I don't—"

"I detest unconvincing lies. I know what he did," the Priest said, pointing a gnarled finger at Felixson. "Never think, either of you, that I am not with you, even when you are not within eyesight."

"No, Lord . . ." Felixson said, his voice thinned with fear.

"You disappoint me, Felixson. And you," the Cenobite said to Norma, "you can stop that wretched hobbling. We have a long journey ahead. A plague fog now waits for us a quarter of a mile from the city's limits. It will ensure that the damned are off the streets and in their homes, if homes they have."

Norma felt the demon's scrutiny abandon her and, as he turned away, Felixson pushed past her.

"God damn you," he whispered to her. "Get behind me and grab hold of my shoulder. If we get separated I won't wait for you."

"I'll be sure to hold on, then," Norma said.

"God. I fucking hate the country," Lana said. She glanced around in disgust at the landscape, a hill lined with trees and shrubs all black in color. The grass, where it grew at all, was white and the dirt it grew in blacker even than the knotted branches of the trees.

Harry suddenly stopped and stood alert, his ears pricked. The group fell silent, everyone listening for the sound of whatever it was that Harry seemed to hear.

"Are those screams?" Caz said.

"We *are* in Hell," Lana remarked.

Holding a hand up to silence his fellow infernal travelers, Harry climbed up to the top of the nearby slope. When he got to the top, he balked at the sight on the horizon.

"Jesus," he muttered. "That's . . . big."

"Whatcha got there?" Lana said, climbing up to join him. "Whoa . . . is that—"

"Fog?" Dale said, finishing Lana's question for her. "In Hell?"

"It's moving," Caz said, his head barely cresting the slope before the sight stopped him in his tracks. "And fast."

"Where's it going?" Lana asked.

"Nowhere. Look," Harry said.

The city, shrouded in fog as it was, looked vast, its buildings significantly more elegant and grandiose than Harry had expected. With its pale stone domes and its pillared plazas, this was clearly Hell's Rome. The city been built on many hills, nearly two-thirds of which rose gently, displaying tier upon tier of immaculate buildings. Trees had been carefully positioned to set their knotted darkness off from the polished beauty of the buildings around which they grew. These trees were dwarfed, however, by even the humblest of buildings on the slope. The city's architect had been a visionary, no doubt of that. There was nothing in Rome—nothing in any of the greatest cities in the world—that could hope to compare with the glories that had been brought into being here.

Some had the simple authority of size: buildings fifty stories tall, the façades of which were not disfigured by so much as a single window. There were statues too, their heads and shoulders easily clearing even the tallest buildings. Whereas the statues of Rome were finely and faithfully crafted likenesses of Christian icons and men who'd ruled the city, the statues here were puzzles. Some were only vaguely recognizable as humanoid; others seemed to freeze in the blur of motion: a stone photograph of an unknown being caught in the throes of ecstasy, or agony, or both.

And everywhere the laws of physics were casually defied: an immense building was held a hundred feet in the air or more by the two steep rows of steps at the front and the back; a trio of pyramids, their squares intricately inscribed, were built so as to seem caught by a seismic jolt that had thrown two of them into the air and left the third supporting them by only the slenderest of means, corner to corner, edge to edge.

And nestled amid it all was a greenish fog that sat, unmoving, in the expansive shantytown in a trench directly in front of the city. The fog cast its greenish hue onto a band of buildings from the monolithic structures close to the summit down to the high walls that marked the limits of the city proper as it sat, willfully motionless, over a portion of the mass of tents and crude shacks and animals that formed the chaotic fringe around the city limits. It was this place, this vast shantytown, that was the source of the screams. This bizarre fog had seemingly settled upon this place, and it was apparent that those who had failed to find their out of its haze were in terrible agony.

"Who's got the best eyes?" Harry said. "It's not me. I can see people moving down there, but they're a blur."

"They're better staying that way," said Caz.

"What's happening?"

"They're fucking insane or something," said Lana.

"They're running around"—Caz shook his head—"beating their

heads against the walls. And, oh God, there's a guy . . . oh Jesus Christ—"

"Are they human?"

"Some of them," Dale said. "Most look like demons to me."

"Yeah," Lana said. "And human beings can't make noises like that."

It was true. The cacophony, which continued to grow louder, was a sickening din—a befouling stew of noise that was beyond the capabilities of the human lungs and throat. The near-death shrieks were mingled with the noises that sounded like an engine or machine in the final phase of self-destruction, gears shredding, and motors shrieking as they tore themselves apart.

"This is more like it," Harry said. "Hell was starting to disappoint me."

"Don't put that out there, man," Caz said. "We don't need any more bad vibes than we've already got. Or . . . I dunno, maybe you do." He looked at Harry, who was squinting to try to get a clearer view of what was happening. "You can't wait to get down there, can you?"

"I want this over with, Caz."

"You sure that's all?"

"What else could there be?" Harry said, keeping his eyes trained on the spectacle.

"Stop looking at the atrocities for two fucking seconds, Harold. This is me. Caz. You know that I'm following you all the way down into this mess no matter what, right? I'm here to get Norma, together, and I ain't leaving without her. But I need you to look me in the fucking eyes right now and tell me the truth. And don't do it for me. Do it for you."

Harry turned to face his friend and uttered a single defiant, "What?"

"Are you enjoying this?" Caz asked.

Harry's face fell. After a moment, he opened his mouth to speak. That's when Lana shouted, "I can't take it!"

Caz and Harry turned to see Lana drop down onto the ground, her arms crossed over the top of her head as though to forcibly hold in her sanity. Caz went on his haunches beside her.

"It's okay," Caz said. "We'll be okay."

"How can you say that? Look at them! Look what this place is doing to them. And they *live* here! We don't stand a chance."

Harry sat down in the long white grass a yard from them, tuning out Caz's placating condolences, as he turned his attention once more to the chaos within the Pit. Harry knew nothing of the poor creatures whose screams rose heavenward and more than likely fell on deaf ears; perhaps they deserved the agonies that had been set upon them. Perhaps not. Either way, their supplications brought him into an unwelcome head-space and they mingled with the rest of the assaults on his senses—the penetrating stench of sulfur mixed with burning flesh, the tattoos beating a wild refrain on his body in a way that brought him once more to that never-distant-enough night. He could hear the demon's voice in his head, even now, a world away.

Spit. Harry heard the word tearing at the inside of his skull. How he wished he could have done something differently that night. If he had, then maybe he'd be able to shake the feeling that he was now exactly where he belonged—where he'd always belonged—in Hell.

"Whatcha thinking about?" Dale's voice cut through his thoughts like a knife. His words were an anchor wrapped in innocence.

"I'm trying to work out how we fit together," Harry said. "Why we're here."

Dale laughed. "You don't have the first idea, do you?"

"No. Do you?"

"Ah. That's the big question, isn't it?"

"You already know."

"I sure do."

"Care to let me in on the secret?"

"Easy: watching isn't the same as seeing."

Harry laughed. "What the hell does that mean?"

"I heard it in a dream."

Apparently Dale assumed the conversation had reached its end here, because without uttering another word he kissed Harry on top of his head and sauntered away. Caz, meanwhile, had somehow coaxed Lana to her feet and was keeping the city at her back.

"I don't want to go down there," she sobbed. "And none of you can make me."

"We wouldn't want to," Caz replied.

There was a raw chorus of birds overhead.

Harry looked up to see that the noise was coming from the longer of two species of winged creatures that were circling above the city. They had congregated with remarkable speed, attracted either by the promising din of agonies from the streets or by the smell, which only now became apparent. The aroma was complicated. There was the twinge of blood in it but also the fragrance of old incense, and another smell that was impossible to fix and for that reason far more tantalizing than the others.

As he sat on the summit, his thoughts still stirred up by the exchange of enigmas (it could scarcely have been called a conversation) he'd just had with a potentially crazy southerner, Harry took in the mingled glories and grotesqueries of Hell. He wasn't any less exhausted than he'd been when he left his apartment in New York, he wasn't any less in need of a ten-year vacation in Hawaii—just him, a hut, and a fishing pole—but if he was going to get there then he was going to have to finish this first.

"Okay," he said. "Let's do this."

13

Being in the fog had very little impression on Norma. The Hell Priest had done as she had asked him, and whatever protection he was using to seal himself off from the fog's effects he had extended to her. She heard, all too clearly, however, the ghastly noises behind her made by those who had been subjected to the fog's influence. Some were simple grunts made by creatures in pain, others begged more articulately for help, but most pitiful of all were those who—upon seeing the Hell Priest's imposing figure emerge from the muck—requested with as much civility as they could muster that he please put them out of their misery.

Suddenly Felixson began to shout. Norma, who had clutched at his garments, felt the fabrics torn from her hands.

"Oh God in Heaven, no!" he shrieked. "I can smell the fog. It's getting in my eyes. My mouth! Lord! Master! Help me!"

Norma stopped dead in her tracks.

"Hello? What happened? I thought Felixson was protected?"

"He was," the demon said, near to Norma's ear. She jumped at the sound of his voice. "But I've stopped."

"What? Why?"

"His story is at its end. His service to me is complete. I have, in you, all that I need."

"You can't! I beg your mercy, on his behalf."

"You do not want to assume such a debt."

"He eased my pain."

"Because he did not wish to carry you."

"I know. I knew even then, when he was doing it. But still, he did it."

"Very well. All he need do is ask. Do you hear, Felixson? Ask, and ye shall receive."

There was an answering sound from the magician, but it did not resemble any words known to Norma. Norma reeled in the direction of Felixson's gasps.

"Speak!" she said. "Felixson, listen to me! Your Lord called your name! Answer him. That's all you have to do." She took a step in the man's direction, her arms extended. The tip of her right shoe came in contact with him first.

"Can you hear me?" she begged, bending forward and searching for the magician.

A gaseous grunt was all she received by way of reply.

"Felixson! Speak the words."

She heard pitiful sounds indicating his final attempts. Then she heard nothing.

"Felixson?" she whispered into the darkness.

"He can't hear you," the Priest said.

"Oh Lord in Heaven," Norma muttered. Her fingers, not yet believing what her mind was still only realizing, continued their search for Felixson's body. She had taken a knee when her fingers made contact with something hot and sticky. Instantly she pulled her hand back, her mind's eye already painting an unwelcome picture of flesh ravaged by the carnivorous fog.

"I don't understand," she said. "This man was loyal to you."

"What have I to gain by feeling anything?"

"Isn't there anything you care about?"

"All is death, woman. All is pain. Love breeds loss. Isolation breeds resentment. No matter which way we turn, we are beaten. Our only true inheritance is death. And our only legacy, dust."

So saying, he turned and walked on, leaving the dead man behind. Norma said a short prayer for Felixson and quickly followed after the Cenobite for fear that if she faltered he would decide she too was no longer worth protecting. Despite her age and sightlessness, it wasn't difficult for Norma to keep up. Whatever protection working had been thrown over her, it seemed to lend her body strength, and she followed in the demon's wake without undue effort.

14

It was called the Bastion of Tyath now, though it had gone by many names before that, each one chosen by the newest ruling despot. But however the interior of the Bastion changed to suit the metaphysical or potential ambition of its occupants, the exterior remained unaltered. It was an uncompromising tower of stone, the blocks of which had been so precisely measured and chiseled that it was virtually impossible, unless you had your face to the Bastion wall, to discover where one stone ended and another began.

Many legends had accrued around it, chiefly regarding its creation, the most popular and probably the likeliest this: that it had been the first building raised in the vicinity, its commissioner, architect, and sole mason an urdemon called Hoethak, who had built it to protect his human wife, a woman called Jacqueline, who was pregnant with a quintet of hybrids—the first fruit of the mating between the sublime angelic, fallen or not, and the ridiculous humans. All had survived—father, mother, children—and from their five dynasties had descended increasingly contaminated bloodlines and swelling lists of vendettas.

Of the eight members of the present regime, only three were in the

Bastion tonight. Their enthusiastic general, Augustine Pentathiyea, an unrepentant lover of war and its rapturous cruelties, sat in the high-backed chair where their regime's noticeably absent authority, Catha Nia'kapo, was usually seated.

The others in the room—Ezekium Suth and Josephine L'thi—were not able to conceal their agitation.

"If Nia'kapo were here," Suth began, "we would have this situation under control by now."

"It is under control," General Pentathiyea replied. He wore his hair long, as did all of the members of the regime, though Pentathiyea's hair was gray, and his purple-black brow ritually scarred with three downward cuts, each the thickness of a finger. They had been coaxed with repeated cutting to stand proud of his forehead. The marks gave him an expression of perpetual fury, though his voice was measured and calm.

"How do you figure?" Suth asked.

"I'd like to hear your theory as well," L'thi offered. She was standing against the far wall of the chamber, her waist-long white hair unkempt, her eyes closed as her detached gaze searched the fog outside, below the Bastion, looking for the felon. "He murdered all but a few of his Order. We should have him arrested and executed."

"A trial would be better," Suth opined. He was by several centuries the oldest in the room, though he did much to conceal the fact, his hair dyed an unnatural intense black, his brows plucked, his skin white where it wasn't rouged. "Something showy to distract the populace."

"Distract them from what?" said Pentathiyea.

"From the fact that we're losing control," L'thi said. "Isn't it time we were honest? If not now, when?"

"L'thi is right, General," Suth said. "If we made a real example of the Cenobite, a long public trial followed by some form of crucifixion, we'd have back the love of our citizens, and—"

"Our enemy is at the gates," L'thi said, interrupting Suth's soliloquy. "And he has a follower."

"Another Cenobite?" Pentathiyea asked. "I thought you said they were all dead."

"I said most. But it's not a Cenobite. It's a human woman."

"Then Hell's most wanted villain is at our doorstep. Ezekium. Do you have anything prepared for this fiend?" Pentathiyea wanted to know.

"As it happens, I do, General! I have devised a metal blanket, which has a lining that will be filled with ice. We'll burn him at the stake. Eventually, of course, the ice will melt, and the fire will have its way, but I've repeated the experiment eleven times now, using men, women, and even infants, just to be certain my calculations were consistent."

"And?"

Ezekium Suth allowed himself a barely perceptible smile. "He'll be fully conscious while the skin is burned off him as his muscles fry in their own juices. Indeed we'll judiciously arrange the fuel for the fire so that he isn't smothered by the smoke, which is too easy a death. Instead, he'll be cremated systematically. But I discovered that this method draws the victim up into a pugilistic pose, so I'll bind him with chains to prevent the posture. It'll oblige his bones to break while they cook inside his flesh."

"You've been thinking about this quite a lot," Pentathiyea said with a hint of distaste.

"One has to dream, General," Suth replied.

"Until a few minutes ago you didn't even know we had the bastard at the gates."

"No, but it was only a matter of time before somebody challenged us, wasn't it? Have faith. The Cenobite won't carry the day. He is one, and we are—"

"—fewer than we should be," L'thi said. "Hasn't anybody wondered why our glorious leader isn't here today? Absent without explanation on the very day that a killing fog comes out of the wastes, and that . . . that *thing* out there, with his face of nails, comes to pay a visit?"

"What are you accusing him of?" the general inquired.

"Who? Nia'kapo or the Cenobite?"

"Buggar the Cenobite! I'm speaking of our leader, Catha Nia'kapo."

"I'm accusing him of being dead, most likely, General. And Quellat, and probably Hithmonio too. All of them missing without explanation on this, of all days? Of course they're dead! The creature outside made it his business to murder as many in power as he could."

"And then what?" Pentathiyea said.

"Aren't you the general here?" L'thi asked. "All you're doing is sitting atop the leader's throne and asking inane questions. This should be your field of expertise."

"It is," Pentathiyea said, rising from his post. "I have led whole armies against the divine horde and seen them beaten back. I once had a place at Lucifer's table. I was Hell's general when it was still a mud pit. And I know exactly what's going to happen next. That demon is coming to kill us. When he's torn the meat from our bones, he will continue his mad quest, wherever it may lead him. In short, we had better depart—no, not just from this chamber, but from Hell itself—if we value our lives at all."

15

As the members of the council discussed their future, the Cenobite who had been the subject of their conversation caused the three triple-bolted iron gates that sealed the Bastion off from the city streets to be thrown open, their locks shattering like ice.

At the same time, the group of weary travelers led by Harry D'Amour entered the city by the easternmost entrance: Janker's Gate. There were watchtowers to the left and right of the compound, but the towers were deserted and the right-hand gate open.

Janker's Gate offered them the least impressive view of the city they had thus far seen. It lay close to the river—the same one they had crossed on a solid iron bridge—and therefore was occupied chiefly by those whose business was with the river: demons who labored to keep alive the damned souls who'd been buried up to their chins in the adjacent mudflats, powerless to protect themselves from the birds that stalked the grounds looking for worms and leeches and finding easier nourishment among the screaming bulbs, eating away their faces peck by peck, eyes, tongue, noses, and nerves, until the short-beaked birds could get no further and left the remaining rations to the infernal varieties of heron and ibis who were better equipped at piercing the empty sockets to reach the fatty and plentiful brain tissue.

But none of those creatures, damned or damning, were now found on the street that led from the Gate. There was plenty of blood, however, to mark their recent presences, the cobbles shiny and the air filled with the fat Doxy Flies that wove around as though intoxicated. They weren't the only life-form feasting here. On the walls, where there were numerous bursts of blood, creatures that possessed the shape and gait of lobsters had emerged from between the bricks and had gathered around these stains, their busy little mouthparts greedily scooping up the bits of blood.

"Is this what the fog did to people?" Caz said.

"I just wanna know where they went," Dale said.

"Was this not in the dream?"

"No," Dale said, his voice falling below a whisper. "And I don't like that one bit."

Lana was doing her best to keep the blood-drunk flies from landing on her, but they seemed immune to her flailing and happily settled in her hair and on her face.

Harry had wandered ahead of everyone, staring on at the street ahead toward the larger and more architecturally ambitious buildings that were visible beyond the modest two-story dwellings of the neighborhood through which they traveled.

"D'Amour?" Dale whispered.

"What?"

"I think we should stick together," he said.

The observation had barely left his mouth when a figure appeared from the alleyway behind him. It caught hold of Lana, who was perfectly able to deal with her attacker; a blow to the throat, a kick to his lower belly, and, as he bent double, an uppercut to his chin and the attacker was down, sprawled on the cobbles.

"What the fuck is that?" Harry said, approaching the unconscious demon.

"I don't want to alarm you, Harold," Caz said, "but that is a demon."

"But what's wrong with him?" Harry said.

For the first time, Harry got a close look at what the fog had wrought. The creature was a demon, Harry saw, well fed and well muscled, dressed only in baggy trousers held up by the ornately decorated belts that younger demons seemed to favor, his prehensile tail emerging from a small slit in the back. Around his neck were several lengths of leather or cord, each of which bore some keepsake. In all of these regards he resembled most of the demons belonging to minor orders whom Harry had encountered in the past.

But Harry saw that the fog had worked a change in this demon, and it was not pretty. At the corners of his mouths and eyes, in the folds of his arms, or between his fingers—wherever, in short, the fog had touched him—it had apparently planted a seed, germinated not by producing same infernal vegetation, but by taking its cue from the spot in which it had been sown and growing a new life-form that was ordained by the place of origin. Thus, the seed lodged between the demon's fingers had brought forth a crop of new fingers, all of which possessed their own beckoning life. And the seed beside the demon's mouth had created new mouths, all of which gaped, many-toothed, within his cheek and his neck. All these anomalies were humbled, however, by the work a seed lodged in his left eye had done, multiplying the number of eyeballs so that from his brow to his cheek were bunches of wet, lidless eyes, their yellowish corneas dissected up, down, and sideways.

The demon reached out suddenly and caught hold of Caz's ankle, his many jointed fingers easily locking around it. Despite the demon's agony—or perhaps because of it—the grip was viselike. In his efforts to free himself, Caz lost his balance and fell back and landed hard on the bloody cobbles. Before anyone had time to react, the maddened demon crawled atop Caz's body, his motion disturbing the flies that had come to rest on his anatomy and creating a ragged, shifting cloud around them both. The demon was a big-bellied creature, and his weight was easily sufficient to keep Caz pinned to the ground.

"Jesus! Fuck! Someone help me!" Caz yelled.

"Where's that damned machete?" Harry said.

"I've got it," said Lana.

"Give it to me!"

Lana tossed the machete to Harry. No sooner had he caught it than the demon—perhaps dimly sensing that he was about to be opposed—reached out for Harry with one of his many-toed feet and caught hold of his throat, new gnarled toes sprouting as he tightened his grip and cut off Harry's oxygen.

As the demon dug his nails deep into the flesh around Harry's windpipe, Harry took a swipe at the demon and buried the blade in the creature's thigh. Shock and pain made the thing loosen his throat hold on Harry, and Harry pulled away. The seeds continued to offer proof of their fecundity; the demon before him was still transforming. The bunches of eyes were swelling, the mouths spreading down the creature's neck and out of his chest. They were all, by some elaborate reconfiguring of the demon's internal anatomy, possessed of health enough to loose a chorus of screams and pleas. Harry intended to grant the thing the only mercy he had on hand.

"Caz! Now!" he said.

As though they had done this a thousand times before, Caz instantly pushed the demon away from his body at the same time Harry swung the machete through a one-hundred-eighty-degree arc. The blow sliced through a third of the demon's neck before it stuck into the creature's vertebrae. Harry worked the blade free, hot blood gushing from the massive wound and into Caz's open mouth.

"Aw. Fuck," said Caz, through liquid coughs.

Harry swung at the demon's head a second time, hoping for mercy's sake to deliver the coup de grâce. But there was too much crazed life in the creature, and he moved away as Harry swung the blade. This time the machete cut through the burgeoning bunch of black and yellow eyes and sank deep into the demon's skull. Thirty eyeballs or more dropped from the cluster and rolled around Harry's feet. The demon's mouths were letting out a single sound now: a long, sustained funereal lament.

Harry took it as a sign that the creature was readying himself for death, and the thought put power into his third swing. It went, more by accident than intention, exactly where the second blow had gone and took off the top half of the enemy's head. The demon lurched, and the severed crown slid off and landed on Caz's chest, several eyes popping from the pressure as it struck. The rest of the pitiful thing sagged for a moment or two in Caz's arms, then keeled over dead.

It took the combined strength of Lana, Harry, and Dale pushing from above and Caz pushing from below to roll the corpse away, but when they finally did Caz pushed himself up into a sitting position, where he paused to wipe some of the blood that had spewed on him and then got to his feet.

"Thank you," he said to Harry. "I thought that was it, man."

"Nobody's dying on this trip," Harry said. "Especially at the hand of some underling. Understood? Lana? Dale? You follow? We're going to get through this—"

Lana was staring down at the corpse of the demon Harry had brought down. "Do they all look like this?" she asked. "Too many eyes? All those mouths?"

"No," said Harry. "That's what I was saying before the bastard sprang back to life. I think that's what the fog did. This isn't normal. Not by a long shot."

"I think we left normal back in New York," Lana said.

"Honey. We left normal long before that," Dale said.

D'Amour nodded in terse agreement. "We've probably got a nice little window to move freely through the city, though, so I suggest we go while the going is still good."

Everyone agreed and they proceeded up the shallow incline that led from Janker's Gate, continuing through the city at a steady pace. They were being watched, Harry knew, every step of the way. At first he only felt it—that tingling sigil on the back of the neck, the ever-trustworthy UI—but soon there were more obvious signs: doors that had been opened a slit were closed sharply when his gaze chanced their way, crude curtains or drapes were dropped back into place, and now and then he heard voices from inside the houses—cries and arguments and sometimes what might have been demonic prayers, offered up in the hope of some fiendish salvation.

At every intersection they crossed, Harry glimpsed figures skipping out of sight into doorways or alleys; a few were even spying on them from the rooftops, risking whatever was left of their lives as they stalked the four earthly life-forms. Suddenly Harry's tattoos went wild. He said nothing, but, out of reflex, his hand went to the place on his neck where the tattoo sang its warning cry.

"Ah Christ," Caz said. "I know what that means."

"What *what* means?" Dale said, his voice barely audible.

"Shit," Harry said. "My tattoos. Caz, I forget you can read me like a book."

"I wrote that book," Caz said.

"Yeah, well. I'm being warned to proceed with caution."

"Harold, we're in Hell. Caution is a fucking given. I put that fucking tattoo on you. And the way your hand shot to that bit of ink tells me that caution doesn't even come close."

"Fine. You want the hard sell? We're not alone, and I think we're fucked. Happy now?" Harry said, walking on.

"Very," Caz replied.

As if on cue, from somewhere near the sound of feet on stone was heard, from another direction a short cry loosed. Seemingly in response, Harry and his friends heard an unholy, deafening din arising from every direction. The loosed sound hadn't been a cry at all. It was a summons, and it was answered in the multitudes.

A horde of terrible voices suddenly punctuated the air with madhouse noises—shrieks, and sobbing, and joyless laughter—all varying imitations of the previous sound, so that within the space of less than a minute the city was no longer silent but filled completely with this cacophony, its source steadily closing on the intersection where Harry and his friends now stood.

16

"Listen," said the Hell Priest.

"What in God's name is that?" Norma said.

They had stumbled together up the Bastion's ninety-one steps, which led them to the massive front door of the regime's sanctuary. It was there now that the Priest attempted to gain entrance.

"I used to live in Los Angeles," Norma said. "Off a winding road called Coldheart Canyon. At night sometimes you'd hear the yipping of a coyote, then a whole chorus of them joining in as they came to share the kill. That's what that sounds like: a bunch of damned coyotes, howling with happiness because they're about to eat."

"That's *exactly* what it is."

"Oh Christ," Norma said. "Harry . . ."

"He should consider himself lucky if he dies here and now," said the Priest, raising one hand and laying his palm flat against the door. "The regime's assassins are afraid. I can hear them weeping on the other side of this door."

She could too, now that she paid closer attention. It was more than simple tears that escaped them. There was terror in their cries.

"They've never seen the void," the Cenobite said, raising his voice so that they could hear him. "They are like children now, waiting for me to come inside and show them the way."

A voice rose above the sobs, its owner doing his best to sound sure of his sanity: "Go back from whence you came, demon!"

"I heard you have troubles, friend," said the Hell Priest.

"The Denials at this Threshold were laid by Lucifer himself. You'll never gain access."

"Then I shall waste no more of your time." So saying, the demon waved his hand over the door and muttered an incantation so soft, Norma wasn't quite sure she heard anything at all. Whatever rite the Priest had issued, it worked its magic, but quick.

"Oh. Oh no! Oh damnation!" said the same voice from behind the door. "Wait—"

"Yes?" the Hell Priest asked.

"Don't go!"

"As you've said, you are safe within your walls. You have no need of me."

"We are under siege! There are things! In here! With us! Terrible things! It's too dark to see! Help us, please!"

"Hallucinations? You don't really think that'll work, do you? They're demons. They know—" Norma said.

"Stop talking to him," a second voice said from within. "He's playing tricks on us." And then, "You're stupid for coming here, Cenobite. The regime has plans for you."

"See?" Norma said, her question answered.

"Wait," the Priest said to her.

"Be quiet!" said the first voice. "Let him in. He has powers. He can help us."

"Yes! Let him in!" said another, his assent taken up by half a dozen others.

"Turn off the Denials, Kafde," said the first guard. "Let the Priest in."

"It's a trick, you damned fool—" the dissenter broke in.

"Enough," the first guard said. There was a sound of ragged motion and then the thump of a body being thrown against the door.

"No! Don't—"

The dissenter never finished his sentence. In place of words came the sound of a violent impact, and then that of his dying body sliding down the door and hitting the floor.

Norma's mouth hung open in shock. "I don't believe it," she said.

"And our journey has not yet even begun," the Hell Priest said.

"Messata," came the voice of the first guard, "get this carcass out of the way while I turn off the Denials. Priest, are you still there?"

"I am," said the Cenobite.

"Step away from the threshold, and be careful." There was a resonant click, and the door swung wide. A large yellow and orange demon greeted him at speed. The soldier was easily twice the Priest's height and dressed in a golden armor. He ushered the Cenobite into the chamber, gesturing frantically all the while. The Hell Priest, followed by Norma, entered the small antechamber occupied by a dozen soldiers, all clad in the same war vestments.

"They're everywhere, these monsters," the guard pleaded. "You must help—"

The Cenobite made a tiny nod and said, "I know. I came for the regime. They are in danger. Where is their chamber?"

The soldier pointed toward a staircase that branched off into dozens of differing directions. "I will lead you. The tower is a vertical labyrinth. You will go mad before you find your way to the second floor. This is the first chamber. Theirs is the sixth. We will fight this scourge together, brother! These fiends will not carry the day. The remaining chambers are each one thousand soldiers strong."

"Then I have much work to do," the Hell Priest said. He then reached into his robe and took out of its folds a Lemarchand Configuration and handed it to the guard. "Here," he said.

"What is that?" the soldier inquired, taking it in hand.

"A weapon. I have several."

He took out another three and passed them to the demon, who then passed them to other soldiers.

"What do they do?" one of them asked.

"Open them," the Hell Priest said.

17

Harry might have taken some comfort at the belief that all but the soul was a human illusion, but there was nothing in his present circumstance that looked illusory. The street at the intersection where he, Caz, Dale, and Lana stood was a nightmare with no foreseeable escape. Each of the humans stared down a different street, but all saw the same unwelcome sight: the monstrously transformed citizens of the unholy city coming at them.

The terrible multiplicities had sprung up from the places where the fog's seeds had lodged themselves, rendering each beast a horror unto itself. All had stripped themselves completely naked, and to add injury to insult, their already-transformed anatomies brought forth strange blood-sopped blossoms and from those blossoms further generations of seeds were now sprouting.

They had all too clear a vision of the seeds at their fecund work; new victims convulsed as their outgrowths swelled and burst, spitting juices in all directions, the flesh they had wetted instantly casting out nets of ripe red veins that were moments later nurturing the creation of new multiplicities.

The second generation's growth was more confident than the first, and more ambitious; the third and fourth, exponential. The forms that they brought into being weren't simply siblings of the anatomy where they'd landed; they were aberrant and fantasized.

And again, as with their predecessors, the urgent need to be naked, to expose every niche and fold to seeding, so that in the space of a minute or two the number of appendages had tripled, the newly infested still shrieking as wave upon wave of agony overtook them.

Strangest of all among the new recruits to this unspeakable regiment were the demonic children, freed from the constraints of hearth and home, their bodies, for all apparent vulnerability, more eager even than those of their parents to reinvent themselves. They wanted to be new species: the seeding providing the perfect reason to unleash every heretical thought the day could make flesh.

Even as their parents reached the limits of their disorder, their children were overtaking them, giving their bodies to the grand experiment with an abandon their elders had tried in their flesh too long to control. Hence the boy with thirty arms or more reaching out from the roots in his back, or the adolescent girl whose sex had split her all the way up to her breastbone, her wet wings undulating as it opened to invite the world to do its worst, or the infant even, seeded into its mother's arms and riding the saddles of her milk-fed breasts, its hand a blistered ball swelled to three times or more its natural size, so that it eclipsed its mother's face completely. As for its limbs, they had quadrupled in number and became in the process little more than bone and sinew, their joints defying nature and turned backward to embrace the mother's body like the many-jointed legs of a spider.

There was nothing of pity here, nor, needless to say, of love, simply the unrelenting hurt and horror of tomorrow's hell being born on the bed of glass and nails where yesterday's hell was in the long, messy process of dying. And the occupants of New Hell had blocked the streets from one side to the other. There was nothing to be done, nowhere to go. The circle of the enemy was around them, complete.

"What's the plan, Harold?"

"Die?" Harry said.

"No," Dale said more in defiance than fright. "Fuck this." And he pressed on toward easily the most crowded of the four directions.

"Dale! Get back here!" Harry shouted.

Dale didn't listen.

"And then there were three," said Lana.

Dale stopped when he reached the first swarm of damned and distorted.

"Oh, just go away," he said.

So saying, he raised his cane and jabbed its pointed tip into the belly of a demon boy. The young demon shrieked, beating a hasty backward retreat on many of his feet. There was a mark, Harry saw: a small black circle that was growing exponentially and quickly becoming a mess of black lightning bolts shooting through the villain's veins. The demon lost his balance and went sprawling down among his comrades.

A female demon charged toward Dale. He was waiting for her, cane in hand. The silver tip pricked a cluster of sapling breasts, and her dozen eyes bulged from their loose-hanging sockets. She unleashed a howl and her skin too quickly became a maze of poisoned flesh. Harry watched everything and was beginning to understand. The flesh from the demon boy's wound had begun to fold back upon itself like blossoming flower petals, exposing the shiny wet muscle beneath.

His skin was retreating with great precision, the square growing, its symmetry spoiled only by the blood that was spilling over as the patch of exposed flesh grew steadily larger.

The same process was happening on the female demon's breasts, where some kind of miracle had left its mark. But the speed at which the square was growing had increased fivefold or more, her multitude of teats all but stripped of skin, her blood-matted chest hanging on the drapes of her breastplate.

Dale jabbed at another demon. And another. Each victim was seized in agony as the place where they had been pierced opened and unmade itself.

"What the fuck is going on?" Lana asked.

"Dale. You're a goddamned genius," Harry said. "I could kiss you."

"Promises, promises," Dale said, impaling another demon. Harry tightened his grip on the machete and headed toward his own beseeded hoard.

"New plan," Harry said. "Grab whatever weapons you have and start cutting."

"Are you sure about this?" Lana asked.

Harry looked back at her and smirked. "Dead sure."

"Probably not the best choice of words, but—" Saying all she had to say, Lana pulled out two knives, gripped them, wrists crossed with elbows out, and walked straight at the oncoming swarm.

"I guess that means me too," Caz said.

He pulled out his weapon and followed suit. Caz took a swing, slicing the seventh forearm of an enormous granddaddy of a demon. The beast clutched at the wound with four of his hands, but the gauze was not enough to stanch the wound. From underneath the cluster of fingers, the demon's flesh unfolded itself, devouring muscle and bone from top to multilayered bottom.

Harry and his group of Harrowers hacked and slashed their way through the bulbous throng, needing only one wound to stop each adversary. There were none among the demons who were granted immunity. They all went down, young and old alike falling, their bodies wracked with spasms, reaching with desperation to catch hold of the killing mote but never far enough to seize the enemy at its work. In a short time there were dying demons lying everywhere, a dozen deep in some places, sprawled over one another: a mass of bodies in the process of self-skinning, pools of blood rising between them all.

Harry glanced back at Dale, Lana, and Caz. "That wasn't so bad," he said.

Caz, panting, stared at his comrades expectantly. "Does anybody want to explain to the big dumb queen what the hell just happened?"

"You forgot to mention gorgeous," Dale said.

Caz looked down at Dale and smiled coyly as he brushed a severed nipple off his shoulder.

"I don't give a shit how it worked," Lana said. "All I need to know is that we're still breathing."

"Clearly," Harry said, "something was causing those poor bastards to sprout multiple pieces of anatomy."

"Clearly," said Lana.

"Whatever was making that happen, it didn't seem to care whether it multiplied appendages, or wounds. Its mission was simply to divide and conquer. The second we opened a hole in those things, the working did the rest for us."

"Got it," Lana said. "Good enough for me."

"Dale, did you know that would happen?" Caz asked, stepping over a small mountain of bleeding cunts.

"I hadn't the foggiest," Dale replied. "I just knew we had to find Norma and that God wouldn't allow us to be stopped now."

"Do me a favor, Dale," Harry said.

"Yes, dear?"

"I know this one went well. But next time you put my life on the line because of what you think God will allow, leave me out of it."

"Spoilsport," Dale said.

"Let's move," Harry said by way of reply.

"I can't wade through all this," Lana said.

"It's just a little blood," Harry remarked, catching hold of Lana's arm. "Come on."

Muttering something under her breath, Lana went with him while Caz and Dale brought up the rear. Together, they stumbled over the mass of bodies, only to find that many of them still had some measure of life in them, the skinning process as yet incomplete.

"That was something," Caz said, watching the continual undoing beneath his soles.

"I've seen stranger things," Harry said.

"You say that about everything," Lana said.

"Not everything."

"Oh yeah? Like what?"

Harry pointed past her, toward the end of the city. Lana turned. The last shreds of fog had cleared away, and for the first time they could see all the way down the street to the impossibly tall black marble building that stood at its end.

"Yeah. That's hard to top," she said.

Without anyone uttering another word, they began walking. The wind had escalated considerably, raising clouds of dirt and litter and, when it gusted with particular vehemence, opening and closing doors along the street. A crudely constricted chimney was toppled from a roof half a block closer to the regime's headquarters, the sliding bricks bringing down slates and eaves with them. The wind brought clouds too, gray shreds like dirty clothes, torn between the roofs and the ever-grinding stone. Some of the clouds even pressed down into the streets and raced along with the wind at the level of the eaves.

The Harrowers put their heads down against the bluster and moved on toward the unguarded gates of the monolithic structure without further challenge.

"How thoughtful," Harry said. "They left the front door open for us."

"Very considerate," Lana said.

"Here's the plan," Harry continued, never breaking stride. "Me and Dale will deal with any demons we find. Caz and Lana, if Norma's in there, you grab her and get her out of there at all costs. Leave us behind if you have to. Any objections?"

Of course, the objections were innumerable, but not one was uttered aloud, and without protestation they entered the tower.

18

"What the fuck is this?" Lana asked.

They had entered the tower not knowing what to expect but anticipating at least the semblance of a fight. What they got, however, was a firsthand look at the aftermath of a massacre, and a recent one at that, judging by the steam that rose from the still-fluttering corpses. The bodies that blocked the passage just inside the front door were already the feeding and breeding place of Hell's green-gold Doxy Flies, the smallest of which were ten times the size of their humble earthling equivalent. And their offspring were correspondingly eager; some of these bodies were already pulsing masses of larval life, devouring what they'd been born into with monstrous appetite.

As Harry listened to the play of his friends' footfalls, he surveyed the blood-drenched canvas before his eyes. He knew this was the work of the Cenobite. These, Harry guessed, were only the beginnings of the visions to which the Hell Priest had requested he bear witness. He was happy he'd declined the offer, not that he'd entertained the notion. But the demon they were chasing was powerful; that much was certain. The problem, however, was that he was far more powerful than Harry had ever wanted to admit. Harry was standing ankle deep in the organs of many large demonic soldiers—warrior demons, clearly, who likely spent the majority of their lives preparing for battle—and they had been felled in the blink of an eye. Harry shuddered.

"Jackpot," Caz said, bringing Harry back from his thoughts.

Broken from his trance, Harry looked up and saw his friend collecting weapons from the dead soldiers. Caz had used his time wisely and had already acquired a considerable collection of belts bristling with knives, all ornately decorated but clearly more than showpieces.

"Hallelujah," Dale sang. "We're trading up."

"Good thinking," Lana said. She drew out a knife that sprouted a second, third, and fourth blade, intersecting the first so as to create an eight-pointed star. "I'll take this one."

"Great," said Harry, giving the chamber a twice-over. "Let's take what we need and get the fuck out of here."

After making their selections from the vast array of infernal weaponry, they advanced toward the first set of stairs and, though each pair of eyes started on the same step, none landed upon same location.

"Uh," said Caz.

"My thoughts exactly," said Lana.

"You think he'd go easy on us for once," Dale said.

"Oh, he has," Harry offered.

Everyone followed Harry's gaze and there they saw a small stream of blood trickling down the face of one of the stone steps.

"Hell's bread crumbs," Harry said.

"You know," said Lana, "most people *wouldn't* follow the blood trail. Not us, though. Jesus Christ."

"Look on the bright side," said Caz. "If there are bears in Hell, they won't come after you first."

"That barely makes sense."

"Bear-ly?" Caz said, grinning.

"Shut up," said Lana.

Harry had already begun to climb the stairs, far too intent on his mission to allay his fears with humor. His sobriety quickly caught on, and

Lana and Caz silenced themselves, following Harry up through the vertical labyrinth. They passed through chamber after chamber without error, always following the beginning of the blood trail at the end of another. For there were many bodies in the various chambers of the Bastion through which they passed: some looked as though they'd turned on one another, others like they'd simply been casually murdered by someone passing by. There were a few who were still faintly alive, but they were all too far gone to answer any question that might have been put to them. On Harry and his followers pressed until they reached the sixth and final chamber at the top of the black tower.

Like every door they'd reached up to this point, this too was wide open, though the chamber Harry and company walked into was vastly different from anything they had seen until now. The area was chaotic—there was no doubt of that—but there was no blood to wade through as there had been in the previous chambers. And there had clearly been a struggle here, but there were no corpses. Pinhead had failed in destroying the regime, and by the looks of the place he hadn't been very happy about it.

"Once more into the proverbial breach, then?" Dale said.

"When in Rome," Harry said as he entered the chamber.

Harry stared across the wreckage in the room, his eyes fixated on a large archway—seemingly the only other means of entry or exit found in the room—at the opposite end of the chamber. Inside this archway, he saw, was a void. No bricks or mortar, but for that matter, no light, objects, colors of any kind; all sense of place was lost there. In the world above, a sight such as this one would have invited madness—in this realm, however, it was yet another one of Hell's tiresome mind games. Harry found it surprising how soon his senses had numbed to the madness of this place.

"Do as the demonic do," Dale said, finishing Harry's thought for him. "That's how the expression goes, right?" Dale walked through the debris, spinning his cane as he moved on.

"What the fuck, man?" Caz said. "What does this thing want? Like, what's the endgame, you know?"

"No," Harry said, drawing closer to the archway of nothingness, "I don't know."

His eyes were fixated on the sight (or lack thereof), and as he approached he realized that the archway wasn't as barren as it had appeared to be. The nothingness was an illusion, and the closer Harry drew the more this nullity before him was beginning to form a flat, monochromatic image. Perhaps the magic of this thing depended upon the nearness of a warm body. Or perhaps it simply begged scrutiny in order for it to work; whatever the case, Harry was now within a stride of two of its location and he could now plainly see a flickering image of one of the streets he and his Harrowers had passed through on their way to the tower. He recognized the location because it wasn't easy to miss the remains of the recently slain and infected damned who were still lying there.

"Can someone tell me what I'm looking at?" Harry said. "Is this magic, or technology?"

"What? Where?" Dale said, turning to look in Harry's direction.

"Whatcha got there, Harold?" Caz said.

Harry opened his mouth as if to say something, but no words escaped his lips. Dale, Lana, and Caz joined Harry at the threshold of the archway. Silently, they all stood staring at the image before them. Finally, Lana spoke.

"Looks kind of like a television. Like a really shitty closed-circuit image."

Harry squinted. He hadn't seen much television in his lifetime, but from what he remembered, it was a very different experience.

"Can I borrow your cane?" Caz said to Dale.

"You can hold my cane as long as you'd like," Dale said, handing Caz his cane with a playful glance.

Caz took the cane, trying to conceal his smile, and quickly turned toward the flickering image. Lifting the cane, he extended his arm, careful not to get too close, and made to press the ivory tip onto the surface of the screen.

"Be careful!" Harry said.

"Harold, I'm fine," Caz replied, and then pressed the tip into the archway. The image rippled where the tip touched the surface, like concentric waves disturbing a serene, translucent lake.

"Ah," said Harry. "It's not either-or. It's both. Technology *and* magic."

"Looks that way," Lana said. "I've never seen anything like it, but that's gotta be some kind of liquid display screen, held upright with some kind of working."

Caz, continuing the experiment, moved the cane across the liquid, causing the image before them to turn like the pages of a book. The view of the streets folded and gave way to a new and entirely unfamiliar vista of the world in which they were outsiders.

"How the fuck—"

"Don't burst a brain cell, Harold," Caz said. "It's like a security camera—*shit!*"

Caz lost the grip of the cane, and it fell into the archway.

"My lucky cane!" Dale shouted. (Though no one was to know, he had a collection of over two hundred lucky canes. All identical. All with the same opulent design. All, according to Dale, equally necessary.) Quickly Caz dropped to his haunches and reached his hand out toward the rippling void.

"I wouldn't do that," Harry said. "A cane's one thing, but—"

"Relax. My ink ain't saying shit. And I'm assuming yours isn't either." Harry said nothing. Caz nodded. "That's what I thought." And, so saying, he thrust his hand into the liquid void and grabbed for the cane.

"Please be careful," Dale said.

Caz turned to Dale and smiled, wordlessly retrieving the cane from the void and bringing it back into the chamber.

"I got a notion," Harry said. "Caz, let me try something."

"You mind?" Caz asked Dale.

"He can touch my cane too," Dale said.

"I'm honored," Harry said as Caz handed him the cane.

Harry inserted the cane into the liquid and flicked it quickly, revealing image upon image. Faster and faster Harry flicked it, and in different directions—up, down, left, right, revealing different locations and images based on each of the differing movements.

"I'll be," said Dale. "It's like the walls have eyes."

"Yeah. And each direction," Harry said, moving the cane at a slower, more deliberate pace, "represents an axis. Looks like we can go left, right, forward, backward."

"In and out?" Dale said.

Caz chuckled.

"Good question," Harry said, and he pressed the cane deeper into the image on the screen—a vast mountain range of craggy, jagged rocks—and the picture zoomed in for a closer look.

"That would be a yes," Harry said, continuing to play with the mechanism. "I don't say this often, but I'm impressed."

"Yup," Caz said "These fuckers definitely got the gizmos— Wait, what was that? Go back! Fuck!"

"What did you see?" Lana said.

"The other way," Caz instructed. "There! Stop!"

Harry brought the image around again and saw, on the screen, the Hell Priest, accompanied by several regime soldiers, each of them at least seven feet tall. Resting comfortably on the shoulders of the tallest soldier was Norma.

"Fuck me dead," Harry said.

Harry and his Harrowers stood there, looking into the void at the image of Norma surrounded by a small army of fiends.

"There you are, momma," said Caz. "We're coming for you."

"You bet your fucking ass we are," said Harry.

"What is that?" Dale asked.

"Oh God," said Lana. "Look at the other soldier. In its hand. Is that—"

"A severed head," said Harry. "I've seen enough of 'em to know."

Harry pushed the cane deeper into the liquid image. The picture of the figures onscreen grew larger.

"I still don't know what we're seeing or how we're seeing it, but it's great to see Norma again," Harry said.

Harry gently eased the cane in farther, ensuring he not lose sight of the Hell Priest and his brigade. Suddenly the Priest and his entourage stopped dead in their tracks. The demon who carried the severed head lifted it up and the Priest slowly and cautiously turned back and began walking toward them.

"What are they doing?" Caz said.

"No fucking clue," Lana said. "This thing doesn't have audio, does it?"

"If it does, I haven't figured out where the mute button is yet."

Harry and his Harrowers watched as the Hell Priest reached for the severed head and lifted it toward his face, putting the mouth to his ears.

"You gotta be fucking kidding," said Caz.

"Afraid not, old friend," Harry said, turning to Caz. "That fucking head is still talking."

"Yeah," said Lana. "And I have a pretty good idea what it said."

And, all too soon, so did the rest of the Harrowers. On Lana's prompting, they had returned their gazes to the screen and saw that the Hell Priest had now lowered the head and was looking out at Harry and his companions as though seeing perfectly clearly the lens through which he was being watched.

"That's fucking spooky," said Caz.

"Right," Harry said, his voice tremulous. "There goes the element of surprise."

19

Norma had done her best to create a rough map in her mind, tracing the journey she'd taken in the company of the Cenobite, the few soldiers he had conscripted from among the survivors of the massacre at the Bastion, and the still-living severed head of a military general named Pentathiyea, one of Hell's highest-ranked officials, whom the Cenobite had beheaded without hesitation or effort. And though the chance of ever making the return journey seemed remoter by the mile, she still held on to the tender hope that she might find a way back.

They had left the Bastion with one of the soldiers carrying Norma on his back. She still had enough powers of persuasion to get her mount, whose name was Knotchee, to quietly describe to her the territory they journeyed over once they were beyond the Bastion. It seemed to be a promising arrangement from the start, with Knotchee using a soldier's unadorned vocabulary to describe the landscape through which they traveled. But his simple eloquence quickly faltered once they got beyond the last of Pyratha's streets and ventured out into the wasteland itself. There was nothing for him to describe except emptiness.

"Are we not on a road of some kind?" Norma asked him.

Knotchee lowered his voice to keep his reply from reaching the Hell Priest's ears.

"The only road we're following is the one in the Lord Tempter's head. And if he loses his way we're all dead."

"That's not very comforting," said Norma.

This silenced the conversation for a long while. When Knotchee took up talking again it was because finally there was a change in the view. Now, however, what he was seeing wasn't so easy to describe, and he fumbled for words. There were huge pieces of wreckage, he said, strewn across the desert, the remains of machines the likes of which he had never seen before. To his soldier's eye it looked as though a war had been fought here, though he freely admitted he could see no killing purpose to which these vast toppled devices could have been put. And if there were demons who might have died during this war he had no way of knowing, since there was not so much as a single bone underfoot.

"Do demons have ghosts?" Norma asked him.

"Of course," Knotchee replied. "There will always be those that won't let go of who they were."

"If this had been a battlefield, there'd be ghosts wandering around."

"Perhaps they are."

"I'd know if there were," Norma replied. "Ghosts and I have a way of crossing paths. And I don't sense them here. Not one. So if this was a battlefield, it was one where all the dead went to a contented rest. And that would be a first for me."

"Then I have no more ideas," the soldier said.

Despite Norma's encouragement, the descriptions grew steadily sparser. But as she was riding on his shoulders, her arms wrapped around his neck, it wasn't hard for Norma to read the signals that were rising off the soldier's body. His skin was getting clammier, his pulse quickening, his breath too. He was afraid. Norma knew better than to impugn his masculinity by attempting to reassure him. She just held tight and kept her peace. The wind rose for a time, its gusts so strong they would have thrown her over if she'd been on her own.

And then, just as the rising velocity of the wind started to cause

Knotchee to stagger, the storm died away completely. There was no slow diminishing of the force. One moment, they were being struck by gust upon gust; the next, the wind seemed to have died away completely.

"What happened?" Norma whispered to Knotchee.

The sound of her own voice gave her some answer to the mystery. The wind hadn't suddenly stopped blowing; they had simply stepped out of it into what sounded, to judge by the noise of their feet on pebbles and her words, like some kind of passageway, the walls of which corrupted the sounds, stretching them or slicing them into slivers.

"The wasteland's gone," he said. "The stories are true. It's all folding up around us, and we're going to get folded up in it." He started to turn around, his breath coming in panicky gasps.

"Don't you dare," Norma said, catching hold of one of his ears and twisting it as hard as she could.

It was the kind of thing an irritated parent might do to a troublesome child, and perhaps for that reason it gained the soldier's attention. He stopped in mid-turn.

"That hurts."

"Good. It's supposed to. Now listen to me: I don't know you from a warm hole in a cold corpse, but there's been enough bloodshed already without adding your body to the heap. Wherever he's taking us, he knows what he's doing."

"If it were possible, I would be humbled," the Hell Priest remarked from quite a distance ahead. It was obvious he'd heard every word Norma and the soldier had shared. "You're right, of course. I haven't come this far to deliver us into oblivion. I have such sights to show you. Soon, you will have answers to questions you have never even dared to ask."

The words cut through Knotchee's panic. His heartbeat ebbed, his skin dried, and he picked up his stride once more. And it was just as the Hell Priest had promised. After thirty or forty yards, the passageway and its confines opened up.

"What do you see?" Norma asked.

There was a long pause. Finally, Knotchee said, "It's so big I'm not sure—"

"Set her down," the Hell Priest said.

Knotchee did as instructed. The pebbles were extremely uncomfortable beneath Norma's bony behind. But within a few minutes of sitting down there was a sound of running feet, off to her right, and shouts of what surely was adoration from those who were approaching.

Knotchee had walked off, leaving Norma to interpret what happened next by the sound alone, which she was used to doing. She guessed that perhaps a dozen or so creatures had come along the beach to pay their respects to the Hell Priest. She heard several dropping down onto the pebbles, whether kneeling or lying she couldn't tell, to demonstrate their reverence, their shouts subdued now to sibilant whispers. Only one voice rose above the worshipful mutterings, that of an aged female who addressed the Hell Priest in a language Norma had no knowledge of.

"Avocitar? Lazle. Lazle matta zu?"

"Ether psiatyr," the Hell Priest replied.

"Summatum solt, Avocitar," the woman said. And then, apparently addressing the others, "Pattu! Pattu!"

"Pick up your baggage, soldier," the Hell Priest said. "The Azeel are prepared for our arrival. They've readied our vessels."

As soon as Knotchee hoisted Norma onto his back he said, "I'll be glad to leave this place." Then more quietly, "And gladder to leave these freaks."

Norma waited until the trek along the beach was under way and she heard the sound of feet on the pebbles to cover her questions before she dared ask her question "What do you mean by 'freaks'?"

"They're inbred," Knotchee said. "Can't you smell them? They're disgusting. When this is over, I'm going to bring a squad out here and clean this filth up."

"But they're demons, like you, aren't they?"

"Not like me. They're misshapen. Heads too big, bodies too small. All of them naked. It's an insult to their heritage. It makes me sick. They must be stomped out."

"What heritage?"

"The Azeel were the first generation of angels after the fall, the sons and daughters of those who had been cast down with our lord Lucifer. Theirs were the hands that built Pyratha. And then, when it was finished, and our lord Lucifer pronounced it good, they went with him to their own land, which he had made for them as reward for their labors. And having gone into their secret country, they were never seen again. Now I know why."

"And where is Lucifer? Does he have his own secret country?"

"He's been gone many, many generations. As for where he is now, it isn't my place to ask, nor is it my right to know. The Lord of Lords is with us every moment, and in every place."

"Even now?"

"In every moment. In every place," the soldier replied. "Now unless you want to walk from here, let this subject sleep."

Norma and the soldier continued in silence, walking along the beach as the Azeel led the Hell Priest and his entourage to their boats.

The Azeel had started chanting now, the chant's rhythmic power, building phrase upon phrase, changed with obsessive devotion. The chant turned Norma's thoughts to pulp; she couldn't hold two notions together.

"They need you to go to the boat, Norma," Knotchee said. "Can I go with her?" he asked somebody, and was given the answer he wanted. "I'll sit in front of you."

Knotchee lifted Norma up off his shoulders and gently deposited her on her wooden seat. She reached out to the left and right of her, running her fingers over the carved beams. The boat did not feel particularly stable. Even though they were in the shallows, it rolled alarmingly whenever someone climbed aboard.

"Where is *he*?" she asked Knotchee.

"In the first boat," he replied. "They carved him a kind of throne."

"How many boats are there?" Norma asked.

"Three," answered Knotchee. "All carved with angels' wings running the length of each side of each boat. Every barb and vein of every feather, perfectly carved. I never saw anything so beautiful in my life. Truly we are blessed to bear witness to such events."

"Funny," said Norma. "I've never been happier to be blind."

The old demon woman who had first addressed them spoke once again:

"When you go, I start big chanting, to conceal any noise you make from Quo'oto."

The name brought barely audible rumblings from the Azeel who were in the boats, desperate little prayers, Norma guessed, to keep Quo'oto away, whatever it was.

"All of you," the demon went on, "not to say a word until you getting to Last Place. Quo'oto hears well."

The observation was echoed in whispers by the entire assembly.

"Quo'oto hears well. Quo'oto hears well. Quo'oto hears well."

The old demon woman said, "Be wise. Be silent. Be safe. We staying here and making like a noise that will drive Quo'oto deeper."

The boats were pushed off from the shore, their hulls scraping on stones for a few seconds before they floated free. Then those who had the oars, one of whom was Knotchee, began to paddle, and if the strength of the wind against Norma's face was anything to judge by, they were skimming through the water at a tremendous pace.

Norma could hear the bow of the boat behind them cutting the water and very occasionally the sound of one of the oars striking one of the waves from the boat in front, but otherwise the first portion of the journey, which took perhaps half an hour, went without incident.

Soon after, however, Norma felt a sudden drop in temperature, and her skin began to crawl with gooseflesh. She could feel it pressing against her face, and chilling her lungs when she next drew breath. Despite this, the boats continued on their expeditious paths through the water, sometimes coming out of a patch of mist for a few teasing moments of warmth, only to plunge back into the bitter air before Norma could even stop her teeth from chattering. The noise she was making was loud enough for one of her fellow passengers to pass forward a piece of canvas that Knotchee placed between her teeth to silence her.

Finally the mist began to thin a little, and then, as the boats came to shore, suddenly it was gone. That's when Knotchee spoke:

"Oh demonation," said Knotchee. "It's beautiful."

"What is?" said Norma, leaning closer to Knotchee, but he gave no reply. "Tell me!" Norma said. "What? What do you see?"

In the span of his life, which had been, to date, far longer than any human life, the Hell Priest had witnessed a great deal that would have cracked lesser minds wide open like fumbled eggs. He once visited a continent in a remote dimension that had contained a single species of mottle-shelled creatures the size of roadkill mongrels, their only food one another or, if pressed to it, their excremental remains. Truly, the Hell Priest was no stranger to the abhorrent. And yet, now that he was in the place where he'd longed to be for many years—the place that had conjured in his mind's eye waking dream upon waking dream—why, he wondered, did he find himself nostalgic for the presence of those corrupted beasts who had only earned his contempt in earlier times?

As soon as he begged the question, he knew the answer, though there wasn't a living soul in Hell (or out of it, for that matter) to whom he would have confessed the truth, which was simply this: now that he was finally here in the Unholy of Unholies, where he had ached for too long to be, he was afraid. He had good reason.

His boat had come ashore, and, fixing his eyes only on the structure, he went to it, like a moth to flame. And now he stood, buried in the oppressive shadow of an edifice so secret, so vast, so complex, that there was nothing in Hell or on Earth (even in those most guarded of chambers in the Vatican, which had been built by men of such genius the chambers defied the laws of physics and were vastly larger on the inside than on the out) that had any hope of comparison with the place where the Hell Priest now stood. The island upon which the structure had been built was called Yapora Yariziac (literally, the Last of All Possibilities), and the name was no lie.

The Hell Priest was finally here, at the end of his journey, with so many betrayals and bloodlettings marking his path, and he actually found himself assailed with doubts. Suppose all his hopes of revelation were confounded? Suppose the Archfiend's majesty had not left any mark on this place for the Cenobite to draw power and understanding from? The sole reason the Hell Priest had come here was to stand in the last testament to Lucifer's genius.

He had expected to feel Lucifer's presence in him, filling up the void in him and, in so doing, showing him the secret shape of his soul. But as it stood, he felt nothing. He'd read somewhere that the makers of Chartres Cathedral, the masons and the carvers of the great façade, had not chiseled their names onto the finished work as an act of humility for the Creator in Whose name the cathedral had been raised.

Was it possible, he wondered now, that Lucifer had done something similar? Actively erasing the echoes of his presence in the name of a higher power? He was suddenly agonizingly aware of the nails that had been hammered into his skull, their points pressing into the clotted jelly of his brain. He had always understood that this portion of his anatomy, being nerveless, could not give him pain. But he felt pain now: bleak, meaningless, stupefying pain.

"This is not right . . ." he said.

There was no echo off the walls of the edifice; they had consumed his words just as they had his hope. He felt something stirring in his belly, then rising through his tormented body, growing in force as it ascended. He had cultivated a distance from his own despair over the years, but it met him at this place and would never again be put out of his sight.

He only repeated himself: "This is not right. . . ."

20

Harry and his friends had left behind them the kind of sights that a thousand lifetimes could not have prepared them for—Pyratha's violent insanities, the plague fog off the wastelands, the secrets and horrors of the Bastion—and had been led into a mystery within a mystery. There was no sound of weeping here—or shrieks, or pleas for mercy for that matter—only the sound of small waves breaking on stones though there was not a body of water to be seen.

Upon leaving the tower and fleeing the city built upon the hills, they had entered a wasteland littered with what looked to be abandoned machinery to the left and right of them. Vast wheels and mammoth coils of chain; toppled structures that had certainly been many stories high, their purpose impossible to fathom. With increasing frequency, lightning struck downward and danced an incandescent tarantella over the metal structures, throwing off showers of sparks in places that in turn started fires among some of the wooden portions of the devices. Many of these conflagrations raged, the smoke they sent up ever thickening the air. As they pressed on, it grew increasingly difficult to see the sky through the brilliance of the lightning, as its shuttering blazes never broke through but only intensified the turmoil.

Finally, the sky, having been unleashing its lightning in silence for three or four minutes, spoke out its thunder, peal upon peal, each roll rising to drown out the one before. The reverberations made the ground shake, and that motion in turn caused several of the pieces of machinery to topple, their massive remains breaking into bits, the smallest of which was still the size of a house.

The group had picked up their speed as the scale of the event continued to escalate around them. Though they were twice obliged to make a detour to avoid pieces of wreckage that came down upon their path, throwing off massive pieces of timber and sheared metal as they did so, the Harrowers quickly reoriented themselves on the other side and picked up the pace again within a few strides.

Harry, forcing himself to maintain the front position, was finding it harder and harder to keep his bearings: his lungs blazed in his chest; his head thumped to the crazed speed of his heart; his feet were a fool's feet, threatening to throw him down in the dirt with every other step.

Lana was several strides behind him, the gap between them steadily closing, but Harry focused his attention as best he could on the road ahead when he thought he saw another archway, much like the one they'd left behind at the top of the Bastion. Harry was certain that his mind was playing tricks on itself and, in his moment of doubt, his body capitulated. He suddenly knew that he wasn't going to make it.

His legs were so weak that they couldn't carry him any farther; he wasn't even sure he wanted them to try. He was only going to slow the rest of them down and put them in harm's way. But he couldn't just stop. He needed to turn to his friends to tell them to go on without him. He'd catch up later, when he'd recovered his strength and put out the blaze in his lungs.

At the threshold of the hallucinated archway, Harry bullied his body into turning around with the intent of addressing his friends. As he spun, his body propelled itself forward, and then the lights went out. The roar and the blaze and the motion of the ground beneath his stumbling feet were a single unendurable assault, and drained of strength, he had stumbled and relinquished himself to gravity. He fell into the gray dirt, and his consciousness seemed to flicker out, taking with it the noise of fire and thunder.

"Watch," ordered a voice in the darkness. Harry didn't want to watch. He'd seen enough. But he knew that voice. It didn't belong to a face, but rather a feeling and a smell. The air was thick with sulfur, and shame washed over him and dragged him down to a place he thought he might never leave. Then he heard a different voice—one containing a different set of associations—and Harry stirred.

"Harold?"

It was Caz. Harry heard him quite clearly. He opened his eyes. Caz was crouching beside him.

"You picked a fine time to fall on your ass, man," Caz said. He spoke quietly, almost a whisper.

Harry pushed himself up out of the dirt and turned to eye the firmaments.

"How long was I out? Where'd the lightning go?"

"A minute, maybe less. One second we could barely see one another, and then there was another archway—like in the middle of fucking nowhere. Look." Caz pointed back toward the top of an incline where there was a fracture in the air. "That's what we came through." There were flickers of lightning at the far end of the passageway between the two landscapes. "And we stepped into this."

Harry hauled his aching body into a sitting position and surveyed the surrounding landscape. The vast machines had gone, as had the gray dust in which they had lain, replaced by a gentle incline of pebbles, reedy trees, and small brush, all of which bounded a body of pristine water. Lana was sitting a few yards from Dale, staring out toward the impossibly clear body of water. Dale had ventured closer to shore, no doubt debating the water's drinkability.

"I don't get it." Harry said. "Where's Pinfuck? We weren't very far behind him and now he's—"

"Bathate ka jisisimo!" shrieked a gravel-laden female voice interrupting Harry's question.

"The fuck?" said Caz.

"I think we'll find out whether we want to or not," said Harry.

The Harrowers barely had time to unsheathe their weapons when a creature came into view from around the bend of the beach. She looked like a misshapen demon; she was squat, no more than three and a half feet tall, and her bald head virtually fetal in its shape and relative proportion to her body. She was naked but caked from head to foot with grime. She stopped as soon as she saw the Harrowers, and despite their defensive stances, a wide smile spread across her face.

"Bathate ka jisisimo?" she said again. Nobody said a word, so she repeated the last word once more, enunciating it as though Harry and company were slow to learn.

"Ji si si mo?"

"Anybody catch that?" Harry asked, getting to his feet, his hand close to the place where his knife was hidden.

"Definitely not," said Lana.

"Negative," said Caz.

There was a fresh patter of pebbles from behind the demon, and a warm brightness spilled down the beach. Several large balls of what looked like braided fire moved into view, hovering two or three feet above the beach and then, as they came abreast of the demon woman, rising up together in one sweeping motion and hanging in a loose circle above the beach.

An entourage appeared—a company of perhaps thirty male and female demons, all of whom were as strangely proportioned as the demon woman. Each of them was naked, except for the same caked-on grime that they had slathered on their bodies and dreadlocked hair so that the locks were now semi-solid.

Harry loosened the grip he had on his weapon and sighed.

"If this is a trap, I'm too tired to give a shit," he said.

The tribe advanced. As they did, another female demon emerged from within the circle. She was old, her breasts hanging completely flat against her body, her dreadlocks long enough to graze the ground.

"Harry D'amour," said the elderly demon woman. "The witness."

"What?" Harry asked. "Who told you that?"

"The Black Inside," said a male demon, standing toward the back of the company, his voice as clear and confident as the others in the tribe. The creature continued speaking: "He coming before. He having blind woman. He said you did coming after. To witnessing."

"Well, he's wrong," Harry said.

"Two hundred and one and thirty demons you have put down," remarked yet another member of the tribe, a younger creature who for no apparent reason boasted a noteworthy erection, which he casually toyed with as he spoke. "Slaughterer of the demonation, Harry D'Amour."

"I don't keep track of those things," Harry said. "But if you're right, and you keep playing with your dick like that, very soon it'll be two hundred thirty-two."

The remark received a current of disapproving murmurs from the assembly.

"This cannot happen," one of them said. "We are too close to the one who sleeps. Is holy ground."

"The one who sleeps?" Dale said under his breath. "I've met drag queens with scarier names."

"Who is the one who sleeps?" Harry asked, tossing Dale a reproving glance.

"He is she is it is everything,"

The phrase earned a round of appreciative whoops from the crowd and was here and there shouted out again: *"He is she is it is everything!"*

"I didn't know Hell was polytheistic," Harry said.

"You find true soon, Harry D'Amour," the old demon woman said. "We, the Azeel, make sailing for you."

She pointed her gnarled finger toward a spot farther down the shore.

There a crew of yet more strangely proportioned demons were pulling ashore three beautifully crafted boats.

"Boats?" Harry said. "And those are for us?"

"Azeel help witness to witness. Black Inside commands."

"This fucking day gets weirder and weirder."

21

The Azeel brought the Harrowers down from the top of the beach toward the boats. Each boat, Harry saw, was big enough to carry at least ten people. Harry and his friends huddled close and, as the old demon woman spoke, Harry found himself increasingly perturbed by Earth's idioms concerning the nether realm. *Why would anyone ever want ice water in Hell?* he wondered to himself. The place was fucking freezing.

"One boat is being for Rescuers," the demon woman said, "in case boat does overturning in the lake's fury, yes?"

"It doesn't look very furious," Lana said.

"Quo'oto," was the Demon Woman's one-word response.

"Geseundheit," said Dale.

"Fine. Then what are the other boats for?" Harry asked, nodding toward the second boat, which was being loaded up with no fewer than nine passengers. All demons. Four of them were young, barely adolescents. They knelt in two rows of two at the front of the boat, their heads down. Behind them was a much older Azeel, a male who looked to be older than the demon woman. He too knelt, his head inclined. Four strong young demons took up the oars.

"Ah," said the demon woman, the end of her tail flicking back and forth like a cat's. "We are having not hopeless. But if bleeding is to be, then they will do bleeding."

"Is she talking about sacrifice?" Lana said. "Because I am not okay with that."

"Harry D'Amour. Witness. Azeel help. Please. If Harry D'Amour is to coming back alive, Azeel will leading to holes of wyrms."

"Not hopeless?" Harry said. "Holes of wyrms? Bleeding? What the fuck are you talking about?"

"Black Inside waits."

Murmurs of reverence spread through the demon gathering.

"Yes, yes, the Black Inside. That's the only thing you keep saying that makes any goddamn sense. Did he have Norma with him?"

The Azeel fell silent. Harry looked at his friends, then back to the demons, and asked again.

"Norma? Human? Blind? Woman? Old?"

Again, his queries were met with confused silence.

"Harry," Lana said, touching his arm. "Let's keep going. They don't know anything."

Harry pressed them one last time.

"The Black Inside. Did he say anything else about me, other than the fact that I'm his witness? Was there a message?"

"Ah," the old demon woman said, excitement in her voice. "Message. Yes! Yes! Black Inside says message. Black Inside says. 'Harry D'Amour to boating' "—as she spoke, the woman pointed to the boats with one gnarled finger—" 'or else No Eyes goes to forever sleep.' "

That was all Harry needed to hear.

"Well then," Harry said, heading to the boat, "let's not keep him waiting."

"Are you sure about this, Harold?" Caz asked.

"You heard the crone. No Eyes. That's Norma. And forever sleep?" Harry said as he climbed aboard the boat. "I don't think I need to explain that to you."

At that, the remaining Harrowers climbed aboard the middle vessel with Harry, and in a matter of just a few rhythmical strokes of the oars the three boats were out in the vast darkness of the lake. When Harry glanced back over his shoulder, he saw that the beach was already little more than a sliver of flickering light, diminishing further with every stroke. Harry watched as the old demon woman, who had stayed onshore, was swallowed up by the horizon, leaving him and his friends in the middle of the vast, preternaturally still waters of Lake Hell.

There followed a period of curious peacefulness; the only sound that could be heard came from the oars dipping into the water and lifting again—dipping, lifting, dipping, lifting—and the soft hiss of boats cutting through the crystal waters. Harry studied intently the darkness into which they were heading, looking for their place of destination. There were immense thunderheads over the lake, or so his eyes seemed to tell him one moment, and the next they didn't seem to be clouds at all, but rather a structure that rose up with such ambition that its topmost spires could only be inches from the stony sky. But no sooner had his eyes grasped the solid structure than that too melted away into nothing. Finally he turned to his friends and spoke.

"So what's at the end of the rainbow? Any guesses?"

"Sanctuary," replied one of the oarsmen.

"For who?"

A second oarsman, urgency in his movements, suddenly raised a finger to his lips and said, "Shhh."

The four oarsmen immediately plucked their oars from the water. The boat glided across the placid body soundlessly, and in the hush Harry understood the demon's warning: he heard a slow, aching grind of vast wheels, as though some mechanism, not used in many hundreds of years, was lifting its gears from some great sleep and proceeding to move an ancient body. The source of the din was impossible to locate; it seemed to be coming from everywhere.

"Quo'oto . . ." Harry murmured.

An oarsman nodded silently, pointing a single finger down, indicating it was beneath the boat.

Narrowing his eyes, Harry slowly peered over the side of the boat and felt his bowels stir. Harry stared unblinking at a pulsating giant, its body writhing deep in the unspoiled waters. He didn't pretend to himself that he had any sense of its scale or shape. The creature looked nothing like any water-dwelling animal he'd ever seen. It resembled instead an enormous millipede, its knotted innards visible through a translucent carapace.

As Harry stared down at the monster, it raised its complicated head and stared back at him. Its head seemed, at first, to be comprised of no more than the same series of scales such as it had along its entire body, except that they were completely opaque. The scaly, featureless face regarded Harry—or at least he imagined he felt its regard—and then, after a minute or more of fruitless study, the opaque shields retracted and finally revealed the true visage of the leviathan.

Its visage was perhaps thirty feet from brow to chin, but there was humanity there, even in so vast a form; its eyes were deep set, and there was a ring of milky whiteness around the black horizontal slit that was focusing on him now. Its nose was not unlike that of a bat, flattened and gaping, but its mouth was completely human. Even now, it seemed to make something very like a smile, uncovering as it did so twin rows of acidic blue teeth. And as it smiled, the dark slits of its pupils opened in a heartbeat, driving every last mote of brightness out. Then, fixed on Harry, it started to rise, peristaltic waves passing through its anatomy to left and right so its myriad legs moved with maximum efficiency, bringing its enormous body (to which, at present, Harry could see no end) up toward the surface. He watched, silently daring the beast to take him.

As it ascended, Harry realized how wrong he'd been about his judgment of the depth of the water. Unused to staring into water so clear, he had assumed the Quo'oto was relatively close to the surface. He was wrong. It was deep, very deep, and the water so unlimited that Harry had no sense of how truly enormous this entity was. The upper two segments were easily the size of a blue whale, and yet for all its scale it moved with extraordinary grace, the motion of its legs and the sinuous sweep of its body almost mesmeric.

It was Caz's voice that stirred Harry from his hypnotic state.

"Oh fuck," Caz said. "I can't look."

"Shh," Dale urged.

"Jesus Christ," Lana said. "This can't really be happening, can it?"

Harry looked up and saw, to his surprise, that his friends were not speaking of the Quo'oto. They still had no knowledge of the gargantuan creature beneath their tiny vessel. Their eyes were fixed instead on the first boat, where the old man sitting behind the young Azeel had risen to his feet. The youths in front of him were already standing, their heads thrown back, presenting their willing throats.

"Yaz Nat, ih. Quo'oto, rih," the elder demon said.

The blade then sliced through the tender young flesh of the first youth. The adolescent demon was given to the waters. His corpse sank quickly thanks to weights tied around his feet. The blood pulsed from the expert cuts the elder demon had made, creating a cloud of swirling crimson. The oarsmen quickly continued the journey, at double the speed.

Watching the young demon struggling to take in his last tortured breaths made Harry feel sick, and his mind began to wander back to that side street in New York when he was forced to watch Scummy take his last gasping cries for help. That had been murder. What was happening now was a sacrifice, though Harry wondered if such a distinction existed for demons.

"Everyone just keep their eyes forward," Harry said, turning his gaze back toward the creature in the depths. "We shouldn't question their rituals."

The turbulence around the boat was increasingly choppy and through the bloodstained water, as the boats passed over the creature, Harry saw the vast form open itself up and suck the corpse into its gaping maw.

"Holy hell," Lana said.

"I told you to look forward," Harry said.

"What is it?" Dale said.

"The problem is," Lana said, "as soon as I say the words 'don't look down' you're going to—"

"Oh my dear lord," said Dale.

"Exactly," said Lana. "I vote we walk back."

"Seconded," Dale said.

Caz was the only one not looking. His eyes were closed, and he was shivering from more than the cold weather. "I've seen enough," he said. "And I know I have more to see. So I'll sit this one out, if y'all don't mind."

Dale reached out and squeezed Caz's hand. Harry glanced up to see that their destination—the opposite end of the lake—was close now. As soon as they came within a short distance of the rocky beach the oarsmen leaped out of the boat and hauled it up onto the shore. There was good reason for haste. The waters just beyond the shore were swelling, and foaming in the frenzy. The second boat came in and, catching a frothy wave stirred up by the Quo'oto's writhing, was upended and all the Azeel upon it thrown into the turmoil. Harry rushed the beach, dragging several demons out of the water. And no sooner had all its occupants reached the shore than the third boat came at them with force. It rode the eruption, whose power was sufficient to drive the fragile vessel all the way out of the water and up onto solid ground. With everyone safely ashore, save for a lone sacrifice, Harry stumbled up the beach, moving between everyone to get a clear view of what existed, as he'd put it, beyond the rainbow. When his eyes landed upon it, he felt his knees go weak.

It was a tower so massive Harry's mind failed to wholly grasp the image. This monument before him rose to such impossible heights that he had difficulty discerning between sky and skyscraper. It was Lucifer's masterwork; there was no doubt about it. From the obsessively decorated stepping-stones upon which Harry was presently standing to the highest of spires whose numbers defied his confounded wits to count, this was clearly the Devil's working, and the sight filled Harry with equal parts dread and awe.

Harry knew very little about architecture but enough to know that Lucifer's labors here had later inspired a whole architecture of the living world and their own Gothic creations. He'd been inside some of them on his travels around Europe, in the Cathedral of the Holy Cross and Santa Eulalia in Barcelona, in Bourdeaux Cathedral, and of course in

Chartres Cathedral, where he'd once taken sanctuary, having just killed in the blizzard-blinded streets a demon who had been seducing infants to their deaths with corrupt nursery rhymes.

But none of those buildings, vast and ambitious and elaborate though they were, held a candle to this mountainous structure. Buttress upon buttress, spire upon spire, the cathedral rose with an arrogance that only a creature systematically confident of his powers would have dared dream, much less make real.

Harry thought back to the vast age-ravaged devices that had littered the route here. They weren't the remnants of war machines, as he had assumed. They were what was left of the devices that had been built to quarry the stones and carry them where the masons could work the raw rock and prepare it for its place in the immense design.

Even with the powers of a fallen angel at Lucifer's disposal, the creation of the cathedral must have been a challenge. To take his fellow fallen angels—and other generations of demons who had come from the fallen's seductions and rapes—and turn them, by force of will and intellect, into the kinds of masons, foundation layers, and spire raisers who would have been required to create this structure must have tested Lucifer's wits and ambition to their limits. But somehow it had been done.

"Has anyone here ever heard of the Harrowing?" Dale asked, breaking the silence.

No one replied.

"It was in the time between Christ's crucifixion and his Resurrection," he went on. "The story goes, Christ went down into Hell, walked among the damned, and set many of them free. Then he returned to Earth and broke the bondage of death. It's supposedly the first and only amnesty Hell has ever known."

"If it's true, and stranger things have happened," Caz said, "then that means there's a way out."

"Deus ex Inferis?" Harry said. "Those are big shoes to fill. Let's hope we don't fall too far."

BOOK THREE

The Mourning Star

We have never heard the devil's side of the story,
God wrote all the book.

—Anatole France

1

Harry passed the word that they all should spread out and look for a way into the cathedral. Lana and Dale, accompanied by a few demons, went one way. Harry and Caz went the other. It occurred to Harry as he made his way around to the side of the cathedral that faced the shore that if ever a thing cried out to the maker of its maker, *"Look what I've done, Father! Aren't you proud?"* it was this abomination. The pleading question, Harry assumed, had remained unanswered.

As he searched the cathedral for any type of entrance, the placid waters of the lake were briefly stirred by the Quo'oto, rolling and raising one of its segmented legs out of the water, a reminder of its lethal presence. Harry turned his attention from the lake to the cathedral, walking back toward the front of the building with Caz shadowing him.

"Son of a bitch," Harry said, turning to Caz, "there's no door on this end."

"None that we can see," Caz said. "But we both know that's not the same thing."

"You're so wise, Caz."

"Don't mock me, Harold. Next time you need a new tattoo, my hand might slip."

"Tell me something, Caz old friend," Harry said, changing the subject. "Why would anyone put all this work into something and keep it hidden from everyone?"

Caz looked up at the obscenity and shrugged his shoulders.

"Wish I knew."

"Yeah," Harry said as he looked up at the heights of the façade. "Maybe there's an opening up there. That would make about as much sense as anything else in this godforsaken—"

"D'Amour! D'Amour!"

"That's Lana," said Caz

"I see her," said Harry.

She was sprinting along the beach.

"What is it?" Harry yelled to her.

Lana yelled a one-word reply: "Door!"

The entrance to the cathedral was at the rear of the building, the doors themselves fifteen feet high and made of dark, weathered timber studded with row upon row of nails whose heads were in the form of pyramids. One of the doors was slightly ajar, though nothing of the building's interior was divulged.

"Anyone else feel that?" Lana asked, touching the back of her neck.

"Definitely." Harry nodded.

Harry had worried that his tattoos, overwhelmed by the danger around him, had exhausted themselves. But now, as he stood before this immense portal, his gaze tracking back and forth over the flow of designs on the arches, he felt the tattoos twitching with full force. Their warnings would not change anything; he had not gone in search of a door only to falter at its threshold.

"All right," Harry said, "just so we're clear on this, there are no heroes here: only dead and not dead. Got it?"

"What happens if you die while you're in Hell?" Dale asked, staring at the crack in the door.

"If you find out," Harry said, "let me know."

And, so saying, he walked into Lucifer's cathedral. As Harry entered, taking three or four steps away from the threshold he paused, waiting for his eyes to make sense of what the interior contained. What he could see when his eyes finally adjusted filled his vision in all directions—from the floor a yard where he stood to the vaulted ceilings held up by twin rows of pillars whose girth would have dwarfed a mature redwood—but precisely what his eyes were witnessing was difficult to comprehend.

Everything that was not essential to the structure itself—the stone, the paved floor, the titanic pillars, the ribbing of the vaults, and the intricate stonework between them—looked spectral, its transparent state allowing him to see through to the layers in all directions. The entire interior seemed to have been filled with the work of hundreds of ambitious scaffold laborers whose efforts defied every law of physics. Gaunt towers rose from floor to ceiling in half a thousand places, lending another solidarity with networks of rods crisscrossed between them. In some places ladders ran up to the heights, while in others there were zigzag stairways that connected tower to tower. And just as he flattered himself that he was getting some grip on the general design, it threw out some startling surprises. In one place the scaffolding seemed to have been possessed by thaumaturgic spiders, creating huge vertical webs that strove for elegance but repeatedly lost themselves to chaos; some were ceaselessly turning spirals, some bearing steps, others bristling with barbs. And all throughout this entire phantasmal interior moved the strangest of machines: forms that resembled gigantic crystalline human skeletons, wearing translucent shells, turning over and over—some in majestic processions, others with solitary grace.

These forms and devices that filled the cathedral were utterly silent, only adding to their mystery. Harry stood watching them for a long time, both mesmerized and vaguely disappointed. None of this sat comfortably with his expectations. His experience of Hell's work on Earth had always been physical. The demonic soul—if such existed—knew the nature of physical being: it was libidinous, and gluttonous, and obsessed with the pursuit of sensation. Harry always imagined that if he ever got close to the Devil he would find that philosophy writ large. He'd always assumed that where sat the Devil so too sat all the excesses of the flesh. But this display of vast whispering forms did not suggest a hotbed of debauchery; rather, this was peaceful—even beautiful in its way. Where the Devil belonged in this world of veils and dreams Harry could not fathom.

"Harold?"

It was Caz's voice that brought him back. Harry looked down from the machines and saw that all eyes were on him.

"Sorry?" he said.

"Did you hear anything I just said?"

He stared at them for a moment, searching for the words to say, and, finding that he had none, simply shook his head in negation.

"Stay with me, okay? We can't lose you," Caz said in a gentle tone.

"Fuck off, Caz. I'm fine. It's just . . . not what I expected."

"Okay. Just checking. I think Dale found the basement."

As if on cue, behind Caz, Dale's head popped into view from below.

"They definitely went this way," he said. "I can still smell 'em. Once more into the breach . . . again."

"I couldn't have said it better myself," said Harry. "Hang on, Norma. We're almost there."

As he spoke, he marched toward the place where Dale's head had emerged. At first it appeared that Dale was floating, but as Harry crossed the vast foyer and drew closer he saw that Dale stood upon a ghostly translucent staircase. Even though he could see that Dale was already standing safely several steps down from him, Harry held out an unwary toe, testing the faint step beneath his foot, and, finding it completely solid, Harry began his descent.

2

"At last, my King lies before me," the Hell Priest exhaled. He was speaking to Norma, who stood next to the demon soldiers in an antechamber at the bottom of Lucifer's vast tower. "Nothing will ever be the same again." Turning to the soldiers, the Hell Priest said, "Your duties are to wait here until you are given contrary instructions."

"Yes, my lord." They spoke in unison, an audible tremor in their voices.

The Cenobite turned his back on them and faced the door. As with everything else in the extravagant cathedral, the door before him was decorated ornately. A craftsman had carved hundreds of lines of hieroglyphics into the wood, their significance beyond the Cenobite's comprehension.

He had educated himself in all languages—even in the semiotics of creatures that barely functioned in the immaterial world, much less that of the solid. And yet a brief scanning of the tiny characters was enough to confirm that the language before him was none he'd ever seen the like of which before. The lesson was plain; however knowledgeable he might have made himself in readiness for this meeting with God's

Most Beloved Angel, there could never be complete readiness, or anything close to it. The digested contents of all the libraries in all of history would not be preparation enough for the encounter that lay ahead.

The Cenobite exhaled lightly and put onto his face an expression of humility. It felt utterly alien to his physiognomy. He was not a creature made for subservience. But he had heard countless stories over the years about how little it took to raise the Devil's ire. He was not about to make that mistake. Not now.

Face fixed, he gripped the handle and turned it. The door responded instantly, though not by opening. A flicker ran back and forth along the minute rows of characters. Here and there glyphs briefly blazed, as though they had caught fire. Some code was at work here, the Hell Priest guessed, letters sacrificed to the flame chosen for some purpose that was beyond his comprehension. The scanning of the lines continued all the way to the bottom of the door and then ceased abruptly.

The Hell Priest waited, concealing his impatience with difficulty. Seconds passed, which became minutes. The door did not move. The Hell Priest was very seldom lost for words or action, but in this moment he was at a loss. Phantom images of events that had brought him to this place and time rose up in his mind's eye, assembling themselves in their entire bespattered splendor: the magicians in their penthouses or their hovels, every one of them spitting out curses as the Cenobite's hooks raked their flesh and bent their bones against nature's intention. All but a few gave up their secrets before being granted a quick dispatch for their compliance.

He saw too the stained and yellowed pages of all the rarest books of magic: books that contained the rites of incantation, and banishment, and laws, and hierarchies, and conjurations, books that he had taken by heart, books that, when he was done with them, had been consigned to the furnace so that he could be the only possessor of the knowledge they had contained.

And all the time—slaughtering, and consuming, and moving on— he'd nurtured the vision of what it would be like when he had learned all there was to learn and was ready to meet the Fallen One, offering himself to the service of greatness. Here he was, ready as he could be, brimming with knowledge and ambition, soaked in murder from scalp to sole—and yet the door would not open.

His fury rose and he raised his hands without awareness of his doing so, unleashing a sound that was the death cries of all those who'd perished so that he might be here. The raised hands closed into fists, and the fists came down upon that intricate, incomprehensible door, carrying in them and behind them the implacable force of knowledge that aspired to deific heights. The sound they made when they struck the door was not that of flesh against wood; it was a sound of seismic proportions, opening fissures in the walls and floors and bringing slabs of marble down from the ceiling. The guards did not disobey their lord's instruction. They stood their ground, striking out at and destroying any falling marble that may have hurt them or their blind cargo.

"What's happening?" Norma wanted to know.

Before any soldier could reply, the Hell Priest's fists came down upon the door a second time, the violence of the blow escalating the damage that the first had done. There was a fissure in the ground a yard or wider crossing the chamber from beside the sealed door to the stairs, which it then ascended, veering from wall to wall. The Hell Priest didn't bother turning back to assess the damage he'd done; the door still mocked him. He paused for a moment to scrutinize the timbers, looking for the merest scratch or crack to indicate that his assault was having some effect. The damn door was unscathed.

He then put his shoulder to it, his entire anatomy swelling with the furies that were running riot in his body. His robes of office, made stiff and brittle by the blood spattered in countless rooms where he had tempted and tortured, split in places, and where the robes were crosslaced with his own flesh the furies now tore new wounds, spilling his own blood down his vestments.

He put his hands into the rivulets, but the blood wasn't coming fast enough to suit his enraged state, so he tore at his chest where his muscle had been permanently skinned and kept from ever healing over by his meticulous scouring of the surface. He went at those chronic wounds with disfiguring vehemence, ripping away the vestments to fully expose his chest where his veins pulsed openly, as though eagerly presenting themselves to pleasure. He then pulled away the shreds of leather and tissue that hung over his belt and selected two of his short-bladed knives—tools he favored for intimate work on particularly defiant individuals—and for the first time in his history, he turned them on himself, using the hooked blade to flick open the veins and the straight one to simply stab into the muscle and bone, then drag the blade up and out before stabbing himself again. The blood leaped from his body. While his veins still gushed, he raised his scarlet fists and slammed them against the door, just as he had done the first time. The blood initiated a new and extremely rapid scanning of the lines of the tiny hieroglyphics; every one of them, it seemed, was combustible.

The Hell Priest, however, wasn't studying the response his assault was having. Fueled by rage, he simply continued to beat the tattoo upon the door, the blood spurting from his chest catching his hands as he slammed them against the wood, over, and over, and over. And then, the sound came, as of a thousand ball bearings all being activated at once.

He stopped suddenly and saw for the first time that the fiery glyphs before him were in motion, flipping over and over, the fire blazing brighter with every turn. He looked down and saw that the pools of blood around his feet were also in motion. In a dozen places at least, the blood had formed separate streams that were disobeying gravity entirely and making their way toward the door. Starting in the bottom right-hand corner and following the indecipherable text from right to left, the glyphs emblazoned on the door briefly burned white-hot and were then consumed, one after the other, until a line was covered, right to left, again and again. The speed of the consumption quickened so that the third line was burned away twice as fast as the first and the sixth twice as fast as the third.

The door was opening.

He had but half a minute to wait before the chamber was revealed to him, and already he felt waves of cold air coming against his face and body. A bitter fragrance stung his sinuses. He turned over in his head the possibility of announcing his presence somehow, but nothing he could conceive of to say sounded anything but pathetic in such momentous circumstances, so he elected to remain mute. The Hell Priest did not doubt that the power waiting inside knew all that it needed to know about its visitor. Better to keep a respectful silence, the Cenobite decided, and speak only when spoken to.

The last line of the glyphs was consumed now, and the door was fully open. He waited, his breath in his throat, thinking perhaps the Devil would offer some words of invitation. None were forthcoming. After some time, the Cenobite took the initiative and stepped over the threshold and into the chamber.

The first thing he noticed was that the light sources in the chamber came from the floor itself; there were thousands of finger-high flames that sprang from invisible sconces in the marble, all burning with a sepulchral chill. Their light illuminated a chamber that bore no resemblance to either the cathedral's grandiloquent exterior or the spectacle of half-made things that had filled its interior.

This place was, the Priest saw, almost as wide as the cathedral above them. Its length, however, was a mystery. The space was occupied by pulleys and pistons, cylinders and crankshafts, all humming in complex configurations over the ceiling, then dropping down to feed into devices that had once clearly been in a delirium of motion. They ran in byzantine patterns, blocking his view and preventing him from calculating the true size of this chamber.

Though the parts had still the shining clarity of well-serviced machines, there was no sign of their having been in motion recently. The pistons were polished but not oiled, and the floor beneath the pipes and the mysterious devices they entered into was dry. There was not so much as a single stain where a drop of fluid had seeped from a joint in need of tightening or from a crack in one of the iron and glass receptacles the size of balled-up human beings that were part of the machinery in a number of places, like parts of an ancient astrolabe. Altogether, they resembled frozen satellites circling a dead sun.

What purpose any of this served was as inscrutable to the Hell Priest as the lines of hieroglyphics on the door. But it wasn't his to understand. He simply followed the parts of the engine as they became larger and therefore, he assumed, of more significance. This truth, however, presented just one problem: the farther he ventured from the door—and thus, he presumed, the closer he came to the creator of all this silent machinery—the more often its mechanisms grew so large they blocked his way completely, and five times he had to investigate until he found a fresh throughway, and by the time he'd done so he was often very far from his projected route. He realized he had come into a labyrinth and he was deep in its coils—not that he cared a whit about the way back; there was no life back there, no pleasure that he would again desire to taste. The sum of his life had led to this maze and the creature waiting at its heart.

Glancing up, he saw that the complex shapes had been cut out of the marble to gain access to the cunningly constructed pipes, so as to have the looseness of sleeping serpents. And there he saw capillaries of glass globes linked by short lengths of tubes no thicker than a finger that dropped in their many hundreds from the ceiling and wound around one another in their lazy descents. There was nothing left in their gleaming beauty that spoke of any recognizable function. He was in a world that had been built by a mind so very far beyond his own that all he could do was hope to glimpse the mysteries it held.

He stopped for a moment or two, just to savor the pleasure that suddenly suffused him. His lord was near. He felt it in his marrow and in the tips of his fingers. He looked up once more and studied the way the ducts led down from the supplementary engines. They were set in the heights of the cathedral and converged—multitudes of beaded pipes and pristine tubes, draining together (or so his limited vision suggested)—no more than ten yards from where he stood.

Had he ever mastered that most elusive piece of magic, which allowed its wielder to pass unharmed through solid matter, he would have walked directly to the part of the convergence where surely his host waited, watching remotely no doubt, to see if the trespasser could prove himself a worthy audience member by getting to the heart of the quieted engines. What would happen then, when he finally reached the throne of his lord? Would a whispered word from the creator set these immense engines into motion and he be rewarded for his tenacity and his ruthlessness by being shown the Devil's masterpiece at work?

He fixed his eyes on the converging arteries and, picking up his pace, made his way toward the spot above which they collected. A turn, another turn, and yet another: the labyrinth teased him with its wiles even now, so close until he turned the last corner and found that his journey was at its end.

3

Harry reached the last step and stood before the Hell Priest's master-work: the shattered remains of the door to Lucifer's bunker. Lana followed shortly after, with Caz and Dale last to arrive. They were all privy to the same sight; something had broken the marbled floor and ceiling wide open just twenty yards from where they had set foot. Cracks spread out in all directions, some of them reaching out far enough to zigzag under the very feet of the weary travelers.

"What the fuck happened here?" Harry said.

At Harry's words, a beleaguered voice called out from within the chamber.

"Harry? Is that you?"

"Norma!" Harry shouted.

"Norma! My God, girl! Where are you?" Caz said.

Norma appeared in the doorway, clutching its frame for support.

"Oh my stars!" she said. "It is you! I didn't believe it, but it is!"

Harry stopped when he saw her state. Though Felixson's magical workings had taken away her pain, they'd done little to heal her broken body, which was now a mass of purpled bruises and weeping wounds.

"Jesus Christ! Did he do this to you? I'll fucking kill—"

"Harry, just hug me, you fool." He did.

"We're gonna get you the fuck out of here. Where's Pin—"

From the dusty shadows behind her stepped the tallest, broadest demons Harry had ever laid eyes upon: Hell's soldiers. Harry reached for his gun. Caz, Dale, and Lana, equally alarmed at the sight of the massive guards, all made for their weapons.

"Norma!" Harry said. "Behind you!"

"Harry D'Amour. Don't you touch that weapon," she chided. "I wouldn't be here if they hadn't carried and protected me. There will be no fight here. I forbid it. You hear me?"

"Norma . . ." Harry said, his distaste for the situation evident in the way he said her name.

"I mean it, Harry," she said as she gestured toward the biggest demon of the bunch. "Knotchee. This is the man I told you about," she said, then, turning to the detective, "Harry, this is Knotchee."

Knotchee squared his shoulders. Harry bit his lip and took his finger off the trigger of his holstered gun. He pointed to the giant demons and said, "I just want you all to know, if she hadn't said what she just said, you wouldn't exist right now."

The demons stood their ground, motionless. Knotchee cracked his knuckles, the bones inside his massive hands popping so loudly the din bounced off the walls of the entryway.

"Okay," Harry said, looking back at his group. "Everyone, make sure Norma gets out of here safely."

"She goes nowhere," Knotchee said.

Harry turned toward the soldier, staring intently at him, while speaking to Norma. "I thought you said these guys were team players, Norma? We're not leaving without you. So tell this fucking mountain to move, or else we will move the fucking mountain."

"Don't threaten me," the demon warned. "I have orders from my lord. A soldier never leaves his post."

Norma turned to Knotchee, laying a gentle hand on his bulbous, veiny forearm.

"I have to go now. Thank you for keeping me safe. Thank you all. But your lord said for you to stay here. Not me."

The other soldiers attempted to protest, but that was as far as they ever got. Norma closed her eyes, and when she did they fell asleep dead away.

"Holy shit, Norma!" said Caz. "I never knew you could do that."

"The old girl still has some tricks up her sleeve," Norma said. "I just wish it would have worked on their lord. We could have ended this fiasco a long time ago. But, my God, he's got power."

"Where is he, Norma?" Harry said.

Norma turned, and with a graceful gesture of her hand indicated the Priest's location inside the chamber.

"Right," Harry said. "Norma, you go with Caz, Lana, and Dale."

"Harry, don't. Let's leave together."

"I can't," Harry said.

"Seriously, Harold?" Caz said. "Leave him. Let's get the fuck out of here." Harry gazed into Lucifer's chamber.

"I have to see," he said.

"No," Dale said. "You have to watch."

"Just go," Harry said. "I'll be okay."

Norma kissed Harry on the cheek, then turned to the Harrowers who began ushering her up the stairs.

"You better fucking come back," Caz said.

"If you do," Lana said," I want details!"

"That makes one of us," Dale said. "I already have enough terrors in my head to keep me rich in nightmares for two lifetimes. See you upstairs, Harry. Hopefully literally. Maybe metaphorically."

Harry silently watched them ascend the stairs and only when he was certain that Norma had been safely delivered into the hands of his friends did he turn to face the chamber. He took a deep breath, then stepped into the room where he would meet the Devil face-to-face.

Harry walked through the maze of technology that was laid out in the vast chamber. His tattoos pulsed as he went, guiding their wearer through the warren of potentially lethal machinery. Slowly, he wove, the sweat beading on his forehead and dripping down the sides of his face. He wondered if he'd ever reach the end. As his tattoos led him through the industrial monstrosity that was this room, his thoughts began to wander. This whole damn thing had started with a puzzle—the simple invention of a humble toymaker—and ever since that moment, Harry's life had been a series of puzzles, mazes, and labyrinths, some physical, some mental, but all challenging beyond belief.

He hoped, after this incident—however it would end—that he at least would be spared from having to solve any more puzzles for a long time to come. And with that thought, Harry's tattoos led him around the final bend. There the Hell Priest stood in front of him, and in front of the Hell Priest, seated on a marble throne, sat the Lord of Hell himself. His robes were white, his skin a mass of purple blotches and yellow stains. His eyes were open, but they saw nothing.

"Dead," the Hell Priest said. "The Lord of Hell is dead."

4

Harry moved closer. As he studied the motionless body, it became apparent that the throne upon which the Devil sat was, for all its fine carving, nothing more than an elaborate death chair. Harry saw now that the machinery through which he had found his way all led ultimately to this fatal throne. The entire room had been set up to activate a fan of spear-length blades, arranged like the feathers of a peacock's tail. These blades had entered the Devil from left, right, and directly below him and summarily exited him in perfect symmetry.

The blades were close to one another and immaculately positioned so that seventeen blades alone emerged from his head, their bright array forming a gruesome halo that stood seven or eight inches off of the Devil's skull. Blood ran down over his face from the seventeen wounds, dried into a purple stain in the curls of his pale blond hair. God, but he had been beautiful, his brow unlined, with almost Slavic features, his cheekbones high, his nose aquiline, and his mouth serene and sensual in equal measure. It was slightly open, as though he might have loosed one last sigh when the suicide machine drove its armory of weapons into him.

There were mirrored arrangements of blades all around his body as well, entering through slits in the marble throne. They pierced his corpse on one side and emerged on the opposite, the glinting, narrow spear-heads seeming to surround his form with signs of glorification, even in death. There was blood from each of these many wounds too, of course, which had soaked into his once-pristine robes, the stains a bright purple in the whiteness of the weave.

"How long . . ." Harry said.

"There is no knowing," the Hell Priest replied. "A thousand days. A thousand years. The flesh of an angel never decays."

"Did you know?"

"No."

"I expected—"

"A mind turned inward for centuries, wholly in search of divinity. In a word: greatness."

"Yes."

"He had seen It, and known It, and been Its most beloved."

"But losing that—"

"Was more than he could bear. I thought he'd seek the Maker's mark inside himself, and take comfort in its presence. But instead . . . this."

"Why the elaborate suicide?" Harry asked, gesturing to their surroundings.

"The Lord God is a vengeful God. Lucifer's death sentence was life everlasting. He was beyond death. He found a means to trick his way past immortality."

As he spoke, the Hell Priest stepped onto the dais and around the side of the throne, where he reached out and seized hold of the end of one of the spears that transfixed Lucifer's corpse. There was a short, sudden sound of numinous voices, and Harry looked back at the Cenobite to see him defiantly holding on to the end of the spear, which was attached, by means of a cable two inches thick, to a defense mechanism that had come into play due to the Hell Priest's proximity to the body. Even in death, Lucifer clearly desired his solitude.

There was a release of energies through the Priest's body that threw him violently about. The Priest stood his ground and so a second shout of voices was released, ten times more violent than the first, the force of the energies passing through the spear commensurately larger. This time, the Hell Priest could not hold on. He was thrown backward, off the dais and through the entrails of the machine.

He had not left the throne without a keepsake, however. He'd held on to the spear long enough to have it slide all the way out of the corpse. As he was pitched across the floor, however, he lost his grip, and the spear ended up no more than a couple of yards from where Harry was standing. The detective stepped a little nearer to it and went down on his aching haunches to look at it more closely. He could not tell what type of metal it was made from. There was a railing iridescence in its substance, which when it had caught Harry's gaze drew him into a place that seemed limitless, as though somehow the angel had caught and sealed a length of infinitude within the spear.

In that moment, the vast engines that filled the chamber beneath the cathedral in all directions made some sense to Harry. He'd seen evidence of almost every kind of magical working with which he was familiar (and many with which he was not) in the labyrinth's devices: ancient icons of primal magic inscribed on devices made of white gold, all shaped to suggest the sexual anatomies of men and women; diagrams that had been etched into polished silver, which were designed—if his memory served—to open doors where there were none. There were more, of course, countless numbers, most of which he'd barely glimpsed. He saw that Lucifer had empowered his final grand act of defiance by drawing together pieces of every magical system that humanity in its hunger for revelation had created, and he had made himself his own executioner, thus successfully bypassing the Will of the Maker.

All this filled Harry's head in a matter of seconds, during which time the Hell Priest had risen from where the blow had pitched him and was coming back at the dais, moving with glacial ease, his hands raised in front of him, motes of glistening darkness pouring from his palms, from the open wounds in his chest, and from his eyes. Harry watched and saw that only at the very last, when the Priest stepped up onto the dais in one stride, did his face betray the fury that was fuelling this counterassault.

He was a creature who held his dignity very high, and the blow from the throne, in casually swatting him away, had violated that dignity. Now he reached deliberately for the throne, despite the power it had just demonstrated, and without hesitation repeated his crime by pulling out a second spear. There was another discharge of energy as he did so, but this time he was ready for it. The black motes that continued to grow in number around and behind him broke like a wave about his head and their dark surf met the force that had emptied from the throne with its own hunger, moving through it like a fervent revolutionary, transforming it as it went.

The Hell Priest was already moving onto the third spear, and the fourth, his face lit from below by the arcs of power leaping from the throne and bursting against his body. If he felt them, he made no sign of the fact; he just went on his business of undoing the death chair's lethal mechanism, one transfixing spear after another. On occasion he separated the serpentine pipe from the handle of the spear into which it fed, releasing a rush of acidic gases. On others he simply pulled the blades directly out of the Devil's corpse, and cast them aside, one upon another, until the dais upon which Lucifer sat had become a nest of metallic snakes forged of alloys unknown to humanity.

The Hell Priest glanced back over his left shoulder and whispered to the assembled darkness, which drew itself closer to him, an anxious ally determined to catch every order that he gave it. Harry watched everything that transpired—his head awash with questions. Was this strange figure—steadily slumping lower in his suicide seat as the blades that had held him were removed—truly the Adversary, Evil Incarnate, the Fallen One, the Satan? He looked too pitifully human sitting there on his death throne. The notion that this thing might have once been God's Most Beloved seemed ludicrous, an urban legend spread by drunken angels. And yet Harry had witnessed enough evidence as to Lucifer's preternatural grasp of occult systems—their code, their sigils, their consequences—to be certain that the creature on the throne was something more than he presently appeared.

Meanwhile the subject of the Hell Priest's whispered conversation with the assembled darkness became apparent as streams of it ran underneath the throne and began the process of removing the spears that had entered the corpse from below. As they went about their labors the Cenobite was pulling blades from the other side of the body, effortlessly transforming the surges of power that flowed from the throne into dark droplets that swelled the thunderhead behind him. Finally, he stood back from the throne, staring down at the Fallen One with hate-filled eyes.

"You expecting him to thank you?" Harry asked.

"There is naught to learn from this pitiful display," the Hell Priest said.

The Cenobite then whispered again to his attendant darkness, and motes of it flew from him like bullets, striking Lucifer's body. For such tiny forms, they possessed uncanny amounts of power. They caught hold of the corpse and raised it up off the throne, its arms outstretched. The allusion to the scene at Golgotha was not lost on Harry; even the way the Devil's head fell forward put in his mind the Man of Sorrows.

While the Fallen One hung there, a hundred or more of the motes swarmed over his body, eating away at the stitches that fashioned the whole of the vestment's many pieces. They came apart effortlessly, revealing behind their sumptuous folds evidence of Lucifer's true nature. Beneath his robes, his entire body was encased in armor wrought from dark metal through which many colors ran like the surface of gasoline on water. Each portion of the armor was immaculately decorated with designs.

For all its exquisite appearance, of course, it had failed in the duty for which it had been forged and hammered: protecting its wearer. That fact, however, meant little to the Hell Priest: it was clear that he meant to have it. And this time the Priest had no need to instruct his creatures. They understood his will perfectly. While Lucifer's body hung before the killing seat, the armor was removed piece by piece from his pale, lithe body.

Harry continued to watch, transfixed, as the Cenobite brought a knife out of a long pocket in front of his left thigh. It was nothing like the other instruments of torture he'd worn on his belt. For one thing it was a much bigger blade, and for another it wasn't caked in blood and chunks of decaying flesh. This weapon glinted in the light. It was obvious to Harry that the knife had never been used. The Priest, it would seem, had been saving it for a special occasion. That occasion now found, the Cenobite slashed at what was left of his black vestments so that they fell away in a foul heap of bloodstained fabric and leather.

He was a patchwork of scars and abrasions, his body resembling—absurd as it seemed—the wall of a cell where countless crazed, raging souls had been incarcerated and all left marks of their presence there: scratches, designs, numbers, faces, there wasn't an inch of the Cenobite's nakedness that did not reveal some piece of testament. He glanced at Harry in this brief moment.

"Angels have a perfect anatomy," the Priest offered. "Few of us are blessed with such a gift."

The Priest then raised the virgin knife and shaved away an inch, perhaps an inch and a half, of the already-skinned muscle of his chest. It curled before his blade, offering itself without protest, the layer of pulpy fat dark yellow, the muscle beneath gray thanks to his bloodletting. Realizing halfway through that the cut was not going to be deep enough to expose the bone, he left off and went for a second slice, which exposed his sternum and a portion of his ribs.

Harry saw that the Cenobite's bones too had been subjected to the questionable horror of being scratched and inscribed in the same fashion as his skin. How that had been achieved was something Harry was neither equipped nor instructed to answer. All he could do was that which the Hell Priest had asked of him: watch.

And watch he did. The Hell Priest continued to saw through the flesh of his chest and on down to his abdomen, opening areas of bleeding muscle with every fresh descent of the blade. At his navel he finally cut the lengthy flank of skin free, and it dropped to the ground in front of him. The Hell Priest feigned indifference, but beads of sweat stood out on his face, gathering in the grooves of his scars.

He took the knife to the fold of excess flesh at his hip and cut off a large piece, which was entirely fat. It had barely hit the ground and he was cutting at the place again, digging deep into the flesh behind the wound he'd already made and using both hands on the knife to make certain the blade kept its course. He came back to the precious cut a full two inches deeper and was rewarded with the sight of blood spurting forth in tiny geysers, then running down the side of his shin. Once he'd turned the corner of his hip he stopped, his breathing hard and raw, sweat running freely from the places where his scars carried it to his jawline.

The Cenobite then turned away, casting his gaze instead on the now naked Lucifer. Each piece of the Devil's armor hung in the air an arm's length from that portion of anatomy where it had been removed. To Harry's eye there was a formal beauty in this, the corpse and its armor entirely static.

As Harry marveled, the Cenobite continued his brutal effort of making new adjustments to his own flesh so as to fit the Devil's suit: first a slice off his other hip, down to the red meat; then up to his arms, slicing away the flesh at the back of his triceps; and passing the knife from left hand to right and back again, cutting effortlessly with either. The area around his feet looked like the floor of a butcher's store. Cobs and slices of fatty meat were scattered everywhere.

Finally, it seemed, the Priest was satisfied. He let the knife drop among the scraps and hackings and then opened his arms, mirroring the position of the Lord of Hell.

"The King is dead," said the Cenobite. "Long live the King."

"Oh shit," Harry said.

Watching the insanity before him unfold, Harry suddenly heard Dale's words echoing in his ears: *Watching isn't the same as seeing.* Harry had spent a lifetime looking. He had watched as Scummy had been burned alive. He had watched a crazed cult leader slaughter his entire congregation. And he had watched a demon drag his friend to Hell. Now Harry realized with terrifying clarity that he no longer wished to be the witness of such sights. This was not the world in which he belonged. Though Hell had come calling on more than one occasion, Harry had always dodged its grip and lived to fight another day. Today, he determined, should be no different. The gripping curiosity to see what came next left Harry in an instant and he decided then that it might be a good time to start running.

5

Harry, running as fast as he could, drew closer to the room's exit when an unsettling din began to fill the room. It was a sound that was difficult to make sense of, drumming that had no real rhythm but came and went from first one side of the cathedral vaults and then the other.

Harry didn't let it slow him down and, as is often the case, the way back proved a far simpler task. In no time at all Harry had navigated his way back into the antechamber at the bottom of the stairs. But, with the terrible din overhead, Harry could hardly feel victorious. He had left his friends in the hopes of keeping them safe. He now hoped with all his might that he hadn't jumped out of Hell's frying pan straight into its fire.

Harry climbed the stairs, preparing himself as best he could for what lay waiting at the top. As long as he kept his focus fixed upon getting his friends out of here, he wouldn't go far wrong. But he had to be quick; they all had to be out of this damn place before the Great Pretender downstairs could make his debut.

There was one last turn on the stairwell, and then Harry was at ground level. Emerging from the hole in the floor, Harry saw his friends standing with the Azeel at the other end of the cathedral, waiting patiently in front of the door.

"Run!" Harry shouted. "Everyone. Fucking run!"

All eyes turned toward Harry, who was winding his way through the forest of phantom forms that thronged the interior.

"Harry!" Norma shouted. "It's all over."

"That's why we need to move! Quick!"

"No, Harold. It's bad," Caz said.

"I fucking know it's bad," Harry said. "You're not listening to me!"

Nobody moved an inch as Harry reached his friends and, running past them, grabbed hold of the ornate polished handle on the door to the cathedral.

"Harry, you're not listening," Lana said.

"No," Harry replied, flinging wide the door. *"You're* not listening. I said—"

Whatever words he'd intended to press past his lips evaporated like water on a desert floor. Harry's eyes widened when he saw what lay outside. As quickly as he opened the door, it was slammed with twice the speed, Harry pressing his back to it in panic.

"There's an army of demons out there," he said. It was then that he realized what the source of the terrible din was.

Dale grabbed Caz's arm out of fear. Caz put an arm around him in an effort to provide comfort.

"Where the fuck did *they* come from?" Harry said.

"Hell, I'd guess. And they are calling for the Priest to give himself up," Dale said.

"Okay. They're not here for us," Harry said to himself. "This could work."

"Work?" Lana said. "Are you completely out of your fucking skull?"

"That's beside the point. We have a very big problem in the basement, and there's an army outside that wants to take care of that problem. The biggest issue now is that we've had the misfortune of being stuck directly between these two fucking obstacles. So, all we need to do is step aside and let them cancel each other out."

"Not your best strategy, Harold," said Caz.

"Harry's right," Norma said. "This fight ain't ours to stop."

And, as if on cue, a series of loud cracks came from under the spot where they all stood, slabs of marble fracturing beneath their feet.

"Fuck me," Harry said. "That'll be King Pinfuck. Listen, the ground's going to give any minute. We need to get out of sight and let whatever is going to happen, happen. The floor will be stronger close to the wall. Let's move."

He barked orders while leading his group to a side of the cathedral, behind two large pillars. By the time they'd reached the pillar nearest to them, the floor was solid beneath their feet.

The din of the approaching army seemed to be coming from both sides of the cathedral. Harry knew that any minute they would be sharing this ground with a great weight of unholy flesh. He just hoped his friends would survive the fallout.

6

The assembly of demons burst into the cathedral with a mingling of veneration and terror. The fog that had concealed most of the building from the outside had left them unprepared for the scale of what awaited them inside. In response, some were so overwhelmed they lost all control over their bodily functions; others dropped to their knees or fell facedown on the slabs, reciting prayers in countless tongues, some simply repeating the same entreaty over and over.

Harry and company had retreated into the shadows, ready for whatever came their way. Every member of his party knew some powerful defensive trick, which they were all quite ready to unleash if the enemy got too close.

But they needn't have worried. The last thing on the mind of this imminent force of demons was a few human interlopers. As the swarms of soldiers filed in, Harry and his friends retreated farther to one of the smaller side chapels, and they gratefully settled there, watching the number of demons entering the cathedral continue to swell, the presence of those at the door forcing the pace of the demons that had first entered. These soldiers had no desire to be pressed on into this mysterious place, with translucent towers and spiraling staircases, against their wills. But such was the size and curiosity of the crowd passing from behind that they could only advance before it and while they advanced let out cries of protest, which were only audible above the murmurs of the assembled masses as incoherent shouts, which were summarily ignored.

Those who had first come into the cathedral and were at the head of the crowd reached the middle of the structure where the violence from below had cracked the marble slabs and weakened the floor. Their collective weight was more than the compromised slabs could support. There were a series of cracking sounds as the fissures spread across the floor in all directions, then dropped away beneath those demons who were forced to venture over this uncertain ground. The din of their cries was loud enough to draw the attention of the leader of this damnedable army: the Unconsumed.

He carved his way through the crowd without meeting resistance, and when he reached the front of the horde the master demon raised his arms and two blazing spirals of light erupted from his hands, rising into the air a dozen yards above his head, where they burst like a vast parasol of iridescent fire, their ridges speeding on past the raw-edged circle of light to burst against the pillars or the walls—whichever they encountered first.

The blaze quickly silenced most of the crowd, but it left unrebuked and unhushed the swelling numbers at the beach, all of whom were being pressured from behind by yet more of the Unconsumed's shapeless army, a vast throng still streaming over the gargantuan tree they had laid over the pristine lake, creating a bridge over which they passed.

The consequences for those already crowding the beach weren't welcome; many had to walk in the shallows of the lake, obliged to venture farther and farther out as the mass of people increased. The Quo'oto was perfectly aware of their situation. It rose to the surface now and then, rolling over sideways as it did so, and, unseen amid the chaos of the assault, silently and routinely snatched several hors d'oeuvres that were stumbling through the water. Inside, of course, there was no knowledge of the mounting chaos on the beaches. The freshly silenced crowd only listened to the words of their leader.

"Silence!" the Unconsumed said, his voice carrying around the interior. "Let us all remember that this is a holy place. There is a power here greater than any below Heaven, and we owe our lives and our devotion to that power."

There was an uncomfortable moment before the first whispers began: "Lucifer, Lord Lucifer."

At the wall of the cathedral, saved from being crumbled by the great mass of demons who had followed the Unconsumed, Harry, his friends, and a small gathering of demons watched as the idol of this great crowd— who were by appearance and number members of every conceivable order of demon—spoke to his followers.

"I fought for you, brothers and sisters," he said. "When you were taxed and every cup of marrow you brought to your table was snatched away again and a great portion of it taken before it was returned I protested. I wept for you, and begged that your agonies be heard and attended to. . . ." He paused, surveying his congregation. "Do you want the truth told? Well?" he said. He had dropped his voice low, to a whisper that nevertheless carried with unnatural force across the cathedral, the proof of its reach in the power of the reply, which came from all directions.

"Yes . . . yes . . ." the crowd said.

"Then I will tell you, because in the end, like all conspiracies, the answer comes down to one."

The word ran murmuring through the huge interior. "One? One. One!"

"Yes, one. One criminal who is at the heart of your miseries. All your suffering. One fiend who passed himself off as a minor tempter of souls, all the while laying his plans against the serenity of the state. The chaos in your streets? He put it there. Is there nothing to buy at your butchers' but bone and gristle? That's because he sells all the finest meat to humankind, who have a taste for themselves that he has nurtured over the years. You will know his face when you lay eyes upon him!"

"Show us!" came a call from somewhere near the door. It was instantly taken up on all sides.

"*Show us!*" they were demanding over and over again. "*Show us! Show us! Show us!*"

The Unconsumed sent up a plume of flame, its color venomous, the light it shed on the upturned forces of the demons illuminating in each evidence of their worst attributes. Their mouths too wide, their eyes tiny darts of malice or simply offering up wide, idiot stares. There were no two faces the same in the many thousands that were illuminated. Each was grotesquely perfected by their revealing light, their ambitions gorged with their joyless faces and burning in their crazed eyes.

The flame the Unconsumed had sent up had virtually silenced the mob *inside* the cathedral, though those outside the entrance continued to bellow and howl.

"Forget them," the Unconsumed said. "They'll have their moment, when I choose and not before. But now, you have asked me to show you the felon who masterminded the many crimes against you. And so you shall see him. This villain had murdered his entire Order. Left a high priest in ruin. He will elude us no more." He threw another flame into the air above his head, where it hung for a moment before plunging back past him, past the platform on which he stood, and down through the gasping marble slabs and onto the secret space below.

Taking his time, so as to squeeze as much drama as possible from the situation, he turned and took a step back from the edge of his platform.

"In here, comrades, is the felon. The thief. The destroyer. His head will roll before this day is done."

"It isn't my time," the Hell Priest said from the gaping hole in the floor.

It was at this moment the Hell Priest rose out of the cracked floor, adorned in Lucifer's armor. Despite the incredible density of the bodies, the crowd still managed to clear a space around the Hell Priest as he made his ascent. When he had fully emerged from the space, he turned to face his supposed executioner.

Without a moment's hesitation the Unconsumed carved a sword of fire and swung it at the Hell Priest, who raised his armored hand and grasped the burning blade. Sparks of white flame spurted from between the Hell Priest's fingers, and he laughed, as though this were the finest sport he'd had in a long time. And while he laughed, and held the blazing sword in his grip, he took time to cast gestures out toward the demon soldiers who stood and watched.

Serpentine chains, hook headed, came weaving between the feet of the spectators, striking with razor edge anyone fool enough to block their way. The condemned knew with the appearance of the first hook what horrors would inevitably follow, and each attempted to outrun the judgment. But the Hell Priest knew his game better than breathing.

Whether his victims fell to their knees and begged salvation, as one did, or tried to outrun the pursuing hooks, as did two more, or simply attempted to go against his enemy as he would any other, with sword and dagger, as did the many, all were lost. The hooks found their eyes, their mouths, their asses, their bellies; and finding them, the hooks dug deep and tore hard, reducing their victims in a matter of seconds into thrashing, incomprehensible knots of twitching muscle.

They made their sounds still, protesting their suffering state, but anything remotely resembling words was beyond them now. The stomach of one had been hooked and hauled up through his throat; the face of another was emerging from his butt hole like a prodigious bowel movement. Their anatomies could not sustain such violent disfigurements. The demons tore, their bodies opening like overripe fruit, spilling their contents as they did so.

Harry had seen this before, but never on so massive a scale. This was full-blown war, all of Hell on one side and a single armored priest on the other. Harry wondered at the ramifications of the chaos that played out before him. If the priest won, would he then take his battle to Earth and the heavens beyond? When would his thirst be slaked? Harry never imagined he'd be on the side of the infernal, watching and even praying for Hell's victory—powerless to do anything else.

Harry remained fixed on the warring figures at the center of this battle. The Hell Priest, content to let his chains dispatch the horde, still had hold of the Unconsumed's fire-edged sword and was bending it back toward its wielder, a trial of strength in which he was steadily gaining the upper hand. He suddenly put all his weight behind the moment, and with a quick twist he had freed the blade from the Unconsumed's grip.

The Hell Priest rose up, the armor feeling good around his body, not like a carapace—hard and brittle—but flowing with him and through him, its power given over to him, wed to him. He was a force unto himself, beyond the reach of any living thing, and though the years that had brought him to this moment had been filled with the most intense personal suffering, it had been worth the agony in order to bring him to this glorious, heart-leaping moment, when Lucifer's armor shot strength into every place where the monkish life he'd lived had left weakness and bliss into the muscles he'd hacked at in order to mold his body to fit the royal armor.

Lords Below and Above, what joy! He'd never felt his flesh and mind and soul in one world like this, a single system, scoured of contradiction. He hadn't lived until this moment.

He saw the Unconsumed from the corner of his eye, his arms raised above his head. Two more swords were being etched out of the incandescent air above the demon's fists, streams of raw lava stuff dropping from their blazing lengths and spreading over the fractured marble floor. The Hell Priest had no fear of walking on liquid fire, not adorned in the full armor of the King of Hell.

He moved toward the Unconsumed and was in front of his enemy in three fire-splattering strides, aiming a sideswipe at his belly. The Unconsumed came back at the Hell Priest with his swords slicing the air like twin threshers. But the Hell Priest was in no mood to retreat; he stood his ground, striking at each of the enemy's swords in turn, the force of his blows enough to slow his adversary's approach a little. But the gusts of wind raised by the threshing swords suddenly caused the flames between the opponents to rise up like a blazing wall, and the Unconsumed came through the fire with his swords spinning.

The Hell Priest raised his own blade to protect his head, and the

Unconsumed's left-handed sword struck it, the impact spitting out serpentine lightning bolts that flew out across the heads of the assembled demons, striking stone dead those stupid enough to reach up and try to grab them. With the Hell Priest's blade locked against one of his own the Unconsumed used the other to strike at his adversary's exposed chest. Surges of power broke over the Hell Priest's armor from the point of impact, their brightness melting into the armor, stealing the energy of the Unconsumed's blow and adding to the armor's power.

The Hell Priest felt the increase of his strength and instantly acted on the knowledge; he took his sword in a two-fisted grip and raced at the Unconsumed, loosing a roar of pleasure. The Unconsumed again raised his left-handed blade to ward off the Priest's attack, but his sword shattered as soon as it was struck, the metal shards going to flakes of fire as they were strewn. The blow was deafening. Every creature in the foyer who had not met an untimely death watched the Unconsumed as he staggered back and gaped at the Cenobite who stood before him.

"What is this magic?" the Unconsumed asked, his voice quivering with cowardice at the prospect of an unfair fight.

"The Crown Jewels of Hell," the Cenobite said.

"It can't be."

"Oh, but it is."

The Unconsumed took several backward steps away from the Cenobite. Quickly he turned to his soldiers and, showering his lips with spittle, howled: "This is the enemy of Hell! He will bring you all to dust if you do not act against him now. I have seen visions. Save Hell before he unmakes us all!"

His words died into darkness, leaving the air empty.

"Visions?" said the Hell Priest as he approached the Unconsumed.

"I've seen your ambitions, Priest," the Unconsumed said, staggering back.

"You couldn't possibly," the Cenobite said. Then, turning to the soldiers, he gestured to his suit of arms. "The armor I wear is a gift from Lucifer, who is reborn in me. My authority is now absolute. My word is now law."

"Madness!" said the Unconsumed. "Soldiers! This is your hour! I have brought you to your enemy. Now it falls to you! You must take him out of this sacred place, and tear him to pieces! Don't listen to his lies. He's afraid of you! Don't you see that? You have righteousness on your side and he has nothing. *Nothing!!* He came here only to steal from our lord Lucifer—hallowed be his name—in his place of meditation. He's admitted to it! The armor belongs to the Morning Star! And I believe our lord would be bountiful in his thankfulness were you to tear it from this vile thief's back."

The Unconsumed's speech worked. The crowd roared an immediate "Aye!" and as they did so the Unconsumed drove the point of his blade into the conflagration above his head. It instantly refracted the light in a blazing show that spat incandescence out across the length and breadth of the cathedral's foyer.

The single, booming "Aye!" became stronger as the beams exploded against the stone walls, blowing ragged holes in them, none of them less than ten feet across, many twice that.

"*Enter all!*" the Unconsumed yelled, his voice possessed of a magnitude that carried his words to the hordes cramming the beach around the building. "And destroy!"

Harry and his friends retreated farther into the shadows as tens of thousands of demons who'd been denied access seethed in through the ruptured walls, their bony backs all pressed together resembling a stream of cockroaches bubbling as they climbed over one another and dropped into the morass of those who'd climbed onto the ledge and fallen over the other side ahead of them.

This mad flood of invading demons filled up a space that was not meant to hold more than a fraction of the crowd, their rage fueled by a visionary hunger to be at the heart of the baptism that they had glimpsed in their dreams all their lives. "Aye!" they had screamed. "Aye!" to the blood and light and "Aye!" to martyrdom, if that was to be the price of their presence here.

The Hell Priest knew that he had a chamber the size of a small nation to witness to, and he knew there was a sight that would bring an end to the spiraling insanity that had been set in motion by the Unconsumed. Let them have proof that the great lord was not mediating from below; let them see for themselves.

"Gaze upon the fallen fruit!" the Cenobite shouted. "Your glorious leader talks of Lucifer's eternal meditation on the nature of sin. Your glorious leader has deceived you. I shall show you the angel Lucifer. In all his soiled glory."

He threw a gesture of force on the ground, which opened beneath him, taking out a hundred or so soldiers with it; then he descended for no more than a few seconds and rose again into view again with Lucifer's corpse held, limp, in one hand. It was a pitiful sight, hanging from the Hell Priest's grip, a sack of broken bones, with a grainy gray face clipped from the book of atrocities, eyes sunk in, mouth gaping, nose crushed against his face so it was little more than two holes.

"This—" the Hell Priest said, his voice once again the raw, intimate whisper that was audible to who were assembled there "—is the lord for whom you fight." He rose as he spoke, climbing effortlessly through the thickening soup of stale and sour that was the air until he was perhaps twenty feet above the crowd. There he turned and let go of the corpse, which tumbled back down the flame-licked dais, through the hole the Hell Priest had used for his descent, and out of sight.

7

An intense hush had grown over the army so that the only sound audible was the steady lapping caress of the flames. The Unconsumed, clearly as surprised to see his fallen lord as the rest of his army, struggled to maintain his rapidly crestfallen soldiers.

"The fiend has murdered our King!" the Unconsumed shrieked. "He must be destroyed! Advance!"

But they did not. Slowly, but in steady droves, the Unconsumed's minions were turning inward to face the Unconsumed, until his entire army faced him, looks of betrayal and condemnation on their faces.

"Have you lost your minds?" the Unconsumed shouted.

"Most likely," the Hell Priest answered. "They see their reflections stripped of lies. The burden of truth is too great, Your Lordship. It is my pleasure to introduce you to *my* army. It is the last thing you will ever see."

The Priest then loosed a war cry that echoed off the walls of the cathedral, repeating in the ears of every being present. He raised his arms and came at the Unconsumed, conjuring a sword in his right hand. In the blink of an eye the Priest took off the Unconsumed's arm just above the elbow and drove his sword through it for good measure. This was the first injury the Unconsumed had sustained in centuries. The shock of the trauma caused him to vomit up a series of flames and he began to babble an incoherent glossolalia.

In taking those few moments to expose the extent of his weakness, the Unconsumed had left himself open to attack from the rest of the army. And they took the opportunity, in a rushed and panicky fashion, eager to get the job done as quickly as possible. The Unconsumed had four blades in his back by the time he turned to face his betrayers, and twice that number of wounds—the most severe a strike at the back of the neck, which had clearly been intended to take off his head and might have done so had he not retaliated by reaching over with his remaining hand and seizing the blade as it cut into his flaming flesh, melting it in an instant.

"Assassins!" he roared, the flame from his severed arm taking the form of a monstrous scythe. It was every bit as powerful as its iron equivalent. It took the legs out from seven of his enemies and bisected an eighth at his waist.

While the Unconsumed used his scythe to deface and butcher the men whose legs he'd sliced off, one who'd so far survived this massacre came at him from behind and with one clean stroke sheared off the scythe arm at the shoulder. The Unconsumed reeled around to face his mutilator, only to meet a hundred more living assassins who came at him without restraint—slicing, hacking, gutting, piercing—their assaults so rapid that the lethal conflagrations stoked in the Unconsumed's marrow, fires that would have made ash of his assassins in a heartbeat, were never unleashed.

The rest was just a graceless, joyless unmaking, the thing on its knees, the thing dropping onto one surviving arm, and then down onto its elbow, and then down onto its side, barely distinguishable from the furnace litter of burning legs, and two pieces of his own arm, also burning, and from everything now a greasy black smoke rising up, which smelled to Harry, when the smoke reached him, like a burning heap of trash.

"And so it ends," the Hell Priest said. "I have had a vision these many years, that when I had readied myself in every way I knew how, I would lead an army out of this abyss which we have suffered for the sins of the Fallen One."

He tapped his brow. "In here are all the great workings that once belonged to the magicians of the Overworld. They did not surrender them lightly. Many fought me bitterly. I was not impatient. I knew this day would come in the fullness of time, and my duty was to come to you on that day with every power our adversaries had ever owned in my head. With the knowledge I own I could kill the world ten thousand times and raise it again ten thousand more and never once repeat the same trick. So now, the road divides. I have pieces of this magic to give to those who will come with me. Who will join me as we lead the lambs to their slaughter?"

The response from the crowd was like the sound of some vast animal, roaring as it woke. As the army unleashed its primal cry, a veil of shadow rose up from the hole in the cathedral floor and the fractured ground beyond it. It rose into the air behind the Hell Priest, some portions of it climbing faster than others, shedding a darkening dust as they did so.

The sight had not been missed by the demons in the cathedral. At first they had assumed it to be another conjuration of their new and glorious leader. But the confident shouts of their assumption soon gave way to superstitious murmurs as the shadow curtain continued to climb, its shed dust spreading the message as every one of the flames atop the torches gathered was extinguished, the smoke of their dying adding to the sum of shadows that thickened the air.

"What impotent magic is this?" the Hell Priest said.

The shadows were overtaking the cathedral. They rose all the way to the ceiling and spread to either wall until there was nothing to illuminate the interior except for the last embers of the dying fire.

And then even they were gone, and the cathedral was a night within a night from end to end. The demons began to voice their doubts.

"Lord, speak to us!" one called.

And another: "Is this a test of our faith?"

"I have faith, Lord."

A thousand murmured, "Yes!"

"We all have faith."

"Take it away, Lord. It blinds us!"

The cries from the crowd stopped suddenly when a flicker of lightning came in the darkness behind the platform, and with it a voice, great and resonant.

"Who has defiled my sanctuary?" said the voice, and the veil of darkness was lifted.

8

The illuminated figure of Lucifer stood naked in the air. It was an extraordinary sight. Harry was astonished to see, now that the King of Hell no longer sat bowed and broken, he stood easily eight feet tall.

Lucifer's anatomy was human, but there were subtle changes to his proportions that lent it an extreme eloquence entirely its own. His limbs were long, as were his neck and nose, his brow uncommonly broad and untouched by a single groove of doubt. His genitals were of uncommon size, his eyes of uncommon blue, his skin of uncommon paleness. His hair was cropped so close to his skull it was barely visible, but it seemed to have a luminescence, as did the faint growth of hair on his face and neck and the hair that spread over his chest and belly and grew lushly at his groin.

Not a soul dared speak. This time, it seemed, even the flames burning within the cathedral stood in silent attendance waiting for Lucifer to utter his next words. When he finally did, light emerged from his throat and illuminated the cloud of fog on which his words were carried.

"I was the best beloved of the Lord God Jehovah," he said, spreading his

arms out to his sides to present himself. *"But I was thrown down out of the loving presence of my father because I was too proud and too ambitious. He meant to punish me with His absence, which was so great a punishment my soul could not endure it. Though I tried, the grief was too great. I wanted an end to the life my Maker had given me. I wanted to be gone forever from being and knowing, which are the pieces of suffering. So I died from this life. I was free. Laid to rest by my own hand in a tomb beneath a cathedral I had built at the edge of Hell . . ."* His voice softened as he spoke about his freedom, dying away until it was barely audible. And then, rising steeply out of that hush, a roar of fury:

"BUT DEATH IS DENIED ME! I WAKE NAKED, IN THE SQUALOR OF MY RUINED CRYPT! AND IN MY SANCTUARY, WHERE I WAS TO PASS AWAY THE AGES IN THE ARMS OF SILENCE, I FIND A MASS, STINKING OF MADNESS AND MURDER, WALLOWING IN BLOOD RAGE—DESPOILING MY PLACE OF OBLIVION."

He was still for a moment, letting the echoes of his outcry, which seemed to last minutes, die away. When he spoke again his voice was not loud, but the syllables resonated in the skulls of everyone in attendance.

"Why am I naked?" the Fallen One said, turning instantly to face the Hell Priest, who stood donning the Devil's armor. The Cenobite said nothing. The Devil smiled. Again, he asked the question, his tone taking on a sickly seduction. *"Why am I naked?"*

Harry watched from the safety of his hideout, refusing the urge to blink.

"Come on," he whispered so quietly that not even Norma, who stood by his side, clutching his arm, could hear. "Kill the bastard!"

The Priest spoke.

"You were dead, my King," the Hell Priest said. "I came for you. My entire life was—"

"—a preparation for the moment we would meet," Lucifer said.

"Yes."

"Not even death can save me from this torture of repetition."

"My lord?"

"I have heard this story. I have seen you. I have seen all of you! In countless incarnations!" the Devil shouted to the crowd who attentively watched his every move. When he spoke again, it was slow and deliberate. *"I do not want this anymore."*

He stepped into the air as he spoke, reaching for the Hell Priest as he did so. But the armor that he'd once worn had new allegiances now, and it responded to Lucifer's approach by unleashing defensive cords of light that unwove themselves as they struck the newfound enemy.

In an instant the Cenobite's fear evaporated. The suit had accepted him as its owner, his magic was infinitely stronger than it had ever been, and the Devil stood before him, naked and wan. The war was not over. The victor had not yet been decided. The Hell Priest took a deep breath and then uttered the fatal summoning syllables of the Eighth Engine:

"Uz . . . Yah . . . I . . . Al . . . Ak . . . Ki . . . Ut . . . Tu . . . Ut . . . Tu . . . J eh . . . Maz . . . Az . . . A . . . Yah . . . Neh . . . Ark . . . Bej . . . Ee . . . Ut . . . Tu."

Barely had the flow of sounds come to a halt than the power in the words rose up, creating a stench, the stink of life and death rolled into one monstrous river of sentient grease, where the secrets of the world's beginning and, no doubt, the secrets of its end were circling together in the same irresistible liqueur. All planet-killing plagues were here, circling in the air around his head—so too their antidotes, were anyone patient enough to track them down in the toxic populace of insanities and sicknesses. This was what the Hell Priest wanted and he sank his hands wrist deep into the Other Muck.

Instantly the Muck responded, not only snaking up over him but also narrowing its painless way into his flesh and bone and marrow so that its swampy substance took possession of him. It was only when it rose up his spine and started to pump its potent stuff into his head that he felt a spasm of unease. To have this primal power in his limbs and heart and belly was one thing; to have it in his mind, where he had always ruled unchallenged, refusing to indulge in even the most modest of mind-altering stuffs in order to keep his thoughts untainted, was not so welcome. The fluid seemed to sense his momentary resistance and, before he could protest any further, it flooded his head completely.

He let out a single grunt, and his body—still held aloft by his elite armor—stiffened. Then the Hell Priest started to slowly rise up into the horizontal position. As he did so the perfect symmetry of his scarified face was destroyed by the creation of new veins clawing their way across his pierced visage, the magic he summoned carving levels of power his anatomy had not been designed to contain on to his body. It not only forged new veins for his face, but it surged through the muscles underneath Lucifer's armor, making them swell until the angelic shell creaked with the pressure from his burgeoning body beneath.

All of this—from the speaking of the syllables to his new position, standing in the air—had taken mere seconds, during which time the Priest's eyes remained closed. When the display came to its end, Lucifer spoke.

"Have you anything else to say?"

"Only this," said the Hell Priest as he opened his eyes, and into his vein-laced hands sprang two curved blades—tricks of his newborn will. The Priest then pitched himself at the onetime King of Hell, and both titans gave free rein to their unrepentant furies.

9

The battlefield inside the cathedral had changed in nature several times. The fight, at first waged by demons who seemingly neither knew nor cared whose side they were on, now transformed into a bloodletting that had entered what was surely the final phase, in which the two central figures circled each other high above the heads of a mass of mutant demons, each collision of their weapons throwing off layers of blazing air.

It was still an astonishment to Harry, seeing the creature—one he'd assumed was a minor tempter in the infernal pantheon—so transformed by the fruit of his crimes (his murders, his thefts, et cetera) that now he was meeting in battle Lucifer himself as though they might be equals. The two forces of nature exchanged no words; they simply clashed and circled and clashed and circled again, each possessed, it seemed, of an unequivocal desire to eradicate the other, to hack from that other life with such ferocity it would be as though the other never existed.

As a result, the clamor of war cries died away; the only sounds audible were the din of Cenobite and the Prince of Darkness delivering their rage-fueled blows. The Priest's newly recruited army had pared down to a core of maybe a thousand demons who silently watched and championed the cause; the rest were gone, because they'd either sustained from Lucifer a fatal blow or simply lost the stomach for the battle and fled the arena. Even the complaints and entreaties of the dying (the demons, like humankind, more often than not called for their mothers in the end) had diminished.

The reason for all this was not hard to fathom; the waves of energy released from the clash of Lucifer and the Hell Priest was one blow more than most of them could take. Now there were just a few survivors at far corners of the cathedral, where the euthanizing waves did not break, and even they were growing steadily weaker as their blood and breath trickled out of their pierced bodies. The immense space, which had but a few hours before been empty and pristine, was now a crumbling slaughterhouse with two forces of immeasurable power battling above the corpse-strewn ground below.

Harry doubted very much that the Hell Priest cared about or even remembered him or his Harrowers at this point. The battle against Lucifer consumed the Hell Priest's attentions entirely. The swords they wielded were not the only weapons at their disposal, of course. Lucifer's eyes, skin, breath, and sweat were all instruments of power in their own right, while the Hell Priest's syllable-summoned energies continued their expansion, surging through the design of the armor, spitting thorny cords of black lightning that wrapped around Lucifer's limbs, tearing open grievous wounds.

There were enough felled bodies now for their departure to go unnoticed. And with the Hell Priest and the Fallen One still engaged in their furies, there would not be a better time to slip away with their lives intact.

"All right. Time to move," Harry said. "We gotta get the fuck out of here before they're done comparing dick sizes. Is everyone ready for this?"

"I'm ready," Norma said. "I can't stand the smell of this place."

"I couldn't agree more," Lana said.

"Hear! Hear!" Dale said. "Let's get this business finished so we can all fuck off home."

Harry and his Harrowers made their way around the fractured ground from which Lucifer had risen up, and moved steadily toward one of the holed walls, unnoticed. Harry kicked one of the bodies out of his way to carve a path for Norma and, as they moved forward, a deep, booming voice addressed them.

"You will bear witness to how this ends!" it said. They all turned to see that the Priest's eyes were upon them; or rather, upon Harry. "The story is nearly at its conclusion. You cannot leave now. Not before the tale is told."

Harry felt his body freeze. Not in attendant terror, but in a physical response to an unheard utterance. He made to move, to shout, to save his friends from the same fate, but he could do none of these things. He could only feel his body turning, against his will, to face the furious battle that raged overhead. The Priest had ensnared Harry. He was in thrall to the Cenobite's edict: witness.

Harry had objected to the Priest's demands but, from the very out-set, had played directly into them, he now realized. He had borne witness to the Priest's great exodus, the resurrection, and was now forced to watch the final victory. The Priest, it was clear, was not about to let Harry escape until this terrible story was at its end. It would seem Dale's prescient advice was for naught. Now, when the will to look away was strongest, Harry was powerless against his body's dictate.

And then he heard his friends' voices in the distance.

"Fuck a duck," Dale said.

"Fuck him!" Caz shouted. "Let's keep moving. What's he gonna do, stop fighting the Devil?"

"Caz!" Lana shouted.

"Don't look back! It's what he wants."

"No! Caz!" Norma protested. "It's Harry!"

"We have to keep—" Harry heard Caz's words escape him and then, "Harold! What the fuck?"

Harry put every ounce of faltering strength into his muscles, screaming at his body to listen to him. One last favor was all he asked, and then he'd be content to do its programmed bidding. His muscles twitched and strained, but he felt them moving, slowly, painfully. At last his eyes met Caz's. Tears fell from Harry's eyes and his lips struggled to find the freedom to speak. In a tortured drawl, Harry uttered a single word:

"Go."

"No fucking way, Harold!" Caz began to protest.

"Promise me!" Harry begged.

Caz reached for him and a shock wave spat forth from Harry's body, sending Caz flying back and to the ground. Harry apologized with his eyes. Had he the power to change this, he would, but he only had power enough for one more word:

"Promise."

At that, his head snapped back into its requested position and he watched the respective blades of Priest and King spark as they struck each other once more. Harry steeled himself, ready to watch this tableau play out to its bitter end, while in the distance he heard his friends continue their getaway, mournful sobs escaping them as they exited the sanctuary.

10

Lucifer and the Hell Priest were still locked in battle, though it was clear from the slow strikes of their weapons, and the way their heads hung down between each strike of blade against blade, that they were fighting with the very last resources of energy they owned.

The Hell Priest had begun to utter what sounded like a cross between a chant and an equation: numbers and words intertwined. As he spoke he moved with startling speed around his enemy, avoiding Lucifer's blade and dropping down as he did so until he was standing on the bodies below. The combination of words and numbers he was giving voice to was working some abnormal change in the dead and the dying. The process of decay seemed to have quickened in their flesh; their muscle was seething as though flies had taken it for their laying place.

He cast his swords away even though Lucifer was circling above him, preparing to swoop and deliver the killing stroke. The Priest then stretched his arms out in front of him, palms down, and lifted his hands up to his chest. Whatever life-in-death he had seeded in the killing fields on which he now stood, he was taking it back and sowing it into himself.

At his feet the dead twitched violently as the Hell Priest's litanies and equations drew back every last bit of demonic force from their desiccated corpses. It made a furnace of his body, in which the bones blazed bright and his organs liquefied any impurity found within the vessel that was his body. The impurities spilled from the confines of his anatomy. He bathed in them as they flooded out of his pores, eyes, ears, nose, mouth, cock, and asshole. His body purged every last bit of imperfect flesh from every opening it could find, creating a being beyond entropy. A being that no longer had need of lungs for breathing and bowels for shitting. A being that fed itself its own blazing substance.

And, as Lucifer touched down and prepared to strike, the Priest's flesh let off a blinding brilliance. Lucifer shielded his eyes, as did every other living thing in the room save for the Hell Priest, who welcomed the death of his old body. He was still spilling the sequences of syllables and numerals that had initiated the working, the corpses beneath him twitching and rolling in response to his instructions, but suddenly, the sequence of words and numbers reached a point of no return, and the blazing transfigurations in the Hell Priest's body became a single rushing motion, each bright strand of ligament momentarily clear to Harry as a soul, stolen from the heap of corpses on which the Hell Priest had prepared his last show of empowerment. Then he was looking at Lucifer, who was eagerly preparing the next phase of this battle.

As the Devil began his assault, however, the Hell Priest reached out with limbs of fire and caught hold of Lucifer by the neck. Lucifer stabbed at him from left and right, but the Priest's body was no longer susceptible to such assaults. Tongues of white fire emptied from the wounds, spilling out and knotting themselves around Lucifer's sword and up around his hands and arms. Lucifer let out a bellow of rage and struggled to free himself, but his enemy's protean body spat fresh cords of flame that caught him by his genitals.

Lucifer made one more attempt to press the point of his sword into the priest, shifting its target from torso to head. The Hell Priest responded by bending Lucifer's arms behind his back on themselves, grinding their joints to bloody dust, and cracking the bones in a dozen places. The sword fell from Lucifer's grip, and the Priest with one quick motion snapped every finger on each of his opponent's hands to be certain they would never pick up another weapon.

Harry watched in breathless anticipation of Lucifer's reprisal. But, much to Harry's horror, none came.

"Is this the end then?" the Hell Priest said.

If Lucifer had any answer, he was beyond giving it in words. All he could do was raise his heavy head to meet the Hell Priest's gaze.

"Death, be not proud . . ." the Hell Priest said.

As he spoke a host of fiery forms sprang from his body—some little more than threads of incandescence, others like the multi-jointed limbs of insects in fire all barbed with flame—which wove between one another in their thousands as they leaped a dozen feet clear of their master's body before turning and speeding back toward their victim.

Harry's trance upon the spectacle alone had been so intense that he had noticed nothing else, and he watched the imminent execution with dread. There were even more piercing extractions from the Hell Priest's body now, all swaying in the same tide as they awaited the instruction to deliver the coup de grâce.

Lucifer seemed unwary of their presence. He no longer strained forward to address his executioner but let his head sway back, his eyes rolled up beneath his fluttering lids, while further cries, all diminishing in volume, escaped his open mouth. With the battle won and the coup de grâce his to deliver when he chose, the Hell Priest surveyed the angelic form before him.

The Cenobite closed his eyes for a moment, his lips moving, as though he was offering up a silent prayer. Then, as he opened his eyes, the weapons of execution that he'd called up out of his own flesh—from the finest thread to the most brutal barb—flew at the Morning Star.

No part of his body was exempt from the assault. The largest of the Hell Priest's weapons punched its way through Lucifer's chest and, writhing wildly, burst out between the scars on his back where his wings had once been rooted. The assault was merciless: one mote struck his Adam's apple, three flew between his teeth with unerring accuracy, another pinned his tongue to his lower lip, and a scalpel-headed dart punctured the sighted sac of his left eye, its bloodied fluids spilling down his face.

Lucifer spasmed and writhed as the first weapons pierced him, but the more he was struck the less he responded, and soon he was no longer moving at all. Wounded in perhaps a half a thousand places, he lay still at the Priest's feet.

The Hell Priest scanned the cathedral, which was still lit by the energies this struggle had loosed. For all the slaughter that had gone on here, there were plenty of survivors. Many wore wounds that would have killed a mortal man, but there were enough who had survived the battle with barely a scratch.

All remaining eyes were on the Hell Priest as he stood triumphant over his enemy. Cords of energy that had spilled from his anatomy to bring Lucifer down hung slackly from his body, still connecting the two, like a napalm umbilicus. The Hell Priest let that hang there, proof to all who had eyes in their heads that he had indeed been the author of Lucifer's second fall.

Then, spreading his arms, he delivered his soliloquy:

"I know that many of you brought ancient enmities into this place. You had scores to settle, and you came here not because you cared who sat on the throne of Hell, but because you wanted to murder some enemy under the cover of battle." There were plenty of guilty glances exchanged here and one or two even made to speak in their defense, but the Hell Priest had more to say. "I am your King now. And as such, I command you to put your vendettas away, forget the past, and follow me out of this place to do a better, more terrible work."

The silent seconds passed. And then a great battle cry of affirmation rose from every direction.

11

The husk of flesh that was now the Morning Star reached out and caught hold of the Hell Priest's foot.

"*Enough,*" he pleaded.

For a moment the Hell Priest simply stared down at his adversary in disbelief, and then he began to struggle to free himself.

But Lucifer, despite his injuries, had no intention of letting the Hell Priest go. He reached up with his other arm, which had acquired in its shattered state the uncanny fluidity of a tentacle, and seized the vestments he'd once lain down to die in. With his grip on them secured, he lifted himself up and stood face-to-face with the Hell Priest, his body still pierced in countless places, blood running freely from his wounds, gathering in rivulets that coursed down his legs.

Lucifer drove his hands into the Hell Priest's abdomen. The Hell Priest screamed as Lucifer took hold of his guts. The weapons the Cenobite's body had produced to bring the Devil down withered now, as the Hell Priest recalled energies that had fueled them, in the hope of putting up some defense against Lucifer, but the Devil had him in his grasp now, and he wasn't about to let his wounder go. Lucifer reached still deeper within the body of the Hell Priest, taunting him as he did so.

"Spit out some magic, fool." He dragged a length of gut out of the Hell Priest's belly and pulled it, uncoiling the demon's entrails. *"And stop that wretched din. I thought you* liked *pain."* He let go of the gut, leaving the loop to fall between the Hell Priest's feet. *"Why would you have these"*— he ran his bloody broken fingers over the nails in the demon's head—*"if it wasn't for the pleasure of the pain?"* He then balled his fists, snapping the broken ligaments of his fingers back into place. He brought thumb and forefinger to the Cenobite's face and selected one of the nails from the creature's cheek. He pulled. With a little persuasion, he worked it out and revealed that more than half of the nail's length had been buried into the Cenobite's bone.

The Hell Priest was too stricken to do anything by way of reply. Lucifer dropped the nail and chose another, working it free and dropping it again, then moving on to a third and fourth. Blood ran down the grid of scum that covered the Cenobite's face. He was no longer screaming. Whatever agony he'd felt as his entrails had been torn from him was inconsequential compared to the defacing he was now enduring. Lucifer was plucking the nails out randomly, his pace quickening. Finally, the demon spoke.

"Please," the Hell Priest begged him.

"A protest you've no doubt heard a thousand thousand times."

"I have."

"You traveled across the wastelands of Hell and battled Lucifer. You are unique, Cenobite. And yet your life is in my hands and you're reduced to a simpering cliché."

"It's . . ."

"Yes?"

The Hell Priest shook his head. Lucifer replied by plucking another nail, and another and another. Desperate to stop him, the Cenobite began his confession again.

"It is who I am."

Lucifer paused to look at the nail he'd just pulled free of the

Cenobite's face. *"This rusted piece of metal? My apologies. You should have it back."* He tore away the collar of the vestments, and drove the nail into the Priest's throat, hammering it all the way in with the heel of his hand.

At that, Harry felt the Cenobite's thaumaturgic grip on his body released. Harry fell to the ground and sucked in great gasping breaths. Even his lungs had been in service to the Priest's whim. Harry collected himself and, content in the knowledge that he had witnessed the end of this scene and indeed the end of an era—and potentially a war that might have spread over Heaven and Earth—he began to crawl in the direction of the nearest felled wall. He had no need to watch the killing blow. He only wished to be again with his loved ones.

As Harry made his way out of the sanctuary, the Hell Priest reached up to Lucifer's face and would surely have put out the angel's un-wounded eye if he'd had the chance, but Lucifer was too quick to lose the advantage. He batted the Hell Priest's hands away.

"You had your moment," he said. *"Now it's gone and it won't come again. Say your prayers, child. It's time for bed."*

Harry exited the cathedral. He could hear all manner of sounds: shouts were heard from demons watching the final struggle of the Hell Priest and Devil, moans unintended from the dying, and other sounds that perhaps emanated from Lucifer's attack on the Cenobite—the tear-ing of fabric and of flesh, the breaking of bones.

Harry clambered up and over the last heap of bodies and came in sight of his exit. There were still demons lingering around the threshold, apparently uncertain of whether they should venture in or not. Harry wove his way between the loiterers and out into the open air. There his friends were waiting for him at the edge of the lake.

"Harold! Thanks fucking Christ!" Caz said as he ran to his friend. "I fucking told them I was giving you five more minutes and I was com-ing in to get you!"

Harry took in the scene. Despite the colossal tree that had been placed across the lake, and the hordes of demons who scrambled to cross it as they fled from the infernal war zone, the lake was a bit more placid than it had been when Harry and his cohorts had first ventured around the cathedral and the Quo'oto had been turning the waters white in its frenzy. The sight of the dark lake and the starless sky above it was wonderfully soothing after the slaughterhouse scenes they'd left behind them. Caz walked Harry toward the water's edge and stood staring out at the tabula rasa before him.

"Done dancing with the Devil, D'Amour?" Dale asked.

"Never," Norma said, answering for Harry. She was more right than he cared to admit.

"What the fuck happened in there?" Lana said.

"It's not important," Harry said. "Here's something you'll only hear me say once: let's follow these demons."

Norma laughed. "That's the fourth time I've heard you say that."

"I missed you, Norma," Harry said. "Let's get you home."

The Harrowers turned toward the makeshift bridge, where the large number of survivors had decided to retreat from the cathedral, many with blood streaming from their wounds and still carrying a knife or a sword to defend themselves if the need arose, but there was little antagonism among the exiting crowd. They were too anxious to be out of the cathedral—away from whatever was now happening inside—to be picking fights with one another, or anyone else for that matter.

As Harry and his Harrowers moved to cross the bridge, from the cathedral Lucifer's booming voice could suddenly be heard:

"I was an angel once! And I had such wings! Oh, such wings!"

Everyone looked toward the cathedral, where cords of light now danced against the few walls that remained.

"But they are just a memory now," he continued, *"and I am left with a pain I cannot endure. Do you hear me? Do you hear me!"*

The repetition of his question was painfully loud, even to those standing outside the cathedral's walls. The building, for all the pillars and buttresses that supported its immensity, shook as the Fallen One's voice grew louder. Stone dust fell in fine dry rains, the escalating growl of stone grinding on stone.

"*I was finished with my life,*" the Devil said, "*finished with this Hell I built. I was dead, and happy. But it seems I cannot be certain of death until I bring all of this down on our heads, and there is no Hell to call me back again.*

"*Hell is finished. Do you understand? If you have other places to go, then go while you can, because there will be nothing left when I am done.* Nothing!"

12

By the time the quartet of Harrowers, plus Norma, began their return journey away from the cathedral, all of Lucifer's audience had grasped the profound seriousness of their situation and were departing by any means available. There were fissures in the walls now, rising from the ground like black lightning, the flying buttresses crumbling as the connecting stonework fractured and fell away, the capitulation of each buttress putting the central structure in even greater risk of complete collapse upon itself.

"What happens when we get off the island?" Caz said as they went. "How do we get back home?"

Harry threw him a despairing glance. "I don't have a fucking clue. But that old demon woman mentioned something about getting home, so I think we need to pay her a visit. As far as I can tell, we *did* make it out alive."

"But will we make it out with our sanity intact? is the question," Norma said.

"All I know," Lana said, "is that I'm taking up alcoholism when this thing is over."

"Make it a double," Dale said.

The exodus from the cathedral was a chaotic flood of frightened demons; many of them, in their haste to be away from the failing building—and even and even more urgently from the creatures inside—were running through the shallows of the lake, so as to avoid the crowded beach. It was only a matter of time before their plunging through the water drew the attention of the Quo'oto.

The beast surfaced suddenly, in a great explosion of foaming water, and seemingly dislocating its lower jaw so that it protruded much farther than the upper, it easily scooped up twenty demons in one pass. Then it threw back its head, tossing its catch down its black throat, and plunged into the lake again only to surface less than a minute later to do the same thing farther down the beach, closer to the front door.

Its appearance did little to dissuade many of the crowd from running out into the water almost immediately, preferring to risk being taken by the beast than to be anywhere near the cathedral. Their frenzy was understandable. The roof was beginning to collapse now, churning up dust that was illuminated by a flickering blue light from within.

There was one piece of good news for the Harrowers: the newly constructed bridge that had been placed across the lake by the army of the Unconsumed made crossing back to the beach easier than having to fight for a boat. It wasn't an elaborate structure, but with the Quo'oto busy digesting the remaining demons Harry and company crossed the body of water and reached the safety of the beach without incident. They ran at speed, Caz carrying Norma all the way. When they finally touched ground, it was not far from the demon encampment from which they had originally launched their boats.

"We have to go to the village," Harry said. "The old lady will be there."

"You all stay here, look after Norma," said Dale. "I'll go. It isn't far."

"I'll go with you," Caz said.

Harry, Lana, and Norma found a place up off the beach under the shelter of what looked to have been a small copse in better days, now reduced to little more than a few desiccated, leafless trees.

"We'll wait here for you," said Harry.

"And if you don't come back in an hour or so I'm going to come looking for you," Lana said. "I don't trust that old woman."

Caz and Dale headed toward the camp while Harry did his best to make Norma comfortable on the uneven ground.

"What are you thinking, Harry?" Lana asked.

"Ha!" Norma barked. "There's a can of worms."

Harry's heart warmed. Norma was back in his arms—bruised but alive—and hearing her familiar maternal tone again made him feel like things just might work in his favor for once. He turned to Lana and spoke.

"Going through that," Harry said, gesturing toward the compromised structure, "makes me feel a little used up inside. But everything's going to be all right, right?" The cathedral's demolition continued, though it had slowed now that its walls were, in several places, little more than heaps of rubble.

"I don't think that's how life works," said Lana. "But at least it's something you can depend on from the moment we enter this fucked-up world. I think babies cry when they're born because they're born with the knowledge of all the terrible shit that's gonna happen to them. That's why I never had kids. Every life is a death sentence. We just forget it later in life, like dreams we lose the second we wake up. Whether we worry about it or not, the shit's still going to fly. The important thing is we're here. At least for now."

"Reassuring," Harry said.

"All the more reason we get out of here as fast as we can." Lana looked along the beach. "I lost sight of the boys. Hopefully they're getting some help from that old bitch."

"There you are, witness."

The Hell Priest appeared suddenly. He walked off the bridge and made his way over to them, the condition of his body so ragged and his face so utterly devoid of its former symmetry and elegance that unless he had spoken Harry would have passed him by unnoticed. Now they stood face-to-face as the crowd turned past them, on up the beach and away into the darkness. D'Amour realized then that his tattoos hadn't let off any alarms in hours. Maybe he'd burned them out. Whatever the case, they'd betrayed him. He crossed in front of Norma to protect her. Lana shot up, readying herself for a fight.

"Jesus Christ," Harry said. "You look like hell."

"My witness . . . my faithful, unerring witness."

"It's gonna make a hell of a book, Pinhead."

"It is a shame that you will not see it to its end now. You live in the dark, D'Amour. And that is where you will remain," the Hell Priest replied. And so saying, he raised his left hand to his face, whispering an indecipherable incantation. His words ignited in the cage of his blackened fingers.

"Still more tricks?" Harry said. "They've done wonders for you so far."

He moved to the right of the demon and took two, perhaps three steps down the beach to better position himself for a fight, but the Hell Priest had other plans, and against his will Harry felt himself once more lose control of his body.

"Fucker!" Harry shouted.

"Harry?" Norma called out.

"*No!*" Lana screamed as she advanced.

"Away, cunt," the Priest said to her. "Or I'll see to it that your punishment far outweighs your crimes."

"Norma. Lana. Let it go," Harry said. "This is between me and Pinfuck."

Harry's eyes began to prick.

"Christ. What are you doing?" His heart quickened, not beating but hammering. And with each hammer blow the pricking worsened, as though invisible hands were steadily pressing white-hot needles into his eyes. He tried to blink, but his lids refused to close. The Hell Priest had turned to watch him, Harry's eyes catching a gleam of the cold blue light that Lucifer was emanating. As the pain increased, darkness crept in from around the edge of Harry's sight.

"Look your last, witness."

Though the Priest still had magic, the strength of his workings had clearly left him, and the working on Harry's body was nowhere near the paralyzing thrall the Priest had held over him in the cathedral. Harry fought the magic and reached out, making contact with the Hell Priest's cold, wet body. His fingers found something to hook themselves under, though whether it was torn flesh or a portion of the Hell Priest's stolen vestments Harry neither knew nor cared.

"What more do you want from me?" D'Amour said. "What am I to you? I need my eyes. I'm a detective."

"You should have thought about that before you turned your back on your duties."

The darkness encroached at ever-greater speed, and Harry could now no longer take in the Hell Priest's face in a single glance but needed to scan it through the iris that was closing his vision down. He could see nothing in the demon's face that suggested there was any reprieve to be had. There was only the cold light reflected off the Fallen One in his eyes. The rest, what had once been a kind of perfection, was ruin.

This has been your life, said some cold, steady voice in him, apparently immune to the terror that had confounded the rest of his thoughts. *You have wandered among evil things, seized by a sickly intoxication that allured you to play the role of hero, while all the time you've been indulging an addiction.* This wretched clarity was more than he could bear. Why now, of all times, did his brain choose to make such a damning judgment? It became a loop that now receded behind the ever-darkening terror.

And then every last pin drop of sight was gone.

13

The noise of the demons' chaotic departure became more ragged after a time as what had been a solid flow eventually diminished. The wounded came now, many gasping for breath as they did their best to climb the beach, often moaning with pain, some even weeping quietly. It was one such demon's whimpering that woke Harry. All track of time was lost as he lay there on the stones, the side of his face stinging from the wounds he'd sustained wherever and whenever he'd landed.

"Hello?" Harry said. "Lana! Norma! Anyone?"

"Harry!" Harry heard Lana's muted voice calling out to him. "You're awake. Oh Jesus—" Her voice was followed by the sound of her approaching footsteps.

"Lana! Is that you?"

"What do you mean? I'm right here."

She was at his side now, touching his face. Harry's eyes were open but could see nothing.

"Fuck. I . . . I think the fucker blinded me."

"Thank God you're awake." Harry heard pain in Lana's voice. "Harry. It's horrible—"

"Hey. Don't worry. Not my first time being blinded by a demon."

"No," Lana said, close to weeping. "Not that."

Harry stopped dead. "Lana?"

"He . . ."

"No!" Harry said. "Lana! Tell me Norma's okay." Lana had given in. Harry could hear her crying now. "Lana! For fuck's sake! Tell me what's happening!"

"She's still alive, but Christ, she's a mess. I tried to stop him once he knocked you unconscious, but . . . I couldn't move, Harry. He'd thrown some fucking words in my face and I was down. All I could do was watch while he . . ."

"What?"

"He fucking violated her, Harry. Right in front of me. And made me watch. I couldn't even close my eyes."

"I'm gonna fucking kill him. I swear, I'll rip out his fucking heart. Where is she?"

"I'll take you." Lana put her hand beneath Harry's elbow.

Harry talked as they walked, some to break the silence in the air, mostly to drown out the noise in his head.

"Something had to give sooner or later," he said. "The number of times I should have been the one in the body bag, but somehow always unharmed. A few broken bones. Never anything serious. Norma used to say I had an angel looking out for me. She said she'd see it sometimes when I came to visit her. But I guess it had other business today."

"Easy now," said Lana.

"I got it," Harry said, climbing the slope of the beach, all the while loose stones were sliding away beneath his boots.

"Slowly—"

"How much further?"

"Two, three strides, then it starts to level off again."

"Can you see Norma?"

"Yeah. She's lying where I left her."

"How is she?"

"She's still breathing. I knew she wouldn't let go till you came back. Thank God you woke. It's just a few more steps."

"Norma! Norma! It's Harry!"

The old lady murmured something.

"Lie still," Harry heard Lana instruct her, but Norma had fashioned a life of creating her own laws and she wasn't about to start taking orders now.

"What did he do, Harry? Tell me. No lies. Just tell me. What did he do?"

Harry heard the pain in her voice. It hit him like a blow to the gut. "I always wondered what the world looked like through your eyes," he said to her. "Now I know."

"Oh . . . child . . ."

Lana took her hand off Harry's elbow and stepped back to allow Harry to settle down into a cross-legged position. Norma immediately reached up and found his face as easily as she would have if she'd been sighted. She stroked his unshaven cheek.

"So you're not hurting?"

"No. But you are, aren't you? Lana told me the fucking—"

"Don't waste your breath, Harry. There's other stuff we need to talk about. Just you and me. Lana, would you give us a moment?"

"Absolutely," Lana said. "I will be waiting nearby. Just yell if—"

"They'll hear me in Detroit if there's a problem," Harry said.

At that, he heard the fading sounds of her feet crunching on the stones as she left Harry and Norma to share their last words together.

"She might be your soul mate, Harry."

"Come on, Norma. We both know I don't get one of those."

"People are complicated. Of course a lot of the time they're putting on faces, at least when they're alive. But once they're dead, you know, they stop all that nonsense. So you'll get to see the truth. And it's so much richer and stranger than you'd ever guess from having looked at their masks."

She was no longer speaking in the raw, hesitant fashion she had been using when Harry first got to her. Now she talked in an urgent whisper.

"I've left all the instructions with a man named George Embessan."

"What instructions?"

"For what happens once I'm gone. Which will be very soon."

"Norma, you're not going—"

"Yes, I am, Harry, and you do neither of us any favors by wasting time with platitudes. My body's meat, pure and simple. All Pinhead did was hasten me toward my exit, for which I am not ungrateful, to be honest. I need to die awhile. Get my appetite for life back before I choose new parents, and set back into the game with all that I've learned hidden away at the back of my soul. It's going to be quite a life next time 'round, knowing all that I know."

"I wish I could be with you."

"You will be. You will."

"No doubt?"

"Would I lie to you?" she said with genuine indignation. "We'll be together. Different faces, same souls. So don't grieve. Just take up where I fell off."

"You mean . . . helping the dead find their way?"

"Damn right. What else are you gonna do with your time?"

Harry allowed a short, disbelieving laugh to escape his throat. "You knew it'd be me."

"No. I didn't, actually. That's a complete revelation."

"I can't help the dead, Norma. I know nothing about them."

"You knew enough to get down into Hell and save my sorry soul."

"And that ended great for all of us."

"You think this is a fuckup?"

"Of course it is," Harry said. "You're dying."

"Harry, Harry," she soothed him, stroking his face. "Listen to me. Things are never the way they seem. You did what you thought you should because you're a good man. You came down into Hell to find me. *Into Hell*, Harry. There aren't many people who'd drive to Jersey for their own mothers, never mind venturing into the abyss for some old, blind, half-crazy woman."

"You're not—"

"*Listen to me*. It wasn't about me in the end. It was never about me. I was just the bait."

"I don't understand."

"I don't either, if it's any comfort. But think about it. Think of how things have changed down here, in this place itself, obviously, and within you, I'd be willing to wager. All because you chose to come looking for me."

"So somebody set all this up. Is that what you're saying?"

"Not at all. That's magical thinking."

"But you said you were bait. And that means there had to be a fisherman, doesn't it?"

Norma took a long moment to think this through before she replied.

"We're all in it together, Harry. We're all pieces of the fisherman. I know that sounds like a bullshit answer, but you'll see, when you start to work with the dead. Everyone's complicit: the most innocent little kiddies; babies who live a day, an hour—they still have a hand in things, even their own deaths. I know that's very hard for you to get your head around right now, but take it from someone that's spent a lot of time with death."

She paused, and Harry heard her make a half-suppressed grunt of pain as she shifted her bruised body.

"I'm still going to kill him," he said.

"I'm fine, Harry," she said, "You don't need to worry about me. Or him. He's just one of the Lost and Afraid. Everyone is so fucked-up." She laughed lightly. "It isn't really funny," she went on, the laughter subsiding. "The World-Soul is sick, Harry, *crazy*-sick. And if we don't each do our part and try to get to the root of its pain and burn it out, then everything is for nothing."

"So what do I do?"

"I can't answer all your questions, Harry," Norma said, her reply tinged with an unsettling remoteness. "They're not all going to get answered. You need . . . you need to accept that."

"How about we split the difference? I'll acknowledge it, but I won't accept it."

Norma reached out and gripped Harry's arm, seizing it with accuracy and a strength that astonished him.

"I'm . . . hap . . . I'm happy . . . just us. . . ."

"You really are happy?" Harry said. He tried to keep the doubt from his voice but knowingly failed.

"Of . . . course . . ."Norma replied. With each syllable her voice grew weaker.

"I'm gonna miss you so goddamn much, Norma."

"I . . . love . . ." She didn't have the strength to finish. She trailed off as the breath that had carried her words ceased with a barely audible click in her throat. He didn't need to speak her name and have his call go unanswered to know that she'd taken her leave.

He reached out tentatively in hope of finding her face so as to close her eyes. To his surprise his fingers found her cheek with the same uncanny accuracy he'd seen her demonstrate; the image of what he was doing appeared in his mind's eye, fixed like a painting: *Attempting to Close the Eyes of a Blind Woman After Death.*

It was easier than he'd wanted it to be. Her eyelids obeyed the slightest touch of his fingertips and closed forever.

BOOK FOUR

Fallout

Out of suffering have emerged the strongest souls.

—E. H. Chapin

1

Lucifer, once the Most Beloved Angel in that incandescent dimension that mortal men called Heaven, exiled from its glories and its powers by his Creator, thrown into a place of rock and darkness where, in defiance of his Creator's torments, he'd made a second Heaven or at least attempted to, which mortal men had come to call Hell, stood amid the wreckage of his cathedral and planned for the second time his farewell to life. He wouldn't make the same mistakes this time as he had the first. There'd be no cathedral to serve as a place of pilgrimage for those who wished to meditate on the injustice and tragedy of his story. Nor would the underworld be populated with the bastard children of the damned and their tormentors, the latter rebels like himself, thrown down from Heaven for conspiring with him to rule from its Throne.

"Enough," he murmured to himself. And then, raising his voice to a bellow that could be heard at the farthest reaches of Hell: *"Enough!"*

The shout caused the stones on the beach to leap up as if in terror, then drop and rattle down the incline toward the lake, whose surface was also stirred into agitated motion. Caz and Dale had failed to return, and rather than wait at the side of their departed den mother, Harry and

Lana set off in search of their friends. They had just reached the Azeel's encampment when Lucifer unleashed his shout and the noise brought the old dreadlocked demon woman out of one of the shacks. She had a knife in her hand, and her locks were in disarray as though she'd been interrupted in the middle of something important and physically demanding.

Upon seeing Harry and Lana at the edge of her property, she waved the knife in the air with wild threat.

"What do you here?" she demanded.

"Have you seen our friends?" Lana asked.

"No. Please now going," the demon woman hissed.

"But your tone is so convincing," Harry said.

"Really," Lana said to the demon woman, "I'm sure you wouldn't mind if I look around, do you?" And, so saying, she headed straight for the demon's tent.

The demon woman's response was to spit full force in her face, the saliva stinging Lana's skin and burning it so viciously that she stumbled and clutched her face in agony.

"Fucking bitch!" Lana said.

"Lana! What's happening?" Harry asked.

The demon woman seized her advantage without hesitation. Clutching her knife, she first sliced up across Lana's chest and then came back down across her belly, spilling blood with both attacks. Before she could wound Lana a third time she retreated clumsily into the dying fire near the tent's entrance, turning up the red-hot embers hidden beneath the ashes. She smelled the stink of boots cooking and felt the heat on her soles, but she wasn't going to stumble back out into the path of the old demon woman's knife, so instead Lana kicked the embers in her direction. The demon loosed a stream of curses as they sprayed in all directions and met with her flesh.

"Don't worry, Harry," Lana said. "I got this."

The demon, as if in response, took two unhindered steps before she came at Lana again, but this time Lana was ready for her and dropped down to avoid the swing of the old woman's blade. Then Lana threw herself at the demon and grabbed her by neck and knife arm, shaking the latter till the demon released her knife. With the demon woman unarmed, Lana released her scaly arm and put both of her hands to the old woman's neck.

"Where are our friends, you ugly old cow?"

The demon woman hissed by way of reply. The wounds she'd given Lana hurt, and the pain fueled her rage. "Fine. I'm just going to kill you," she said, half meaning it, "and throw you in the fire, then find them myself."

"Crazy woman man! Slaughterer of demonation!"

"I'm happy you've been paying attention, cunt," Lana said, tightening her hold on the woman's throat.

The old demon woman's strong bony fingers pulled at Lana's hands, desperately trying to loosen Lana's grip. But the half of Lana that truly intended to strangle the life from the demon had her pressing her thumbs side by side against the demon woman's windpipe. The old woman started to make a nasty rattling gasp, and her hands lost their strength and slid away from Lana's, whose sanity prevailed as she finally let go of the demon completely. The old woman dropped to the ground, using the first available breath to begin cursing Lana again.

Lana picked up the old woman's knife and tucked it through her belt.

"Sticks and stones, bitch," she said. "Come on, Harry."

"Wait." Harry held Lana at bay, turned in the direction from which he'd last heard the demon woman's hissed curses, and addressed her. "You said something about wyrms leading the way out. Tell me what that means. Are they wormholes we can travel through? Answer me!"

"You die now is what meaning!" the demon woman said.

The toe of Lana's boot met the demon woman's mouth and the demon flew back several yards, landing in a twisted heap.

"Wrong," said Lana, rubbing her face to clear it of the last bits of the demon's toxic phlegm. Lana then grabbed Harry's arm and led him into the tent. There was a small fire burning inside, the smoke vented through a hole in the middle of the roof, and by its light she saw Caz and Dale, kneeling with their backs to the fire, staring at the blank wall. Their hands were crossed behind them, as if they were tied, though they weren't. Lana went to them.

"Christ! Guys! Talk to me!"

"Are they alive?"

"Yeah. She has them tied up or . . . under some sort of trance. But they're alive."

Lana grabbed Caz's hands in an attempt to establish contact and break the manacles of his mind. A shudder passed through his body by way of response and he made a muted wordless sound, as though talking in his sleep. Lana went down on her haunches with her back against the shack wall and looked at Caz's face. His eyes were wide and his mouth closed tight. He stared straight ahead of her—beyond her—his gaze unshifting.

"Caz. It's Lana. Can you—"

"Hey, you fucking guys!" Harry broke in. "We've got to go. Lucifer is making a hell of a bark and I don't want us to be here when he decides to bite."

Caz made the same wordless noise he'd made before. Lana moved her open palm back and forth in front of both Dale's and Caz's eyes. Neither of them blinked.

"Assholes. Listen to Harry! You're not tied even up," Lana said. "That old bitch just got you believing you are. And you're not gagged either. Are you hearing me?"

Again, the muted noise from behind sealed lips.

"It's a trick, that's all," Harry said. "Some stupid incantation. Caz, your tattoos should be able to get you out of this one."

Harry and Lana waited for some response. None came.

"Nothing," Lana said. "What the fuck are we gonna do? We can't carry them out like this!"

"Wait," Harry said. "Their eyes are open, yes?"

"Yeah," Lana said. "They're not even blinking. It's creepy as hell."

"Are they staring at anything in particular? Is something in their line of sight?"

Lana glanced at the wall in front of Caz and Dale and saw that painted on the tattered sheet of canvas from which the wall was made was a quartet of hieroglyphs, arranged so close to one another that they almost touched. Dale's and Caz's eyes were fixed upon the glyphs.

"Ha," Lana said. "Harry, you're a goddamn genius! There's something painted on the wall. And they're staring right at it. What should I do?"

"Erase them. Wash them off. Obscure them. It doesn't matter. Just make them gone."

"Can do," Lana said, putting her hand to her chest wound and wetting her palm with blood.

She went to the wall and wiped the blood over the hieroglyphs, obscuring them completely. The release was immediate. The invisible ropes, gags, and blindfolds all lost their grip on Caz's and Dale's imaginations. The two men blinked, as though waking from a dream, and looked round at Harry and Lana, their faces screwing up in confusion.

"Hey, y'all," Dale said. "When did you get here?"

"When you two queens failed to show," Harry said, "we came looking."

"Good thing too," Lana said. "A few more minutes and I think you would have been that old demon bitch's dinner."

"Jesus," Caz said. "Really? The last thing I remember is getting to the edge of the village and then . . . this."

"I'd be willing to wager that old bitch knew some even older magic," Harry said. "I don't know how else she would have made it past your tattoos."

"Harold, why aren't you looking at me?"

"It is rather odd," Dale chimed in. "And where's Norma?"

Harry pursed his lips and gave a single slight shake of his head by way of reply. Dale grabbed Caz's hand and squeezed hard. Caz squared his jaw and took in a deep breath. No words were needed. The message had been received.

"Right," Caz said. "I'll have my own private apocalypse later. Right now, what's the plan?"

"The plan," Lana said, poking her head out of the tent, "is to find that wormhole the old bitch was—" But the old demon woman was gone, no trace of her to be found. "Fuck. I should have just killed her."

"Nah," Harry said. "It's better that she's somewhere, rotting for the rest of eternity."

The Harrowers headed back the way they came while Lana told them what Pinhead had done to Harry and Norma.

"I can't believe it," Caz said.

"Neither can I," said Harry. "But we can't focus on that right now, or we'll never do what it is we have to do."

"Which is?" Caz asked.

"Find a way out of this place," Harry said. "That old demon woman said there was a way out."

"She also said she'd help us," Caz said.

"Maybe she meant turn us into helpings," Dale said. "Old cow didn't exactly have a grasp of the language."

No sooner had the words escaped his lips than a bright light illuminated their entire field of vision. The ground shook and the stones beneath their feet rattled.

"What the fuck was that?" Harry asked.

"I don't know," Caz said, "but it was bright as shit."

The Harrowers headed off between the trees, swallowed up by darkness in a few strides.

"That's gotta be Lucifer again, right?" Harry asked.

They came to a clearing and the source of the light suddenly became all too evident.

"Oh Jesus God," Dale said.

"Lucifer isn't in the cathedral anymore," Lana said. "He's glowing."

"Glowing?" Harry asked.

"And he's floating over the lake," Dale said, "kicking up the waters something fierce."

"I think I knew that . . ." Harry said. "My ears seem to be making up for my eyes. I can hear the water going crazy."

"Crazy is right. He's . . ." Caz stopped. "Wow."

"What?" said Harry.

"He's flying now. Up. Fast," said Lana. "And that fucking sea beast—"

"The Quo'oto?" Harry said.

"That's the one!" Lana replied. "It's coming up after him. Goddamn it's big. It's riding a reverse whirlpool or something. Fuckin' A . . ."

The words to describe the sight seemed to fail them all. It was too immense a spectacle: the circling waters in a foaming frenzy, the massive serpentine form of the Quo'oto rising out of the vortex empowered by its spiraling energies, and the light from Lucifer's body growing brighter as he climbed the air, with the Quo'oto following close behind him. The creature was defying the limitations of its anatomy with this flight, but Lucifer had it hooked by some invisible barb and drew it up from above just as the waters had cast it skyward from below.

Harry stared sightlessly at the spectacle, doing his best to make sense of all the commotion.

"Guys? What the fuck?"

"I never thought I'd say this, but my words are failing me," Dale said.

"How about trying? Anyone? I want to *see*!"

"The Quo'oto's the size of ten trains, I swear," Lana said.

"And it's following him," Caz followed.

"Going?"

"Out of the lake and up."

"Why?"

Before anyone could venture a guess, Lucifer answered the question for them.

2

Lucifer, the Fallen One, the star of morning, had lived and died in his underworld beneath a hated sky. God had set it in the heavens above Lucifer's prison kingdom as a stone might be rolled in front of a tomb, to seal in the dead's corruption so that it could never befoul the world.

Now, finally, rather than take his battle inward, Lucifer reacted outwardly for the first time in millennia and struck out at the stone ceiling, his strength fueled purely by rage. The Quo'oto was still rising up out of the vortex, its body far vaster than even the Lord of Hell had anticipated. Yet he drew it up without effort, though it roared its displeasure at being ejected from its natural habitat; its breath stinking of the dead meat in its entrails, it wanted Lucifer in its belly more than anything its hungry eyes had ever settled on, and for that reason alone it didn't fight to free itself from the hold that had been placed on it. Soon it would catch up with the Morning Star and swallow him whole. He was so close, just a tiny distance beyond its gaping maw. Any moment it would have him.

But no. Lucifer kept rising, and the Quo'oto came after him, coil upon coil rising skyward from the vortex now a thousand feet below.

On the beach the Harrowers who still retained their sight watched the spectacle in silence. At that moment all the commotion, those layers of sound that had steadily escalated as Lucifer prepared to start the waters spinning—now ceased. Even the roar of the vortex became remote. The hush lasted two, three, four heartbeats. Then Lucifer drove the Quo'oto into the sky's limit and the beast crashed into the surface. Upon its impact, there came a single thunderous boom, which started some distance away and then reverberated across the heavens. The Quo'oto loosed an unholy chthonic cry of pain—its last living act—and died, plummeting from the sky toward its watery grave.

"What the fuck was that?!" Harry screamed, his hands going to his ears.

"Jesus. It . . . uh, hit the sky," said Lana.

"The stone?"

"Hard," said Caz. "And there's a crack opening up. More than one, actually. A lot more. Fuck. There's cracks spreading over the whole damn rock."

"And where's Lucifer?"

"He's right up against the stone, forcing the cracks open with his light."

"And the Quo'oto?"

"Dead. Falling. I've never seen anything like it."

"I got the picture," Harry said.

"He's going to crack the sky open," Lana said.

"Are we going?" Dale wanted to know. "Or are we waiting for the musical number?"

"We're going," Caz said. "Right, Harry?"

"I've seen all I want to see," Harry replied, unsmiling.

"So let's get gone," Lana said.

"Lead me to Norma," Caz said. "And we're as good as ghosts."

There was a fresh fusillade of noise from overhead as new cracks opened in the stone, spreading from the fissures that were already gaping in the surface. A litter of fragments dropped from the cracks, seeming inconsequential for the first few seconds of their descent but rapidly revealing their true immensity. It wasn't only their size that was deceptive; so too was their course. The relation between the fracturing stone above and the lay of the land below was misleading. Shards of stone that seemed certain to fall on the beach near (if not directly upon) them fell many miles back, somewhere in the vicinity of Pyratha, or thereabouts, while pieces that seemed destined to land a long way off came down in the water close to the shore. The largest of these slivers—a piece of rock the size of a dozen houses or more—hit the water a hundred yards out from the shore, the impact sufficient to throw up a plume of water that challenged the cathedral for height.

The drizzle of falling shards was rapidly becoming a deluge, as Lucifer's inquiring light pressed deeper into the fractured surface of the sky, breaking off more and more fragments of Heaven. One slab, easily as big as a car, headed straight for the beach where Harry and company were currently standing

"You've got to be shitting me," said Caz.

"What's—"

"No time for questions!" Lana barked as she shoved Harry out of the way. The slab sailed past D'Amour's head, missing his scalp by a whisper, and disappeared, without a sound, into a line of trees behind them. Everyone stopped dead in their tracks.

"Whoa," said Harry. "That felt big. Where the hell was the crash?"

The car-sized slab of sky had sufficient size that its landing would have been enough to make every tree sway from its roots up to its topmost branch, shaking down leaves as it did so. Instead, the slab sailed over the heads of the Harrowers and was swallowed whole as though it had never existed.

"Did y'all see what I just saw?" Dale said, his jaw slack.

"No," said Harry. "And I'm starting to think you guys are doing this on purpose."

"Holy shit," Lana said. "Harry, I think we found our way out."

"Holes of worms, leading the way home! Fuckin' A!" Caz said. "Wormholes, Harold! You were right! That's what the old bitch was talking about. We have our way out of this! Come on!"

Lana led the way to Norma's body. Upon seeing his friend's crushed and lifeless body, Caz faltered for a moment but stayed the course.

"Jesus Christ," he said. "I wasn't ready for that."

"This was never in my dreams," Dale said, his voice shaky.

After a moment of recalibration he bent over, picked up his old friend, and draped her corpse over his left shoulder.

"Let's do it," Caz said. "We said we wouldn't leave without her."

Together they marched out across the inland edge of the trees and into a landscape of piled obsidian boulders. Here the deteriorating heavens shattered with loud cracks as they struck the obsidian. The shrapnel that sped off in all directions from these bits was potentially lethal, ricocheting off the black boulders like bullets. Heads down, the Harrowers wove among the boulders to find their wyrm hole.

"Jesus," Harry said. "How much longer is this gonna keep up?"

"From the looks of it, I think he aims to flatten all of Hell," Caz said.

"That does appear to be the plan," Dale agreed.

On the heels of Dale's reply came three monstrous thunderclaps, louder by magnitudes than anything that had preceded them. They echoed back and forth between earth and sky, their volume not diminishing with each echo but instead becoming still louder, echoes of echoes of echoes soon so numerous they birthed an almost single, solid sound.

"Run!" Lana said.

"Oh shit. Here comes Judgment Day!" Caz yelled.

Despite the danger from the flying fragments, Caz stood up and threw back his head so as to at least see the immense spectacle clearly, for a few seconds. Lucifer's assaults had finally raised the stone, breaking it into pieces that were still monumental in their fractured state. To Caz's eyes the cataclysm seemed to be happening in slow motion, the vast pieces sliding apart with a lazy elegance.

"I think I see it!" Lana said.

"Tell me we're close!" Harry yelled.

"If I'm right, yeah!" Lana yelled. "There's a spot ahead, between two boulders where the rocks aren't ricocheting. That's gotta be it, right?"

Caz pulled his reluctant eyes off the sky and glanced in Harry's direction. He and Lana were on their haunches six or seven strides away, reaching out to investigate the empty air space between the boulders where the rocks were disappearing in front of them.

"Works for me," Harry said. "In case it's not what we think it is, if you hear me scream—"

"Then what? Stay here?" Lana said. "Just fucking move it, Galahad. There is no plan b."

Before Caz could watch his friends enter the wyrm hole, there was another thunderous clap. Caz turned his head to see the source of the sound and, in that moment, finally understood a piece of what drove Harry to do the things he did. Caz found himself suddenly hungry for another glimpse of the dying sky. The pieces were falling faster now, preceded by a hail of stones monsoonal in its ferocity. It was all Caz could do not to stand still and watch the spectacle unfold before his wondering eyes.

"Caz!" Dale was right beside him, pulling on Caz's arm. "We gotta go now, hon," he said. "Or not at all."

As Dale pulled Caz toward the wyrm hole, a massive block of shed stone struck one of the obsidian boulders nearby. It shattered, throwing immense pieces in all directions. Caz turned and saw that Harry and Lana were already gone—disappeared into the wyrm hole when he wasn't looking. He hoped that wasn't the last time he'd see his friends.

Then, from the corner of his eye Caz saw one of the shards coming at them and started to shout a warning, but before he could speak Dale pulled him into the cleft between the two boulders. Abruptly the dark, roaring landscape and its splintered, falling sky were gone and he and Dale were in another place entirely, where only smears of light, speeding across their path or over the uneven ground they stood on, offered any clue to their location.

"So this is a wormhole?" Caz said.

"I reckon," Dale said. "Never been in one till now."

"It's hard to make sense of what's where," Caz said. "Harry? Lana?" There was no reply. "Where the hell did they go? Do you see them?"

"Honey, I don't see shit. I just hope this doesn't dump us somewhere in the middle of the Atlantic."

"No," said Caz. "We're going to step out into Times Square and it'll all have been a dream."

His remark was punctuated by one almighty, albeit muted, crash from the other side of the threshold as the remains of the stone dropped out of the sky over Hell, crushing the infernal landscape beneath its bulk. The reverberations leaped at the threshold and dispersed their energies through the broken ground, sparking lights that cavorted in the walls that rose to such heights they seemed to converge.

Seemingly very far away from Hell's landscape now, Caz and Dale traveled onward as the noise of the infernal cataclysmic scene and its attendant vibrations dropped off into silence and stillness.

"Bon voyage, Perdition," Dale said. "Until we meet again."

3

The wyrm hole didn't deliver them into the icy waters of the Atlantic. But neither did it set them down on a quiet New York sidewalk where they could have readily found a way to transport Norma's corpse back to her apartment. No, the wyrm hole was exquisitely arbitrary. It first offered Lana, Harry matching her step for step behind her, a tantalizing glimpse of a city street (not New York perhaps, but civilization nevertheless). It did not, however, let them exit there. She had barely reported the street to Harry when a shoal of lights blazed by, erasing the reassuring sight.

"I guess that wasn't our stop," Lana said, trying to keep her tone from sounding hopeless. Whatever desperation she presently felt, it was nothing, she was sure, compared with the thoughts circling in the darkness of Harry's head.

"Where are Caz and Dale?" Harry asked. "Any sign of them?"

"No. But I'm sure they're not far behind us," she lied. "Don't worry. We've got another stop coming up."

She wasn't lying that time. Even as she spoke, a new door was presenting itself. It was a far less reassuring scene than the city street that had preceded it: a landscape of black rock and unsullied snow, its drifts being stirred into blinding white veils by a relentless wind.

"If this is our stop we're fucked," she said.

It wasn't. Once again she had barely glimpsed the scene when it was erased by the same shoal of lights. A little time passed while they walked on down the wyrm hole in silence. Lana was in the lead, with Harry's right hand lightly laid on her left shoulder, just to keep Harry from falling as he walked on the uneven ground.

A third doorway came into view, and the landscape at least looked warmer than the one preceding it: an American highway, to judge by the signs, running through a desert landscape. The image solidified, signifying to Lana that this was it. The ground of the wyrm hole then threw a length of its light-streaked darkness out into the yellow-orange dust at the side of the highway.

"Not quite a red carpet," Lana said, "but it does the job. We should hurry, before this fucking thing changes its mind."

Lana brought Harry out into the heat of a desert noon and glancing back at the wyrm hole saw Caz, Norma slung over his shoulder, and Dale as they too stepped off its light-smeared ground to find that there was nothing but empty air, shimmering with heat. Then the wyrm hole vanished.

"Where were you?" Lana shouted to them. "I thought you were both dead!"

"I thought you were sure they were behind us," Harry said, a wry smile on his face.

"Don't break my balls. I had to keep us moving."

"How long have you been waiting here?" Caz said.

"We haven't," Harry said. "You stepped out right after we did. But it could have been hours apart to you. I don't expect a wyrm hole to adhere to our laws of time and space."

"Well, it's damn good to see you everyone again," Caz said. "I can't believe we made it."

"We didn't all make it," Harry said.

"I know, Harold," Caz said, clutching Norma closer to his body. "You don't have to remind me. I'm happy we're all at least together. I didn't know where that thing would spit us out. Or if it would take us all to the same place. Does anyone know where we are?"

"Out of the fire," said Dale. "And into the frying pan."

"I'll drink to that," Lana said as he peered down the length of the highway, which ran without so much as a one-degree accommodation down its entire visible length. "Wherever we are, or wherever we go from here, nothing will be as bad as what we just faced,"

"There's a building a few miles away, in that direction," Dale said.

"I don't see it," Caz told him.

"Me neither," Harry said.

"There's that trademark wit," Lana said. "Anyway, I see the building too. It's far, but it's there. It might lead us to a city."

"I guess we go that way, then," Caz said.

"We could wait for some traffic," Harry offered. "Get somebody to pick us up."

"Please," Dale said. "I'd like to meet the driver who'd stop to pick up a dandy, a dyke, a blind man covered in blood, and a nearly seven-foot-tall queen carrying a dead black woman."

"Suddenly, I'm glad I'm blind," Harry said.

"Yes, you are."

"So we're walking, then."

"Let's."

With the plan agreed upon, they started down the straight highway. They walked for a time, and as they walked a few autos heading in their direction passed them by. Each vehicle slowed down more than a little to take a good look at the spectacle. But after having looked, each driver moved on with haste, kicking up choking clouds of yellowish dust as they sped away.

But after the seventh car passed them and sped out of sight, Harry began to hear the sound of gospel music. As it grew in volume, he turned his head toward his friends and said, "Please tell me I'm not the only one who hears that. I'm not ready to be called to Heaven. Not so soon after leaving Hell."

"No," Caz said. "I hear it too."

"Me three," Dale said. "Matter of fact, I think it's coming right for us."

At that, a large black sedan with a foot-tall crucifix serving as a hood ornament was barreling down the highway.

"Christians," Caz said. "No hope there, I'm afraid."

Caz turned his attention back to the road ahead and shifted Norma's weight on his shoulder. Norma's body had seemed so very light when he'd first shouldered it, mere skin and bones. But he was a lot weaker now, and though he moved her body from his left shoulder to his right and back again (and sometimes, to ease up on his shoulders, he simply carried her draped over his arms), there was no real relief. He had no intention of laying the body down, not without any real notion of their whereabouts.

He would never forgive himself if any harm were to come to Norma's remains just because he'd neglected them for a moment. Forgiving himself for allowing her to die would be hard enough, he knew. So he trudged on, focusing his diminishing energies on the piece of ground ahead of him where he would presently set down his foot. Then on to the next piece of terrain, indistinguishable from the previous piece except in one vital regard: it brought him closer to the end of this insane journey to Hell and back—closer to his tiny store at 11th and Hudson and the smell of the inks and the prospect of another breathing canvas standing naked before him, shaking, some of them, with happy anticipation of the adventure ahead. Oh, to be there now! To crack a beer—no, fuck the beers, right now he would kill for a glass of ice-cold milk.

"Are you folks looking for a ride?" The voice smashed into Caz's thoughts like a brick wall. The Harrowers turned to see that the voice had come from the driver of the black stretch limousine.

"Please God, yes," Harry said.

A young, pale-skinned, bespectacled man in a short-sleeved white shirt and a narrow black tie opened the passenger door and got out.

"The name's Welsford. You folks look like you need some help, and the Reverend Kutchaver wants you to accept his invitation and step inside and out of this monstrous heat."

"And we happily accept," Harry replied, "but I should tell you that one of our number is dead."

"Yes. I tried pointing that out to the reverend, but—"

"Hallelujah," came a voice from the back of the car. "One of our beloved sisters has gone to meet her Maker! This is a happy, happy day. Bring her in and make her comfortable."

Caz labored to get into the limousine with Norma's body while preserving the dignity of the attempt, but it was hard work single-handed, and very plainly the Reverend Kutchaver, who was sitting in the far corner of the backseat (a very large white man in his late fifties, dressed in a very expensive suit), had no intention of offering any physical assistance.

Caz draped Norma's corpse half-laid, half-sitting opposite the reverend, and he then guided Harry to the long seat that ran down the length of the limousine.

"A little more, Harold," Caz said. "Right there!"

"Are you blind, young man?" the reverend asked.

"Only recently," said Harry.

"Oh Lord, oh Lord," the reverend said. "You are all mightily afflicted."

"You could say that," Caz said as he got out to allow Lana and Dale into the vehicle. Only then did Caz himself get in and, positioning his body between Norma and Dale, closed the door. "We're all aboard."

"Y'all look like you've been through it," said the reverend.

Dale groaned. Harry took the conversational reins.

"Thank you for stopping. If you could just drop us off at some place where we can make arrangements to get back to New York—"

"New York?" said the reverend's assistant. "You are a long way from home."

"Where are we?" said Harry.

"That is a good question," said the reverend. "Where in the blazes are we, Welsford? It feels as though we've been driving for hours."

"Arizona, Reverend," Welsford replied. Then, turning to Harry and company: "The reverend is due at a church in Prescott in"—he consulted his watch—"one hour and twenty-two minutes."

"Then if it's all right with you-all we'll happily travel with you to Prescott," Harry said, "and make our arrangements from there."

The assistant glanced nervously at Kutchaver, who seemed not to have even heard Harry's proposal. Welsford was staring with intense fascination at the rest of the Harrowers.

"Is that all right with you, Reverend?" Welsford asked.

"What?"

"If they come with us to Prescott?"

"Prescott . . ." Kutchaver said, lost in his thoughts.

"Is that a yes or a no?"

The reverend didn't reply to the question; his attention remained riveted at the sight of Caz and Dale, who were now holding hands. Finally the reverend said, with an almost tender intimacy in his voice, "And you, brothers, what are your stories?"

Neither man replied. Harry knew what was coming next and, weary as he was, he found himself looking forward to the rude awakening the dear reverend was about to receive. He had picked the wrong day to bring these wayward sinners to his Lord.

"Poor children," the reverend said. "Being tricked into believing you are born like that. The hardships you must have endured. But God always has purpose, my sons. However difficult it may be for us to understand it."

"He does?" said Caz.

"Of course, child. Of course. Whatever sins you have committed, He invites you to lay them down and accept His forgiveness and His protection. Oh Glory to God in the highest—I see it so clearly now. This is why you're here! Thank You, Lord—"

"Here we go," Harry said, a smile spreading across his face.

The reverend kept up the hard sell.

"Thanks be to the Lord for delivering you all into my care, so that I may save your souls!"

Now it was Caz who groaned.

"God never tests us beyond what we can bear!" the reverend continued. "I promise you, sure as I sit here before you, if you do not repent, you will never see the light of Heaven. But I can save you. There is still time, children! Do you wish to be saved from the flames of Hell?"

"There is no Hell," Harry said. "Not anymore."

"Oh, but there is," the reverend replied. "I have had many visions of that place. I have witnessed its furnaces. I have counted its chimneys. I have watched damned sodomites like you." He pointed at Caz. "And you"—now at Dale—"driven by demons whose faces were foul beyond words."

"Scary," Harry said.

"It is. And I swear by the blood of Christ, the Devil is in you—is in all of you—but in Christ's name, I can drive him out. I can—"

The reverend was interrupted by the sound of Harry laughing. "Jesus Christ. Ever hear the expression 'know your audience'?" Harry said, the air in the limo growing thick. "I swear, on the soul of that dear woman sitting next to you, that we just came from the Hell you're describing. We followed a demon there to bring my friend back alive. We saw populations destroyed by a plague fog. We saw armies wiped out by magic workings. We saw the Devil himself dead, and then resurrected as he rode a gargantuan sea beast into the sky, where he cracked open the roof of Hell and brought the sky down on everyone's heads. We barely escaped with our lives. We're hungry, we're beaten, and we're in mourning. We don't have the patience for a sermon right now, Rev. So either shut the fuck up or get the fuck out, because this car is going to New York."

"I-I-I," the reverend stammered. "I-I . . . Driver!"

The reverend violently slapped at the glass partition that separated the driver from the rest of the vehicle. *"Driver!"*

"Everything okay back there?" the driver called out.

"No," Welsford said, his voice shrill. "Stop the car!"

The driver dutifully eased the vehicle over to the side of the empty highway and got out, slamming his door, and then walked the length of the vehicle to open the reverend's door. The driver bent low and peered into the limo. He found everyone sitting politely in their seats.

"What's the problem, Reverend?"

"These travelers are beyond hope! Destined for Hell and content to drag every living soul they encounter with them."

"Of course they are," said the driver, placating his boss. "So what, you want them out?"

"Yes!" screamed the reverend.

The driver threw the passengers a sympathetic look. "All right. The reverend says out, you're out."

"We'll get out in New York," Harry said.

"Don't get smart with me, guy. This here's the reverend's ride, and he's going to Prescott and then on to—I forget where the hell comes next. But New York is not on the list. So you need to find yourselves a different ride."

"Or a different driver," Caz said behind the driver's back. He had slipped out of the passenger side while the driver made his way to the back of the limo, and he had not emerged from Hell without his knife. He waved it at the driver, whose response was quick and unequivocal.

"Take the car. Just don't hurt me, okay? I got five kids. No wife but five fucking kids. You want to see? I got pictures." He reached into his jacket.

"I'm sure you're an excellent breeder," Caz said. "But I don't need pictures of the kids. I just need you to help the reverend out of the car."

"Out?"

"Oh, he can stay, but I don't think he wants to ride all the way to New York with a car full of unrepentant sinners."

The reverend didn't need Caz to repeat himself. He had the answer already in mind.

"Get me the fuck out of this car," he said. "It's not going to New York. It's going to the lake of fire and I don't want to be riding in it when it gets there!" He stuck out his overly bejeweled fat-fingered hand. "Help me here, Jimmy, or Julius or whatever the fuck your name is."

"Frederick."

"Just get me the fuck out of this car."

"Please don't take the Savior's name in vain, Reverend," Caz said.

"Ah, fuck you," the reverend said.

The reverend reached up and might have caught hold of the door if Caz hadn't found his hand first and, supplementing Frederick's strength, hauled all three hundred and seven pounds of Reverend Kutchaver up out of the considerable depression he'd made in the limo seat. Once they had the worst of the work done, Frederick let go of his half of the burden and Caz took the hint and did the same. The reverend loosed a shrill shout and went down on his hands and knees in the litter of the rock shards at the edge of the highway.

"Welsford, you idiot. Where are you? I fell down. Help me up or I swear to Christ I will fire you and make goddamn sure that no one will hire you if you live to be a hundred and fucking fifty."

Welsford scrambled to help his beloved employer and preened over him like a sycophantic lover. The sight was enough to make Caz laugh out loud.

"What's so fucking funny?" the reverend demanded of Caz as Welsford fussed over him, brushing dirt from his suit with short little strokes of his hand.

"It's an inside joke," Caz said. "Oh yeah, and I'll be needing everyone's phones, of course."

Once all forms of communication had been confiscated, Caz climbed into the driver's seat, then rolled down the window and drove off, leaving the sanctimonious reverend and his staff in the Arizona dust.

"Caz," Harry said as the car barreled down the length of highway.

"Yes, Harold?"

"God bless you."

4

Lucifer lay under a great weight of shattered stone, his body so exquisitely knitted that it had remained whole beneath the fall of Hell's heavens. The voices that stirred him from his comatose state were not human; rather they spoke in the fluting voices of his own tribe of angels, though their debate (which he understood perfectly well despite the passage of centuries) was scarcely evidence that they were messengers of love.

"We should have been here to see this, Bathraiat. Somebody should have been keeping an eye on things and raised the alarm the moment the stone became unstable. I would have wanted a seat up front for this! Can you imagine the panic, and the screaming and the praying—"

"Demons don't pray, Thakii!"

"Of course they pray."

"You really are a cretin, aren't you? Who the fuck would they pray *to*?"

"They had a leader. Some rebel. Shite! I don't remember his name. You know me and names. He was a dickhead and everybody says so. And old Bitch Tits kicked him down here. He started some rebellion."

"Lucifer?"

"That's the one. Lucifer. They prayed to Lucifer."

"Why?"

"Didn't he build this place?"

"So? Who cares?"

"*I* care."

"You *care*? About somebody other than yourself? What kind of shite is that?"

"I'm not saying I care as in 'tears-and-lamentation' care. I care that the fuckwit who had this come to pass—and it's a big job—I'm saying whoever that selfish fuckwit was, he could have told a few friends and we all could have been sitting on the sidelines watching the slaughter like civilized creatures. Instead we were standing around doing nothing in a state of ignorance—"

"Shut up, will you?"

"I can do whatever—"

"Shut your mouth, brother, and open your eyes. Do you see what I see? There! Under that rock!"

At that, Lucifer drew a deep breath, and the massive stone that pressed down on his body loosed a single loud crack as it split from end to end.

"God. In. Heaven," the one called Bathraiat said.

The two angels looked up at Lucifer. Their natures were not capable of shame. What could perfect beings such as they ever have to be ashamed of? But their instincts, however coarsened by lack of use they were, told them this was no ordinary demon.

"It's him," Bathraiat said.

"But he looks so—"

"Shut up, brother," Bathraiat hissed. "Be best if you kept your opinions to yourself."

"You're not afraid of him, are you?"

"I said shut the mouth."

"You know what? Fuck you," Thakii said, and then turning to Lucifer, "and especially fuck you, Lucifer almighty. We were having a fine time till you showed up."

Having spoken his mind, the angel started to turn away, but one word uttered by Lucifer—"Don't"—was enough to stop the angel in mid-motion.

"What?" said Thakii.

"You are numbered among the dead, angel," Lucifer said.

"I am?" Thakii looked puzzled. Then smiled in blissful adoration and ceased.

The energies from which he had been nurtured, inheriting their willfulness and their lusts and their escalating confusions, immediately began to vacate his body and go in search of new pastures to seed. The light in the warm flesh of his muscles flickered out as all the strength in him perished. He curled in upon himself, his head becoming elongated and shrinking as he collapsed like a building set with charges. If there was any pain in his demise he let out no complaint.

The other angel, whose skin was subtly imprinted with what looked like eyes, delineated in red with black irises, blinked in acceptance.

"It is boring, day after day," the creature said. "I get to feeling that anything is preferable to this."

"Anything?"

"Yes," the angel said, deliberately providing the executioner with his cue.

"Dead," Lucifer said.

The other angel nodded and, curling in upon himself, was unmade twice as quickly.

Lucifer climbed up into the tallest pinnacle of sky-stone and did his best to assess his whereabouts. But it was by no means easy. The deluge of fractured stone had effectively flattened every last topographical detail that might have helped him to work out where he was and in which direction he had hope of making an unseen departure. He had no desire to find any others here. He simply wanted anonymity for a while, to sit in a quiet place and try to figure out what to do with the unwanted resurrection that had been gifted to him.

But first he needed to get up and out of Hell's wasteland without drawing any further attention to himself. The number of angelic presences here was growing; he saw them stepping down out of the darkness all around him, eager to witness the ruins of Hell. He took advantage of their morbidity—plotting a path of departure that would keep him away from the grisly sites that drew the angels' clammy attentions and instead took him away through narrow cracks between the heaped stones.

Once he'd put some distance between himself and the worst of it all, it was easy. He found a dead soldier in a robe that was large enough for him to envelop himself. He removed the soldier's clothing and wrapped it around his own body to keep the light in his flesh from attracting the gazes of the curious as he made his way up out of Hell and into the world of men.

5

D'Amour sat in darkness. Whatever the time, day or night, darkness. Being blind in Hell had seemed scarcely real, but once he got back into New York—back into his apartment and later his office—he began to comprehend how merciless the Hell Priest's final curse on him had been. Like everyone blessed with the gift of sight, he had taken it for granted. He had lived with his eyes. They made it possible for him to exist in the eternal present. As long as he could see ahead, he could at least attempt not to look back. Now he had to rely upon memory to find his way around his world, and memory took him out of the present and forced him to constantly cast his mind into the murky waters of the past. He had never been very good at it, but regardless, he wanted the now again.

With no reason to think there'd be an end to his curse, Harry decided to close the agency. It wasn't as though Harry needed the money anymore either. As soon as Caz and Harry were ruled out as suspects in Norma's death, the matters of her estate were settled. For a woman living in such humble circumstances, Norma had been quite well-off. Harry was surprised to find that she owned the building in which she lived, along with half the buildings in the vicinity, several gas stations, a handful of car dealerships, and an island off the coast of California. She'd left everything to Harry.

Still, even with his newfound wealth, the decision to close up shop was brutal on Harry, and Caz was his only lifeline to sanity. When the decision was finally made, they went to Harry's office together and ran through the jobs that had still been outstanding when they'd taken off in pursuit of Norma. There were a couple that Harry felt he'd virtually wrapped up and would be able to finish with Caz there to give him some help. But most of the jobs were simply not feasible in his blind state, and he made the calls to all the clients in question, explaining that he had met with an accident and was unable to finish the job he'd accepted. Where there were advanced fees, he promised to return them.

"It feels like I've died," he said to Caz when he'd finished.

"Well, you didn't."

"And I should be grateful, right?"

"Right."

"Well, I'm not."

"I love you, Harold, but I don't have the energy to cheer you up. Why don't we put the pity party on hold while you tell me what you want to do with all this shit?"

"This shit is my life, Caz. Try to show a little compassion."

"You're starting to sound like a bigger queen than me. Brooding only looks good in the movies. Trust me, in real life, it's fucking annoying. Let's start going through the files to figure out what you want to keep? You need to get out of the office by the end of next week."

"I should have kept it."

"And done what with it? Open a driving school?"

"All right, all right: I get it."

Harry reached out and grabbed for the bottle of Scotch on his desk.

"Did you move my Scotch?"

"Sure did."

"Why?"

"You were slurring at your clients."

Harry sat for a moment, digesting Caz's words, then changed the subject.

"How's married life?"

"Kinky," Caz said. "Dale is the best thing that ever happened to me. You should call Lana. You guys have a lot in common. Mostly, you're both stubborn assholes."

"Yep," said Harry, wishing he had something to swig.

6

The sky-stone had broken into three massive parts as far as the Hell Priest could discern. It had shed pebbles no larger than a hand and slabs big enough to be minor moons.

All of Hell had been virtually flattened by the falling sky, which left the Cenobite guessing his location as he traveled. He sensed now that he had finally discovered the remains of the city, and his instinct was confirmed when he came upon a split in the rock that was barely a crack at one end and yawned to the distance of perhaps a quarter mile at the other. He walked toward the narrow end of the fissure while peering down into its depths. There wasn't enough light, even for one whose eyes were as sensitive as his, to make out anything below, at least not until several planes of yellow flame burst from the crevice and illuminated the rubble.

He saw here the houses of the richest demons: the Crawley Crescent, with its perfect sweep of white marble houses that had once faced out toward an ancient stand of Thriasacat trees to which legend attached the notion that should they ever ail, then the city would also ail. And should they die, so then would the city. Here now was the proof, lying crushed at the bottom of the fissure and lit by the same fire that had first illuminated the depths. He could see several Thriasacat branches, stripped of foliage and split, the sweet swell of their sap hanging in the air.

The Hell Priest was not for the most part superstitious, but there were a few cases that crossed the boundaries of his distrust and had become a profound part of his understanding of the world. The legend of the Thriasacat trees had here been proved true. Strange to say—given that he'd witnessed the stone falling and known that nothing beneath it could have survived—he had held on to the remote idea that the stand of Thriasacat trees would have escaped by some miracle. But no. The sky had killed everything.

And he had played a part in all of this. Were it not for his ambitions there would have been no need to raise Lucifer against him. And if Lucifer had stayed asleep in death, there would still be a sky in the sky. So this was of his making: this silence, this death. It was what he thought he had wanted all along.

7

Caz finished packing Harry's things, then left to tend to Dale. Waiting for his friend to return, Harry sat, the window open a crack, and listened to the flux of the traffic as the lights changed at the intersection. The afternoon was slipping away; the passage of blue sky visible between the buildings would be steadily darkening. The traffic would be even heavier now as the flow was swollen by people heading home or out for dinner, their heads still buzzing with what the day had brought. Sure, work could be a pain in the ass, but it was purpose, and what was a life, any life, *his life*, without purpose?

"Nothing . . ." he muttered to himself, and, uncorking the Scotch Caz finally had relinquished upon leaving, put the bottle to his lips. As he did so, a glimmer of light appeared at the corner of his eye. He lowered the bottle, his heart suddenly beating quick time. He'd *seen* something. His sight *wasn't* extinguished after all!

Very slowly, so as not to upset the healing going on in his head, he turned toward whatever was coming back into view. That's when he saw her.

"Norma?"

"Hi, Harry."

She looked healthy, more like the Norma Paine whom Harry had first met so many years ago. Her body wasn't insubstantial, like some cheap Hollywood phantom. She was perfectly solid. But it was she and only she who had come into view, a body framed by darkness.

"I can see you. Christ, I can *see* you. I always tried imagining what ghosts looked like to you, but I wasn't even close. Oh, Norma, I can't believe you're here."

"It's good to see you too, Harry. I've missed you."

"Can we . . . I mean . . . can I hug you?"

"I'm afraid not. But we can sit here and talk as long as you want. I don't have a curfew. I can come and go as I please."

"Come and go from where?"

"That's between me and . . . the Architect of my New Accommodations. Just know that I'm very comfortable where I am now. And believe me, it was worth waiting for. But I had to come back and see you, Harry. I miss you so much. And I have a few tips I want to pass on. Dos and don'ts, if you will, when dealing with the recently deceased. I thought I'd be dying of natural causes at a hundred and one. That's how old my momma was when she died. And my grandmother too. So I was pretty damn certain I'd do the same, by which time I would have taught you everything I knew about, you know, getting the dead to move on. And you'd just take over from there."

"Wait—"

"You can't contain your excitement, right? You get to save people who were kicked into the Hereafter a little too suddenly. They're wandering around half-crazy, Harry, trying to figure out what in the name of sweet Jesus they're supposed to do now. And, good news, you're their only hope!"

"Slow down. I don't—"

"You certainly have your choice of offices," she said. "A lot of them have a panoramic view of the city."

"Yeah, where the hell did all the money come from?"

"I got a lot of money given to me over the years, Harry. All from relatives of dead folks I helped. They heard what I'd done for their family members and wanted to say thank you. I gave it all to you."

"I know. And it was entirely too generous, Norma—"

"Generosity had nothing to do with it. I gave you that money so you could afford to do what you need to do. Don't make me take it back. I can do that, you know."

"You might have to. I don't think I can do what you're asking of me."

"You feeling sorry for yourself again because of a little darkness in your life? I heard you with Caz. He was right. All that brooding? Ain't healthy. Don't make me lecture you from beyond the grave. I've done enough of it already."

Harry smiled. "God, I missed that. But it has nothing to do with being blind, Norma. You made it look easy. But you're so much stronger than me. How does a lost soul help lost souls?"

Norma smiled and the darkness in the room diminished.

"Who better?" she said. "And while you're thinking about it, open up your blinds and look down."

"When I open that window, I'm going to see what you saw every day of your sightless life, aren't I?"

"Maybe," she said, smiling.

Harry turned his chair around and stood up, reaching with uncertain fingers for the cords of the antiquated venetian blinds, which were knotted and truculent and near impossible to open even when he'd had eyes to help him separate them. Today was no exception. Harry gave up tugging on the cords and reached down to lift the blinds with his hand. When he did so, he looked down at the street as Norma had requested, and he knew that nothing would ever be the same again. It felt like the bottom dropped out beneath his feet and he'd fallen ten stories in the blink of an eye.

"They're everywhere," he said.

EPILOGUE

Prima Facie

*Man cannot discover new oceans unless he has
the courage to lose sight of the shore.*

—André Gide, *The Counterfeiters*

1

Lucifer came up into the world with an unerring sense of how the lines of power were laid and which was best to follow if he wanted to get into the heart of the human story the same way he had so often in the early days. The lines converged in the city of Welcome, Arizona, where he'd lingered for two days to sit in on the trial of a man who'd murdered several children in the region and partaken of their flesh.

There was nothing new about the spectacle: the parents of the dead children sat in the court, pouring out wordless venom toward the murderer; the madman sought refuge in his madness; and outside the courthouse demonstrators threw makeshift nooses over the branches of the sycamores that grew amid the square. When Lucifer was certain that there was nothing for him here, he skipped unnoticed through the crowd, pausing to look up at the churning trees, their boughs creaking in the gusting wind that snatched away fall's early deaths.

Then he was on his way again, following the flow of energies that seeped up out of the ground. He knew already what city awaited him at the end of his journey. He'd seen its name many times in the newspapers he plucked out of trash cans or out from under the arm of some human being. New York, it was called, and all that he'd read about it made it seem the greatest city in the known world, somewhere he could linger awhile and taste the times. For long distances he walked, because the line did not lie beside a highway. But when it did he never waited long for a ride. A woman driving alone picked him up when he was still three hundred miles from his destination. She said her name was Alice Morrow. They talked a little, of nothing significant, then lapsed into silence. Ten minutes passed. Then Alice said, "I had a night-light when I was little, which I kept beside my bed to make sure the bogeyman didn't get me. Your eyes have the same light in them. I swear."

They stopped at a motel for one night, Alice paying for his room and for food. He ate pizza. Thereafter, it would be all he ever ate. In the night, he lay naked on his bed and waited for her. She did not come immediately, but after two hours she knocked at his door and said something about wanting to see his eyes in the dark. Alice and he had sexual congress six times before dawn, and by the fifth she was in love with him. In the middle of the next day she asked him if he had a place to stay in New York and when he told her no she seemed happy, as if this confirmed the rightness of what she felt.

They arrived in New York at one in the morning, the city an astonishment to Lucifer. Alice checked them into a hotel, promising that tomorrow she would take him out and buy him some good clothes. The long drive had exhausted her, but sleep would not come. She went to his room, where he was waiting, twin night-lights flickering in his head.

"Who are you?" she asked him.

"Nobody yet," he whispered.

2

The Cenobite was climbing the steps to the fortresses, which were littered with pieces of stone but still climbable, when a shock wave passed through the air and ground. He turned to see bright bursts of gold and scarlet flame spouting from the fissures in the stone that had demolished the city, the force of the eruptions sufficient to make the fissures gape, which unleashed still-greater torrents of fire. He watched for a little time and returned to his climb, his long, thin shadow, thrown by fires, preceding him to the top step. He was two steps shy of reaching the top himself when a second shock wave, much more violent than the first, erupted. The tremors didn't die away this time. They steadily became more powerful. Very cautiously the Cenobite took a backward step while keeping his eyes on the flame. The vista of stone, smoke, and tremors was changing in nature, the shocks giving way to tidal motions that had the scale of tsunami surf.

Another shock wave threw him off his feet, and he fell. The cracked slab of the threshold dropped away beneath him into the throw of the wave, making his fall all the longer. When he landed, the bones of his face cracked in a dozen places, and the sudden rush of pain, which had been such a reliable source of pleasure in years long lost, was now only agony. His system rebelled. His body was marked by its own tsunamis, driving deep into the cankerous pit of its stomach and deeper still, into its gut, where rot turned to shards of stone. It was as if his body were attempting to turn itself inside out. He loosed a sound that was part belch, part sob, and then vomited, a rush of blood that was nearly black and as thick as phlegm. Through the noise of its splattering he heard a far deeper sound, and some fraction of him that was able, even in the midst of this violent decay, to assess circumstances with detached thought.

That's the end beginning.

The violence of his vomiting left him powerless to control his body, his battered face so distrusted by his scream that his lips tore like wet paper. There was nothing left in him now except his last poor hope of willing his eyes to open, so he might look and see whatever final vision Hell had for him.

He drew every last mote of will from the furrows of his collapsing body and gathered them, turning them to a single purpose.

"I will open my eyes," he ordered himself.

Reluctantly, his body obeyed him. He unstuck his lids, sealed with the gray glue of his dissolving flesh, and focused his eyes on whatever was in front of them. He had the whole panorama in view: the flames emptying to a higher point than ever, as the motion in the ground put new stresses on the stone.

He had been watching for just a few seconds when the tidal shifts in the ground abruptly ceased, the thundering that accompanied them ceasing at the same instant.

The Hell Priest's pulse quickened in anticipation of whatever lay on the far side of this silence. It came soon enough. A simple sound, as of some immense blow, struck in the tormented ground. It caused the pieces of the stone that had crushed the city to be lifted off their bed of rubble, their vast weight effortlessly thrown up by the power unleashed in that single blow. At the top of their ascent they seemed to pause for a beat. Then they dropped—their magnitude so great that the ground upon which the city had been raised simply cracked as the stones bearing the city's remains started their descent. The fires found the mother lode of whatever fuel had fed them and the geysers of flame leaped so high they would have licked the sky if it had still been there.

The burst of light illuminated the cataclysm below with brutal clarity. But there was nothing down there left to witness. Just the stones falling away with the abyss. The Cenobite looked at the fire instead, and in that instant the fire looked back at him.

He was watching, he knew, the unmaking of Hell. The place was being wiped away by some great, invisible hand. Perhaps it would be rebuilt. Perhaps a new system would be put in place. It was not for him to know. The thoughts contented him. He had challenged a higher power, and he had lost. It was the natural order of things. In that challenge, he had wreaked havoc, and now he was dying, along with everyone else in this contemptible place. Content in the knowledge that his legacy would forever be one of agony and loss, he opened himself to oblivion.

His eyelids closed—buckled, really—the bones in his face so fragile they shattered under the weight of his very lids as he dropped to the threshold of existence. His last breath had already left him. And as he fell, life did the same.

3

Besides Norma's impressive television collection, the only other physical items Harry had inherited from Norma's apartment were the many talismans and charms that she accrued doing during her years as New York's Queen of the Dead, almost all of them sent to her by the relatives of spectral clients, thanking her for the help that she had given to a spouse, or a sibling, or, most distressing of all, a child.

As it had been Harry who had read the letters these items came with to Norma, he was profoundly respectful of how much love and gratitude had been poured into the gifts. Each item had been charged with all the power of those feelings, making up a vast collection of potent protectors. Not a single one was discarded.

With so much to be moved from Harry's apartment and office, Caz knew the task would take several weeks if it was to be left to Dale and himself. He talked it over with Harry and asked if he could bring some extra muscle to get the job done quickly, so that Caz could open up his shop again and start earning some money. Harry had no problem with this; he only asked that Caz be the one to box up and carry the contents of the two deep-bottomed drawers to the right and left of his chair.

"What have you got in there that's so special?"

"Just a few keepsakes. Souvenirs from various scrapes I got into. I don't want anybody but you to deal with all the stuff in those drawers, okay? Do you know who will be helping with the move yet?"

"Yeah. Some friends of mine. They can be trusted."

"Are they . . . ?"

"*Ex*–fuck buddies, Harold. I'm a new man, remember?"

"That's right. I keep forgetting that Dale has made an honest man of you."

"It doesn't hurt that he's hung like a giraffe."

"I was a detective for a long time, Caz. I already assumed as much."

Caz's friends Armando and Ryan arrived the next day. Lana was there too, invited by Caz, unbeknownst to Harry, who forcibly made nothing of it and put them all to work in the storeroom, with the duty of packing up in boxes everything on the cluttered shelves and in the cabinets. The room was L-shaped, with the portion that wasn't visible from the office abandoned to chaos by Harry several years before. Most of it, Harry had admitted to Caz, was boxes of old office supplies, which he'd intended for his secretary back in the day when he'd still believed his life was going to be a painless, lucrative round of divorce cases and insurance investigations.

Lana, Armando, and Ryan were working up a sweat in the L-shaped room, the door between the two rooms open a crack, but there was very little conversation. They shifted many boxes that were indeed packed with office supplies that told their own melancholy story. Only one item was slipped through to Caz.

"Take a look at this. There's a whole box of them," Lana said, passing Caz a Christmas card. If there was any sadder proof of Harry's high hopes for his business it was this slickly painted card with an innocuous painting of pine trees and snow by moonlight with a printed message inside wishing the recipient:"The Best Christmas till Next Christmas! Season's Greetings from the D'Amour Detective Agency."

Caz laughed. "I'd bet he never sent a single one of these out."

"What's the joke?" Caz turned. Harry was pushing the door open wider.

"Just talking about Christmas," Caz replied a little lamely. He put the card down on Harry's desk. "It wasn't important."

"Everybody okay?"

"We're sweaty and dusty and ready for something to eat," said Lana, "but we're getting through it."

"Shall I order Chinese? Or there's a good Thai place a few blocks over that delivers? Or pizza?"

"I vote Thai!" Armando yelled through from the storage room.

"Thai's fine with me," Lana said. "Will you get some Thai beer? I've worked up a powerful thirst."

"Not a problem," Harry said. "Is the phone still in the same place?"

"You want me to do it?" Caz asked.

"No, Caz. I'm blind, not crippled."

Harry made a confident move toward the desk, avoiding with uncanny ease the heaped-up files that littered his path. He got to his chair and sank down in it.

"You know this is a damn comfortable chair. Will you put it by the window for me, Caz?"

"You mean in the Big Room? In place of Norma's chair?"

"Yeah."

"Done."

Harry slid the chair toward his desk and picked up the phone, dialing the number from memory.

"I'm just going to order a bunch of things they do really well. Is that okay?"

"Ryan doesn't like stuff too spicy," Armando said. "Right, Ryan?"

There was a grunt from Ryan.

"Are you okay back there?"

"Yeah. Just . . . concentrating."

"On what?"

"Nothing. Just make sure it isn't too spicy."

"Already noted," Harry said. "Damn." He put the phone down. "Dialed the wrong number."

He pulled the phone over so it was right in front of him and ran his fingers over the buttons. "Why the hell did I do that? My head feels—"

He stopped.

"You need me to check the number?" Caz said.

"Listen," Harry murmured. "You hear that?"

"What?"

"That tinkling music." Harry stood up, dropping the receiver on the desk beside the phone. "You don't hear it, Caz? Lana?" He was moving around the other side of the desk toward the stockroom door, kicking over several piles of paperwork in his haste. Lana opened the door as wide as she could, squashing the garbage behind it against the wall.

"Be careful," she said to Harry. "The floor's covered—"

Too late. Harry's foot caught on one of the boxes and he stumbled forward, dropping onto his hands and knees in the litter of envelopes and rubber bands that had spilled from the box he'd kicked.

"Oh God, Harry," Lana said. "Are you okay?"

"I'm fine!"

He reached out to his right, memory guiding his fingers to the handle of the top drawer of the much-dented filing cabinet. The drawer was unlocked, however, and empty. It slid out, and Harry would have hit the floor a second time if Lana hadn't thrown her weight against the drawer and slammed it closed. There was still a moment while Harry regained his equilibrium. The music continued its tintinnabulation: the sticky-sweet little cycle of melody quickening like a madhouse waltz.

"Where's Ryan?" Harry said.

"He's back there," Armando told him. Armando was talking from the corner of the room, Harry guessed, a vantage point from which he could have both Harry and Ryan in view. The far end of the room was the most chaotic. Four black plastic garbage bags, disgorged notes without files, and files without notes, discarded cameras that had been thrown in a box along with hundreds of rolls of exposed but undeveloped film. And buried behind all this chaos, a few items that Harry had felt obliged to hang on to but hadn't wanted to think about every day because they had unpleasant associations; toxic souvenirs of his journeys to the end of the world and his wits.

He quietly cursed himself for failing to remember the danger that was buried amid the trash here: a scalpel he'd confiscated from a demon who'd caused mischief by passing itself off as a cut-rate plastic surgeon; some keepsakes from a demonic casino he had closed. He'd held on to all of these, but—

"No," Harry whispered. "That's not possible. I left it in Louisiana."

Harry had cautiously found his way around the corner now. It was unmistakable. It was the chime of the box, Lemarchand's infernal masterpiece.

The music it was producing was to enrapture the man who was in the midst of opening it.

"Ryan?" Harry said. "What have you got?"

Ryan grunted by way of reply. He was obviously in the throes of the box's hypnotic working.

"Harold, what is it?" Caz shouted. "You're freaking me out, man!"

"Ryan! I know what you've found is fun to play with, but you need to put it down."

Ryan actually spoke up now, in defense of his ownership.

"I found it in the trash!"

"I know," Harry said as calmly as he could. "But it needs to go back there."

"You heard Harry," Caz said. He'd come to the spot just behind Harry's left shoulder where he'd reliably been throughout the march through Hell. "Harry doesn't fuck around," Caz went on. "Just hand over the fucking box. I don't know what you're fucking with, but neither do you."

"The hieroglyphics are beautiful. . . ."

"It's Teufelssprache," Harry said. "It's German. The guy who decided it all was a man in Hamburg. He's dead now. But he named the code before he died."

"Teufelssprache," Lana said. "Fuck. That's—"

"Devilspeak, yeah. And I've had my fill."

"And what does it say?" Ryan asked.

"Give me the box back and I'll tell you."

"No," Ryan said.

"Ryan, listen to yourself," Caz said. He squeezed Harry's shoulder for a moment as he spoke, signaling that he was about to make a move.

"All I hear is the pretty music."

"Bullshit." Caz moved suddenly and Harry heard a scuffle, then a pained shot from Ryan, and the source of the lunatic melody dropped to the floor and rolled away from the struggle, ending up close to Harry's feet.

Harry dropped down onto his haunches, his clammy-palmed hands locating the box instantly. As he picked it up, Ryan yelled:

"That's mine, you fuck!"

"Get back, Harry!" Caz yelled.

Harry turned, but Ryan reached out and grabbed his arm, his fingernails digging deep enough through shirt and skin to make Harry bleed. Harry pulled away, Ryan's nails gouging him in the process, and stumbled in what he hoped was the right direction. Lana caught him and took his arm.

"Where's Armando?" Harry said.

"He ran," Lana said. "Soon as you said 'Devilspeak.' Where are we going?"

"Into the office."

It was only four steps to the door; five and they were through it. Behind them Ryan was still cursing Harry, but he put it out of his head and concentrated on the matter in hand. The puzzle apparently no longer needed any human agency in its solving. It was doing that for itself, opening in Harry's hands as he walked with it, its tune scratching at the back of his skull to get in there and cause some trouble the way it had with Ryan. The little door of curved bone near the back of the device was open, just a crack, and Harry felt the familiar stream of Teufelssprache that had made Ryan crazy wind its way into his head.

At its root were the remnants of angelic speech, which had risen into music when their passions were fired. But the words had been poisoned, the music corrupted. After his trip into the inferno, Harry knew now that what was coursing into his head was sewer filth, stinking with plague and despair. He wanted it out.

"Desk?" he said to Lana. "One sweep. Just clear it all off. Quickly!"

Lana caught the urgency in Harry's voice and she did as he'd said, sweeping whatever papers and photographs Caz had been organizing back into the chaos underfoot. From every corner of the room, and from the boards beneath the threadbare carpet, came a ragged litany of growls and creaks as the fabric of the old building was tested by the mechanisms that the solving of the puzzle had activated. Somewhere in the nonamesland between crawl-space and dream-space, where the brute simplicity of brick and timber lost faith in itself, something slid over the threshold.

Harry carefully set the box down on his old desk. He'd spent much of his adult life behind it, too much time wasted puzzling over the twin mysteries of cruelty and grace. Now all that was old news. The only puzzle left that mattered had finished solving itself, right there on his desk. The music had slowed again, the pitch dropping to a guttural mutter.

What happened next was candy for the sighted. It drew an admiring, "Fuck, look at that," from Lana.

"What?"

"Light. Coming out of the top of the puzzle. Going straight up. And bright. Wait . . . it's dropping."

"Keep clear of it."

"It's nowhere near either of us. It's sliding down onto the wall where your big map of New York is pinned up. Now it's stopped."

"Describe it."

"It's just a long, narrow line of light. One end at the bottom of the wall, the other—"

"Six feet up."

"A bit higher maybe. What *is* this?"

"A door. To Hell. Open just a crack."

"Another one?" Lana said. "Caz!"

"I'm right here," Caz said. He was at the door between the rooms.

"Have you got Ryan?" Harry asked.

"More or less. He's subdued."

"Get him out of here. Get everybody out."

"No, fuck this. We did our time. They can't do this to us again!"

"I don't think it works like that. Tell me: what's going on through there?"

"The light's dying away," Lana said. "It got really bright for a few seconds and now is just fading. Maybe you stopped it before it got going?"

"No."

The solid structure of the room didn't greet the door's defiant appearance in its midst without complaint. Bricks, forced askew to accommodate the trespassing door, had cracked from top to bottom and now ground their broken halves together. Black lightning fractures crossed the ceiling and zigzagged down the walls, flakes of paint shed from overhead, flickering as they fell.

A gust of wind, befouled by the stench of rot, blew in from Hell and caught the door as it came, throwing it open. The room complained vehemently having to suddenly make room for the entire door, the walls shaking in their fury, particularly the map wall, where the cracks were an inch wide around the doorframe. Timbers creaked and splintered as the comforting geometry of the real was recalculated by the supernatural; brick dust, ground into a fine red haze, filled up the room, the gusts from the other side making it curl and eddy.

"What can you see through the door?"

"Not much," Caz said. "If I go to the threshold, will I get sucked back in?"

"That's not how it worked for me," Harry said.

"Shouldn't there be a bell? I remember you telling me there was a bell tolling."

"Yeah," said Harry. "Like a funeral bell."

He lifted his head back, listening closely for the sound. It wasn't there. "No bells in Hell?" he said.

"No, nothing in Hell," Caz said, peering into the portal. "Harold, if that box is supposed to open a doorway to Hell, either Hell ain't there anymore or the box dialed the wrong number."

"I'm coming to you," Harry said.

He stood up and Lana took hold of his arm again. She helped him around the side of his desk, moving cautiously over the littered floor. When they got to the corner of the desk Harry paused for a moment, then turned and reached back to pick up the puzzle box. He didn't handle it with reverence now, which fact it recognized by letting out a shrill shriek, the sound so sudden Harry almost dropped the thing. It modulated immediately, the shriek becoming the sobbing of an infant.

"Caz?"

"I'm right here."

"Three steps, Harry," Lana said. "Yeah, that's it. Two. One. Okay. There's a stone step a couple of inches ahead of you. That's the threshold."

Harry tapped the step with the toe of his boot. Then he set the Configuration down onto the step. The box rolled over a couple of times and then stopped, its anguished mewling dying away. He didn't need his sight to evoke the wasteland that lay beyond the threshold. Harry faced the blustering wind. Lucifer's country smelled of death and disease. There were no appeals, no judgments, no prayers or shrieks—just the occasional buzz of a fly, looking for somewhere to lay its eggs, and the remote rumble of thunder from storm clouds pregnant with poison rain.

"Smells like Hell," Harry said. "I guess it's gone. Thank God."

"Any idea what to do about this fucking door?" Caz said.

"Just one. You used to be a football player, right?"

"I never told you that. How'd you—"

"Kick the box."

"What?"

"The box, Caz. Kick it as far as you can."

Harry felt Caz's grin of pleasure. "Gimme some room." Harry and Lana backed up a couple of steps.

He couldn't see Caz's kick of course, but Harry felt and heard it. The rush of air as Caz ran past him, the sound of his boot connecting with the puzzle box, and a barely contained yelp from Caz, who growled to Harry:

"Fuck! That fucking thing did *not* want to be kicked."

The tremors started again in mid-sentence, the room shaking, drizzles of paint flakes and brick dust beginning afresh. Harry stood at the threshold, Caz on one side, Lana griping his arm firmly on the other, as he listened to the door close once and for all.

4

Harry tentatively threaded between the towers of televisions, which he had turned off two hours ago, as it began to get dark, and found his way to the chair in front of the window that faced the river, setting a bottle of single malt on the floor beside him. Harry had been given, at his request, a meticulous description of the view spread before him by Caz, but before he could bring it into his mind's eye something bright moved left to right across what would once have been his field of vision. It had barely passed from view when a second blur of light came after it. This time Harry followed it with his spirit-sight to the corner of the room and then lost it as it turned the corner, leaving for his study, beads of luminosity shedding as it traveled out of sight.

But, even as they fell from sight, a massive shoal of bright forms burst into view, drawing his gaze back over to the left. The forms wove between one another as they came, and stopped in front of Harry's chair so that they could scrutinize him with their glistening eyes and allow him to have sight of them. They were the dead, of course, some still wearing their fatalities like ragged insignia on their bright anatomies, others, their killing traumas perhaps internal, unmarked, but all dead, all ghosts, and all lost, he assumed, or else why had their wanderings brought them to him?

Norma had given him two five-hour-long lessons on how to deal with his deceased visitors when they came.

"And they will come," she'd said. "You can be certain of that. Because I'll go among the lost dead and tell them where to find help."

She'd done her work well. Now the rest was up to him. He took a swig of Scotch and very slowly, so as not to cause any panic among the ghosts, he got up out of his chair. It was six steps to the window. He took five, still moving cautiously, and saw the throng of wayward spirits below. He was suddenly seized with the overwhelming knowledge that life was good. If he ever needed a reminder, all he had to do was gaze down at the hopeless deceased spirits seeking answers below. So what if he couldn't see? The sighted memories he had weren't all that pleasant to begin with. It seemed that the time-tested metaphor of passing through the fire held true. Harry was on the other side of it, burned but cleansed. Maybe tonight he'd even call Lana and ask her out on that date everyone had been trying to talk him into setting. Or maybe he'd do it tomorrow. Hell was easy; romance was hard.

Harry took a deep breath and again turned his mind to the task at hand. He then reached out with his right hand, laying it on the cold glass of the large window.

"My name's Harry," he said, hoping his words would be audible to them. "I'm here to help, if you have questions, and to direct you if you're lost. I can't guarantee that I'll have all, or any, of the answers, though. I'm new at this job. But I will do my damnedest—sorry, my best—I'll do my best to get your problems solved so you can go on your way. Please, come closer."

The invitation was barely out of his mouth when the entire shoal came at him, the suddenness of their approach sending Harry stumbling back toward his chair. They flew through the room, their presence instantly chilling the air by several degrees. Then they circled him, picking up speed with each circuit, dividing around Harry as they swept by him. Norma had warned him he might find the first couple of nights a little raucous until word got around that he was the real thing, but she hadn't advised him on how to deal with such situations. No matter; Harry had corralled enough demons in his time to know how to handle an energetic spirit.

"All right!" he yelled. "You've seen the room! Now all of you get the hell out of here! I mean it! I want this room completely cleared! Do you hear me? I said completely cleared!"

The shoal divided now, as those who were instantly intimidated by Harry's orders fled for the open air, leaving three or four troublemakers to keep circling, deliberately clipping him as they flew past him.

"If you don't get out right now," Harry said, "nobody gets a word of advice from me. You understand? I don't care how fucked-up your death was or how lost you feel. I'll keep everything I know to myself."

The phantoms slowed their flight, exchanging glances that Harry couldn't interpret, and then turned, faces to Harry's window, and flew directly at the glass and out into the night air.

The fracas had not gone unnoticed; far from it. Outside, Harry saw there were spirits converging toward the Big Room from every compass point. A few came in the company of other wanderers, but most were solitaries.

"Okay," Harry said quietly. "Another hit of Scotch, then I get going."

He returned to his chair, picked up the bottle, opened it, and put it to his lips, pausing for a second or two in sweet anticipation, then took a good-sized hit.

There are worse things I could do with my life, he thought as he set the bottle down once more.

Then he turned to look at the window and caught sight of the most distressing of his visitors he'd yet witnessed. A woman, with a child at her side—a boy, Harry thought, though he couldn't be sure as the crowd eclipsed them too quickly. He sat down and surveyed the many faces before him. How many were there now? Forty? Fifty? He wouldn't get through them all tonight. A lot of them would have to wait until tomorrow, by which time, of course, word would have spread and there'd be plenty of new wanderers. No wonder Norma had been so covetous of her brandy and so happy to have her televisions on hand, to give her some time to herself and drown out the din of needy souls.

There was hectic motion in the crowd, and a child—surely the boy he'd seen with the woman at his side—slipped through.

"Welcome," Harry said. "Please come in."

"What about my aunt Anna? She's very well behaved."

"She can come too."

The boy turned and waved the woman in. She entered, shaking. Funny, Harry had never imagined ghosts did that.

"Hello, Anna," he said.

"Hello, Mister . . ."

"D'Amour."

"See," the boy said to his aunt. "It's French for 'love,' like I said."

"I lost my faith for a little while out there," the woman said. "I didn't think there was anybody to help us."

"There wasn't, for a while," said Harry. "But I'm here now. I see you."